Frank B. Whipple

Algeria Stud Farm

property of W.L. Scott, Erie, Pa.

Frank B. Whipple

Algeria Stud Farm
property of W.L. Scott, Erie, Pa.

ISBN/EAN: 9783337293529

Printed in Europe, USA, Canada, Australia, Japan

Cover: Foto ©Andreas Hilbeck / pixelio.de

More available books at **www.hansebooks.com**

1889.

ALGERIA STUD FARM,

PROPERTY OF

W. L. SCOTT,

ERIE, PA.

NOTE.—An asterisk (*) indicates that the horse is imported. When double parentage occurs, the pedigree of the last named is given.

Tabulated and Compiled by Frank B. Whipple, Erie, Pa.

PRINTED BY
HERALD PRINTING AND PUBLISHING CO.,LTD.
ERIE, PA.

IMPORTED RAYON D'OR.—(RAY OF GOLD.)

Chestnut horse, foaled 1876. Bred at Dangu Stud Harns, France. Imported in 1882 by W. L. Scott.

- **Araucaria.**
  - **Flageolet.**
    - **Plutus.**
      - **Trumpeter.**
        - **Orlando.**
          - Touchstone
            - Camel, by Whalebone.
            - Banter, by Master Henry.
          - Vulture.
            - Langar, by Selim.
            - Kite, by Bustard.
        - **Cavatina.**
          - Redshank.
            - Sandbeck, by Catton.
            - Johanna, by Selim
          - Oxygen.
            - Emilius, by Orville.
            - Whizgig, by Rubens.
      - **Daughter of Planet.**
        - **Planet.**
          - Bay Middleton.
            - Sultan by Selim.
            - Cobweb, by Phantom.
          - Plenary.
            - Emilius, by Orville.
            - Harriet, by Pericles.
        - **Alice Bray.**
          - Venison.
            - Partizan, by Walton.
            - Fawn, by Smolensko.
          - Darkness.
            - Glencoe by Sultan.
            - Fanny, by Whisker.
    - **La Favorite.**
      - **Monarque.**
        - **The Baron, Sting, or The Emperor.**
          - Defence.
            - Whalebone, by Waxy.
            - Defiance, by Rubens.
          - Delight.
            - Reveller, by Comus.
            - Design, by Tramp.
        - **Poetess.**
          - Royal Oak.
            - Catton, by Golumpus.
            - Daughter of Smolensko.
          - Ada.
            - Whisker, by Waxy.
            - Anna Belle, by Shuttle.
      - **Constance.**
        - **Gladiator.**
          - Partisan.
            - Walton, by Sir Peter Teazle.
            - Parasol, by Pot-8-os.
          - Pauline.
            - Moses, by Whalebone.
            - Quadrille, by Selim.
        - **Lanterne.**
          - Hercules.
            - Rainbow, by Walton.
            - Aimable, by Election.
          - Elvira.
            - Eryx, by Milo.
            - Coral, by Orville.
  - **(dam line)**
    - **Ambrose.**
      - **Touchstone.**
        - **Camel.**
          - Whalebone.
            - Waxy, by Pot-8-os.
            - Penelope, by Trumpator.
          - Daughter of
            - Selim, by Buzzard.
            - Maiden, by Sir Peter.
        - **Banter.**
          - Master Henry.
            - Orville, by Beningbrough.
            - Miss Sophia, by Stamford.
          - Boadicea.
            - Alexander, by Eclipse.
            - Brunette, by Amaranthus.
      - **Annette.**
        - **Priam.**
          - Emilius.
            - Orville, by Beninbrough.
            - Emily, by Stamford.
          - Cressida.
            - Whiskey, by Saltram.
            - Young Giantess, by Diomed.
        - **Poten-tate's Dam.**
          - Don Juan.
            - Orville, by Beninbrough.
            - Peterea, by Sir Peter.
          - Moll in the Wad.
            - Hambletonian, by King Fergus.
            - Spitfire, by Pipator.
    - **Pocahontas.**
      - **Glencoe.**
        - **Sultan.**
          - Selim.
            - Buzzard, by Woodpecker.
            - Alexander Mare, by Alexander
          - Bacchante.
            - Williamson's Ditto, by Sir Peter.
            - Sister to Calomel, by Mercury.
        - **Tramp-oline.**
          - Tramp.
            - Dick Andrews, by Joe Andrews.
            - Daughter of Gohanna.
          - Web.
            - Waxy, by Pot-8-os.
            - Penelope, by Trumpator.
      - **Marpessa.**
        - **Morley.**
          - Orville.
            - Beningbrough, by King Fergus.
            - Evelina, by Highflyer.
          - Eleanor.
            - Whiskey, by Saltram.
            - Young Giantess, by Diomed.
        - **Clare.**
          - Marmion.
            - Whiskey, by Saltram.
            - Young Noisette, by Diomed.
          - Harpalice.
            - Gohanna, by Mercury.
            - Amazon, by Driver.

Seventh dam, Fractious by Mercury (Eclipse); Eighth dam by Woodpecker (Herod); Ninth dam, Everlasting by Eclipse (Marske); Tenth dam, Hyaena by Snap (Snip); Eleventh dam, Miss Belsea by Regulus (Godolphin Arabian); Twelfth dam by Bartlet's Childers (Darley Arabian); Thirteenth dam by Honeywood's Arabian; Fourteenth dam, Dam of the Two True Blues by the Byerly Turk.

IMPORTED RAYON D'OR.

(WINNER OF THE CLEARWELL, LEVANT AND GLASGOW STAKES IN 1878; THE ST.
JAMES' PALACE STAKES, THE SUSSEX, ZETLAND, SELECT CHAMPION, GREAT FOAL
STAKES, THE GREAT CHALLENGE STAKES AND DONCASTER ST. LEGER, IN 1879;
THE PRIX DU CADRAN AND PRIX RAINBOW AT PARIS, AND THE POST STAKES, THE
PRINCE OF WALES STAKES AND THE ROUS MEMORIAL STAKES, IN ENGLAND
IN 1880.)

From the Horse Breeders' Guide and Hand Book, by Col. S. D. Bruce.

"RAYON D'OR (Ray of Gold), by Flageolet, son of Plutus, bred in Dangu Stud,
France, foaled 1876, dam Araucaria, dam of Chamant, Camelia, etc., by Ambrose,
son of Touchstone, out of Pocahontas, dam of Stockwell, Rataplan, King Tom, etc.,
by *Glencoe. Rayon d'Or made his debut in England as a two-year-old by winning
the Levant Stake, half a mile, at Goodwood, carrying 122 pounds, beating Flavius,
Galantha and two others. At Doncaster, in September, he won a sweepstake, at
three-quarters of a mile, with 129 pounds, beating Charibert and Reconciliation. At
the Newmarket Second October Meeting won the Clearwell Stakes, carrying 131
pounds, with such horses as Ringleader and Bay Archer, 122 pounds each, second
and third, and three others; the Glasgow Stakes, at the Newmarket Houghton Meeting, three-quarters of a mile, beating Ringleader and Glencairn. During the winter
and spring which followed, Rayon d'Or was much fancied both for the 2,000 guineas
and Derby, but his running was a disappointment. He was third to Charibert and
Cadogan for the 2,000 guineas, and was unplaced for the Derby, won by Sir Bevys.
At Ascot, on the first day, he was third for the Prince of Wales Stakes, to Wheel of
Fortune and Adventure, but on the third day he won the St. James' Palace Stakes
with 122 pounds, over the severe "Old Mile," beating Charibert, Ruperra and seven
others. At Goodwood Rayon d'Or won the Sussex Stakes, one mile, beating Ruperra,
Leap Year and Exeter, and won the great Doncaster St. Leger, Ruperra second and
Exeter third, and fourteen others unplaced, including the winner of the Derby, Sir
Bevys. The next day Rayon d'Or "walked over" for the Zetland Stakes, Mr. Crawford's Pell Mell Colt saving his stake. At the Newmarket First October Meeting won
the Great Foal Stakes with 131 pounds, beating Discord, Palmbearer and three others,
but at the same meeting was beaten by Bay Archer for the Newmarket St. Leger, he
yielding 7 pounds, after which Rayon d'Or won the Select Stakes, Rowley Mile, beating Discord and three others; the Champion Stakes, across the flat, one mile, 2 furlongs, 73 yards, beating Placida, the Oaks winner, Exeter and five others, and the
Great Challenge Stakes, Bretby Course, six furlongs, beating Lollypop, Placida,
Parole and others. He ended his three-year-old career by running third for a handicap "Across the Flat" to Out of Bounds, who carried 110 pounds to Rayon d'Or's
126 pounds. His earning for the year amounted to $87,735. As a four-year-old
Rayon d'Or began by winning the Prix du Cadran, 2 miles and 5 furlongs, beating
Zut, Salteador and others, and the Prix Rainbow, 3 miles and a furlong, beating Zut
and Clocher at the Paris Spring Meeting in March. He was immediately afterward
sent to England, where, on the 16th of April, at Newmarket, he "walked over" for
the Post Stakes (the two middle miles). At the Newmarket First Spring meeting—
two weeks later—he "walked over" for the Prince of Wales Stakes (the Cesarewitch
Course). At Ascott he won the Rous Memorial Stakes over the New Mile, carrying

132 pounds ; but in running for the Hardwicke Stakes at the same meeting over the Swinley Course (mile and a half) he was beaten a head by Exeter, to whom he was giving 10 pounds. This race closed his turf career, placing to his credit a total of $122,140.65.

Flageolet, his sire, was a superior race-horse. He won his first race in France at two years old, defeating a large field. Won the Hopeful Stakes, one-half mile, at Newmarket, 128 pounds; won the Rutland Stakes, three-quarters of a mile, 129 pounds, beating His Grace and two others ; won the Forlorn Stakes, Rowley mile, 128 pounds, beating Lord Mayo, 122 pounds ; won Burwell Stakes, 5 furlongs, 128 pounds, defeating Amalie Von Edelreich, 122 pounds; was unplaced in Middle Park Plate, won by Surinam. Ran second to Andred in the Prendergast Stakes, Surinam and three others behind him. Won the Criterion Stakes, three-quarters of a mile, defeating Paladin, Kaiser and four others. As a three-year-old ran second to Boiard in the Prix du Jockey Club (French Derby), and second to him in the Grand Prix de Paris in 1873. He was also second to Apollon in the Prix du Cedre, same year. Crossing the Channel, he was unplaced in the 2,000 guineas, won by Gang Forward ; ran second to Cremorne in the Gold Cup at Ascott ; won the Goodwood Cup, in which he beat both Favonius and Cremorne, the Derby winners of 1871 and 1872. He ran second to Uhlan in Brighton Cup ; won the Grand Duke Michael Stakes at Newmarket First October Meeting ; won a free handicap sweepstakes across the flat, and the Jockey Club Cup at the Newmarket Houghton Meeting. As a four-year-old he ran second to Boiard twice in France ; won the Claret Stakes at Newmarket, England ; was second to Boiard in the Gold Cup, and third to King Lud and Boiard in the Alexandra Plate, both at Ascot. This closed his turf career. Plutus, his sire, was unplaced in the Derby of 1866, but won some races and ran creditably in others.

Araucaria, Rayon d'Or's dam, was the dam of Camelia, winner of the 1,000 guineas, and ran a dead heat and divided the Oaks Stakes with Enguerrande. Chamant, by Mr. Lorillard's Mortemer, out of Araucaria, won the Middle Park Plate and the Dewhurst Plate in England at two years old, and at three won the 2,000 guineas. The blood on the sire side is a combination of Touchstone through Orlando, a Derby winner, Bay Middleton, son of Sultan, a Derby winner, Venison and Glencoe, through Darkness, a winner of the Ascot Stakes. On the dam's side, Touchstone, St. Leger winner, Priam, Derby winner, and Glencoe, through Pocahontas, dam of Stockwell, Rataplan, King Tom, etc. An analysis of the tabulated pedigree will show that he is richly and fashionably bred ; he has a double cross of Glencoe, a triple cross of Diomed, a double cross of Touchstone, fortified by the blood of Whalebone, doubled in upon the Herod and Eclipse blood on both sides to the Byerly Mare, dam of the Two True Blues. Rayon d'Or is probably the most magnificent specimen of his race ever imported. He is the highest priced horse ever shipped across the Atlantic. His cost delivered at his home is little short of $40,000. In color he is a rich, true chestnut, with a large, rather faint, star in his forehead, standing 16 hands, 3½ inches in height. He has a beautiful head, very broad between the eyes, with a fine, clean and tapering ear ; neck, long but broad where it enters the head ; shoulders well set and broad, with great depth of girth ; good, round barrel, with splendid back, hip and loin. His hips will be found broad, with great length from the point of the hip to the whirlbone, and thence to stifle and hocks, the latter clean cut and well placed, and the finest, soundest and best set of legs ever seen under a horse ; in fact, it is one of his great excellent points, and certainly nothing is more essential to a good race-horse. Rayon d'Or (Ray of Gold) deserves his name.

The winnings of the get of Rayon d'Or in 1886, their first appearance on the American turf, were $1,965 ; in 1887, $32,955.

RAYON D'OR'S WINNERS IN 1888.

NAME.	Age	DAM.	Starts	First	Second	Third	Winnings.
Gypsy Queen, b f........	2	Liahtunah..............	16	5	2	4	$ 12,720
Defense, blk c.............	3	Imp. Presto.............	17	2	3	3	9,615
†Tipstaff, ch c............	2	Verdict	11	1	2	2	7,250
Bronzomarte, ch g.......	4	Imp. Doncaster Lass....	42	7	7	6	5,305
Quotation, b f......	3	Quarantine.................	11	15	5	10	4,597
Ransom, ch c............	2	Nellie Ransom.............	10	2	1	2	4,305
Laura Stone b. f...........	2	Valleria...........	21	6	9	3	4,165
Roi d'Or, ch g..........	4	Imp. Blue Cap..........	26	14	5	2	4,165
Belle d'Or, ch f..........	3	Belle Meade.............	22	5	3	3	4,100
Tudor, b g.............	3	Clemency..............	23	9	3	3	3,860
Tea Tray, ch c	3	Ella T..............	18	1	3	6	3,615
Marauder, ch c............	3	Maudina................	8	.....	3	2	2,430
‡Somerset, br g..........	4	Nannie H..............	24	5	4	3	1,420
Tenny, b c.................	2	Belle of Maywood.......	17	2	5	3	1,530
Flageoletta, b f..........	4	Imp. Clover................	15	1	2	4	1,185
Arundel, b g.............	4	Long Nine.................	18	3	2	3	1,100
Lady Hemphill, b f.....	2	Imp Miss Neilson.......	17	1	2	3	710
Sparling, ch c.............	2	Lucy Wallace.............	19	2	1	3	620
*Pat Oakley, ch c.......	4	Nell Gwynne..............	29	1	6	4	505
Quibler, ch g.............	3	Quits	20	2	1	1	450
Julien, b c................	2	Imp. Judith.............	10	1	3	3	425
Gendarme, b g............	2	Bona Fide.............	6	.....	1	......	300
Louis d'Or, b c............	2	Nettie Sterling............	4	1	1	......	300
Cold Stream, ch c.........	4	Pride of the Village.....	12	.....	2	1	240
Jake Miller, b c..........	2	Monopoly	15	.....	1	6	220
Alchemist, ch g...........	3	Lilly R.............	10	1	......	2	160
Harbor Lights, ch g.....	3	Imp. Lisou.............	10	1	......	......	150
†Village Maid, ch f.....	2	Adelaide.............	10	.....	3	1	105
Ionia, b f......	2	Ione	8	.....	1	1	50
Kingsford, ch c...........	3	Ione	10				
Ayala, ch g......	2	Brenda.............	9				
Cotillion, ch f..............	2	Reel Dance.............	5				
Chateau d'Or, ch g......	4	Luella.............	2		2		
Bellaire, ch c.............	2	Florence I.............	2				
The Belle, ch f..........	2	Blue Grass Belle.........	2				
Aftermath, b g..........	2	Imp. Clover.............	1				
Grand totals........			530	88	81	86	$ 75,627

*Jumper.   †By Rayon d'Or or Kantaka.   ‡By Rayon d'Or or Algerine.

Of the eighty-eight races won, two were half a mile ; two, four and a half furlongs ; four, five furlongs ; one, five and a half furlongs ; twenty-six, six furlongs ; one, six and a half furlongs ; six, seven furlongs ; three, seven and a half furlongs ; twenty, one mile ; eight, one mile and a sixteenth ; seven, one mile and a furlong ; three, one mile and a quarter ; one, one mile and five-sixteenths ; one, two miles ; one, half-mile heats ; one six-furlong heats, and one, mile heats

Gypsy Queen won the Spinaway Stake, Saratoga, five furlongs, 1:03, value $2,925 ; the Saratoga Stake, Saratoga, six furlongs, 1:16, value $5,020 ; the Tennessee Stake, Saratoga, six furlongs, 1:16½, value $1,950, and the Misses' Stake, Saratoga, six furlongs, 1:16, value $1,875.

Belle d'Or won the Annual Homebred Stake, Baltimore, one mile, 1:45, value $1,050, and the Chesapeake Stake, Baltimore, one mile and a quarter, 2:19, value $950.

Defense won the Tidal Stake, Coney Island, one mile, 1:42¼, value $7,720.

Laura Stone won the Ivy Leaf Stake, Nashville, half a mile, :50, value $1,000, and the Kensington Handicap, Chicago, six furlongs, 1:16½, value $1:240.

Ransom won the Camden Stake, Monmouth Park, six furlongs, 1:17¼, value $2,955, and Tipstaff won the Sapling Stake, Monmouth Park, six furlongs, 1:15¼, value $6,350.

ALGERINE.

Bay Horse, foaled 1873. Bred by Maj. Thomas W. Doswell, of Virginia.

Abd-el-Kader.

Nina.—Planet's Dam.

*Australian.

West Australian.
- Melbourne.
  - Humphrey Clinker. { Comus, by Sorcerer. / Clinkerina, by Clinker.
  - Daughter of { Cervantes, by Don Quixote. / Daughter of Golumpus.
- Mowerina.
  - Touchstone. { Camel, by Whalebone. / Banter, by Master Henry.
  - Emma. { Whisker, by Waxy. / Gibside Fairy, by Hermes.

Emilia.
- Young Emilius.
  - Emilius. { Orville, by Beningbrough. / Emily, by Stamford.
  - Shoveler. { Scud, by Beningbrough. / Goosander, by Hambletonian.
- Persian.
  - Whisker. { Waxy, by Pot-8-os. / Penelope, by Trumpator.
  - Variety. { Selim or Soothsayer. / Sprite, by Bobtail.

Rescue.

Berthune.
- Sidi Hamet.
  - Virginian. { Sir Archy, by * Diomed. / Meretrix, by Magog.
  - Lady Burton. { Sir Archy, by *Diomed. / Sultana, by Prest. Jefferson's Barb Horse.
- Susette.
  - Aratus. { Director, by Sir Archy. / Betsey Haxall, by * Sir Harry.
  - Jenny Cockracy. { Potomac, by *Diomed. / Timoleon's dam, by * Saltram.

Alice Carneal.
- *Sarpedon.
  - Emilius. { Orville, by Beningbrough. / Emily, by Stamford.
  - Icaria. { The Flyer, by VanDyke, jr. / Parma, by Dick Andrews.
- Rowena.
  - Sumpter. { Sir Archy, by *Diomed. / Daughter of *Robin Redbreast.
  - Lady Grey. { Robin Gray, by * Royalist. / Maria, by Melzar.

Boston.

Timoleon.
- Sir Archy.
  - * Diomed. { Florizel, by Herod. / Sister to Juno, by Spectator.
  - *Castianira. { Rockingham, by Highflyer. / Tabitha, by Trentham.
- Daughter of
  - *Saltram. { Eclipse, by Marske. / Virago, by Snap.
  - Daughter of { Symmes' Wildair, by * Fearnaught. / Daughter of Tyler's Driver, (by *Othello)

Sister to Tuckahoe.
- Ball's Florizel.
  - * Diomed. { Florizel, by Herod. / Sister to Juno, by Spectator.
  - Daughter of { *Shark, by Marske. / Daughter of Harris' Eclipse.
- Daughter of
  - *Alderman. { Pot-8-os, by Eclipse. / Lady Bolingbroke, by Squirrel.
  - Daughter of { *Clockfast, by Gimcrack. / Daughter of Symmes' Wildair.

*Frolicksome Fanny.

Lottery.
- Tramp.
  - Dick Andrews. { Joe Andrews, by Eclipse. / Daughter of Highflyer.
  - Daughter of { Gohanna, by Mercury. / Fraxinella, by Trentham.
- Mandane.
  - Pot-8 O's. { Eclipse, by Marske. / Sportsmistress, by Sportsman.
  - Young Camilla. { Woodpecker, by Herod. / Camilla, by Trentham.

Sister to Catterick.
- Whisker.
  - Waxy. { Pot-8-os, by Eclipse. / Maria, by Herod.
  - Penelope. { Trumpator, by Conductor. / Prunella, by Highflyer.
- Daughter of
  - Bay Trophonius. { Beningbrough, by King Fergus / Daughter of Stamford.
  - Daughter of { Sibpe, by Highflyer. / Lardella, by Young Marske.

Seventh dam by Cade (Godolphin Arabian); Eighth dam, Beaufremont's dam by Tartar (Partner); Ninth dam by Brother to Fearnaught (Bay Bolton;) Tenth dam, Miss Wyndham by Wyndham (Old Huntboy); Eleventh dam by Belgrade Turk; Twelfth dam, Old Scarborough Mare by Makeless (Oglethorp Arabian); Thirteenth dam, Daughter of Brimmer (D'Arcy Yellow Turk).

ALGERINE.

(WINNER OF THE BELMONT STAKES AT JEROME PARK IN 1876.)

From the Horse Breeders' Guide and Hand Book, by Col. S. D. Bruce.

"ALGERINE, by Abd-el-Kader, son of *Australian, was bred by Major Thomas W. Doswell, Bullfield Stud, Hanover Junction, Va.; foaled 1873, dam Nina, the dam of Planet, Exchequer, Ninette, Ecliptic, etc., by Old Boston. Algerine did not run as a two-year-old ; he made his bow to the public in the Preakness Stakes at Baltimore in 1876, 1½ miles, and was third to Shirley and Rappahannock in 2:44¾. At Jerome Park he won the Belmont Stakes, 1½ miles, in 2:40½, beating Fiddlesticks, the winner of the Withers Stakes, Barricade, brother to Bassett (Charley Howard) and Red Coat, each carrying 110 pounds. He was unplaced in the Dixie Stakes, 2 miles, at Baltimore, won by Vigil in 3:41½, track muddy. As a four-year-old he started five times, ran second to Parole in the Maturity Stakes at Jerome Park, 3 miles, in 5:39 ; second to St. James, 2 miles, in 3:49½ ; was unplaced in the All-Aged Sweepstake, 1½ miles, won by Tom Ochiltree in 2:43. Won club purse, 2-mile heats, at Baltimore, in 4:02½, 3:50, 4:00; track very heavy. Barricade won the second heat ; was unplaced in the Bowie Stake, 4-mile heats, won by Ten Broeck in 7:42½, 7:40. Abd-el-Kader, his sire, although badly hipped, was a fine race-horse at all distances ; he won a dash of 4 miles at Saratoga in 1869, in 7:31¾, a very creditable performance. Nina, the dam of Algerine, was one of the best race-mares of her day ; she was a winner at all distances, from one to four-mile heats, in good time, and produced Planet, one of the best horses in the country, at all distances, and for his chances a successful sire. Algerine is a blood bay, 15¾ hands, with black points, and no white about him. He is strongly inbred to Sir Archy, and on the sire's side is a grandson of the great West Australian, winner of the tripple events, 2,000 guineas, Derby and St. Leger, in 1853. Boston, the sire of his dam, was the best horse of any day. Algerine has no colts yet upon the turf, but from good mares should get winners and stayers ; he traces on both sides of sire and dam many times, to Herod and Eclipse, through the famous Waxy and Dick Andrews, and with the Archy and Diomed blood on both sides, through Diomed's best sons."

The entire produce of Algerine, living to be two years old, numbers but thirty-two, three of which are of double parentage. Twenty of these have gone to the post and furnished the large proportion of fifteen winners, viz : Aurelia, Brian Boru, I. H. D., Allarene, Somerset, Krishna, Tunis, J. C. Burnet, Irish Dan, Sirocco, Velvet, Simoon, Radha, Binnacle and Torso.

WANDERER.

Chestnut horse, foaled 1868. Bred at Woodburn Stud, Kentucky.

- **Lexington.**
  - **Boston.**
    - **Timoleon.**
      - **Sir Archy.**
        - Diomed. { Florizel, by Herod. / Sister to Juno, by Spectator. }
        - *Castianira. { Rockingham, by Highflyer. / Tabitha, by Trentham. }
      - **Daughter of**
        - *Saltram. { Eclipse, by Marske. / Virago, by Snap. }
        - Daughter of { Symme's Wildair, by *Fearnaught. / Daug. of Tyler's Driver (by *Othello) }
    - **Sis. to Tuckahoe.**
      - **Ball's Florizel.**
        - *Diomed. { Florizel, by Herod. / Sister to Juno, by Spectator. }
        - Daughter of { *Shark, by Marske. / Daughter of Harris' Eclipse. }
      - **Daughter of**
        - *Alderman. { Pot-8-os, by Eclipse, / Lady Bolingbroke, by Squirrel. }
        - Daughter of { *Clockfast, by Gimcrack. / Daughter of Symme's Wildair. }
  - **Alice Carneal.**
    - ***Sarpedon.**
      - **Emilius.**
        - Orville. { Beningbrough, by King Fergus. / Evelina, by Highflyer. }
        - Emily. { Stamford, by Sir Peter. / Daughter of Whiskey. }
      - **Icaria.**
        - The Flyer. { Van Dyke, Jr., by Walton. / Azalia, by Beningbrough. }
        - Parma. { Dick Andrews, by Joe Andrews. / May, by Beningbrough. }
    - **Rowena.**
      - **Sumpter.**
        - Sir Archy. { *Diomed, by Florizel, / *Castianira, by Rockingham. }
        - Flirtilla's dam. { Robin Redbreast, by Sir Peter. / Daughter of *Obscurity. }
      - **Lady Grey.**
        - Robin Grey. { *Royalist, by Saltram. / Belle Mariah, by Grey Diomed. }
        - Maria. { Melzar, by *Medley. / Daughter of Highflyer. }
- **Coral.**
  - **Vandal.**
    - ***Glencoe.**
      - **Sultan.**
        - Selim. { Buzzard, by Woodpecker. / Castrel's dam, by Alexander. }
        - Bacchante. { Williamson's Ditto, by Sir Peter. / Sister to Calomel, by Mercury. }
      - **Trampoline.**
        - Tramp. { Dick Andrews, by Joe Andrews. / Daughter of Gohanna. }
        - Web. { Waxy, by Pot-8-os. / Penelope, by Trumpator. }
    - **Alaric's dam.**
      - **Tranby.**
        - Blacklock. { Whitelock, by Hambletonian. / Daughter of Coriander. }
        - Daughter of { Orville, by Beningbrough. / Miss Grimstone, by Weasel. }
      - **Lucilla.**
        - Trumpator. { Sir Solomon, by Tickle Toby. / Daughter of Hickory. }
        - Lucy. { Orphan, by Ball's Florizel. / Lady Grey, by Robin Grey. }
  - **Glencairne.**
    - **Cotherstone.**
      - **Touchstone.**
        - Camel. { Whalebone by Waxy. / Daughter of Selim. }
        - Banter. { Master Henry, by Orville. / Boadicea, by Alexander. }
      - **Emma.**
        - Whisker. { Waxy, by Pot-8-os. / Penelope, by Trumpator. }
        - Gibside Fairy. { Hermes, by Mercury. / Vicissitude, by Pipator. }
    - **Glenluce.**
      - **Slane.**
        - Royal Oak. { Catton, by Golumpus. / Daughter of Smolensko. }
        - Daughter of { Orville, by Beningbrough. / Epsom Lass, by Sir Peter. }
      - **Daughter of**
        - Sultan. { Selim, by Buzzard. / Bacchante, by Williamson's Ditto. }
        - Trampoline. { Tramp, by Dick Andrews. / Web, by Waxy. }

Seventh dam, Penelope, by Trumpator; eighth dam, Prunella, by Highflyer; ninth dam, Promise, by Snap; tenth dam, Julia, by Blank; eleventh dam, Spectator's dam, by Partner; twelfth dam, Bonny Lass, by Bay Bolton; thirteenth dam, by Darley Arabian; fourteenth dam by The Byerly Turk; fifteenth dam by the Taffolet Barb; sixteenth dam by Place's White Turk; seventeenth dam, Natural Barb Mare.

WANDERER.

(WINNER OF THE RAILROAD STAKES AT NASHVILLE, 1872; THE MONMOUTH CUP AT LONG BRANCH, AND WESTCHESTER CUP AT JEROME PARK, 1873.)

From the Horse-Breeders' Guide and Hand Book, by Col. S. D. Bruce.

"WANDERER, by Lexington, son of Boston, bred in the Woodburn Stud, Ky., foaled 1868, dam Coral, dam of Uncas by Vandal, son of Glencoe out of *Cairngorme by Cotherstone, winner of the 2,000 guineas and Derby, son of Touchstone winner of the St. Leger.

Wanderer is descended from one of the most noted racing families of England, tracing back through an own sister to *Glencoe to the famous Web by Waxy. The family has furnished some of the most noted race-horses and successful sires of the English turf. From it came Whalebone, winner of the Derby in 1810; Whisker, winner of the same event in 1815; Cobweb, winner of the Oaks and 1,000 guineas in 1824; Riddlesworth, winner of the 2 000 guineas and Derby in 1836; Glencoe, winner of the 2,000 guineas in 1831; Bay Middleton, winner of the 2,000 guineas and Goodwood Cup in 1834; Blue Gown, winner of the Derby in 1868; Silvio, winner of both Derby and St. Leger in 1877, and a host of others.

Wanderer made his first appearance as a three-year-old and was unplaced in the Belmont Stakes at Jerome Park, and the Jersey Derby at Long Branch, both events having been won by his half brother, Harry Bassett. At Long Branch he won a club purse, mile heats, in 1:48¾, 1:48¼, defeating a field of seven. In his four-year-old form, at New Orleans, he won a race of mile heats in 1:51, 1:47¼, 1:47½, beating Frank Ross, winner of the first heat, Niagara and Glenrose; won the Railroad Stakes at Nashville, Tenn., two-mile heats, in 3:41¼, 3:38½, beating Hollywood, Frogtown, etc., and walked over for club purse, two-mile heats. As a five-year-old he won the Monmouth Cup at Long Branch, 2½ miles, in 4:34¼, beating Preakness, Hubbard and others; won the Westchester Cup at Jerome Park, 2¼ miles, in 4:04, beating True Blue, Eolus and others. At Saratoga, ran second to Hubbard, 3 miles in 5:34, beating Harry Bassett and King Henry. Same meeting ran second to Arizona, 1½ miles, in 2:38, beating Boss Tweed and Eolus. As a six year-old won club purse at Savannah, Ga., 2 miles, in 3:43½, beating Granger and four others, and also same meeting, a club purse, 1¼ miles, in 2:18¾, beating Ortolan and Tabitha. At Nashville, Tenn., won the Johnson Stakes, 2¼ miles, in 4:06½, beating Planchette, St. George and two others. At Jerome Park ran second to Shylock, son of Lexington, in the Westchester Cup, 2¼ miles, in 4:13, beating Lizzie Lucas, Abd-el-Koree and two others, track heavy. Saratoga, won club purse, 2¼ miles, in 4:00½, beating Fellowcraft, Jack Frost, Galway and Katie Pease. Same place, ran second to Fellowcraft, 4 miles, in 7:19½, the fastest race at the distance ever run up to that date. In this race Wanderer beat Katie Pease and was timed the distance in 7:20.

Wanderer has been quite a success in the stud, having only a few mares, he sired One Dime a winner 1⅛ mile in 1:55½, 1¼ miles in 2:09¼, mile heats in 1:44½, 1:44½. Elkhorn Stakes, 1¾ miles in 3:05¼. Minnie C. (Mrs. Chubbs), winner of the filly stakes at Lexington. Juanita, 1¼ miles in 2:10. Lizzie S, filly stakes at Lexington, half mile in 0:49 Coquette Stakes at St. Louis, three-quarters of a mile in 1:18½; five furlongs in 1:02; three-quarters of a mile in 1:16½; one mile in 1:43. Mary Lamphier, Farragut, Nomad, Wakefield, Cash Clay, Waterford, Prophet, Rambler, Wandering, winner one mile in 1:45¼, and Capital Stakes, one mile in 1:44¾, and others all winners. His colts are the best the dams have produced. He is a rich golden chestnut, with the marks of his sire; is handsomely shaped and of very blood-like appearance, muscular and highly finished. His sire was the best race-horse and stallion this country has produced; his dam is by the best son of *Glencoe and traces through his own sister to Glencoe and Web by Waxy to a Natural Barb Mare. This is one of the pure sources through which the blood of Lexington and Glencoe should be preserved."

IMPORTED KANTAKA.

Chestnut horse, foaled 1860. Bred by Mr. W. Blenkiron, England. Imported by Mr. P. Lorillard.

Seclusion. (Hermit's dam).

Sire: Scottish Chief
- Lord of the Isles.
  - Touchstone.
    - Camel.
      - Whalebone. — { Waxy, by Pot-8-os. / Penelope, by Trumpator. }
      - Daughter of — { Selim, by Buzzard. / Maiden, by Sir Peter. }
    - Banter.
      - Master Henry. — { Orville, by Beningbrough. / Miss Sophia, by Stamford. }
      - Boadicea. — { Alexander, by Eclipse. / Brunette, by Amaranthus. }
  - Fair Helen.
    - Panta-loon.
      - Castrel. — { Buzzard, by Woodpecker. / Daughter of Alexander. }
      - Idalia. — { Peruvian, by Sir Peter / Musidora, by Meteor. }
    - Rebecca.
      - Lottery. — { Tramp, by Dick Andrews. / Mandane, by Pot-8-os. }
      - Daughter of — { Cervantes, by Don Quixote. / Anticipation, by Beningbrough. }
- Miss Ann.
  - The Little Known.
    - Muley.
      - Orville. — { Beningbrough, by King Fergus. / Evelina, by Highflyer. }
      - Eleanor. — { Whiskey, by Saltram. / Young Giantess, by Diomed. }
    - Lacerta.
      - Zodiac. — { St. George, by Highflyer. / Abigail, by Woodpecker. }
      - Jerboa. — { Gohanna, by Mercury. / Camilla, by Trentham. }
  - Bay Missy.
    - Camilla.
      - Sultan. — { Selim, by Buzzard. / Bacchante, by Williamson's Ditto. }
      - Cobweb. — { Phantom, by Walton. / Filagree, by Soothsayer. }
    - Cain.
      - Young Phantom. — { Phantom, by Walton. / Emmeline, by Waxy. }
      - Sister to Speaker — { Camillus, by Hambletonian. / Sister to Prime Minister, by Sancho. }

Dam: Seclusion
- Bay Middleton.
  - Tadmor.
    - Mar-garet.
      - Paulowitz. — { Sir Paul, by Sir Peter. / Evalina, by Highflyer. }
      - Daughter of — { Paynator, by Trumpator. / Daughter of Delpini, by Highflyer. }
    - Ione.
      - Edmond. — { Orville, by Beningbrough. / Emmeline, by Waxy }
      - Medora. — { Selim, by Buzzard. / Daughter of Sir Harry, by Sir Peter. }
  - Palmyra.
    - Sultan.
      - Selim. — { Buzzard, by Woodpecker. / Daughter of Alexander. }
      - Bacchante. — { Williamson's Ditto, by Sir Peter. / Sister to Calomel, by Mercury. }
    - Hester.
      - Camel. — { Whalebone, by Waxy. / Daughter of Selim, by Buzzard. }
      - Monimia. — { Muley, by Orville. / Sister to Petworth, by Precipitate. }
- Miss Sellon.
  - Cowl.
    - Bay Middleton.
      - Sultan. — { Selim, by Buzzard. / Bacchante, by Williamson's Ditto. }
      - Cobweb. — { Phantom, by Walton. / Filagree, by Soothsayer. }
    - Cruci-fix.
      - Priam. — { Emilius, by Orville. / Cressida, by Whiskey. }
      - Octaviana. — { Octavian, by Stripling. / Daughter of Shuttle, by Marske. }
  - Belle Dame.
    - Bel-shazzar.
      - Blacklock. — { Whitelock, by Hambletonian. / Daughter of Coriander. }
      - Manuella. — { Dick Andrews, by Joe Andrews. / Mandane, by Pot-8-os. }
    - Ellen.
      - Starch. — { Waxy Pope, by Waxy. / Miss Stavely, by Shuttle. }
      - Cuirass. — { Oiseau, by Camillus. / Castianea, by Gohanna. }

Seventh dam, Grey Skim by Woodpecker; Eighth dam, Silver's dam by Herod; Ninth dam, Young Hag by Skim; Tenth dam, Hag by Crab: Eleventh 4am, Ebony by Childers; Twelfth dam, Ebony by Basto; Thirteenth dam, The Massey Mare by Mr. Massey's Black Barb.

IMPORTED KANTAKA.

KANTAKA, by Scottish Chief, son of Lord of the Isles, by Touchstone, was bred by Mr. W. Blenkiron, England, foaled 1880, dam Seclusion (Hermit's dam), by Tadmor. Kantaka was bought as a yearling in England by Mr. P. Lorillard for the sum of $5,000, and was trained there by Mr. Lorillard's trainers, Mr. Puryear and Mr. Pincus, but never ran on account of injuries received in his exercise. He is represented, however, by Messrs. Puryear and Pincus as one of the most promising yearlings they ever trained. By an examination of his pedigree it will be seen that he is one of the finest bred horses in the world, being more than a half brother to Hermit, winner of the English Derby in 1867, and who during the the past ten years has risen into fame as the leading sire of England, having sired Peter, Shotover, St. Blaise, Tristan, Thebais, Clairvaux, St. Marguerite, Queen Adelaide and St. Helena.

On the sire's side, Scottish Chief is by Lord of the Isles, by Touchstone, and Hermit's sire, Newminster, is by Touchstone. Kantaka is a true chestnut, 15 hands and 3 inches high.

Kantaka is young in the stud and has had but eleven starters at this writing (June 15, '89), five of them securing winning brackets, viz : Canteen, G. D. Boyden, Dock Wick, Irish Dan (Kantaka or Algerine), and Tipstaff (Rayon d'Or or Kantaka.)

ADELAIDE.
Chestnut mare, foaled 1873. Bred by Mr. Alexander, Ky.

- **Dolly Carter.**
  - **Mavis.**
    - ***Glencoe.***
      - **Sultan.**
        - **Selim.**
          - Buzzard. { Woodpecker, by Herod. / Misfortune, by Dux. }
          - Castrel's dam. { Alexander, by Eclipse. / Daughter of Highflyer. }
        - **Bacchante.**
          - Williamson's Ditto. { Sir Peter, by Highflyer. / Arethusa, by Dungannon. }
          - Sister to Calomel { Mercury, by Eclipse. / Daughter of Herod. }
      - **Trampoline.**
        - **Tramp.**
          - Dick Andrews. { Joe Andrews, by Eclipse / Daughter of Highflyer. }
          - Daughter of { Gohanna, by Mercury. / Fraxinella, by Trentham. }
        - **Web.**
          - Waxy. { Pot-8-os, by Eclipse. / Maria, by Herod. }
          - Penelope. { Trumpator, by Conductor. / Prunella, by Highflyer. }
    - **Wagner.**
      - **Sir Charles.**
        - Sir Archy. { *Diomed, by Florizel. / *Castianira, by Rockingham. }
        - Daughter of { *Citizen, by Pacolet. / Daughter of *Alderman. }
      - **Maria West.**
        - Marion. { Sir Archy, by *Diomed. / Daughter of *Citizen. }
        - Ella Crump. { *Citizen, by Pacolet. / Daughter of Huntsman. }
  - **Daughter of**
    - **Meloc.**
      - American Eclipse. { Duroc, by *Diomed / Miller's Damsel, by *Messenger. }
      - Young Maid of the Oaks. { *Expedition, by Pegassus. / Maid of the Oaks, by *Spread Eagle. }
    - **Daughter of**
      - Blackburn's Whip. { *Whip, by Saltram. / Specklebrack, by Randolph's Celer. }
      - Daughter of { Sumpter, by Sir Archy. / Virago, by *Shark. }

- ***Australian.***
  - **West Australian.**
    - **Melbourne.**
      - **Humphrey Clinker.**
        - Comus. { Sorcerer, by Trumpator. / Houghton Lass, by Sir Peter. }
        - Clinkerina. { Clinker, by Sir Peter. / Pewet, by Tandem. }
      - **Daughter of**
        - Cervantes. { Don Quixote, by Eclipse. / Evelina, by Highflyer. }
        - Daughter of { Golumpus, by Gohanna. / Daughter of Paynator. }
    - **Mowerina.**
      - **Touchstone.**
        - Camel. { Whalebone, by Waxy. / Daughter of Selim. }
        - Banter. { Master Henry, by Orville. / Boadicea, by Alexander. }
      - **Emma.**
        - Whisker. { Waxy, by Pot-8-os. / Penelope, by Trumpator. }
        - Gibside Fairy. { Hermes, by Mercury. / Vicissitude, by Pipator. }
  - **Emilia.**
    - **Young Emilius.**
      - **Emilius.**
        - Orville. { Beningbrough, by King Fergus. / Evelina, by Highflyer. }
        - Emily. { Stamford, by Sir Peter. / Daughter of Whiskey. }
      - **Shoveler.**
        - Scud. { Beningbrough, by King Fergus. / Eliza, by Highflyer. }
        - Goosander. { Hambletonian, by King Fergus. / Rally, by Trumpator. }
    - **Persian.**
      - **Whisker.**
        - Waxy. { Pot-8-os, by Eclipse. / Maria, by Herod. }
        - Penelope. { Trumpator, by Conductor. / Prunella, by Highflyer. }
      - **Variety.**
        - Selim, or Soothsayer. { Sorcerer, by Trumpator. / Goldenlocks, by Delpini. }
        - Sprite. { Bobtail, by Precipitate. / Catherine by Woodpecker. }

Seventh dam, *Gunilda (called Virago) by Star; Eighth dam, Virago by Panton Arabian; Ninth dam, Crazy by Lath; Tenth dam, Sister to Snip by Childers; Eleventh dam, Sister to Soreheels by Basto; Twelfth dam, Sister to Mixbury by Curwen's Bay Barb, etc., etc.

ADELAIDE.

At two years old started three times, running second to Parole in both the Saratoga and Alabama Stakes, and third to Sultana in the Two-Year-Old Sweepstakes at Saratoga. At three years old started but once, running unplaced in mile-and-a half purse to Ore Knob at Jerome Park.

PRODUCE.

1878, ch. c., ADALBERT, by Kingfisher.

1879, Missed to Kingfisher.

1880, ch. c., ADAMANTIUS, by Count d'Orsay.

1881, ch. f. (dead), by Fiddlesticks.

1882, ch. f., ADELA, by Count d'Orsay.

1883, Missed to Kingfisher.

1884, ch. c., ALARIC, by *Illused. (Gelded.

1885, Missed to *Illused.

1886, ch. f., VILLAGE MAID, by *Rayon d'Or, or *Kantaka.

1887, Missed to *Rayon d'Or.

1888, Dead ch. c., by *Rayon d'Or.

1889, ch. c.,   by *Rayon d'Or.

1890,   by *Rayon d'Or.

ARABELLA (IMPORTED). Bred by Mr. Blenkiron, England. Imported 1882, by Mr. W. L. Scott, Erie, Pa.

Chestnut mare, foaled 1873.

- **Miss Winkle.**
  - **The Flying Dutchman.**
    - **Bay Middleton.**
      - **Sultan.**
        - Selim. — { Buzzard, by Woodpecker / Castrel's dam, by Alexander.
        - Bacchante. — { Williamson's Ditto, by Sir Peter. / Sister to Calomel, by Mercury.
      - **Cobweb.**
        - Phantom. — { Walton, by Sir Peter. / Julia, by Whiskey.
        - Filagree. — { Soothsayer, by Sorcerer. / Web, by Waxy.
    - **Barbelle.**
      - **Sandbeck.**
        - Catton. — { Golumpus, by Gohanna. / Lucy Grey, by Timothy.
        - Orvillina. — { Beningbrough, by King Fergus. / Evelina, by Highflyer.
      - **Davioletta.**
        - Amadis. — { Don Quixote, by Eclipse. / Fanny, by Sir Peter.
        - Selima. — { Selim, by Buzzard. / Daughter of Pot-8-os.
  - **Dutch Skater / Fulvie.**
    - **Gladiator.**
      - **Partisan.**
        - Walton. — { Sir Peter, by Highflyer. / Arethusa, by Dungannon.
        - Parasol. — { Pot-8-os, by Eclipse. / Prunella, by Highflyer.
      - **Pauline.**
        - Moses. — { Whalebone, or Seymour. / Daughter of Gohanna.
        - Quadrille. — { Selim, by Buzzard. / Canary Bird, by Whiskey or Sorcerer.
    - **Bontique.**
      - **Giges.**
        - Priam. — { Emilius, by Orville. / Cressida, by Whiskey.
        - Eva. — { Sultan, by Selim. / Eliza Leeds, by Comus.
      - **Belvidere.**
        - Actæon. — { Scud, by Beningbrough. / Diana, by Stamford.
        - Belvoirina. — { Stamford, by Sir Peter. / Sister to Silver, by Mercury.
- **The Belle.**
  - **Newminster.**
    - **Touchstone.**
      - **Camel.**
        - Whalebone. — { Waxy, by Pot-8-os. / Penelope, by Trumpator.
        - Daughter of — { Selim, by Buzzard. / Maiden, by Sir Peter.
      - **Banter.**
        - Master Henry. — { Orville, by Beningbrough. / Miss Sophia, by Stamford.
        - Boadicea. — { Alexander, by Eclipse. / Brunette, by Amaranthus.
    - **Beeswing.**
      - **Dr. Syntax.**
        - Paynator. — { Trumpator, by Conductor. / Daughter of Marc Anthony.
        - Daughter of — { Beningbrough, by King Fergus. / Jennie Mole, by Carbuncle.
      - **Daughter of**
        - Ardrossan. — { John Bull, by Fortitude. / Miss Whip, by Volunteer.
        - Lady Eliza. — { Whitworth, by Agonistes. / Daughter of Spadille.
  - **Miss Fairfield.**
    - **Slane**
      - **Royal Oak.**
        - Catton. — { Golumpus, by Gohanna. / Lucy Grey, by Timothy.
        - Daughter of — { Smolensko, by Sorcerer. / Lady Mary, by Beningbrough.
      - **Daughter of**
        - Orville. — { Beningbrough, by King Fergus. / Evelina, by Highflyer.
        - Epsom Lass. — { Sir Peter, by Highflyer. / Alexina, by King Fergus.
    - **Grey Tommy's dam.**
      - **Hampton.**
        - Sultan. — { Selim, by Buzzard. / Bacchante, by Williamson's Ditto.
        - Rachel — { Whalebone, by Waxy. / Moses' dam, by Gohanna.
      - **Daughter of**
        - Comus. — { Sorcerer, by Trumpator. / Houghton Lass, by Sir Peter.
        - Daughter of — { Smolensko, by Sorcerer. / Sister to Orphan, by Camillus.

Seventh dam by Gabriel (by Dorimant); Eighth dam, Legacy by King Fergus; Ninth dam, Mortonia by Herod; Tenth dam by Northumberland; eleventh dam by Regulus; Twelfth dam by Lord Morton's Arabian; Thirteenth dam by Mixbury; Fourteenth dam by Mulso's Bay Turk; Fifteenth dam by Bolton; Sixteenth dam by Coneyskins; Seventeenth dam by Hutton's GreyBarb; Eighteenth dam by The Byerly Turk; Nineteenth dam by Bustler.

IMPORTED ARABELLA.

At two years old started in nine races in England ; at Alexandra Park won the Selling Two-Year-Old Plate, beating Florence, Pantaloon and four others ; same place won the Caen Wood Plate, beating Blue Gown-Catherine filly, Pantaloon and Honey-Bee ; ran second in two, third in one and unplaced in four.

----- ------ -----

PRODUCE.

1883, Missed to Scottish Chief.

1884, b. c., DOMINICK B., by Algerine. (Gelded.)

1885, ch. f.,   by Algerine or *Rayon d'Or. (Died in '87.)

1886, b. c., IRELAND, by Algerine.

1887, b. f., (Dead), by Algerine.

1888, ch. f., GADABOUT by Wanderer.

1889, ch. f.,   by Wanderer

1890,   by Algerine.

ALL HANDS AROUND.

(Chestnut mare, foaled 1880. Bred by James A. Grinstead, Kentucky.)

War Dance.
- **Lexington.**
  - **Boston.**
    - **Timoleon.**
      - Sir Archy. { * Diomed, by Florizel. / * Castianira, by Rockingham.
      - Daughter of { * Saltram, by Eclipse. / Daughter of Symme's Wildair.
    - **Sister to Tuckahoe.**
      - Ball's Florizel. { * Diomed, by Florizel. / Daughter of * Shark.
      - Daughter of { * Alderman, by Pot-8-os. / Daughter of * Clockfast.
  - **Alice Carneal.**
    - *** Sarpedon.**
      - Emilius. { Orville, by Beningbrough. / Emily, by Stamford.
      - Icaria. { The Flyer, by Van Dyke, jr. / Parma, by Dick Andrews.
    - **Rowena.**
      - Sumpter. { Sir Archy, by * Diomed. / Daughter of * Robin Redbreast.
      - Lady Grey. { Robin Grey, by * Royalist. / Maria, by Melzar.
- **Reel.**
  - *** Glencoe.**
    - **Sultan.**
      - Selim. { Buzzard, by Woodpecker. / Castrel's dam, by Alexander.
      - Bacchante. { Williamson's Ditto, by Sir Peter. / Sister to Calomel, by Mercury.
    - **Trampoline.**
      - Tramp. { Dick Andrews, by Joe Andrews. / Daughter of Gohanna.
      - Web. { Waxy, by Pot-8-os. / Penelope, by Trumpator.
  - *** Gallopade.**
    - **Catton.**
      - Golumpus. { Gohanna, by Mercury. / Catherine, by Woodpecker.
      - Lucy Grey. { Timothy, by Delpini. / Lucy, by Florizel.
    - **Camilline.**
      - Camillus. { Hambletonian, by King Fergus. / Faith, by Pacolet.
      - Daughter of { Smolensko, by Sorcerer. / Miss Cannon, by Orville.

Turantella.
- *** Australian.**
  - **West Australian.**
    - **Melbourne.**
      - Humphrey Clinker { Comus, by Sorcerer. / Clinkerina, by Clinker.
      - Daughter of { Cervantes, by Don Quixote. / Daughter of Golumpus.
    - **Mowerina.**
      - Touchstone. { Camel, by Whalebone. / Banter, by Master Henry.
      - Emma. { Whisker, by Waxy. / Gibside Fairy, by Hermes.
  - **Emilia.**
    - **Young Emilius.**
      - Emilius. { Orville, by Beningbrough. / Emily, by Stamford.
      - Shoveler. { Scud, by Beningbrough. / Goosander, by Hambletonian.
    - **Persian.**
      - Whisker. { Waxy, by Pot-8-os. / Penelope, by Trumpator.
      - Variety. { Selim, by Soothsayer. / Sprite, by Bobtail.
- **Schottische.**
  - **Albion.**
    - **Cain or Actaeon.**
      - Send. { Beningbrough, by King Fergus. / Eliza, by Highflyer.
      - Diana. { Stamford, by Sir Peter. / Daughter of Whiskey.
    - **Pan-thera.**
      - Comus. { Sorcerer, by Trumpator. / Whitelock, by Hambletonian.
      - Manuella. { Dick Andrews, by Joe Andrews. / Mandane, by Pot-8-os.
  - **Dance.**
    - **Silencer.**
      - Sultan. { Selim, by Buzzard. / Bacchante, by Williamson's Ditto.
      - Trampoline. { Tramp, by Dick Andrews. / Web, by Waxy.
    - **Cotillion.**
      - * Leviathan. { Muley, by Orville. / Daughter of Windle.
      - * Gallopade. { Catton, by Golumpus. / Camillina, by Camillus.

Seventh dam by Smolensko; eighth dam, Miss Cannon, by Orville; ninth dam by Weathercock; tenth dam, Cora, by Matchem; eleventh dam by Turk; twelfth dam by Cub; thirteenth dam by Allworthy; fourteenth dam by Starling; fifteenth dam by Bloody Buttocks; sixteenth dam by Greyhound; seventeenth dam, Brocklesby Betty, by Curwin's Bay Barb; eighteenth dam, Leed's Hobby Mare, by Lister Turk.

ALL HANDS AROUND.

At two years old started ten times, winning Two-Year-Old Selling Stakes at Saratoga, second four times, running second to Miss Woodford in both the Spinaway and Misses' Stakes, and unplaced five times. At three years old started eleven times, winning the Clarendon Hotel Stakes, and mile and a furlong purse at Saratoga, ran second once, third three times, and unplaced five times. At four years old started eight times, winning two Handicap Sweepstakes at Sheepshead Bay, ran third once and unplaced five times.

PRODUCE.

1886. ch. c., by *Rayon d'Or. (Died in '87.)

1887, Missed to *Rayon d'Or.

1888, ch. c., BOLERO, by *Rayon d'Or.

1889, ch. c., by *Rayon d'Or.

1890, by *Rayon d'Or.

ASTERIA.

Chestnut mare, foaled 1884. Bred in Erlenheim Stud.

ASTERIA

- ***Kantaka**
  - **Scottish Chief**
    - **Lord of the Isles**
      - **Touchstone**
        - Camel. — Whalebone, by Waxy. / Daughter of Selim.
        - Banter. — Master Henry, by Orville. / Boudicea, by Alexander.
      - **Fair Helen.**
        - Pantaloon. — Castrel, by Buzzard. / Idalia, by Peruvian.
        - Rebecca. — Lottery, by Tramp. / Daughter of Cervantes.
    - **Miss Ann.**
      - **The Little Known.**
        - Muley. — Orville, by Beningbrough. / Eleanor, by Whiskey.
        - Lacerta. — Zodiac, by St. George. / Jerboa, by Gohanna.
      - **Bay Missy.**
        - Bay Middleton. — Sultan, by Selim. / Cobweb, by Phantom.
        - Camilla. — Young Phantom, by Phantom. / Sister to Speaker, by Camillus.
  - **Seclusion (Hermit's dam).**
    - **Tadmor.**
      - **Ione.**
        - Cain. — Paulowitz, by Sir Paul. / Daughter of Paynator.
        - Margaret. — Edmond, by Orville. / Medora, by Selim.
      - **Palmyra.**
        - Sultan. — Selim, by Buzzard. / Bacchante, by Williamson's Ditto.
        - Hester. — Camel, by Whalebone. / Mominia, by Muley.
    - **Miss Sellon.**
      - **Cowl.**
        - Pay Middleton. — Sultan, by Selim. / Cobweb, by Phantom.
        - Crucifix. — Priam, by Emilius. / Octavia, by Octavian.
      - **Belle Dame.**
        - Belshazzar. — Blacklock, by Whitelock. / Manuella, by Dick Andrews.
        - Ellen. — Starch, by Waxy Pope. / Cuirass, by Oiseau.
- **Zieka.**
  - ***Australian.**
    - **West Australian.**
      - **Melbourne.**
        - Humphrey Clinker. — Comus, by Sorcerer. / Clinkerina, by Clinker.
        - Daughter of — Cervantes, by Don Quixote. / Daughter of Golumpus.
      - **Mowerina.**
        - Touchstone. — Camel, by Whalebone. / Banter, by Master Henry.
        - Emma. — Whisker, by Waxy. / Gibside Fairy, by Hermes.
    - **Emilia.**
      - **Young Emilius.**
        - Emilius. — Orville, by Beningbrough. / Emily, by Stamford.
        - Shoveler. — Scud, by Beningbrough. / Goosander, by Hambletonian.
      - **Persian.**
        - Whisker. — Waxy, by Pot-8-os. / Penelope, by Trumpator.
        - Variety. — Selim, or Soothsayer. / Sprite, by Bobtail.
  - **Mazurka.**
    - **Lexington.**
      - **Boston.**
        - Timoleon. — Sir Archy, by *Diomed. / Daughter of *Saltram.
        - Sister to Tuckahoe. — Ball's Florizel, by *Diomed. / Daughter of *Alderman.
      - **Alice Carneal.**
        - *Sarpedon. — Emilius, by Orville. / Icaria, by The Flyer.
        - Rowena. — Sumpter, by Sir Archy. / Lady Grey, by Robin Grey.
    - **Miss Morgan.**
      - ***Yorkshire.**
        - St. Nicholas. — Emilius, by Orville. / Seamew, by Scud.
        - Miss Rose. — Tramp, by Dick Andrews. / Daughter of Sancho, by Don Quixote.
      - **Sally Morgan.**
        - *Emancipation. — Whisker, by Waxy. / Daughter of Ardrossan.
        - Lady Morgan. — John Richards, by Sir Archy. / Matchless, by *Expedition.

Seventh dam, by Sir Solomon; eighth dam, Aurora, by *Honest John; ninth dam, Zelipha, by *Messenger: tenth dam, Dido, by *Bay Richmond; eleventh dam, Slamerkin, by *Wildair; twelfth dam, *Mare by Cub; thirteenth dam, Amaranthus' dam, by *Second; fourteenth dam by Starling: fifteenth dam (sister to Vane's Little Partner), by Croft's Partner); sixteenth dam, (sister to Guy) by *Greyhound: seventeenth dam, Brown Farewell, by Makeless; eighteenth dam by Brimmer; nineteenth dam by Place's White Turk; twentieth dam by Dodsworth; twenty-first dam, Layton Barb mare.

ASTERIA.

At two years old started four times, running second to Lady Primrose in a three-quarter-mile Sweepstakes, at Coney Island, eight starters, and unplaced three times permanently injuring herself in her last race.

PRODUCE.

1889, ch. f.,   by *Rayon d'Or.

1890,   by Wanderer.

BENEDICTION (IMPORTED).

Chestnut mare, foaled 1857. Bred by Lord Lovelace, England. Imported 1881, by Mr. W. Easton.

- **Lord Lyon, 1863.**
  - **Stockwell, 1849.**
    - **The Baron.**
      - **Irish Birdcatcher.**
        - Sir Hercules. { Whalebone, by Waxy. / Peri, by Wanderer.
        - Guiccioli. { Bob Booty, by Chanticleer. / Flight, by Escape.
      - **Echidna, 1838.**
        - Economist. { Whisker, by Waxy. / Floranthe, by Octavian.
        - Miss Pratt. { Blacklock, by Whitelock. / Gadabout, by Orville.
    - **Pocahontas, 1837.**
      - **Glencoe, 1831.**
        - Sultan. { Selim, by Buzzard. / Bacchante, by Wm's Ditto.
        - Trampoline. { Tramp, by Dick Andrews. / Web, by Waxy.
      - **Marpessa, 1830.**
        - Muley. { Orville, by Benningbrough. / Eleanor, by Whiskey.
        - Clare. { Marmion, by Whiskey. / Harpalice, by Gohanna.
  - **Paradigm.**
    - **Paragone, 1843.**
      - **Touchstone, 1831.**
        - Camel. { Whalebone, by Waxy. / Daughter of Selim.
        - Banter. { Master Henry, by Orville. / Boadicea, by Alexander.
      - **Hayden, 1837.**
        - Tomboy. { Jerry, by Smolensko. / Beeswing's dam, by Ardrossan.
        - Rochana. { Velocipede, by Blacklock. / Miss Garforth, by Walton.
    - **Ellen Horne.**
      - **Redshank.**
        - Sandbeck. { Catton, by Golumpus. / Orvilina, by Benningbrough.
        - Johanna. { Selim, by Buzzard. / Skyscraper Mare.
      - **Delhi.**
        - Plenipotentiary. { Emilius, by Orville. / Harriet, by Pericles.
        - Pawn, jr. { Waxy, by Pot-8-os. / Pawn, by Trumpator.
- **Benefactress.**
  - **Ada DeClare.**
    - **Lord Albemarle.**
      - **The Emperor.**
        - Whalebone. { Waxy, by Pot-8-os. / Penelope, by Trumpator.
        - Defiance. { Rubens, by Buzzard. / Little Folly, by Highland Fling.
      - **Daughter of Defence.**
        - Reveller. { Comus, by Sorcerer. / Rosette, by Benningbrough.
        - Design. { Tramp, by Dick Andrews. / Defiance, by Rubens.
    - **Coral.**
      - **Sir Hercules.**
        - Whalebone. { Waxy, by Pot-8-os. / Penelope, by Trumpator.
        - Peri. { Wanderer, by Gohanna. / Thalestres, by Alexander.
      - **Ruby.**
        - Rubens. { Buzzard, by Woodpecker. / Castrel's dam, by Alexander.
        - Daughter of { Williamson's Ditto, by Sir Peter. / Agnes, by Shuttle.
  - **Maid of Newton.**
    - **Voltigeur or De Clare.**
      - **Touchstone.**
        - Camel. { Whalebone, by Waxy. / Daughter of Selim.
        - Banter. { Master Henry, by Orville. / Boadicea, by Alexander.
      - **Daughter of**
        - Catton. { Golumpus, by Gohanna. / Lucy Grey, by Timothy.
        - Daughter of { Orville, by Benningbrough. / Miss Grimstone, by Weasel.
    - **Miss Bowe.**
      - **Sir John.**
        - Tramp. { Dick Andrews, by Joe Andrews. / Daughter of Gohanna.
        - Daughter of { Waxy, by Pot-8-os. / Bizarre, by Peruvian.
      - **Lapwing.**
        - Bustard. { Castrel, by Buzzard. / Mishap, by Shuttle.
        - Daughter of { Muley, by Orville. / Rosanne, by Dick Andrews.

Seventh dam, Rosette by Benningbrough; Eighth dam, Rosamond by Tandem; Ninth dam, Tuberose by Herod; Tenth dam, Grey Starling by Starling; Eleventh dam, Coughing Polly by Bartlett's Childers; Twelfth dam, sister to Thunderbolt, by Counsellor; Thirteenth dam, by Snake; Fourteenth dam, by Luggs; Fifteenth dam, by Davill's Old Woodcock.

IMPORTED BENEDICTION.

Never ran.

PRODUCE.

1883, Missed to Aureolus.

1884, ch. c., DE CORDOVA, by *Rayon d'Or.   (Gelded.)

1885, Missed to *Rayon d'Or.

1886, ch. f., ALLARENE, by Algerine,

1887, Slipped foal August, '86, by Algerine.

1888, Missed to Wanderer.

1889, ch. c.,   by Wanderer.

1890,   by Algerine.

BORDELAISE (IMPORTED).

Bay mare, foaled 1875. Bred by Mr. McMorland, England. Imported 1882, by Mr. W. L. Scott, Erie, Pa.

{ Tramp
{ Dick Andrews, by Joe Andrews.
{ Daughter of Gohanna.

{ Mandane.
{ Pot-8-os, by Eclipse.
{ Young Camilla, by Woodpecker.

{ Muley.
{ Orville, by Benningbrough.
{ Eleanor, by Whiskey.

{ Miss Stevenson.
{ Scud or Sorcerer.
{ Daughter of Precipitate.

{ Emilius.
{ Orville, by Benningbrough.
{ Emily, by Stamford

{ Cressida.
{ Whiskey, by Saltram.
{ Young Giantess, by Diomed

{ Orville.
{ Benningbrough, by King Fergus.
{ Evelina, by Highflyer.

{ Daughter of
{ Buzzard, by Woodpecker.
{ Hornpipe, by Trumpator.

{ Humphrey Clinker.
{ Comus, by Sorcerer.
{ Clinkerina, by Clinker.

{ Daughter of
{ Cervantes, by Don Quixote.
{ Daughter of Golumpus.

{ Touchstone.
{ Camel, by Whalebone.
{ Banter, by Master Henry.

{ Emma.
{ Whisker, by Waxy.
{ Gibside Fairy, by Hermes.

{ Sir Hercules.
{ Whalebone, by Waxy.
{ Peri, by Wanderer.

{ Guiccioli.
{ Bob Booty, by Chanticleer.
{ Flight, by Escape.

{ Clarion.
{ Sultan, by Selim.
{ Clara, by Filho da Puta.

{ Annette.
{ Priam, by Emilius.
{ Daughter of Don Juan.

{ Whalebone.
{ Waxy, by Pot-8-os.
{ Penelope, by Trumpator.

{ Daughter of
{ Selim, by Buzzard.
{ Maiden, by Sir Peter.

{ Master Henry.
{ Orville, by Benningbrough.
{ Sophia, by Stamford.

{ Boadicea.
{ Alexander, by Eclipse.
{ Brunette, by Amaranthus

{ Blacklock.
{ Whitelock, by Hambletonian.
{ Daughter of Coriander.

{ Manuella.
{ Dick Andrews, by Joe Andrews.
{ Mandane, by Pot-8-os.

{ Whalebone.
{ Waxy, by Pot-8-os.
{ Penelope, by Trumpator.

{ Daughter of 1819.
{ Frolic, by Hedley.
{ Daughter of Selim and Maiden.

{ Lottery.
{ Tramp, by Dick Andrews.
{ Mandane, by Pot-8-os.

{ Morgiana.
{ Muley, by Orville.
{ Miss Stevenson, by Scud or Sorcerer.

{ Priam.
{ Emilius, by Orville.
{ Cressida, by Whiskey.

{ Daughter of
{ Orville, by Benningbrough.
{ Daughter of Buzzard.

{ Irish Birdcatcher.
{ Sir Hercules, by Whalebone.
{ Guiccioli, by Bob Booty.

{ Whim.
{ Drone, by Master Robert.
{ Kiss, by Waxy Pope.

{ Clarion.
{ Sultan, by Selim.
{ Clara, by Filho da Puta.

{ Annette.
{ Priam, by Emilius.
{ Daughter of Don Juan.

Weatherbit, 1842. Sheet Anchor. Lottery. Morgiana. Weatherside, 1860. Weatherbit, 1842. Miss Letty. Chanticleer, 1858. Lady Alice, 1855. Agnes. Sheet Anchor. Aline. Brown Bread, 1862. Miss Letty, 1854. Priam. Daughter of. Orville. Daughter of. Humphrey Clinker. Daughter of. Touchstone. Emma. West Australian, 1850. Brown Agnes, 1857. Miss Agnes, 1850. Irish Birdcatcher. Agnes. Sir Hercules. Guiccioli. Clarion. Annette. Claret, 1862. Touchstone, 1831. Mountain Sylph, 1837. Belshazzar. Stays. Camel. Banter. Whalebone. Daughter of. Master Henry. Boadicea. Blacklock. Manuella. Whalebone. Daughter of 1819.

Weatherbit, 1842. Mowerina. Sheet Anchor.

IMPORTED BORDELAISE.

At two years old started in eight races, winning the Maiden Two-Year-Old Stakes at Sandown Park, England, beating a field of nine, ran third once and unplaced six times. At three years old started five times, second once and unplaced four times.

PRODUCE.

1880, ch. f., BACCHANTE, by Saturnalia.

1881, b. f., by Wild Oats. ⎫ In England.

1882, Missed to Chancellor. ⎭

1883, b. f., WAITAWAY, by Rosicrucian. (Imp. in utero.)

1884, b. c, ETHON, by *Rayon d'Or. (Gelded.)

1885, b. f., by *Rayon d'Or or *Kantaka (Died in 1887.)

1886, ch. c., by *Kantaka.

1887, Missed to *Rayon d'Or.

1888, b. c., TOURIST, by Wanderer. (Gelded.)

1889, b. c., by Algerine.

1890, by *Kantaka.

BLUE CAP (IMPORTED).

Chestnut mare, foaled 1878. Bred by Mr. J. T. McKenzie, England. Imported in 1881, by Mr. Wm. Easton.

- **Blue Gown.**
  - **Beadsman.**
    - **Weatherbit.**
      - **Sheet Anchor.**
        - Lottery. { Tramp, by Dick Andrews. / Mandane, by Pot-8-os.
        - Morgiana. { Muley, by Orville. / Miss Stephenson, by Scud or Sorcerer.
      - **Miss Letty.**
        - Priam. { Emilius, by Orville. / Cressida, by Whiskey.
        - Daughter of { Orville, by Benningbrough. / Golden Legs, dam, by Buzzard.
    - **Mendicant.**
      - **Touchstone.**
        - Camel. { Whalebone, by Waxy. / Daughter of Selim.
        - Banter. { Master Henry, by Orville. / Boadicea, by Alexander.
      - **Lady Moore Carew.**
        - Tramp. { Dick Andrews, by Joe Andrews. / Daughter of Gohanna.
        - Kite. { Bustard, by Castrel. / Olympia, by Sir Oliver.
  - **Bas Bleu.**
    - **Stockwell.**
      - **The Baron.**
        - Irish Birdcatcher. { Sir Hercules, by Whalebone. / Guiccioli, by Bob Booty.
        - Echidna. { Economist, by Whisker. / Miss Pratt, by Blacklock.
      - **Pocahontas.**
        - Glencoe. { Sultan, by Selim. / Trampoline, by Tramp.
        - Marpessa. { Muley, by Orville. / Clare, by Marmion.
    - **Vexation.**
      - **Touchstone.**
        - Camel. { Whalebone, by Waxy. / Daughter of Selim.
        - Banter. { Master Henry, by Orville. / Boadicea, by Alexander.
      - **Vat.**
        - Langar. { Selim, by Buzzard. / Daughter of Walton.
        - Wire. { Waxy, by Pot-8-os. / Penelope, by Trumpator.
- **Young Desdemona.**
  - **Thormanby.**
    - **Windhound, or Melbourne.**
      - **Humphrey Clinker.**
        - Comus. { Sorcerer, by Trumpator. / Houghton Lass, by Sir Peter.
        - Clinkerina. { Clinker, by Sir Peter. / Pewet, by Tandem.
      - **Daughter of**
        - Cervantes. { Don Quixote, by Eclipse. / Evelina, by Highflyer.
        - Daughter of { Golumpus, by Gohanna. / Daughter of Paynator.
    - **Alice Hawthorn.**
      - **Muly Molock.**
        - Muley. { Orville, by Benningbrough. / Eleanor, by Whiskey.
        - Nancy. { Dick Andrews, by Joe Andrews. / Spitfire, by Benningbrough.
      - **Rebecca.**
        - Lottery. { Tramp, by Dick Andrews. / Mandane, by Pot-8-os.
        - Daughter of { Cervantes, by Don Quixote. / Anticipation, by Benningbrough.
  - **Foible.**
    - **Faugh-a-Ballagh.**
      - **Sir Hercules.**
        - Whalebone { Waxy, by Pot-8-os. / Penelope, by Trumpator.
        - Peri. { Wanderer, by Gohanna. / Thalestris, by Alexander.
      - **Gucciolli.**
        - Bob Booty. { Chanticleer, by Woodpecker. / Ierne, by Bagot.
        - Flight. { I. Escape, by Commodore. / Young Heroine, by Bagot.
    - **Daughter of**
      - **Cadland.**
        - Andrew. { Orville, by Benningbrough. / Morel, by Sorcerer.
        - Sorcery. { Sorcerer, by Trumpator. / Cobbea, by Skyscraper.
      - **Widgeon.**
        - Whisker. { Waxy, by Pot-8-os. / Penelope, by Trumpator.
        - Daughter of { Dick Andrews, by Joe Andrews. / Desdemona, by Sir Peter.

* Seventh dam, Heroine, by Phœnomenon ; Eighth dam, Princess (Sister to Pegasus), by Eclipse ; Ninth dam, by Bosphorus ; Tenth dam, sister to Grecian Princess, by Forester ; Eleventh dam, by the Coalition Colt ; Twelfth dam, by Bustard ; Thirteenth dam, Lord Leigh's Charming Molly (Sister to Diana), by Second ; Fourteenth dam, by Stanyan's Arabian; Fifteenth dam, by King William's No-Tongued Barb; Sixteenth dam, by Makeless ; Seventeenth dam, Royal Mare.

IMPORTED BLUE CAP.

Never started, and was never trained.

— —

PRODUCE.

1884, ch. c., ROI D'OR, by *Rayon d'Or.   (Gelded.)

1885, ch. c., TORCHLIGHT, by *Rayon d'Or.

1886, ch. f., BLUE GRASS, by *Rayon d'Or.

1887, ch c.   (Died August, '87.)

1888, ch. c., RUSHLIGHT, by Wanderer.

1889, ch. f.,   by *Rayon d'Or.

1890,   by *Rayon d'Or.

BELLE OF ELTHAM (IMPORTED).

Bay mare, foaled 1877. Bred by Mr. W. Blenkiron, England. Imported 1882, by Mr. W. L. Scott, Erie, Pa.

Sire (upper branch)

- **Newminster**
  - **Touch-stone**
    - **Camel**
      - Whalebone — { Waxy, by Pot-8-os. | Penelope, by Trumpator. }
      - Daughter of · — { Selim, by Buzzard. | Maiden, by Sir Peter. }
    - **Banter**
      - Master Henry — { Orville, by Beningbrough. | Miss Sophia, by Stamford }
      - Boadicea — { Alexander, by Eclipse. | Brunette, by Amaranthus. }
  - **Bees-wing**
    - **Doctor Syntax**
      - Paynator — { Trumpator, by Conductor. | Daughter of Marc Anthony, }
      - Daughter of — { Beningbrough, by King Fergus. | Jennie Mole, by Carbuncle. }
    - **The Lame Mare**
      - Ardrossan — { John Bull, by Fortitude. | Miss Whip, by Volunteer. }
      - Lady Eliza — { Whitworth, by Agouistes. | Daughter of Spadille. }
- **Victorious**
  - **Clara's dam**
    - **Jerry**
      - Smolensko — { Sorcerer, by Trumpator. | Wowski, by Mentor. }
      - Louisa — { Orville, by Beningbrough. | Thomasina, by Timothy. }
    - **Mar-pessa**
      - Muley — { Orville, by Beningbrough | Eleanor, by Whiskey }
      - Clare — { Marmion, by Whiskey. | Harpalice, by Gohanna. }
  - **Daughter of**
    - **Vol-taire**
      - Blacklock — { Whitelock, by Hambletonian. | Daughter of Coriander. }
      - Daughter of — { Phantom, by Walton. | Daughter of Overton. }
    - **Light-ning's dam**
      - Blucher — { Waxy, by Pot-8-os. | Pantina, by Buzzard. }
      - Opal — { Sir Peter, by Highflyer. | Olivia, by Justice. }

Dam: Night Shade (lower branch)

- **Kingston**
  - **Veni-son**
    - **Parti-san**
      - Walton — { Sir Peter, by Highflyer. | Arethusa, by Dungannon. }
      - Parasol — { Pot-8-os, by Eclipse. | Prunella, by Highflyer. }
    - **The Fawn**
      - Smolensko — { Sorcerer, by Trumpator. | Wowski, by Mentor. }
      - Jerboa — { Gohanna, by Mercury. | Camilla, by Trentham. }
  - **Queen Anne**
    - **Slane**
      - Royal Oak — { Catton, by Golumpus. | Daughter of Smolensko. }
      - Daughter of — { Orville, by Beningbrough. | Epsom Lass, by Sir Peter. }
    - **Garcia**
      - Octavian — { Stripling, by Phœnomenon. | Daughter of Oberon. }
      - Daughter of — { Shuttle, by Y. Marske. | Katherine, by Delpini. }
- **Eltham Beauty**
  - **Touch-stone**
    - **Camel**
      - Whalebone — { Waxy, by Pot-8-os. | Penelope, by Trumpator. }
      - Daughter of — { Selim, by Buzzard. | Maiden, by Sir Peter. }
    - **Banter**
      - Master Henry — { Orville, by Beningbrough. | Miss Sophia, by Stamford. }
      - Boadicea — { Alexander, by Eclipse. | Brunette, by Amaranthus. }
  - **Prussic Acid**
    - **Vol-taire**
      - Blacklock — { Whitelock, by Hambletonian. | Daughter of Coriander. }
      - Daughter of — { Phantom, by Walton. | Daughter of Overton. }
    - **Arse-nic**
      - The Colonel — { Whisker, by Waxy. | Daughter of Delpini. }
      - Arsena — { Morisco, by Muley. | Arethissa, by Quiz. }

Seventh dam, Persepolis by Alexander; Eighth dam, sister to Tickle Toby by Alfred; Ninth dam, Celia by Herod; Tenth dam, Proserpine, own sister to Eclipse, by Marske; Eleventh dam, Spiletta by Regulus; Twelfth dam, Mother Western by Smith's son of Snake; Thirteen dam by Lord D'Arcy's old Montague; Fourteenth dam by Hautboy; Fifteenth dam by Brimmer.

ı

IMPORTED BELLE OF ELTHAM.

At two years old started but once, running unplaced to Polly Carew in Maiden Two-Year-Old Plate at Epsom, England. At three years old started twice, running unplaced to Lord Ronald in South Western Stakes at Hampton, five starters, and unplaced to Beaconsfield in Paddock Stakes at Sandown Park, eleven starters.

–

PRODUCE.

1883, b. c., HARRY BROWN (Bell Ringer), by Coltness (imp. in utero.) (Gelded.)

1884, br. f., COROLA, by Algerine.

1885, Missed to *Rayon d'Or.

1886, b. f., BELLE LORING, by *Kantaka.

1887, b. f., RUNAWAY, by Algerine.

1888, b. f., PROMENADE, by Wanderer.

1889, b. f.,   by Algerine.

1890,   by Wanderer.

BLUE GRASS BELLE. Chestnut mare, foaled 1880. Bred by Mr. Jas. A. Grinstead, Kentucky.

- **War Dance**
  - **Lexington**
    - **Boston**
      - **Timoleon**
        - Sir Archy. { *Diomed, by Florizel. / *Castianira, by Rockingham.
        - Daughter of { *Saltram, by Eclipse. / Daughter of Symme's Wildair.
      - **Sister to Tuckahoe**
        - Ball's Florizel. { *Diomed, by Florizel. / Daughter of *Shark.
        - Daughter of { *Alderman, by Pot-8-os. / Daughter of *Clockfast.
    - **Alice Carneal**
      - ***Sarpedon**
        - Emilius. { Orville, by Beningbrough. / Emily, by Stamford.
        - Icaria. { The Flyer, by VanDyke, jr. / Parma, by Dick Andrews.
      - **Rowena**
        - Sumpter. { Sir Archy, by *Diomed. / Daughter of *Robin Redbreast.
        - Lady Grey. { Robin Gray, by *Royalist. / Maria, by Melzar.
  - **Reel**
    - ***Glencoe**
      - **Sultan**
        - Selim. { Buzzard, by Woodpecker. / Castrel's dam, by Alexander.
        - Bacchante. { Williamson's Ditto, by Sir Peter. / Sister to Calomel, by Mercury.
      - **Trampoline**
        - Tramp { Dick Andrews, by Joe Andrews. / Daughter of Gohanna.
        - Web. { Waxy, by Pot-8-os. / Penelope, by Trumpator.
    - ***Gallopade**
      - **Catton**
        - Golumpus. { Gohanna, by Mercury. / Catherine, by Woodpecker.
        - Lucy Grey. { Timothy, by Delpini. / Lucy, by Florizel.
      - **Camillina**
        - Camillus. { Hambletonian, by King Fergus. / Faith, by Pacolet.
        - Daughter of { Smolensko, by Sorcerer. / Miss Cannon, by Orville.
- **Rallet**
  - **Planet**
    - **Revenue**
      - **Trustee**
        - Catton. { Golumpus, by Gohanna. / Lucy Grey, by Timothy.
        - Emma. { Whisker, by Waxy. / Gibside Fairy, by Hermes.
      - **Rosalie Somers**
        - Sir Charles. { Sir Archy, by *Diomed. / Daughter of *Citizen.
        - Mischief. { Virginian, by Sir Archy. / Daughter of *Bedford.
    - **Nina**
      - **Boston**
        - Timoleon. { Sir Archy, by *Diomed. / Daughter of *Saltram.
        - Sister to Tuckahoe. { Ball's Florizel, by *Diomed. / Daughter of *Alderman.
      - ***Frolicksome Fanny**
        - Lottery. { Tramp, by Dick Andrews. / Mandane, by Pot-8-os.
        - Sister to Catterick. { Whisker, by Waxy. / Daughter of Bay Trophonius.
  - **Balloon**
    - ***Yorkshire**
      - **St. Nicholas**
        - Emilius. { Orville, by Beningbrough. / Emily, by Stamford.
        - Seamew. { Scud, by Beningbrough. / Goosander, by Hambletonian.
      - **Miss Rose**
        - Tramp. { Dick Andrews, by Joe Andrews. / Daughter of Gohanna.
        - Daughter of { Sancho, by Don Quixote. / Daughter of Coriander.
    - **Heraldry**
      - **Herald**
        - Plenipotentiary. { Emilius, by Orville. / Harriet, by Pericles.
        - Delpini. { Whisker, by Waxy. / My Lady, by Comus.
      - **Margaret Woods**
        - *Priam { Emilius, by Orville. / Cressida, by Whiskey.
        - Maria West { Marion, by Sir Archy. / Ella Crump, by *Citizen.

Seventh dam by Huntsman; Eighth dam by Symme's Wildair; Ninth dam by *Fearnaught; Tenth dam by *Janus.

BLUE GRASS BELLE

Started eight times at two years old, winning five-furlong purse at Saratoga, beating Barbarian, Carlyle and seven others ; ran second once, third twice and unplaced four times. At three years old started fifteen times, won a mile and a furlong purse, ten starters, at Chicago, ran second twice, third six times, and unplaced six times. At four years old started nine times, winning three times, *i. e.*, the Baltimore Cup, two Handicap Sweepstakes at Sheepshead Bay, beating Barnes, Chanticleer and six others ; second to Duke of Montalban in the Washington Cup, second to Gen. Monroe in the Coney Island Cup, and unplaced four times.

PRODUCE.

1886, ch. f., THE BELLE, by *Rayon d'Or.

1887, ch. f., PANDORA, by *Rayon d'Or.

1888, Missed to *Rayon d'Or.

1889, ch. f.,   by *Rayon d'Or.

1890,   by *Rayon d'Or.

BONA FIDE

Bay filly, foaled 1878. Bred by Gen. Wm G. Harding, Tennessee.

- *** Bonnie Scotland**
  - **Iaco.**
    - **Don John.** *(Tramp or Waverly)*
      - **Whalebone.** { Waxy, by Pot-8-os. / Penelope, by Trumpator. }
      - **Margaretta.** { Sir Peter, by Highflyer. / Sister to Crasker, by Highflyer. }
      - **Hetman Platoff's dam.**
        - **Comus.** { Sorcerer, by Trumpator. / Houghton Lass, by Sir Peter. }
        - **Marciana.** { Stamford, by Sir Peter. / Marcia, by Coriander. }
    - **Scandal.**
      - **Selim.**
        - **Buzzard.** { Woodpecker, by Herod. / Misfortune, by Dux. }
        - **Castrel's dam.** { Alexander, by Eclipse. / Daughter of Highflyer. }
      - **Daughter of**
        - **Haphazard.** { Sir Peter, by Highflyer. / Miss Hervey, by Eclipse. }
        - **Daughter of** { Precipitate, by Mercury. / Colibri, by Woodpecker. }
  - **Queen Mary.**
    - **Gladiator.**
      - **Partisan.**
        - **Walton.** { Sir Peter, by Highflyer. / Arethusa, by Dungannon }
        - **Parasol.** { Pot-8-os, by Eclipse. / Prunella, by Highflyer. }
      - **Pauline.**
        - **Moses.** { Whalebone or Seymour. / Sister to Castanea, by Gohanna. }
        - **Quadrille.** { Selim, by Buzzard. / Canary Bird, by Sorcerer. }
    - **Daughter of**
      - **Plenipotentiary.**
        - **Emilius.** { Orville, by Beningbrough. / Emily, by Stamford. }
        - **Harriet.** { Pericles, by Evander. / Daughter of Selim }
      - **Myrrha.**
        - **Whalebone.** { Waxy, by Pot-8-os. / Penelope, by Trumpator. }
        - **Gift.** { Young Gohanna, by Gohanna. / Sister to Grazier, by Sir Peter. }
- **Euchre.**
  - **Brown Dick.**
    - *** Margrave.**
      - **Muley.**
        - **Orville.** { Beningbrough, by King Fergus. / Evelina, by Highflyer. }
        - **Eleanor.** { Whiskey, by Saltram. / Young Giantess, by Diomed. }
      - **Chatham's dam.**
        - **Election.** { Gohanna, by Mercury. / Chestnut Skim, by Woodpecker. }
        - **Fair Helen.** { Hambletonian, by King Fergus. / Helen, by Delpini. }
    - **Fanny King.**
      - *** Glencoe.**
        - **Sultan.** { Selim, by Buzzard. / Bacchante, by Williamson's Ditto. }
        - **Trampoline.** { Tramp, by Dick Andrews. / Web, by Waxy. }
      - **Mary Smith.**
        - **Sir Richard** { Pacolet, by * Citizen. / Daughter of Topgallant. }
        - **Daughter of** { Tennessee Oscar, by * Wonder. / The Ledbetter mare, by Sir Archy. }
  - **Odd Trick**
    - **Lexington.**
      - **Boston.**
        - **Timoleon.** { Sir Archy, by * Diomed. / Daughter of * Saltram. }
        - **Sister to Tuckahoe.** { Ball's Florizel, by * Diomed. / Daughter of * Alderman. }
      - **Alice Carneal**
        - *** Sarpedon.** { Emilius, by Orville. / Icaria, by The Flyer. }
        - **Rowena.** { Sumpter, by Sir Archy. / Lady Grey, by Robin Grey. }
    - **Little Trick**
      - *** Priam.**
        - **Emilius.** { Orville, by Beningbrough. / Emily, by Stamford. }
        - **Cressida.** { Whiskey, by Saltram. / Young Giantess, by Diomed }
      - **Daughter of**
        - *** Bluster** { Orlando, by Whiskey. / Daughter of Pegasus. }
        - **Bet Bosley.** { Wilkes' Wonder, by * Diomed. / Daughter of Chanticleer. }

Seventh dam by * Sterling; Eighth dam by Clodius; Ninth dam by * Silvereye; Tenth dam by * Jolly Roger; Eleventh dam by Partner; Twelfth dam by * Monkey; Thirteenth dam imported mare of Harrison, of Brandon, &c. * imported.

BONA FIDE.

At two years old started in three races and was unplaced in each. Did not run at three years old. At four years old started five times, running third in one and unplaced in four.

————————

PRODUCE.

1884, twins, ch. f. and b. c., by *Rayon d'Or. (Both dead.)

1885, ch. f., by *Rayon d'Or. (Dead.)

1886, b. c., GENDARME, by *Rayon d'Or. (Gelded.)

1887, b. c., OSSA, by *Rayon d,Or.

1888, ch. c., by *Kantaka. (Died October, '88.)

1889, b. c., by *Kantaka. (Died '89.)

1890, by *Kantaka.

BRENDA.

Chestnut mare, foaled 1878. Bred by Gen. W. G. Harding, Tenn.

Belladonna — * Bonnie Scotland — Iago / Queen Mary

- **Iago**
  - **Don John.**
    - **Tramp or Waverly**
      - Whalebone. { Waxy, by Pot-8-os. / Penelope, by Trumpator.
      - Margaretta. { Sir Peter, by Highflyer. / Sister to Crasker, by Highllyer.
    - **Hetman Platoff's dam.**
      - Comus. { Sorcerer, by Trumpator. / Houghton Lass, by Sir Peter.
      - Marciana. { Stamford, by Sir Peter. / Marcia, by Coriander.
  - **Scandal.**
    - **Selim.**
      - Buzzard. { Woodpecker, by Herod. / Misfortune, by Dux.
      - Castrel's dam. { Alexander, by Eclipse. / Daughter of Highllyer.
    - **Daughter of**
      - Haphazard. { Sir Peter, by Highllyer. / Miss Hervey, by Eclipse.
      - Daughter of { Precipitate, by Mercury. / Colibri, by Woodpecker.

- **Queen Mary.**
  - **Gladiator.**
    - **Partisan.**
      - Walton { Sir Peter, by Highflyer. / Arethusa, by Dungannon
      - Parasol. { Pot-8-os, by Eclipse. / Prunella, by Highflyer.
    - **Pauline.**
      - Moses. { Whalebone or Seymour. / Sister to Castanea, by Gohanna.
      - Quadrille. { Selim, by Buzzard. / Canary Bird, by Sorcerer.
  - **Daughter of**
    - **Plenipotentiary.**
      - Emilius. { Orville, by Beningbrough. / Emily, by Stamford.
      - Harriet. { Pericles, by Evander. / Daughter of Selim
    - **Myrrha.**
      - Whalebone. { Waxy, by Pot-8-os. / Penelope, by Trumpator.
      - Gift. { Young Gohanna, by Gohanna. / Sister to Grazier, by Sir Peter.

Anodyne — Brown Dick — Fanny King / * Margrave — Ann Chase — Morgiana

- **Brown Dick.**
  - **Fanny King.**
    - **Muley.**
      - Orville. { Beningbrough, by King Fergus. / Evelina, by Highllyer.
      - Eleanor. { Whiskey, by Saltram. / Young Giantess, by Diomed.
    - **Chatham's dam.**
      - Election. { Gohanna, by Mercury. / Chestnut Skim, by Woodpecker.
      - Fair Helen { Hambletonian, by King Fergus. / Helen, by Delpini.
  - *** Margrave.**
    - *** Glencoe.**
      - Sultan. { Selim, by Buzzard. / Bacchante, by Williamson's Ditto
      - Trampoline. { Tramp, by Dick Andrews. / Web, by Waxy.
    - **Mary Smith.**
      - Sir Richard. { Pacolet, by * Citizen. / Daughter of Topgallant.
      - Daughter of { Tennessee Oscar, by * Wonder. / The Ledbetter mare, by Sir Archy.

- **Ann Chase.**
  - *** Albion.**
    - **Coin or Octaeon.**
      - Scud. { Beningbrough, by King Fergus. / Eliza, by Highflyer.
      - Diana. { Stamford, by Haphazard. / Daughter of Whiskey.
    - **Pan-thea.**
      - Comus or Blacklock. { Whitelock, by Hambletonian. / Daughter of Coriander.
      - Manuella. { Dick Andrews, by Joe Andrews. / Mandane, by Pot-8-os.
  - *** Levinathan.**
    - **Muley.**
      - Muley. { Orville, by Beningbrough. / Daughter of Whiskey.
      - The Dandy's Dam. { Windle, by Beningbrough. / Daughter of Anvil.
  - **Morgiana.**
    - **Pacolet.**
      - Pacolet. { * Citizen, by Pacolet. / Daughter of Tippoo Saib.
      - Black Sophia. { Top Gallant, by Gallatin. / Daughter of Lamplighter.

Seventh dam by Beedee (Son of Hall's Union); Eighth by Bowie (Son of * Janus). (NOTE:—"The above pedigree (of Morginna) is, as given the compiler by Col. Elliott, during his lifetime. Edgar gives the following pedigree, under Morgiana by Pacolet: We think Col. Elliott right; she was one of the best brood mares in America: First dam by Hobb's Augustus (Son of Old Clodius); Second by Dolan; Third by Meade's Celer; Fourth by * Bay Richmond; Fifth by * Fearnaught; Sixth by Goldfinder; Seventh by Lee's Old Mare Anthony."
—Bruce American Stud Book, vol. 1, p. 245.)

BRENDA.

Did not run at two years old. At three years old started seven times, winning twice, second twice, and unplaced three times.

PRODUCE.

1883, b. c., by Voltigeur.   (Died December, '83.)

1884, b. c.,   by Voltigeur.

1885, ch. c., by Storey.   (Died '86.)

1886, ch. c., AYALA (Brendor), by *Rayon d'Or.   (Gelded.)

1887, ch. c., CRAWFISH, by *Rayon d'Or.

1888, ch. c., by *Kantaka.   (Died '89.)

1889, Dead ch. c., by *Kantaka.

1890, .   by *Kantaka.

BELLE OF MAYWOOD.

Bay mare, foaled 1878. Bred by Mr. John Mattingly, Kentucky.

- **Julia Mattingly.**
  - **Hunter's Lexington.**
    - **Lexington.**
      - **Boston.**
        - **Timoleon.**
          - Sir Archy. { * Diomed, by Florizel. / * Castianira, by Rockingham. }
          - Daughter of { * Saltram, by Eclipse. / Daughter of Symme's Wildair. }
        - **Sister to Tuckahoe.**
          - Ball's Florizel. { * Diomed, by Florizel. / Daughter of * Shark. }
          - Daughter of { * Alderman, by Pot-8-os. / Daughter of * Clockfast. }
      - **Alice Carneal.**
        - **Sarpedon.**
          - Emilius. { Orville, by Beningbrough. / Emily, by Stamford. }
          - Icaria. { The Flyer, by Van Dyke, jr. / Parma, by Dick Andrews. }
        - **Rowena.**
          - Sumpter. { Sir Archy, by * Diomed. / Daughter of * Robin Redbreast. }
          - Lady Grey. { Robin Grey, by * Royalist. / Maria, by Melzar. }
    - **Sally Lewis.**
      - *** Glencoe.**
        - **Sultan.**
          - Selim. { Buzzard, by Woodpecker. / Castrel's dam, by Alexander. }
          - Bacchante. { Williamson's Ditto, by Sir Peter. / Sister to Calomel, by Mercury. }
        - **Trampoline.**
          - Tramp { Dick Andrews, by Joe Andrews. / Daughter of Gohanna. }
          - Web. { Waxy, by Pot-8-os. / Penelope, by Trumpator. }
      - **Motte.**
        - *** Barefoot.**
          - Tramp. { Dick Andrews, by Joe Andrews. / Daughter of Gohanna. }
          - Rosamond. { Buzzard, by Woodpecker. / Roseberry, by Phoenomenon. }
        - **Lady Tompkins.**
          - American Eclipse. { Duroc, by * Diomed. / Miller's Damsel, by * Messenger. }
          - Katy Ann. { Ogle's Oscar, by * Gabriel. / Medoc's dam, by * Expedition. }
  - **John Morgan.**
    - *** Sovereign.**
      - **Emilius.**
        - Orville. { Beningbrough, by King Fergus. / Evelina, by Highflyer. }
        - Emily. { Stamford, by Sir Peter. / Daughter of Whiskey. }
      - **Fleur-de-Lis.**
        - Bourbon. { Sorcerer, by Trumpator. / Daughter of Precipitate. }
        - Lady Rachel. { Stamford, by Sir Peter. / Young Rachel, by Volunteer. }
    - **Motto.**
      - *** Glencoe.**
        - Sultan. { Selim, by Buzzard. / Bacchante, by Williamson's Ditto. }
        - Trampoline. { Tramp, by Dick Andrews. / Web, by Waxy. }
      - **Motte.**
        - * Barefoot. { Tramp, by Dick Andrews. / Rosamond, by Buzzard. }
        - Lady Tompkins. { American Eclipse, by Duroc. / Katy Ann, by Ogle's Oscar. }
- **Blue Bell.**
  - **Blue Filler (Piat).**
    - *** Contract.**
      - **Chorister.**
        - Catton. { Golumpus, by Gohanna. / Lucy Grey, by Timothy. }
        - Helen. { Hambletonian, by King Fergus. / Susan, by Overton. }
      - **Jenny Grey.**
        - Robin Grey. { * Royalist, by Saltram. / Belle Mariah, by Grey Diomed. }
        - Richmond Jenny. { * Diomed, by Florizel. / Daughter of * Shark. }
    - *** Hedgeford.**
      - Filho-da-Puta. { Haphazard, by Sir Peter. / Mrs. Barnett, by Waxy. }
      - Miss Craigie. { Orville, by Beningbrough. / Marchioness, by Lurcher. }
  - **Lady Tompkins.**
    - American Eclipse. { Duroc, by * Diomed. / Miller's Damsel, by * Messenger. }
    - Katy Ann. { Ogle's Oscar, by * Gabriel. / Young Maid of the Oaks, by * Expedition. }

Seventh dam, Old Maid of the Oaks by * Spread Eagle; Eighth dam, Annette (Nancy Air's dam) by * Shark; Ninth dam by Rockingham; Tenth dam by Baylor's Gallant; Eleventh dam by True Whig; Twelfth dam by * Regulus; Thirteenth dam by * Diamond.

BELLE OF MAYWOOD.

Never ran.

———————

PRODUCE.

1884, b. or br. c., STILLETTO (Branch), by Duke of Montrose.

1885, b. f.,   by Duke of Montrose.

1886, b. c., TENNY, by *Rayon d'Or.

1887, ch. c., RAFTER, by *Kantaka.

1888, b. f., MAYWOOD, by *Rayon d'Or.

1889, ch. c., by *Rayon d'Or.   (Died '89.)

1890,   by *Rayon d'Or.

BLANDONA.

Foaled May 30th, 1882. Bred by Mr. R. F. Johnson, Ky.

Whalebone.	{ Waxy, by Pot-8-os. / Penelope, by Trumpator. }
Peri.	{ Wanderer, by Gohanna. / Thalestris, by Alexander. }
Bob Booty.	{ Chanticleer, by Woodpecker. / Ierne, by Bagot. }
Flight.	{ Irish Escape, by Commodore. / Young Heroine, by Bagot. }
Castrel.	{ Buzzard, by Woodpecker. / Selim's dam, by Alexander. }
Idalia.	{ Peruvian, by Sir Peter. / Musidora, by Meteor. }
Laurel.	{ Blacklock, by Whitelock. / Wagtail, by Prime Minister. }
Maid of Honor.	{ Champion, by Selim. / Etiquette, by Orville. }
Duroc.	{ *Diomed, by Florizel. / Amanda, by Grey Diomed. }
Miller's Damsel.	{ * Messenger, by Mambrino. / Daughter of Pot-8-os. }
Henry.	{ Sir Archy, by *Diomed. / Daughter of *Diomed. }
Young Romp.	{ Duroc, by Diomed. / Romp, by Duroc. }
Sir Archy.	{ * Diomed, by Florizel. / * Castianira, by Rockingham. }
Eliza.	{ Bedford, by Dungannon. / Mambrina, by Mambrino. }
Brimmer or Bluebeard.	{ *Bluebeard, by *Starling. / Daughter of Mendoza. }
Woodpecker's Dam.	{ Buzzard, by Woodpecker. / The Fawn, by Craig's Alfred. }
Humphrey Clinker.	{ Comus, by Sorcerer. / Clinkerina, by Clinker. }
Daughter of	{ Cervantes, by Don Quixote. / Daughter of Golumpus. }
Touchstone.	{ Camel, by Whalebone. / Banter, by Master Henry. }
Emma.	{ Whisker, by Waxy. / Gibside Fairy, by Hermes. }
Emilius.	{ Orville, by Beningbrough. / Emily, by Stamford }
Shoveler.	{ Scud, by Beningbrough. / Goosander, by Hambletonian. }
Whisker.	{ Waxy, by Pot-8-os. / Penelope, by Trumpator. }
Variety.	{ Selim or Soothsayer. / Sprite, by Bobtail. }
Timoleon.	{ Sir Archy, by * Diomed. / Daughter of * Saltram. }
Sister to Tuckahoe.	{ Ball's Florizel, by * Diomed. / Daughter of * Alderman. }
* Sarpedon.	{ Emilius, by Orville. / Icaria, by The Flyer. }
Rowena.	{ Sumpter, by Sir Archy. / Lady Grey, by Robin Grey. }
Sultan.	{ Selim, by Buzzard. / Bacchante, by Wm's Ditto. }
Trampoline.	{ Tramp, by Dick Andrews. / Web, by Waxy. }
Trustee.	{ Catton, by Golumpus. / Emma, by Whisker. }
Vandal's Dam.	{ Tranby, by Blacklock. / Lucilla, by Trumpator. }

Intermediate connecting columns (read right to left): Sir Hercules, Guiccioli, Pantaloon, Daphne, American Eclipse, Daughter of, Kertrand, Lady Fortune, Melbourne, Mowerina, Young Emilius, Persian, Boston, Alice Carneal, *Glencoe, Levity, Crucifix, Lightsome, Lexington, Emilia, *Australian, Blanche J., Faugh-a-Ballagh, *Leamington, Daughter of, Brawner's Eclipse, Queen Mary, West Australian, Nantura, Longfellow.

Seventh dam, Lucy by Orphan: Eighth dam, Lady Grey by Robin Grey: Ninth dam, Maria by Melzar: Tenth dam by *Highflyer: Eleventh dam by *Fearnaught; Twelfth dam by Ariel (Brother to Partner); Thirteenth dam by *Jack of Diamonds: Fourteenth dam, Old Diamond (called Duchess) by Cullen's Arabian; (Both Jack of Diamonds and Old Diamond were imported by Gen. Spottswood, and both were by Cullen's Arabian): Fifteenth dam, Grisewood's Lady Thigh by Croft's Partner: Sixteenth dam by Greyhound: Seventeenth dam (Sophonisba's dam) by Curwen's Bay Barb: Eighteenth dam by D'Arcy's Chestnut Arabian: Nineteenth dam by Whiteshirt; Twentieth dam Montague Mare.

BLANDONA.

Never ran.

———————— ——

PRODUCE.

1886, b. c., VERONA, by *Kantaka.   (Gelded.)

1887, b. f., DONNA, by *Rayon d'Or.

1888, b. f., KATONA, by *Kantaka.

1889, Barren to *Rayon d'Or.

1890,   by Algerine.

CLOVER (IMPORTED.)

Bay Mare, foaled 1858. Bred by the Baroness Rothschild, England.

Pedigree columns (left to right: Verdure / Macaroni; Sweetmeat, Jocose; Gladiator, Lollypop, Pantaloon, Banter; Parti-san, Pauline, Starch or Voltaire, Belinda, Castrel, Idalia, Master Henry, Boadicea; King Tom, Harkaway, Glencoe, Pocahontas, Newminster, Touchstone, Windhound, Lady Hawthorn, Alice Hawthorn, Maybloom; Econo-mist, Fanny Dawson, Marpessa, Beeswing):

Name	Sire / Dam
Walton.	Sir Peter, by Highflyer. / Arethusa, by Dungannon.
Parasol.	Pot-8-os, by Eclipse. / Prunella, by Highflyer.
Moses.	Whalebone or Seymour. / Daughter of Gohanna.
Quadrille.	Selim, by Buzzard. / Canary Bird, by Sorcerer.
Blacklock.	Whitelock, by Hambletonian. / Daughter of Coriander.
Daughter of	Phantom, by Walton. / Daughter of Overton.
Blacklock.	Whitelock, by Hambletonian. / Daughter of Coriander.
Wagtail.	Prime Minister, by Sancho. / Daughter of Orville.
Buzzard.	Woodpecker, by Herod. / Misfortune, by Dux.
Daughter of	Alexander, by Eclipse. / Daughter of Highflyer.
Peruvian.	Sir Peter, by Highflyer. / Daughter of Boudrow.
Musidora.	Meteor, by Eclipse. / Maid of all Work, by Highflyer.
Orville.	Beningbrough, by King Fergus. / Evelina, by Highflyer.
Miss Sophia.	Stamford, by Sir Peter. / Sophia, by Buzzard.
Alexander.	Eclipse, by Marske. / Grecian Princess, by Forester.
Brunette.	Amaranthus, by Old England. / Mayfly, by Matchem.
Whisker.	Waxy, by Pot-8-os. / Penelope, by Trumpator.
Floranthe.	Octavian, by Stripling. / Caprice, by Anville.
Nabocklish.	Rugantino, by Commodore. / Butterfly, by Master Bagot.
Miss Tooley.	Teddy the Grinder, by Asparagus. / Lady Jane, by Sir Peter.
Sultan.	Selim, by Buzzard. / Bacchante, by Williamson's Ditto.
Trampoline.	Tramp, by Dick Andrews. / Web, by Waxy.
Muley.	Orville, by Beningbrough. / Eleanor, by Whiskey.
Clare.	Marmion, by Whiskey. / Harpalice, by Gohanna.
Camel.	Whalebone, by Waxy. / Daughter of Selim.
Banter.	Master Henry, by Orville. / Boadicea, by Alexander.
Doctor Syntax.	Paynator, by Trumpator. / Daughter of Beningbrough.
Daughter of	Ardrossan, by John Bull. / Lady Eliza, by Whitworth.
Pantaloon.	Castrel, by Buzzard. / Idalia, by Peruvian.
Phryne.	Touchstone, by Camel. / Decoy, by Filho-da-Puta.
Muley Moloch.	Muley, by Orville. / Nancy, by Dick Andrews.
Rebecca.	Lottery, by Tramp. / Daughter of Cervantes.

Seventh dam, Anticipation by Beningbrough; Eighth, Expectation by Herod: Ninth by Skim: Tenth by Janus; Eleventh, Spinster by Crab; Twelfth, Widdrington Mare by Partner; Thirteenth, Sister to Squirrel's dam by Bloody Buttocks; Fourteenth, Sister to Guy by Greyhound (Barb); Fifteenth, Brown Farewell by Makeless; Sixteenth by Brimmer; Seventeenth, Trumpet's dam by Place's White Turk: Eighteenth by the Dodsworth Barb; Nineteenth, Layton Barb Mare.

CLOVER.

Never ran.

—— — ——

PRODUCE.

1882, b. c., AFTER-MATH, by Kisber.   (Imp. in utero ; died '84.)

1883, Barren.

1884, b. f., FLAGEOLETTA, by *Rayon d'Or.

1885, Missed to *Rayon d'Or

1886, b. c.. AFTER-MATH, by *Rayon d'Or.   (Gelded.)

1887, Missed to *Rayon d'Or.

1888, twin b. fillies, by *Rayon d'Or.   (One dead)

1889, slipped ch. f. Nov. '88, by *Rayon d'Or.

1890,   by Wanderer.

CLEMENCY (IMPORTED.)

Bay mare, foaled 1879. Bred by the Duke of Westminster, England. Imported 1882, by Mr. W. L. Scott, Erie, Pa.

- **Springfield.**
  - **St. Albans, 1857.**
    - **Stockwell, 1849.**
      - **The Baron, 1842.**
        - Irish Birdcatcher. { Sir Hercules, by Whalebone. / Guiccioli, by Bob Booty. }
        - Echidna. { Economist, by Whisker. / Miss Pratt, by Blacklock. }
      - **Poca-hontas, 1837.**
        - Glencoe. { Sultan, by Selim. / Trampoline, by Tramp. }
        - Marpessa. { Muley, by Orville. / Clare, by Marmion. }
    - **Bribery, 1851.**
      - **The Libel, 1842.**
        - Pantaloon. { Castrel, by Buzzard. / Idalia, by Peruvian. }
        - Pasquinade. { Camel, by Whalebone. / Banter, by Master Henry. }
      - **Split-vote.**
        - St. Luke. { Bedlimate, by Welbeck. / Eliza Leeds, by Comus. }
        - Electress. { Election, by Gohanna. / Daughter of Stamford. }
  - **Viridis.**
    - **Marsyas.**
      - **Or-lando, 1841.**
        - Touchstone. { Camel, by Whalebone. / Banter, by Master Henry. }
        - Vulture. { Langar, by Selim. / Kite, by Bustard. }
      - **Mali-bran.**
        - Whisker. { Waxy, by Pot-8-os. / Penelope, by Trumpator. }
        - Garcia. { Octavian, by Stripling. / Daughter of Shuttle. }
    - **Maid of Palmyra.**
      - **Pyrrhus I., 1843.**
        - Epirus. { Langar, by Selim. / Olimpia, by Sir Oliver. }
        - Fortress. { Defence, by Whalebone. / Jewess, by Moses. }
      - **Pal-myra.**
        - Sultan. { Selim, by Buzzard. / Bacchante, by Williamson's Ditto. }
        - Hester. { Camel, by Whalebone. / Monimia, by Muley. }
- **Clemence.**
  - **Newminster, 1848.**
    - **Touch-stone, 1831.**
      - **Camel, 1822.**
        - Whalebone. { Waxy, by Pot-8-os. / Penelope, by Trumpator. }
        - Daughter of { Selim, by Buzzard. / Maiden, by Sir Peter. }
      - **Banter, 1826.**
        - Master Henry. { Orville, by Beningbrough. / Miss Sophia, by Stamford. }
        - Boadicea. { Alexander, by Eclipse. / Brunette, by Amaranthus. }
    - **Beeswing, 1833.**
      - **Dr. Syntax, 1811.**
        - Paynator. { Trumpator, by Conductor. / Daughter of Marc Anthony. }
        - Daughter of { Beningbrough, by King Fergus. / Jennie Mole, by Carbuncle. }
      - **Daughter of**
        - Ardrossan. { John Bull, by Fortitude. / Miss Whip, by Volunteer. }
        - Lady Eliza. { Whitworth, by Agonistes. / X Y Z's dam, by Spadille. }
  - **Eulogy.**
    - **Euclid.**
      - **Emilius.**
        - Orville. { Beningbrough, by King Fergus. / Evelina, by Highflyer. }
        - Emily. { Stamford, by Sir Peter. / Daughter of Whiskey. }
      - **Maria.**
        - Whisker. { Waxy, by Pot-8-os. / Penelope, by Trumpator. }
        - Gibside Fairy. { Hermes, by Mercury. / Vicissitude, by Pipator. }
    - **Martha Lynn.**
      - **Mulatto.**
        - Catton. { Golumpus, by Gohanna. / Lucy Grey, by Timothy. }
        - Desdemona. { Orville, by Beningbrough. / Fanny, by Sir Peter. }
      - **Leda.**
        - Filho da Puta. { Haphazard, by Sir Peter. / Mrs. Barnett, by Waxy. }
        - Treasure. { Camillus, by Hambletonian. / Daughter of Hyacinthus. }

Seventh dam. Flora by King Fergus: Eighth dam, Atalanta by Matchem; Ninth dam, Less of the Mill by Oronooko: Tenth dam by Old Traveller; Eleventh dam, Miss Makeless by Young Greyhound: Twelfth dam by Partner; Thirteenth dam, Miss Doe's dam by Woodcock: Fourteenth dam by Croft's Bay Barb; Fifteenth dam, Desdemona's dam by Makeless; Sixteenth dam by Brimmer; Seventeenth dam by Dickey Pierson: Eighteenth dam, Burton Barb mare.

CLEMENCY.

Started but twice and then at two years old ; at Manchester, England, "walked over" for Two-Year-Old Selling Stakes, and at Kempton Park ran third to Dean Swift in Hampton Two-Year-Old Selling Plate, five starters.

PRODUCE.

1883, lost foal at sea, by Coltness.

1884, br. c., by Algerine or *Rayon d'Or.   (Dead.)

1885, b. c , TUDOR, by *Rayon d'Or.

1886, Missed to *Rayon d'Or.

1887, twins, c. and f., by *Rayon d'Or.   (Both dead.)

1888, b. f., TUDIE, by Wanderer.

1889, b. c.,   by Algerine.

1890   by *Rayon d'Or.

IMPORTED CATHEDRA.

Bay mare, foaled 1873. Bred by Mr. C. Snewing, England. Imported by W. L. Scott in 1882.

Vicar's Daughter.

- **Paul Jones.**
  - Buccaneer.
    - Wild Dayrell.
      - Ion.
        - Cain { Paulowitz, by Sir Paul. / Daughter of Paynator. }
        - Margaret. { Edmond, by Gohanna. / Medora, by Selim. }
      - Ellen Middleton.
        - Bay Middleton. { Sultan, by Selim, / Cobweb, by Phantom. }
        - Myrrha. { Malek, by Blacklock. / Bessy, by Young Gouty. }
    - Cruizer's Dam.
      - Little Red Rover.
        - Tramp. { Dick Andrews, by Joe Andrews. / Daughter of Goharna. }
        - Miss Syntax. { Paynator, by Trumpator. / Daughter of Beningbrough. }
      - Eclat.
        - Edmond. { Orville, by Beningbrough. / Emmeline, by Waxy. }
        - Squib. { Soothsayer, by Sorcerer. / Bernice, by Alexander. }
  - Queen of the Gipsies.
    - Chanticleer.
      - Irish Birdcatcher.
        - Sir Hercules. { Whalebone, by Waxy. / Peri, by Wanderer. }
        - Guiccioli. { Bob Booty, by Chanticleer. / Flight, by Irish Escape. }
      - Whim.
        - Drone. { Master Robert, by Buffer. / Daughter of Sir Walter Raleigh. }
        - Kiss. { Waxy-Pope, by Waxy. / Daughter of Champion. }
    - Rambling Kate.
      - Melbourne.
        - Humphrey Clinker. { Comus, by Sorcerer. / Clinkerina, by Clinker. }
        - Daughter of { Cervantes, by Don Quixote. / Daughter of Golumpus. }
      - Phryne.
        - Touchstone { Camel, by Whalebone. / Banter, by Master Henry. }
        - Decoy. { Filho-da-Puta, by Haphazard. / Finesse, by Peruvian. }
- **My Niece.**
  - Surplice.
    - Touchstone.
      - Camel.
        - Whalebone. { Waxy, by Pot-8-os. / Penelope, by Trumpator. }
        - Daughter of { Selim, by Buzzard. / Maiden, by Sir Peter. }
      - Banter.
        - Master Henry { Orville, by Beningbrough. / Miss Sophia, by Stamford. }
        - Boadicea. { Alexander, by Eclipse. / Brunette, by Amaranthus. }
    - Crucifix.
      - Emilius. { Orville, by Beningbrough. / Emily, by Stamford. }
      - Cressida. { Whiskey, by Saltram. / Young Giantess, by Diomed. }
      - Octavian. { Stripling, by Phenomenon. / Daughter of Oberon. }
      - Daughter of { Shuttle, by Young Marske. / Zara, by Delpini. }
  - Vanity.
    - Cowl.
      - Bay Middleton.
        - Sultan. { Selim, by Buzzard. / Bacchante, by Williamson's Ditto. }
        - Cobweb. { Phantom, by Walton. / Filagree, by Soothsayer. }
      - Crucifix.
        - Priam. { Emilius, by Orville. / Cressida, by Whiskey. }
        - Octaviana. { Octavian, by Stripling. / Daughter of Shuttle. }
    - ~Val.
      - Camel.
        - Whalebone. { Waxy, by Pot-8-os. / Penelope, by Trumpator. }
        - Daughter of { Selim, by Buzzard. / Maiden, by Sir Peter. }
      - Daughter of
        - Langar. { Selim, by Buzzard. / Daughter of Walton. }
        - Wire. { Waxy, by Pot-8-os. / Penelope, by Trumpator. }

Seventh dam, Prunella by Highflyer; Eighth dam, Promise by Snap; Ninth dam, Julia by Blank; Tenth dam, Spectator's dam by Partner; Eleventh dam, Bonny Lass by Bay Bolton; Twelfth dam by the Darley Arabian; Thirteenth dam by the Byerly Turk; Fourteenth dam by Taffolet Barb; Fifteenth dam by Place's White Turk; Sixteenth dam, Natural Barb Mare.

CATHEDRA.

Started but once as a two-year-old, running second to Lord Malden in Maiden Two-Year-Old Plate at Croyden, seven starters. At three years old started but twice, running unplaced in Welter Cup at Hampton and unplaced in Summer Handicap at Sandown.

PRODUCE.

1879, b. f., (dead), by Esca.

1880, b. f. SISTER ELLEN by Moorlands.

1881, b. c., by Moorlands.

1882, b. c., by Moorlands,

In England.

1883, b. f, CALICO by Moorlands. (imp. in utero.)

1884, b. c. SIROCCO, by Algerine. (Gelded.)

1885, b. c., by Algerine.

1886, Missed to *Kantaka.

1887, Missed to *Kantaka.

1888, b. f WANDERING NUN, by Wanderer.

1889, b. c., (dead), by Wanderer.

1890, by Wanderer.

CLAUDIA.

Bay mare, foaled in 1876. Bred by Capt. G. W. Stewart, Ky.

{ Sir Archy. { * Diomed, by Florizel.
{ * Castianira, by Rockingham.

Daughter of { * Saltram, by Eclipse.
{ Daughter of Symme's Wildair.

Ball's Florizel. { * Diomed, by Florizel.
{ Daughter of * Shark.

Daughter of { * Alderman, by Pot-8-os.
{ Daughter of * Clockfast.

Emilius. { Orville, by Beningbrough.
{ Emily, by Stamford.

Icaria. { The Flyer, by Van Dyke, jr.
{ Parma, by Dick Andrews.

Sumpter. { Sir Archy, by * Diomed.
{ Daughter of * Robin Redbreast.

Lady Grey. { Robin Grey, by * Royalist.
{ Maria, by Melzar.

Selim. { Buzzard, by Woodpecker.
{ Castrel's dam, by Alexander.

Bacchante. { Williamson's Ditto, by Sir Peter.
{ Sister to Calomel, by Mercury.

Tramp. { Dick Andrews, by Joe Andrews.
{ Daughter of Gohanna.

Web. { Waxy, by Pot-8-os.
{ Penelope, by Trumpator.

Golumpus. { Gohanna, by Mercury.
{ Catherine, by Woodpecker.

Lucy Grey. { Timothy, by Delpini.
{ Lucy, by Florizel.

Camillus. { Hambletonian, by King Fergus.
{ Faith, by Pacolet.

Daughter of { Smolensko, by Sorcerer.
{ Miss Cannon, by Orville.

Cattou. { Golumpus, by Gohanna.
{ Lucy Grey, by Timothy.

Emma. { Whisker, by Waxy.
{ Gibside Fairy, by Hermes.

Sir Charles. { Sir Archy, by * Diomed.
{ Daughter of * Citizen.

Mischief. { Virginian, by Sir Archy.
{ Daughter of * Bedford.

Timoleon. { Sir Archy, by * Diomed.
{ Daughter of * Saltram.

Sister to Tuckahoe. { Ball's Florizel, by * Diomed.
{ Daughter of * Alderman.

Lottery. { Tramp, by Dick Andrews.
{ Mandane, by Pot-8-os.

Sister to Catterick. { Whisker, by Waxy.
{ Daughter of Bay Trophonius.

Selim. { Buzzard, by Woodpecker.
{ Castrel's dam, by Alexander.

Bacchante. { Williamson's Ditto, by Sir Peter.
{ Sister to Calomel, by Mercury.

Tramp. { Dick Andrews, by Joe Andrews.
{ Daughter of Gohanna.

Web. { Waxy, by Pot-8-os.
{ Penelope, by Trumpator.

Blacklock. { Whitelock, by Hambletonian.
{ Daughter of Coriander.

Daughter of { Orville, by Beningbrough.
{ Miss Grimstone, by Weasel.

Trumpator. { Sir Solomon, by Tickle Toby.
{ Daughter of Hickory.

Lucy. { Orphan, by Ball's Florizel.
{ Lady Grey, by Robin Grey.

Seventh dam, Maria by Melzar; Eighth dam by * Highflyer; Ninth dam by * Fearnaught; Tenth dam by * Jack of Diamonds; Eleventh dam by * Ariel; Twelfth dam, * Diamond (called Dutchess), by the Cullen Arabian; Thirteenth dam, Lady Thigh by Croft's Partner; Fourteenth dam by Greyhound; Fifteenth dam by Curwen Bay Barb; Sixteenth dam by D'Arcy Chestnut Arabian; Seventeenth dam by Whiteshirt; Eighteenth dam, Old Montague Mare.

CLAUDIA.

Did not start as a two-year-old. At three years old started twenty-five times, winning nine times, as follows: Mile-and-a-quarter purse at Cincinnati ; the Neil House
Stakes and Columbus Stakes at Columbus; a mile purse and a mile-and-a-half purse at
Chillicothe; the Michigan Derby at Detroit ; a mile-and-a-half purse and a mile purse
at Coney Island, and ran a dead heat with Glenmore in mile-and-three-quarters Sweepstakes at same place. Ran second three times, third three times, and unplaced ten
times. At four years old started six times, ran third five times and unplaced
once. At five years old started seven times, won once, second twice, third once and
unplaced three times.

PRODUCE.

1883, b f., MAY D., by Voltigeur.
1884, b. f.,   by Versailles.
1885, ch. c., UMPIRE, by Versailles.
1886, ch. c.,   by *Rayon d'Or. (Died July, '86,)
1887, Missed to *Rayon d'Or.
1888, ch. f., CUTALONG, by *Rayon d'Or.
1889, (dead filly), by *Rayon d'Or.
1890,   by *Rayon d'Or.

CLIO.
Chestnut mare, foaled 1884. Bred by W. L. Scott, Erie, Pa.

- **Quits.**
  - **Rayon D'Or.**
    - **Flageolet.**
      - **Plutus.**
        - **Daughter of Trumpeter.**
          - **Orlando.** — Touchstone, by Camel. / Vulture, by Langar.
          - **Cavatina.** — Redshank, by Sandbeck. / Oxygen, by Emilius.
        - **Planet.** — Bay Middleton, by Sultan. / Plenary, by Emilius.
        - **Alice Bray.** — Venison, by Partisan. / Darkness, by Glencoe.
      - **La Favorite.**
        - **Monarque.**
          - **The Baron Sting, or the Emperor.** — Defense, by Whalebone. / Delight, by Reveller.
          - **Poetess.** — Royal Oak, by Catton. / Ada, by Whisker.
        - **Constance.**
          - **Gladiator.** — Partisan, by Walton. / Pauline, by Moses.
          - **Lanterne.** — Hercules, by Rainbow. / Elvira, by Eryx.
    - **Araucaria.**
      - **Ambrose.**
        - **Touchstone.**
          - **Camel.** — Whalebone, by Waxy. / Daughter of Selim.
          - **Banter.** — Master Henry, by Orville. / Boadicea, by Alexander.
        - **Annette.**
          - **Priam.** — Emilius, by Orville. / Cressida, by Whiskey.
          - **Potentate's Dam.** — Don Juan, by Orville. / Moll in the Wad, by Hambletonian.
      - **Pocahontas.**
        - **Glencoe.**
          - **Sultan.** — Selim, by Buzzard. / Bacchante, by Williamson's Ditto.
          - **Trampoline.** — Tramp, by Dick Andrews. / Web, by Waxy.
        - **Marpessa.**
          - **Muley.** — Orville, by Beningbrough. / Eleanor, by Whiskey.
          - **Clare.** — Marmion, by Whiskey. / Harpalice, by Gohanna.
  - **Columbia.**
    - ***Sovereign.**
      - **Eclipse.**
        - **Orlando.**
          - **Camel.** — Whalebone, by Waxy. / Daughter of Selim.
          - **Banter.** — Master Henry, by Orville. / Boadicea, by Alexander.
        - **Vulture.**
          - **Langar.** — Selim, by Buzzard. / Daughter of Walton.
          - **Kite.** — Bustard, by Castrel. / Olympia, by Sir Oliver.
      - **Gaze.**
        - **Bay Middleton.**
          - **Sultan.** — Selim, by Buzzard. / Bacchante, by Williamson's Ditto.
          - **Cobweb.** — Phantom, by Walton. / Filigree, by Soothsayer.
        - **Fly-catcher.**
          - **Godolphin.** — Partisan, by Walton. / Ridicule, by Shuttle.
          - **Sister to Cobweb.** — Phantom, by Walton. / Filigree, by Soothsayer.
    - ***Silence.**
      - **Trampoline.**
        - **Sultan.**
          - **Selim.** — Buzzard, by Woodpecker. / Castrel's dam, by Alexander.
          - **Bacchante.** — Williamson's Ditto, by Sir Peter. / Sister to Calomel, by Mercury.
        - **Trampoline.**
          - **Tramp.** — Dick Andrews, by Joe Andrews. / Daughter of Gohanna.
          - **Web.** — Waxy, by Pot-8-os. / Penelope, by Trumpator.
- **Fleur de Lis.**
  - **Emilius.**
    - **Emilius.** — Orville, by Beningbrough. / Emily, by Stamford.
    - **Fleur de Lis.** — Bourbon, by Sorcerer. / Lady Rachel, by Stamford.
- **Maria West, Wagner's dam.**
  - **Marion.** — Sir Archy, by *Diomed. / Daughter of *Citizen.
  - **Ella Crump.** — *Citizen, by Pacolet. / Daughter of Huntsman.

Seventh dam by Symme's Wildair; eighth dam by *Fearnaught; ninth dam by *Janus.

CLIO.

Never ran.

––––––––––––

PRODUCE.

1888, ch. f., CLYTIE, by *Kantaka.

1889, ch. f.,   by *Kantaka.

1890,   by Wanderer.

CHARITY.

Chestnut mare, foaled 1853. Bred by W. L. Scott, Erie, Pa.

{ Whalebone. { Waxy, by Pot-8-os. / Penelope, by Trumpator.
{ Peri. { Wanderer, by Gohanna. / Thalestris, by Alexander.
{ Bob Booty. { Chanticleer, by Woodpecker. / Ierne, by Bagot.
{ Flight. { Irish Escape, by Commodore. / Young Heroine, by Bagot.
{ Castrel. { Buzzard, by Woodpecker. / Selim's dam, by Alexander.
{ Idalia. { Peruvian, by Sir Peter. / Musidora, by Meteor.
{ Laurel. { Blacklock, by Whitelock. / Wagtail, by Prime Minister.
{ Maid of Honor. { Champion, by Selim. / Etiquette, by Orville.
{ Timoleon. { Sir Archy, by * Diomed. / Daughter of * Saltram.
{ Sister to Tuckahoe. { Ball's Florizel, by * Diomed. / Daughter of * Alderman.
{ *Sarpedon. { Emilius, by Orville. / Icaria, by The Flyer.
{ Rowena. { Sumpter, by Sir Archy. / Lady Grey, by Robin Grey.
{ Sultan. { Selim, by Buzzard. / Bacchante, by Williamson's Ditto.
{ Trampoline. { Tramp, by Dick Andrews. / Web, by Waxy.
{ Barefoot. { Tramp, by Dick Andrews. / Rosamond, by Buzzard.
{ Lady Tompkins. { American Eclipse, by Duroc. / Katy Ann, by Ogle's Oscar.
{ Humphrey Clinker. { Comus, by Sorcerer. / Clinkerina, by Clinker.
{ Daughter of { Cervantes, by Don Quixote. / Daughter of Golumpus.
{ Touchstone. { Camel, by Whalebone. / Banter, by Master Henry.
{ Emma. { Whisker, by Waxy. / Gibside Fairy, by Hermes.
{ Emilius. { Orville, by Beningbrough. / Emily, by Stamford.
{ Shoveler. { Scud, by Beningbrough. / Goosander, by Hambletonian.
{ Whisker. { Waxy, by Pot-8-os. / Penelope, by Trumpator.
{ Variety. { Selim or Soothsayer. / Sprite, by Bobtail.
{ Emilius. { Orville, by Beningbrough. / Emily, by Stamford.
{ Seamew. { Scud, by Beningbrough. / Goosander, by Hambletonian.
{ Tramp. { Dick Andrews, by Joe Andrews. / Daughter of Gohanna.
{ Daughter of { Sancho, by Don Quixote. / Blacklock's dam, by Coriander.
{ Duroc. { *Diomed, by Florizel. / Amanda, by Grey Diomed.
{ Miller's Damsel. { * Messenger, by Mambrino. / Daughter of Pot-8-os.
{ Sumpter. { Sir Archy, by * Diomed. / Flirtilla's dam by * Robin Redbreast.
{ Jenny Slamerkin. { Tiger, by Blackburn's Whip. / Hannah Harris, by *Buzzard.

Sir Hercules. Faugh-a-Ballagh.
Guiccioli. *Leamington.
Pantaloon. Daughter of
Daphne.
Boston. Sensation.
Lexington.
Alice Carneal.
*Glencoe. Susan Beane.
Motto. Sally Lewis.
Melbourne. West Australian.
Mowerina. *Australian.
Young Emilius. Emilia.
Persian.
St. Nicholas. *Yorkshire.
Miss Rose. Maria Innis.
American Eclipse. Ann Innis.
Miss Obstinate.

Emma.

Seventh dam, Indiana, by Butler's Columbus; Eighth dam, Jane Hunt by Hampton's Paragon; Ninth dam, Moll by *Figure; Tenth dam, Maria Slamerkin by *Wildair; Eleventh dam, *Mare by Cub; Twelfth dam, Amaranthus' dam by Second; Thirteenth dam by Starling; Fourteenth dam, Sister to Vane's Little Partner by Croft's Partner; Fifteenth dam, Sister to Guy by Greyhound; Sixteenth dam, Brown Farewell by Makeless; Seventeenth dam by Brimmer; Eighteenth dam by Place's White Turk; Nineteenth dam by Dodsworth; Twentieth dam, Layton Barb Mare

CHARITY.

At two years old started five times, winning the Flatbush Stakes at Coney Island; third to The Bard in the Red Bank Stakes at Monmouth Park, eight starters; third in the Adieu Stakes, Coney Island, sixteen starters; second to Dew Drop in the Nursery, and unplaced in the Great Eastern Handicap. At three years old started ten times, winning the Fourth of July Handicap, nine starters, and the Raritan Stakes, beating The Bard and three others, at Monmouth Park; second to Bandala in the Ladies' Stakes, Jerome Park; second to Rupert in the Long Branch Handicap; second to Dew Drop in the Monmouth Oaks; second to Little Minch in the Midsummer Handicap, twelve starters, at Monmouth Park; third in the Alabama Stakes at Saratoga, and unplaced three times.

PRODUCE.

1890,   by *Rayon d'Or.

CLIPSIANNA. Chestnut mare, foaled 1881. Bred by T. J. Megibben.

- **Springbok.**
  - ***Australian.**
    - **West Australian.**
      - *Melbourne.*
        - Humphrey Clinker. — { Comus, by Sorcerer, / Clinkerina, by Clinker.
        - Daughter of — { Cervantes, by Don Quixote, / Daughter of Golumpus.
      - *Mowerina.*
        - Touchstone. — { Camel, by Whalebone. / Banter, by Master Henry.
        - Emma. — { Whisker, by Waxy. / Gibside Fairy, by Hermes.
  - **Emilia.**
    - *Young Emilius.*
      - Emilius. — { Orville, by Beningbrough. / Emily, by Stamford.
      - Shoveler. — { Scud, by Beningbrough. / Goosander, by Hambletonian.
    - *Persian.*
      - Whisker. — { Waxy, by Pot-8-os. / Penelope, by Trumpator.
      - Variety. — { Selim, or Soothsayer. / Sprite, by Bobtail.
- **Hester.**
  - **Lexington.**
    - *Boston.*
      - Timoleon. — { Sir Archy, by *Diomed. / Daughter of *Saltram.
      - Sister to Tuckahoe. — { Ball's Florizel, by *Diomed. / Daughter of *Alderman.
    - *Alice Carneal.*
      - Sarpedon. — { Emilius, by *Orville. / Icaria, by The Flyer.
      - Rowena. — { Sumpter, by Sir Archy. / Lady Grey, by Robin Grey.
  - **Heads-I-Say.**
    - *Glencoe.*
      - Sultan. — { Selim, by Buzzard. / Bacchante, by Williamson's Ditto.
      - Trampoline. — { Tramp, by Dick Andrews. / Web, by Waxy.
    - *Heads or Tails.*
      - Lottery. — { Tramp, by Dick Andrews. / Mandane, by Pot-8-os.
      - Active. — { Partisan, by Walton. / Eleanor, by Whiskey.
- **Eclipsa.**
  - ***Eclipse.**
    - **Orlando.**
      - *Touchstone.*
        - Camel. — { Whalebone, by Waxy. / Daughter of Selim.
        - Banter. — { Master Henry, by Orville. / Boadicea, by Alexander.
      - *Vulture.*
        - Langar. — { Selim, by Buzzard. / Daughter of Walton.
        - Kite. — { Bustard, by Castrel. / Olympia, by Sir Oliver.
  - **Gaze.**
    - *Bay Middleton.*
      - Sultan. — { Selim, by Buzzard. / Bacchante, by Williamson's Ditto.
      - Cobweb. — { Phantom, by Walton. / Filigree, by Soothsayer.
    - *Fly-catcher.*
      - Godolphin. — { Partisan, by Walton. / Ridicule, by Shuttle.
      - Sister to Cobweb. — { Phantom, by Walton. / Filigree, by Soothsayer.
- **Avis.**
  - ***Sovereign.**
    - *Emilius.*
      - Orville. — { Beningbrough, by King Fergus. / Evelina, by Highflyer.
      - Emily. — { Stamford, by Sir Peter. / Daughter of Whiskey.
    - *Fleur-de-lis.*
      - Bourbon. — { Sorcerer, by Trumpator. / Daughter of Precipitate.
      - Lady Rachel. — { Stamford, by Sir Peter. / Young Rachel, by Volunteer.
  - **Thrush.**
    - **Leviathan.*
      - Muley. — { Orville, by Beningbrough. / Daughter of Whiskey.
      - The Dandy's dam. — { Windle, by Beningbrough. / Daughter of Anvil.
    - *Object.*
      - Marshall Ney. — { Pacolet, by *Citizen. / Virginia, by *Dare Devil.
      - Pigeon. — { Pacolet, by *Citizen. / *Mare, by Waxy.

Seventh dam, Mother Shipton, by Anvil; eighth dam, Jemima, by Satelite; ninth dam, Maria, by Herod; tenth dam, Lizette, by Snap; eleventh dam, Miss Windsor, by Godolphin Arabian; twelfth dam, sister to Wyvill's Volunteer, by Young Belgrade; thirteenth dam by Bartlet's Childers.

CLIPSIANNA.

Never ran.

PRODUCE.

1885-'86-'87, Barren to *Uhlan.

1888, ch. c.,   by Aristides.

1889, b. f.,   by *Uhlan.

1890,   by *Rayon d'Or.

DAPHNE.

Chestnut mare, foaled 1884. Bred by W. L. Scott, Erie, Pa.

Sire: *Rayon D'Or.

- Flageolet.
  - Plutus.
    - Daughter of Trumpeter.
      - Orlando. { Touchstone, by Camel. / Vulture, by Langar.
      - Cavatina. { Redshank, by Sandbeck. / Oxygen, by Emilius.
    - Planet. { Bay Middleton, by Sultan. / Plenary, by Emilius.
    - Alice Bray. { Venison, by Partisan. / Darkness, by Glencoe.
  - La Favorite.
    - Monarque.
      - The Baron Sting, or the Emperor. { Defense, by Whalebone. / Delight, by Reveller.
      - Poetess. { Royal Oak, by Catton. / Ada, by Whisker.
    - Constance.
      - Gladiator. { Partisan, by Walton. / Pauline, by Moses.
      - Lanterne. { Hercules, by Rainbow. / Elvira, by Eryx.
- Araucaria.
  - Ambrose.
    - Touchstone.
      - Camel. { Whalebone, by Waxy. / Daughter of Selim.
      - Banter. { Master Henry, by Orville. / Boadicea, by Alexander.
    - Annette.
      - Priam. { Emilius, by Orville. / Cressida, by Whiskey.
      - Potentate's Dam. { Don Juan, by Orville. / Moll in the Wad, by Hambletonian.
  - Pocahontas.
    - Glencoe.
      - Sultan. { Selim, by Buzzard. / Bacchante, by Williamson's Ditto.
      - Trampoline. { Tramp, by Dick Andrews. / Web, by Waxy.
    - Marquessa.
      - Muley. { Orville, by Beningbrough. / Eleanor, by Whiskey.
      - Clare. { Marmion, by Whiskey. / Harpalice, by Gohanna.

Dam: Mary Clark.

- Leamington.
  - Faugh-a-Ballagh.
    - Sir Hercules.
      - Whalebone. { Waxy, by Pot-8-os. / Penelope, by Trumpator.
      - Peri. { Wanderer, by Gohanna. / Thalestris, by Alexander.
    - Guiccioli.
      - Bob Booty. { Chanticleer, by Woodpecker. / Ierne, by Bagot.
      - Flight. { Escape, by Commodore. / Young Heroine, by Bagot.
  - Daughter of
    - Pantaloon.
      - Castrel. { Buzzard, by Woodpecker. / Selim's dam, by Alexander.
      - Idalia. { Peruvian, by Sir Peter. / Musidora, by Meteor,
    - Daphne.
      - Laurel. { Blacklock, by Whitelock. / Wagtail, by Prime Minister.
      - Maid of Honor. { Champion, by Selim. / Etiquette, by Orville.
- Eagless.
  - Lexington.
    - Boston.
      - Timoleon. { Sir Archy, by *Diomed. / Daughter of *Saltram.
      - Sister to Tuckahoe. { Ball's Florizel, by *Diomed. / Daughter of *Alderman.
    - Alice Carneal.
      - *Sarpedon. { Emilius, by Orville. / Icaria, by The Flyer.
      - Rowena. { Sumpter, by Sir Archy. / Lady Gray, by Robin Gray.
  - Daughter of *Glencoe.
    - Sultan. { Selim, by Buzzard. / Bacchante, by Williamson's Ditto.
    - Trampoline. { Tramp, by Dick Andrews. / Web, by Waxy.
    - Spark.
      - Grey Eagle. { Woodpecker, by Bertrand. / Ophelia, by Wild Medley.
      - Mary Morris. { Medoc, by Am. Eclipse. / Miss Obstinate, by Sumpter.

Seventh dam, Jennie Slamerkin, by Tiger; eighth dam, Paragon, by *Buzzard; ninth dam, Columbia, by Columbus; tenth dam by Hampton's Paragon; eleventh dam by *Figure; twelfth dam, Maria Slamerkin, by *Wildair; thirteenth dam, *Mare by Cub; fourteenth dam, Amaranthus' dam, by Second; fifteenth dam by Starling; sixteenth dam by Croft's Partner; seventeenth dam by Greyhound; eighteenth dam, Brown Farewell, by Makeless; nineteenth dam by Brimmer; twentieth dam by Place's White Turk; twenty-first dam by Dodsworth; twenty-second dam, Layton Barb mare.

DAPHNE.

At two years old started seven times, winning once, second twice, third once, and unplaced three times. At three years old started five times, running unplaced each time.

PRODUCE.

1889, ch. f., (Died in 1889.) by *Kantaka.

1890,   by *Kantaka.

DI VERNON.

Bay mare, foaled 1882. Bred by P. Lorillard, Rancocas Stud, N. J.

Duke of Magenta

- Lexington
  - Boston
    - Timoleon
      - Sir Archy.
        - Diomed, by Florizel.
        - Castianira, by Rockingham.
      - Daughter of
        - Saltram, by Eclipse.
        - Daughter of Symme's Wildair.
    - Robin Brown's dam.
      - Ball's Florizel.
        - Diomed, by Florizel.
        - Daughter of *Shark.
      - Daughter of
        - *Alderman, by Pot-8-os.
        - Daughter of *Clockfast.
  - Alice Carneal.
    - Sarpedon.
      - Emilius.
        - Orville, by Beningbrough.
        - Emily, by Stamford.
      - Icaria.
        - The Flyer, by Van Dyke, Jr.
        - Parua, by Dick Andrews.
    - Rowena.
      - Sumpter.
        - Sir Archy, by Diomed.
        - Flirtilla's dam, by Robin Redbreast.
      - Lady Grey.
        - Robin Grey, by Royalist.
        - Maria, by Melzar.
- Magenta.
  - *Yorkshire.
    - St. Nicholas.
      - Emilius.
        - Orville, by Beningbrough.
        - Emily, by Stamford.
      - Sennow.
        - Scud, by Beningbrough.
        - Goosander, by Hambletonian.
    - Miss Rose.
      - Tramp.
        - Dick Andrews, by Joe Andrews.
        - Daughter of Gohanna.
      - Daughter of
        - Sancho, by Herod.
        - Blacklock's dam, by Coriander.
  - Marian.
    - Glencoe.
      - Sultan.
        - Selim, by Buzzard.
        - Bacchante, by Williamson's Ditto.
      - Trampoline.
        - Tramp, by Dick Andrews.
        - Web, by Waxy.
    - Minerva Anderson.
      - *Luzborough.
        - Williamson's Ditto, by Sir Peter.
        - Daughter of Dick Andrews.
      - Daughter of
        - Sir Charles, by Sir Archy,
        - Daughter of Bess' Brimmer.

Jessie Dixon

- Hilda.
  - *Eclipse.
    - Orlando.
      - Touchstone.
        - Camel.
          - Whalebone, by Waxy.
          - Daughter of Selim.
        - Banter.
          - Master Henry, by Orville.
          - Bondicea, by Alexander.
      - Vulture.
        - Langar.
          - Selim, by Buzzard.
          - Daughter of Walton.
        - Kite.
          - Bustard, by Castrel.
          - Olympia, by Sir Oliver.
    - Gaze.
      - Bay Middleton.
        - Sultan.
          - Selim, by Buzzard.
          - Bacchante, by Williamson's Ditto.
        - Cobweb.
          - Phantom, by Walton.
          - Filigree, by Soothsayer.
      - Fly-catcher.
        - Godolphin.
          - Partisan, by Walton.
          - Ridicule, by Shuttle.
        - Sister to Cobweb.
          - Phantom, by Walton.
          - Filigree, by Soothsayer.
- Puss.
  - Arlington.
    - Boston.
      - Timoleon.
        - Sir Archy, by *Diomed.
        - Daughter of *Saltram.
      - Sister to Tuckahoe.
        - Ball's Florizel, by *Diomed.
        - Daughter of *Alderman.
    - Stella.
      - Contention.
        - Sir Archy, by *Diomed,
        - Daughter of *Dare Devil.
      - Daughter of
        - *Speculator, by Dragon.
        - Pompadour, by °Vailiant.
  - John Blount.
    - Marion.
      - Sir Archy, by *Diomed.
      - Daughter of *Citizen.
    - Maid of the Brook.
      - Sir Alfred, by *Sir Harry.
      - Daughter of Phenomenon.
  - Canary.
    - Sir Charles.
      - Sir Archy, by *Diomed.
      - Daughter of *Citizen.
    - Daughter of
      - Trafalgar, by *Mufti.
      - Polly Bridges, by *Buzzard.

Seventh dam, Raffle, by Bellair; eighth dam, Narcissa, by Symme's Wildair; ninth dam, Melpomene, by Burwell's Traveler; tenth dam, Virginia, by Mark Anthony; eleventh dam, Polly Byrd, by *Jolly Roger; twelfth dam, *Bonnie Lass, by Bay Bolton; thirteenth dam by the Darley Arabian; fourteenth dam, by the Byerly Turk; fifteenth dam by Place's White Turk; sixteenth dam by Taffolet Barb; seventeenth dam, Natural Barb Mare.

DI VERNON.

Never ran.

PRODUCE.

1886, Barren to *Uhlan.

1887, b. c., GEN. HOLLAND), by Aristides.

1888, Barren to *Uhlan.

1889, b. f.,   by *Uhlan.

1890,   by *Rayon d'Or.

DONCASTER LASS (IMOPRTED.)

Bay mare, foaled 1878. Bred by Mr. H. Waring, England. Imported 1882, by Mr. W. L. Scott, Erie, Pa.

- **Doncaster**
  - **Stockwell**
    - **The Baron**
      - *Bird-catcher*
        - **Sir Hercules.** — { Whalebone, by Waxy. / Peri, by Wanderer. }
        - **Guiccioli.** — { Bob Booty, by Chanticleer. / Flight, by Escape. }
      - *Ech-idna*
        - **Economist.** — { Whisker, by Waxy. / Floranthe, by Octavian. }
        - **Miss Pratt.** — { Blacklock, by Whitelock. / Gadabout by Orville. }
    - **Pocahontas**
      - *Glencoe*
        - **Sultan.** — { Selim, by Buzzard. / Bacchante, by Ditto. }
        - **Trampoline** — { Tramp, by Dick Andrews. / Web, by Waxy. }
      - *Marpessa*
        - **Muley.** — { Orville, by Benningbrough. / Eleanor, by Whiskey. }
        - **Clare.** — { Marmion, by Whiskey. / Harpalice, by Gohanna. }
  - **Marigold**
    - **Teddington**
      - *Orlando*
        - **Touchstone.** — { Camel by Whalebone. / Banter, by Master Henry. }
        - **Vulture.** — { Langar, by Selim. / Kite, by Bustard. }
      - *Miss Twickenham*
        - **Rockingham.** — { Humphrey Clinker, by Comus. / Medora, by Swordsman. }
        - **Electress.** — { Election, by Gohanna. / Daughter of Stamford. }
    - **Sister to Singapore**
      - *Ratan*
        - **Buzzard.** — { Blacklock, by Whitelock. / Delphini Mare. }
        - **Daughter of** — { Picton, by Smolensko. / Daughter of Selim. }
      - *Daughter of*
        - **Melbourne.** — { Humphrey Clinker, by Comus. / Daughter of Cervantes. }
        - **Lisbeth.** — { Phantom, by Walton. / Elizabeth, by Rainbow. }

- **Our Mary Ann**
  - **Voltigeur**
    - **Voltaire**
      - *Black-lock*
        - **Whitelock.** — { Hambletonian, by King Fergus. / Rosalind, by Phenomenon. }
        - **Daughter of** — { Coriander, by Pot-8-os. / Wildgoose, by Highflyer. }
      - *Daughter of*
        - **Phantom.** — { Walton, by Sir Peter. / Julia, by Whiskey. }
        - **Daughter of** — { Overton, by King Fergus. / Gratitude's dam, by Walnut. }
    - **Martha Lynn**
      - *Mulatto*
        - **Calton.** — { Golumpus, by Gohanna. / Lucy Grey, by Timothy. }
        - **Desdemona.** — { Orville, by Benningbrough. / Fanny, by Sir Peter. }
      - *Leda*
        - **Filhoda Puta.** — { Haphazard, by Sir Peter. / Mrs. Barnett, by Waxy. }
        - **Treasure.** — { Camillus, by Hambletonian. / Daughter of, by Hyacinthus. }

- **Gaiety**
  - **Fangh-a-Ballagh**
    - *Sir Hercules*
      - **Whalebone.** — { Waxy, by Pot-8-os. / Penelope, by Trumpator. }
      - **Peri.** — { Wanderer, by Gohanna. / Thalestris, by Alexander. }
    - *Guiccioli*
      - **Bob Booty.** — { Chanticleer, by Woodpecker. / Ierne, by Bagot. }
      - **Flight.** — { Escape, by Commodore. / Y. Heroine, by Bagot. }
  - **Cast Steel**
    - *Touchstone*
      - **Camel.** — { Whalebone, by Waxy. / Daughter of Selim. }
      - **Banter.** — { Master Henry, by Orville. / Boadicea, by Alexander. }
    - *Whisker*
      - **Whisker.** — { Waxy, by Pot-8-os. / Penelope, by Trumpator. }
      - **The Twinkle** — { Walton, by Sir Peter. / Daughter of Orville. }

Seventh dam, Lisette by Hambletonian; Eighth dam, Constantia by Walnut; Ninth dam, Contessina by Y. Marske; Tenth dam, Tuberose by Herod; Eleventh dam, Grey Starling by Starling; Twelfth dam Coughing Polly by Bartlett's Childers Thirteenth dam by Counsellor, etc.

DONCASTER LASS.

Never started but once and then ran unplaced to Isolina in Selling Plate, seven starters, at Newmarket, England.

———————

PRODUCE.

1883, b. f., SCOTTISH LASS, by Scottish Chief.   (Imp. in utero.)

1884, ch. c., BRONZOMARTE, by *Rayon d'Or.   (Gelded.)

1885, Missed to *Rayon d'Or.

1886, b. or br. c., by *Rayon d'Or.   (Died in 1887.)

1887, Missed to *Rayon d'Or.

1888, ch. f., STRAY LASS, by Wanderer.

1889, ch. f.,   by Wanderer.

1890,   by Wanderer.

DORMOUSE. Brown mare, foaled 1885. Bred by W. L. Scott, Erie, Pa.

- ***Rayon D'Or.**
  - **Flageolet.**
    - **Plutus.**
      - Orlando. { Touchstone, by Camel. / Vulture, by Langar.
      - Cavatina. { Redshank, by Sandbeck. / Oxygen, by Emilius.
    - **Daughter of Trumpeter.**
      - Planet. { Bay Middleton, by Sultan. / Plenary, by Emilius.
      - Alice Bray. { Venison, by Partisan. / Darkness, by Glencoe.
  - **La Favorite.**
    - **Monarque.**
      - The Baron Sting, or the Emperor. { Defense, by Whalebone. / Delight, by Reveller.
      - Poetess. { Royal Oak, by Catton. / Ada, by Whisker.
    - **Constance.**
      - Gladiator. { Partisan, by Walton. / Pauline, by Moses.
      - Lanterne. { Hercules, by Rainbow. / Elvira, by Eryx.
- **Araucaria.**
  - **Ambrose.**
    - **Touchstone.**
      - Camel. { Whalebone, by Waxy. / Daughter of Selim.
      - Banter. { Master Henry, by Orville. / Boadicea, by Alexander.
    - **Annette.**
      - Priam. { Emilius, by Orville. / Cressida, by Whiskey.
      - Potentate's Dam. { Don Juan, by Orville. / Moll in the Wad, by Hambletonian.
  - **Pocahontas.**
    - **Glencoe.**
      - Sultan. { Selim, by Buzzard. / Bacchante, by Williamson's Ditto.
      - Trampoline. { Tramp, by Dick Andrews. / Web, by Waxy.
    - **Marpessa.**
      - Muley. { Orville, by Beningbrough. / Eleanor, by Whiskey.
      - Clare. { Marmion, by Whiskey. / Harpalice, by Gohanna.
- **Fannie Moore.**
  - **Lightning.**
    - **Lexington.**
      - **Boston.**
        - Timoleon. { Sir Archy, by *Diomed. / Daughter of *Saltram.
        - Sis. to Tuckahoe. { Ball's Florizel, by *Diomed. / Daughter of *Alderman.
      - **Alice Carneal.**
        - Sarpedon. { Emilius, by Orville. / Icaria, by The Flyer.
        - Rowena. { Sumpter, by Sir Archy. / Lady Grey, by Robin Grey.
    - **Blue Bonnet.**
      - ***Hedgford.**
        - Filho-da-Puta. { Haphazard, by Sir Peter. / Mrs. Barnet, by Waxy.
        - Miss Craigie. { Orville, by Beningbrough. / Marchioness, by Lurcher.
      - **Grey Fanny.**
        - Bertrand. { Sir Archy, by *Diomed. / Eliza, by *Bedford.
        - Daughter of. { *Buzzard, by Woodpecker. / Arminda, by *Medley.
  - **Lady Sovereign.**
    - ***Sovereign.**
      - **Emilius.**
        - Orville. { Beningbrough, by King Fergus. / Evelina, by Highflyer.
        - Emily. { Stamford, by Sir Peter. / Daughter of Whiskey.
      - **Fleur-de-lis.**
        - Bourbon. { Sorcerer, by Trumpator. / Daughter of Precipitate.
        - Lady Rachel. { Stamford, by Sir Peter. / Young Rachel, by Volunteer.
    - **Croppy.**
      - **Medoc.**
        - Am. Eclipse. { Duroc, by *Diomed. / Miller's Damsel, by *Messenger.
        - Young Maid of the Oaks. { *Expedition, by Pegasus. / Old Maid of the Oaks, by *Spread Eagle.
      - **Daughter of.**
        - Thornton's Rattler. { Sir Archy, by *Diomed. / Sumpter's dam, by *Robin Redbreast.
        - Daughter of. { *Spread Eagle, by Volunteer. / Daughter of Boxer.

Seventh dam, Rose of Sharon, by *Pantaloon; eighth dam, Queen of Diamonds, by Merde's Celer; ninth dam, Philadelphia, by Mende's Pilgrim; tenth dam by Lee's Mare Anthony; eleventh dam by Silverere; twelfth dam by *Jolly Roger; thirteenth dam by *Monkey; fourteenth dam by *Childers.

DORMOUSE.

Never ran.

— — —

PRODUCE.

1889, Barren to *Kantaka.

1890, by *Kantaka.

EMMA.

Chestnut mare, foaled 1871. Bred by Mr. A. J. Alexander, Kentucky.

- **EMMA** — by *Australian, out of Maria Innis.
  - ***Australian.**
    - **West Australian.**
      - **Melbourne.**
        - Humphrey Clinker
          - Comus. { Sorcerer, by Trumpator. / Houghton Lass, by Sir Peter.
          - Clinkerina. { Clinker, by Sir Peter. / Pewet, by Tandem.
        - Daughter of
          - Cervantes. { Don Quixote, by Eclipse. / Evelina, by Highflyer.
          - Daughter of { Golumpus, by Gohanna. / Daughter of Paynator.
      - **Mowerina.**
        - Touchstone
          - Camel. { Whalebone, by Waxy. / Daughter of Selim and Maiden.
          - Banter. { Master Henry, by Orville. / Boadicea, by Alexander.
        - Emma
          - Whisker. { Waxy, by Pot-8-os. / Penelope, by Trumpator.
          - Gibside Fairy. { Hermes, by Mercury. / Vicissitude, by Pipator.
    - **Emilia**
      - **Young Emilius.**
        - Emilius
          - Orville. { Beningbrough, by King Fergus. / Evelina, by Highflyer.
          - Emily. { Stamford, by Sir Peter. / Daughter of Whiskey, by Saltram.
        - Shoveler
          - Scud. { Beningbrough, by King Fergus. / Eliza, by Highflyer.
          - Goosander. { Hambletonian, by King Fergus. / Rally, by Trumpator.
      - **Persian.**
        - Whisker
          - Waxy. { Pot-8-os, by Eclipse. / Maria, by Herod.
          - Penelope. { Trumpator, by Conductor. / Prunella, by Highflyer.
        - Variety
          - Selim, or Soothsayer. { Sorcerer, by Trumpator. / Golden Locks, by Delpini.
          - Sprite. { Bobtail, by Precipitate. / Catherine by Woodpecker.
  - **Maria Innis.**
    - ***Yorkshire.**
      - **St. Nicholas.**
        - Emilius
          - Orville. { Beningbrough, by King Fergus. / Evelina, by Highflyer.
          - Emily. { Stamford, by Sir Peter. / Daughter of Whiskey.
        - Seamew
          - Scud. { Beningbrough, by King Fergus. / Eliza, by Highflyer.
          - Goosander. { Hambletonian, by King Fergus. / Rally, by Trumpator.
      - **Miss Rose.**
        - Tramp
          - Dick Andrews. { Joe Andrews, by Eclipse. / Daughter of Highflyer.
          - Daughter of { Gohanna, by Mercury. / Fraxinella, by Trentham.
        - Daughter of
          - Sancho. { Don Quixote, by Eclipse. / Daughter of Highflyer.
          - Blacklock's dam. { Coriander, by Pot-8-os. / Wildgoose, by Highflyer.
    - **Ann Innis.**
      - **American Eclipse.**
        - Duroc
          - *Diomed. { Florizel, by Herod. / Sister to Juno, by Spectator.
          - Amanda. { Grey Diomed, by *Medley. / Daughter of Virginia Cade.
        - Miller's Damsel
          - *Messenger. { Mambrino, by Engineer. / Daughter of Turf, by Matchem.
          - Daughter of { Pot-8-os, by Eclipse. / Daughter of Gimcrack.
      - **Miss Obstinate.**
        - Sumpter
          - Sir Archy. { *Diomed, by Florizel. / Castianira, by Rockingham.
          - Robin mare. { *Robin Redbreast, by Sir Peter. / Daughter of *Obscurity.
        - Jenny Slamerkin
          - Tiger. { Blackburn's Whip, by *Whip. / Jane Hunt, by Hampton's Paragon.
          - Hannah Harris. { *Buzzard, by Woodpecker. / Indiana, by Butler's Columbus.

Seventh dam, Jane Hunt, by Hampton's Paragon; Eighth dam, Moll by *Figure; Ninth dam, Maria Slamerkin, by *Wildair; Tenth dam, *Mare by Cub; Eleventh dam, Amaranthus' dam, by Second; Twelfth dam by Starling; Thirteenth dam (sister to Vane's Little Partner), by Croft's Partner; Fourteenth dam, (sister to Guy) by Greyhound; Fifteenth dam, Brown Farewell, by Makeless; Sixteenth dam by Brimmer; Seventeenth dam by Place's White Turk; Eighteenth dam by Dodsworth; Nineteenth dam, Layton Barb mare.

EMMA.

Did not run as a two-year-old. At three years old started three times, winning once, third once, and unplaced once. At four years old started twice and was unplaced both times.

— ---

PRODUCE.

1877, b. c., JUDGE MURRAY, by Vauxhall.

1878, b. f., MAGGIE DUFFY, by Charley Howard.

1879, ch. c., J. O. NAY, by Fellowcraft.

1880, ch. c., H. MURRAY, by Alarm.

1881 and 1882, barren.

1883, ch. f., CHARITY, by Sensation.

1884, Missed to *Rayon d'Or.

1885, Missed to *Kantaka and *Rayon d'Or.

1886, (twins) ch. f., EMULATE, by *Kantaka. (One died.)

1887, dead c., by *Rayon d'Or.

1888, Barren to *Rayon d'Or.

1889, Barren to *Kantaka and *Rayon d'Or.

1890, by *Kantaka.

ELLA T.
Bay mare, foaled 1876. Bred by Wm. T. Herne, Kentucky.

Pedigree chart:

- Bonny Kate
  - War Dance
    - Lexington
      - Boston
        - Timoleon
          - Sir Archy. { *Diomed, by Florizel. / *Castianira, by Rockingham.
          - Daughter of { *Saltram, by Eclipse. / Daughter of Symme's Wildair.
        - Sister to Tuckahoe
          - Ball's Florizel. { *Diomed, by Florizel. / Daughter of *Shark.
          - Daughter of { *Alderman, by Pot-8-os. / Daughter of *Clockfast.
      - Alice Carneal
        - Sarpedon
          - Emilius. { Orville, by Beningbrough. / Emily, by Stamford.
          - Icaria. { The Flyer, by VanDyke, jr. / Parma, by Dick Andrews.
        - Rowena
          - Sumpter. { Sir Archy, by *Diomed. / Daughter of *Robin Redbreast.
          - Lady Gray. { Robin Gray, by *Royalist. / Maria, by Melzar.
    - *Glencoe
      - Sultan
        - Sellin. { Buzzard, by Woodpecker. / Castrel's dam, by Alexander.
        - Bacchante. { Williamson's Ditto, by Sir Peter. / Sister to Calomel, by Mercury.
      - Trampoline
        - Tramp { Dick Andrews, by Joe Andrews. / Daughter of Gohanna.
        - Web. { Waxy, by Pot-8-os. / Penelope, by Trumpator.
  - Reel
    - Gallopade
      - Catton
        - Golumpus. { Gohanna, by Mercury. / Catherine, by Woodpecker.
        - Lucy Gray. { Timothy, by Delpini / Lucy, by Florizel.
      - Camillina
        - Camillus. { Hambletonian, by King Fergus. / Faith, by Pacolet.
        - Daughter of { Smolensko, by Sorcerer. / Miss Cannon, by Orville.
    - Sir Hercules.
      - Whalebone. { Waxy, by Pot-8-os. / Penelope, by Trumpator.
      - Peri. { Wanderer, by Gohanna. / Thalestris, by Alexander.
    - Guiccioli.
      - Bob Booty. { Chanticleer, by Woodpecker. / Ierne, by Irish Escape.
      - Flight. { Escape, by Highflyer. / Young Heroine, by Bagot.

- Eagle
  - *Knight of St. George
    - Irish Birdcatcher.
      - Sir Hercules.
        - Brutandorf. { Blacklock, by Whitelock. / Mandane, by Pot-8-os.
        - Daughter of { Comus, by Sorcerer. / Mariana, by Stamford.
      - Peri.
        - Sir Hercules. { Whalebone, by Waxy. / Peri, by Wanderer.
        - Mary Ann. { Waxy Pope, by Waxy. / Witch, by Sorcerer.
    - Malese.
      - Water Witch.
        - Hetman Platoff.
          - Duroc. { *Diomed, by Florizel. / Amanda, by Gray Diomed.
          - Miller's Damsel. { *Messenger, by Mambrino. / Daughter of Pot-8-os, by Eclipse.
  - Zenith.
    - Belle Anderson.
      - American Eclipse.
        - Sir William, of Transport. { Sir Archy, son of *Diomed. / Transport, by Virginius.
        - Butterfly. { Sumpter, by Sir Archy. / Daughter of *Buzzard.

- Eagletta
  - Gray Eagle.
    - Woodpecker. { Bertrand, by Sir Archy. / Daughter of *Buzzard.
    - Ophe'ia. { Wild Medley, by Mendozo. / Daughter of Sir Archy, by Diomed.
  - Mary Home.
    - Tiger { Blackburn's Whip, by *Whip. / Jane Hunt, by Wade Hampton's Paragon.
    - Lady Robin. { Robin Gray, by *Royalist. / Daughter of Quicksilver, by *Medley.

Seventh dam by Meade's Celer, son of *Janus.

ELLA T.

Ran only as a two-year-old, starting in nine races, winning six, third once, and unplaced twice.

PRODUCE.

1881, b. f., TWILIGHT, by Algerine.

1882, b. c., KRISHNA, by Algerine. (Gelded.)

1883, (twins), b. c., COYOTE, by Algerine. (One died.)

1884, Missed to *Rayon d'Or.

1885, ch. c., TEA-TRAY, by *Rayon d'Or.

1886, b. c., REALIZATION, by *Rayon d'Or. (Died April, 1886.)

1887, b. c., BANQUET, by *Rayon d'Or. (Gelded.)

1888, ch. c.,   by *Kantaka. (Died October, 1888.)

1889, ch. c.,   by *Rayon d'Or.

1890,   by *Rayon d'Or.

EMULATE.

Chestnut mare (a twin), foaled 1856. Bred by W. L. Scott, Erie, Pa.

		Camel.	Whalebone, by Waxy. / Daughter of Selim.
Touchstone.	Lord of the Isles.	Banter.	Master Henry, by Orville. / Boadicea, by Alexander.
Scottish Chief.	Fair Helen.	Pantaloon.	Castrel, by Buzzard. / Idalia, by Peruvian.
		Rebecca.	Lottery, by Tramp. / Daughter of Cervantes.
Miss Ann.	The Little Known.	Muley.	Orville, by Beningbrough. / Eleanor, by Whiskey.
		Lacerta.	Zodiac, by St. George. / Jerbon, by Gohanna.
Ilay Missy.	Bay Middleton.		Sultan, by Selim. / Cobweb, by Phantom.
	Camilla.		Young Phantom, by Phantom. / Sister to Speaker, by Camillus.

*Kentuke.

		Cain.	Paulowitz, by Sir Paul. / Daughter of Paynator.
Tadmor.	Ione.	Margaret.	Edmond, by Orville. / Medora, by Selim.
Pal-myra.	Sultan.		Selim, by Buzzard. / Bacchante, by Williamson's Ditto.
	Hester.		Camel, by Whalebone. / Monimia, by Muley.
Cowl.	Bay Middleton.		Sultan, by Selim. / Cobweb, by Phantom.
	Crucifix.		Priam, by Emilius. / Octavinna, by Octavian.
Belle Dame.	Belshazzar.		Blacklock, by Whitelock. / Manuella, by Dick Andrews.
	Ellen.		Starch, by Waxy Pope. / Cuirass, by Oiseau.

Seclusion (Hermit's dam). / Miss Sellon.

Mel-bourne.	Humphrey Clinker.		Comus, by Sorcerer. / Clinkerina, by Clinker.
	Daughter of		Cervantes, by Don Quixote. / Daughter of Golumbus.
Mow-erina.	Touchstone.		Camel, by Whalebone. / Banter, by Master Henry.
	Emma.		Whisker, by Waxy. / Gibside Fairy, by Hermes.

West Australian. / *Australian.

Young Emilius.	Emilius.		Orville, by Beningbrough. / Emily, by Stamford.
	Shoveler.		Scud, by Beningbrough. / Goosander, by Hambletonian.
Persian.	Whisker.		Waxy, by Pot-8-os. / Penelope, by Trumpator.
	Variety.		Selim, or Soothsayer, by Sorcerer. / Sprite, by Bobtail.

Emilia.

St. Nicholas.	Emilius.		Orville, by Beningbrough. / Emily, by Stamford.
	Seamew.		Scud, by Beningbrough. / Goosander, by Hambletonian.
Miss Rose.	Tramp.		Dick Andrews, by Joe Andrews. / Daughter of Gohanna.
	Daughter of		Sancho, by Don Quixote. / Blacklock's dam, by Coriander.

*Yorkshire.

American Eclipse.	Duroc.		*Diomed, by Florizel. / Amanda, by Grey Diomed.
	Miller's Damsel.		*Messenger, by Mambrino. / Daughter of Pot-8-os.
Miss Slamerkin.	Sumpter.		Sir Archy, by *Diomed. / Robin mare, by *Robin Redbreast.
	Jenny Slamerkin		Tiger, by Blackburn's Whip. / Hannah Harris, by *Buzzard.

Emma. / Maria Innis. / Ann Innis. / Miss Obstinate.

Seventh dam, Indiana, by Butler's Columbus; eighth dam, Jane Hunt, by Hampton's Paragon; ninth dam, Moll, by *Figure; tenth dam, Maria Slamerkin, by *Wildair; eleventh dam, *Mare by Cub; twelfth dam, *Amaranthus' dam, by Secund; thirteenth dam by Starling; fourteenth dam (sister to Vane's Little Partner), by Croft's Partner; fifteenth dam (sister to Guy), by Greyhound; sixteenth dam, Brown Farewell, by Makeless; seventeenth dam by Brimmer; eighteenth dam by Place's White Turk; nineteenth dam by Dodsworth; twentieth dam, Layton Barb mare.

Never ran.

EMULATE.

PRODUCE.

1890,   by *Rayon d'Or.

FANCY. Brown mare, foaled in 1883. Bred by D. Swigert, Ky.

- **Acoustic.**
  - **Virgil.**
    - **Vandal.**
      - *** Glencoe.**
        - **Sultan.**
          - Selim. { Buzzard, by Woodpecker. / Castrel's dam, by Alexander.
          - Bacchante. { Williamson's Ditto, by Sir Peter. / Sister to Calomel, by Mercury.
        - **Tramp-oline.**
          - Tramp. { Dick Andrews, by Joe Andrews. / Daughter of Gohanna.
          - Web. { Waxy, by Pot-8-os. / Penelope, by Trumpator.
      - **Tranby Mare.**
        - **Tranby.**
          - Blacklock. { Whitelock, by Hambletonian. / Daughter of Coriander.
          - Daughter of { Orville, by Beningbrough. / Miss Grimstone, by Weasel.
        - *** Lucila.**
          - Trumpator. { Sir Solomon, by Tickle Toby. / Daughter of Hickory.
          - Lucy. { Orphan, by Ball's Florizel. / Lady Grey, by Robin Grey.
    - **Hymenia.**
      - *** Yorkshire.**
        - **St. Nicholas.**
          - Emilius. { Orville, by Beningbrough. / Emily, by Stamford.
          - Seamew. { Scud, by Beningbrough. / Goosander, by Hambletonian.
        - **Miss Rose.**
          - Tramp. { Dick Andrews, by Joe Andrews. / Daughter of Gohanna.
          - Daughter of { Sancho, by Don Quixote. / Blacklock's dam, by Corinnder.
      - **Little Peggy.**
        - **Cripple.**
          - Medoc. { Am. Eclipse, by Duroc. / Young Maid of the Oaks, by * Expedition.
          - Grecian Princess. { Cook's Whip by * Whip. / Jane Hunt, by Hampton's Paragon.
        - **Peggy Stewart.**
          - Cook's Whip. { * Whip, by Saltram. / Specklebnck, by Randolph's Celer.
          - Mary Bedford. { Duke of Bedford, by * Bedford. / Daughter of * Speculator.
  - *** Australian.**
    - **West Australian.**
      - **Mel-bourne.**
        - Humphrey Clinker. { Comus, by Sorcerer. / Clinkerina, by Clinker.
        - Daughter of { Cervantes, by Don Quixote. / Daughter of Golumpus.
      - **Mow-erina.**
        - Touchstone. { Camel, by Whalebone. / Banter, by Master Henry.
        - Emma. { Whisker, by Waxy. / Gibside Fairy, by Hermes.
    - **Emilia.**
      - **Young Emilius.**
        - Emilius. { Orville, by Beningbrough. / Emily, by Stamford
        - Shoveler. { Scud, by Beningbrough. / Goosander, by Hambletonian.
      - **Persian.**
        - Whisker. { Waxy, by Pot-8-os. / Penelope, by Trumpator.
        - Variety. { Selim or Soothsayer. / Sprite, by Bobtail.
- **Nemesis.**
  - *** Eclipse.**
    - **Orlando.**
      - Touchstone. { Camel, by Whalebone. / Banter, by Master Henry.
      - Vulture. { Langar, by Selim. / Kite, by Bustard.
    - **Gaze.**
      - Bay Middleton. { Sultan, by Selim. / Cobweb, by Phantom.
      - Flycatcher. { Godolphin, by Partisan. / Sister to Cobweb, by Phantom.
  - **Echo.**
    - **Lexing-ton.**
      - Boston. { Timoleon, by Sir Archy. / Sister to Tuckahoe, by Ball's Florizel.
      - Alice Carneal. { *Sarpedon, by Emilius. / Rowena, by Sumpter.
    - **Maria Innis.**
      - * Yorkshire. { St. Nicholas, by Emilius. / Miss Rose, by Tramp.
      - Ann Innis. { American Eclipse, by Duroc. / Miss Obstinate, by Sumpter.

Seventh dam, Jenny Slamerkin by Tiger; Eighth dam, Hannah Harris (Paragon) by * Buzzard: Ninth dam, Indiana by Butler's Columbus; Tenth dam, Jane Hunt, by Wade Hampton's Paragon; Eleventh dam. Moll by * Figure; Twelfth dam, Old Slamerkin by_4 Wildair; Thirteenth dam, * Cub mare by Cub: Fourteenth dam, Amaranthus' dam by Second; Fifteenth dam, Leede's dam by Starling; Sixteenth dam, Sister to Vane's Little Partner by Croft's Partner; Seventeenth dam, Sister to Guy by Greyhound; Eighteenth dam, Brown Farewell by Makeless; Nineteenth dam, Sister to Brimmer; Twentieth dam by Place's White Turk; Twenty-first dam by Dodsworth; Twenty-second dam, Layton Barb Mare.

FANCY.

Never ran.

PRODUCE.

1887, Missed to *Rayon d'Or.

1888, b. c.,   by *Kantaka. (Died September, 1888.)

·1889, br. f., (Died 1889), by *Rayon d'Or.

1890,   by *Rayon d'Or.

FANNIE MOORE.
Gray mare, foaled 1872. Bred by J. C. VanMeter, K'y.

Lady Sovereign.

Lightning.

Lexington.

Blue Bonnet.

* Sovereign.

Croppy.

Boston.
- Timoleon.
  - Sir Archy. { * Diomed, by Florizel. / * Castianira, by Rockingham. }
  - Daughter of { * Saltram, by Eclipse. / Daughter of Symme's Wildair. }
- Sister to Tuckahoe.
  - Ball's Florizel. { * Diomed, by Florizel. / Daughter of * Shark. }
  - Daughter of { * Alderman, by Pot-8-os. / Daughter of * Clockfast. }

Alice Carneal.
- Sarpedon.
  - Emilius. { Orville, by Beningbrough. / Emily, by Stamford. }
  - Icaria. { The Flyer, by Van Dyke, jr. / Parma, by Dick Andrews. }
- Rowena.
  - Sumpter. { Sir Archy, by * Diomed. / Daughter of * Robin Redbreast. }
  - Lady Grey. { Robin Grey, by * Royalist. / Maria, by Melzar. }

* Hedgford.
- Miss Cragle.
  - Filho-da-Puta.
    - Haphazard. { Sir Peter, by Highflyer. / Miss Hervey, by Eclipse. }
    - Mrs. Barnet. { Waxy, by Pot-8-os. / Daughter of Woodpecker. }
  - Orville. { Beningbrough, by King Fergus. / Evelina, by Highflyer. }
  - Marchioness. { Lurcher, by Dungannon. / Miss Cogdcn, by Phoenomenon. }

Grey Fanny.
- Bertrand.
  - Sir Archy. { * Diomed, by Florizel. / * Castianira, by Rockingham. }
  - Eliza. { * Bedford, by Dungannon. / * Mambrina, by Mambrino. }
- Daughter of.
  - * Buzzard. { Woodpecker, by Herod. / Misfortune, by Dux. }
  - Arminda. { * Medley, by Gimcrack. / Daughter of * Bolton. }

Emilius.
- Orville.
  - Beningbrough. { King Fergus, by Eclipse. / Daughter of Herod. }
  - Evelina. { Highflyer, by Herod. / Termagant, by Tantrum. }
- Emily.
  - Stamford. { Sir Peter, by Highflyer. / Horatio, by Eclipse. }
  - Daughter of { Whiskey, by Saltram. / Grey Dorimant, by Dorimant. }

Fleur-de-lis.
- Bourbon.
  - Sorcerer. { Trumpator, by Conductor. / Young Giantess, by Diomed. }
  - Daughter of { Precipitate, by Mercury. / Daughter of Herod. }
- Lady Rachel.
  - Stamford. { Sir Peter, by Highflyer. / Horatio, by Eclipse. }
  - Young Rachel. { Volunteer, by Y. Belgrade. / Rachel, by Highflyer. }

Medoc.
- Am. Eclipse.
  - Duroc. { * Diomed, by Florizel. / Amanda, by Gray Diomed. }
  - Miller's Damsel. { *Messenger, by Mambrino. / Daughter of Pot-8-os, by Eclipse. }
- Y. Maid of the Oaks.
  - * Expedition. { Pegasus, by Eclipse. / Active, by Woodpecker. }
  - Old Maid of the Oaks. { * Spread Eagle. / Annette, by * Shark. }

Daughter of.
- Thornton's Rattler.
  - Sir Archy. { * Diomed, by Florizel. / * Castianira, by Rockingham. }
  - Sumpter's dam. { * Robin Redbreast, by Sir Peter. / Daughter of * Obscurity. }
- Daughter of.
  - * Spread Eagle. { Volunteer, by Y. Belgrade. / Daughter of Highflyer. }
  - Daughter of { Boxer. († See Note). / Rose of Sharon, by * Pantaloon. }

Seventh dam, Queen of Diamonds by Meade's Celer; Eighth dam, Philadelphia by Meade's Pilgrim; Ninth dam by Lee's Mare Anthony; Tenth dam by * Spread

* Silvereye; Eleventh dam by * Jolly Roger; Twelfth dam by * Monkey; Thirteenth dam by * Childers.

(†) NOTE.—Croppy's pedigree was always in doubt; the sire of her grand-dam is not reliable, being given in the Stud Book in various ways—by * Spread Eagle; by Seymour's Spread Eagle; by Seymour's Eagle; etc..etc.—and no Boxer produce appears under Rose of Sharon.

FANNIE MOORE.

Never ran.

PRODUCE.

1878, gr. f., MISS McCLINCH, by Waverly.

1879, gr. f., JENNIE V., by Waverly.

1880, Barren.

1881, gr. c., LAST DANCE, by War Dance. (Dead.)

1882, gr f., FANCHETTE, by *Thunderstorm.

1883, Barren.

1884, br. or roan f., POMONA, by Ten Broeck.

1885, br. f., DORMOUSE, by *Rayon d'Or.

1886, Missed to *Rayon d'Or.

1887, br. c., DREAMER, by *Rayon d'Or.

1888, br. c., THE MOOR, by *Rayon d'Or. (Gelded.)

1889, b. or br. c.   by *Rayon d'Or.

1890,   by Algerine.

FAUN. Bay mare, foaled 1883. Bred by D. Swigert, Ky.

				Selim.	Buzzard, by Woodpecker. Castrel's dam, by Alexander.
		* Glencoe	Sultan.	Bacchante.	Williamson's Ditto, by Sir Peter. Sister to Calomel, by Mercury.
Vandal.			Tramp-oline.	Tramp	Dick Andrews, by Joe Andrews. Daughter of Gohanna.
				Web.	Waxy, by Pot-8-os. Penelope, by Trumpator.
	Tranby Mare.	* Tranby.	Blacklock.		Whitelock, by Hambletonian. Daughter of Coriander.
			Daughter of		Orville, by Beningbrough. Miss Grimstone, by Weasel.
		Lucilla.	Trumpator.		Sir Solomon, by Tickle Toby. Daughter of Hickory.
Virgil.			Lucy.		Orphan, by Ball's Florizel. Lady Grey, by Robin Grey.
	Hymenia.	* Yorkshire.	St. Nicholas.	Emilius.	Orville, by Beningbrough. Emily, by Stamford.
				Seamew.	Scud, by Beningbrough. Goosander, by Hambletonian.
			Miss Rose.	Tramp.	Dick Andrews, by Joe Andrews. Daughter of Gohanna.
				Daughter of	Sancho, by Don Quixote. Blacklock's dam, by Coriander.
		Little Peggy.	Cripple.	Medoc.	Am. Eclipse, by Duroc. Young Maid of the Oaks, by * Expedition.
				Grecian Princess.	Cook's Whip by * Whip. Jane Hunt, by Hampton's Paragon.
			Peggy Stewart.	Cook's Whip.	* Whip, by Saltram. Speckleback, by Randolph's Celer.
				Mary Bedford.	Duke of Bedford, by * Bedford. Daughter of * Speculator.
Blunder.					
	Lexington.	Boston.	Sir Archy to Timoleon.	Sir Archy.	*Diomed, by Florizel. *Castianira, by Rockingham.
				Daughter of	*Saltram, by Eclipse. Daughter of Symme's Wildair.
			Sister to Tuckahoe.	Ball's Florizel.	*Diomed, by Florizel. Daughter of *Shark.
				Daughter of	*Alderman, by Pot-8-os. Daughter of *Clockfast.
		Alice Carneal.	* Sarpedon.	Emilius.	Orville, by Beningbrough. Emily, by Stamford.
				Icaria.	The Flyer, by VanDyke, jr. Parma, by Dick Andrews.
			Rowena.	Sumpter.	Sir Archy, by *Diomed. Daughter of *Robin Redbreast.
Bionde.				Lady Grey.	Robin Gray, by * Royalist. Maria, by Melzar.
	* Glencoe.	Sultan.	Selim.		Buzzard, by Woodpecker. Alexander Mare, by Alexander.
			Bacchante.		Williamson's Ditto, by Sir Peter. Sister to Calomel, by Mercury.
		Tramp-oline.	Tramp.		Dick Andrews, by Joe Andrews. Daughter of Gohanna.
Sister to Tangent.			Web.		Waxy, by Pot-8-os. Penelope, by Trumpator.
Cherry Elliott.	Wagner.	Sir Charles.			Sir Archy, by *Diomed. Daughter of * Citizen.
		Maria West.			Marion, by Sir Archy. Ella Crump, by * Citizen.
		Sumpter.			Sir Archy, by * Diomed. Daughter of * Robin Redbreast.
		Rosemary			Tiger, by Blackburn's Whip. Mary Bedford, by Duke of Bedford.

Seventh dam by *Speculator; Eighth dam by *Dare Devil; Ninth dam, *Trumpetta by Trumpator; Tenth dam, Sister to Lambinos by Highflyer; Eleventh dam by Eclipse; Twelfth dam, Vauxhall's dam by Young Cade; Thirteenth dam by Bolton Littlejohn; Fourteenth dam, Durham's Favorite by Son of Bald Galloway; Fifteenth dam, Daffodil's dam by Sir E Gascolgne's Arabian.

FAUN.

At two years old, started six times, running second to Bess in the Louthful Stakes at Washington, beating Biggonet and five others ; second to Inspector B. at Coney Island, beating Shamrock, The Bard, and three others ; second to Peru colt at Monmouth Park, and unplaced three times. At three years old started twenty-six times, winning five times, second five times, third twice, and unplaced fourteen times.

PRODUCE.

1889, ch. f., (Died June, 1889), by *Rayon d'Or.

1890, Not bred.

FLAVIA.

Brown mare, foaled 1883. Bred by Mr. D. Swigert, Ky.

- **Fay Templeton.**
  - **Virgil.**
    - **Vandal.**
      - ***Glencoe.**
        - **Sultan.**
          - Selim. { Buzzard, by Woodpecker. / Castrel's dam, by Alexander. }
          - Bacchante. { Williamson's Ditto, by Sir Peter. / Sister to Calomel, by Mercury. }
        - **Trampoline.**
          - Tramp. { Dick Andrews, by Joe Andrews. / Daughter of Gohanna. }
          - Web. { Waxy, by Pot-8-os. / Penelope, by Trumpator. }
      - **Tranby Mare.**
        - ***Tranby.**
          - Blacklock. { Whitelock, by Hambletonian. / Daughter of Coriander. }
          - Daughter of { Orville, by Beningbrough. / Miss Grimstone, by Weasel. }
        - **Lucilla.**
          - Trumpator. { Sir Solomon, by Tickle Toby. / Daughter of Hickory. }
          - Lucy. { Orphan, by Ball's Florizel. / Lady Grey, by Robin Grey. }
    - **Hymenia.**
      - **St. Nicholas.** / ***Yorkshire.**
        - Emilius. { Orville, by Beningbrough. / Emily, by Stamford. }
        - Scamew. { Scud, by Beningbrough. / Goosander, by Hambletonian. }
      - **Miss Rose.**
        - Tramp. { Dick Andrews, by Joe Andrews. / Daughter of Gohanna. }
        - Daughter of { Sancho, by Don Quixote. / Blacklock's dam, by Coriander. }
      - **Little Peggy.**
        - **Cripple.**
          - Medoc. { Am. Eclipse, by Duroc. / Young Maid of the Oaks, by *Expedition. }
          - Grecian Princess. { Cook's Whip, by * Whip. / Jane Hunt, by Hampton's Paragon. }
        - **Peggy Stewart.**
          - Cook's Whip. { * Whip, by Saltram. / Speckleback, by Randolph's Coler. }
          - Mary Bedford. { Duke of Bedford, by * Bedford. / Daughter of * Speculator. }
  - ***Phaeton.**
    - **King Tom.**
      - **Hark-away.**
        - Economist. { Whisker, by Waxy. / Floranthe, by Octavian. }
        - Daughter of { Nabocklish, by Rugantino. / Miss Tooley, by Teddy-the-Grinder. }
      - **Poca-hontas.**
        - *Glencoe. { Sultan, by Selim. / Trampoline, by Tramp. }
        - Marpessa. { Muley, by Orville. / Clare, by Marmion. }
    - **Merry Sunshine.**
      - **Storm.**
        - Touchstone. { Camel, by Whalebone. / Banter, by Master Henry. }
        - Ghuznee. { Pantaloon, by Castrel. / Languish, by Cain. }
      - **Daughter of**
        - Falstaff. { Touchstone, by Camel. / Decoy, by Filho-da-Puta. }
        - Sister to Pompey. { Emilius, by Orville. / Variation, by Bustard. }
- **Danger's Dam.**
  - **War Dance.**
    - **Lexington.**
      - Boston. { Timoleon, by Sir Archy. / Sister to Tuckahoe, by Ball's Florizel. }
      - Alice Carneal. { *Sarpedon, by Emilius. / Rowena, by Sumpter. }
    - **Reel.**
      - *Glencoe. { Sultan, by Selim. / Trampoline, by Tramp. }
      - *Gallopade. { Catton, by Golumpus. / Camillina, by Camillus. }
  - **Daughter of**
    - **Mahomet.**
      - *Sovereign. { Emilius, by Orville. / Fleur de Lis, by Bourbon. }
      - Flight. { *Leviathan, by Muley. / Charlotte Hamilton, by Sir Charles. }
    - **Fay.**
      - *Yorkshire. { St. Nicholas, by Emilius. / Miss Rose, by Tramp. }
      - *Fury. { *Priam, by Emilius. / Sister to *Ainderby, by Velocipede. }

Seventh dam, Kate by Catton; Eighth dam, Miss Garforth by Walton; Ninth dam by Hyacinthus; Tenth dam, Zara by Delpini; Eleventh dam, Flora by King Fergus; Twelfth dam, Atalanta by Matchem; Thirteenth dam, Lass of the Mill by Oroonoko; Fourteenth dam by Old Traveler; Fifteenth dam, Miss Makeless by Young Greyhound; Sixteenth dam by Old Partner; Seventeenth dam, Miss Doe's dam by Woodcock; Eighteenth dam by Croft's Bay Barb; Nineteenth dam, Desdemona's dam by Makeless; Twentieth dam by Brimmer; Twenty-first dam by Dickey Pierson; Twenty-second dam, Burton Barb Mare.

FLAVIA.

Ran only at two years old, starting six times, running second once and unplaced five times.

PRODUCE.

1888, ch. c., FLAGRANT, by *Kantaka. (Gelded.)

1889, ch. c., by *Kantaka.

1890, by *Rayon d'Or.

FLAGEOLETTA.

Bay mare, foaled 1884. Bred by W. L. Scott, Erie, Pa.

*Rayon D'Or.

Flageolet. — Plutus.

Daughter Trumpeter of —
- Orlando. { Touchstone, by Camel. / Voltire, by Langar.
- Cavatina. { Redshank, by Sandbeck. / Oxygen, by Emilius.

- Planet. { Bay Middleton, by Sultan. / Plenary, by Emilius.
- Alice Bray. { Venison, by Partisan. / Darkness, by Glencoe.

La Favorite.

Monarque —
- The Baron Sting, or the Emperor. { Defense, by Whalebone. / Delight, by Reveller.
- Poetess. { Royal Oak, by Catton. / Ada, by Whisker.

Constance —
- Gladiator. { Partisan, by Walton. / Pauline, by Moses.
- Lanterne. { Hercules, by Rainbow. / Elvira, by Eryx.

Araucaria.

Ambrose. — Touchstone.
- Camel. { Whalebone, by Waxy. / Daughter of Selim.
- Banter. { Master Henry, by Orville. / Boadicea, by Alexander.

Annette.
- Priam. { Emilius, by Orville. / Cressida, by Whiskey.
- Potentate's Dam. { Don Juan, by Orville. / Moll in the Wad, by Hambletonian.

Pocahontas.

Glencoe.
- Sultan. { Selim, by Buzzard. / Bacchante, by Williamson's Ditto.
- Trampoline. { Tramp, by Dick Andrews. / Web, by Waxy.

Marpessa.
- Muley. { Orville, by Beningbrough. / Eleanor, by Whiskey.
- Clare. { Marmion, by Whiskey. / Harpalice, by Gohanna.

*Clover.

Verdure*

Macaroni. — Sweetmeat.

Jocose. — Gladiator.
- Partisan. { Walton, by Sir Peter. / Parasol, by Pot-8-os.
- Pauline. { Moses, by Whalebone. / Quadrille, by Selim.

Lollypop.
- Starch or Voltaire { Blacklock, by Whitelock. / Daughter of Phantom.
- Belinda. { Blacklock, by Whitelock. / Wagtail, by Prime Minister.

Pantaloon.
- Castrel. { Buzzard, by Woodpecker. / Daughter of Alexander.
- Idalia. { Peruvian, by Sir Peter. / Musidora, by Meteor.

Banter.
- Master Henry. { Orville, by Beningbrough. / Miss Sophia, by Stamford.
- Boadicea. { Alexander, by Eclipse. / Brunette, by Amaranthus.

King Tom.

Harkaway.
- Economist. { Whisker, by Waxy. / Floranthe, by Octavian.
- Fanny Dawson. { Nabocklish, by Rugantino. / Miss Tooley, by Teddy the Grinder.

Pocahontas.
- Glencoe. { Sultan, by Selim. / Trampoline, by Tramp.
- Marpessa. { Muley, by Orville. / Clare, by Marmion.

Marlboom.

Newminster.
- Touchstone. { Camel, by Whalebone. / Banter, by Master Henry.
- Beeswing. { Doctor Syntax, by Paymaster. / Daughter of Ardrossan.

Lady Hawthorn.
- Windhound. { Pantaloon, by Castrel. / Phryne, by Touchstone.
- Alice Hawthorn. { Muley Moloch, by Muley. / Rebecca, by Lottery.

Seventh dam by Cervantes; eighth dam, Anticipation, by Beningbrough; ninth dam, Expectation, by Herod; tenth dam by Skim; eleventh dam by Janus; twelfth dam, Spinster, by Crab; thirteenth dam, Widdrington Mare, by Partner; fourteenth dam, sister to Squirrel's dam, by Bloody Buttock's; fifteenth dam, sister to Guy, by Greyhound (Barb); sixteenth dam, Brown Farewell, by Makeless; seventeenth dam by Brimmer; eighteenth dam, Trumpet's dam, by Place's White Turk; nineteenth dam by the Dodsworth Barb; twentieth dam, Layton Barb Mare.

FLAGEOLETTA.

At two years old started twice, running unplaced in the Criterion and Select Stakes. At three years old started twenty-five times, winning a Sweepstakes at Brooklyn, beating Hypasia and three others ; won a Free Handicap Sweepstakes at Monmouth Park ; won the Challenge Stakes at Coney Island, beating Strideaway and four others, including Stuyvesant ; won Handicap Sweepstakes at Brooklyn, seven starters; ran second to Firenzi in the Ladies' Stakes, Jerome Park ; second to Firenzi in the Gazelle Stakes, Brooklyn ; second to Grisette in the Alabama Stakes, Saratoga ; second to Grisette in one-eighth mile purse at Saratoga, five starters ; second to Kingston in Sweepstakes at Coney Island, beating Stuyvesant and seven others ; second to Touche Pas in a Sweepstakes at Coney Island, beating Connemara and seven others ; second to Stockton at Jerome Park, eight starters ; third twice and unplaced twelve times. At four years old started fifteen times, winning Free Handicap Sweepstakes at Monmouth Park, beating Benedictine, Strideaway and five others, one mile in 1:42½ ; ran second three times, third four times, and unplaced seven times.

PRODUCE.

1890,   by Wanderer.

FLORENCE FONSO.
Chestnut mare, foaled 1883. Bred by W. L. Scott, Erie, Pa.

Florence I. — King Alfonso — *Phaeton

- King Tom — Pocahontas
  - **Economist.** { Whisker, by Waxy. / Floranthe, by Octavian.
  - **Daughter of** { Nabocklish, by Rugantino, / Miss Tooley, by Teddy-the-Grinder.
- Merry Sunshine — Storm — Daughter of
  - **Glencoe.** { Sultan, by Selim. / Trampoline, by Tramp.
  - **Marpessa.** { Muley, by Orville. / Clare, by Marmion.
  - **Touchstone.** { Camel, by Whalebone. / Banter, by Master Henry.
  - **Ghuznee.** { Pantaloon, by Castrel. / Languish, by Cain.
  - **Falstaff.** { Touchstone, by Camel. / Decoy, by Filho-da-Puta.
  - **Sister to Pompey** { Emilius, by Orville. / Variation, by Bustard.

Capitola — Vandal — Alaric's Dam

- **Sultan.** { Selim, by Buzzard. / Bacchante, by Williamson's Ditto.
- **Trampoline.** { Tramp, by Dick Andrews. / Web, by Waxy.
- ***Tranby.** { Blacklock, by Whitelock. / Daughter of Orville.
- **Lucilla.** { Trumpator, by Sir Solomon. / Lucy, by Orphan.

Daughter of — *Margrave — Mistletoe

- **Muley.** { Orville, by Beningbrough. / Eleanor, by Whiskey.
- **Chatham's Dam.** { Election, by Gohanna. / Fair Helen, by Hambletonian.
- **Cherokee.** { Sir Archy, by *Diomed. / Roxana, by Hephestion.
- **Black-Eyed Susan.** { Tiger, by Blackburn's Whip. / Daughter of Albert.

Melbourne — West Australian — *Australian

- **Humphrey Clinker.** { Comus, by Sorcerer. / Clinkerina, by Clinker.
- **Daughter of** { Cervantes, by Don Quixote. / Daughter of Golumpus.
- **Touchstone.** { Camel, by Whalebone. / Banter, by Master Henry.
- **Emma.** { Whisker, by Waxy. / Gibside Fairy, by Hermes.

Emilia — Young Emilius — Persian

- **Emilius.** { Orville, by Beningbrough. / Emily, by Stamford.
- **Shoveler.** { Scud, by Beningbrough. / Goosander, by Hambletonian.
- **Whisker.** { Waxy, by Pot-8-os. / Penelope, by Trumpator.
- **Variety.** { Selim or Soothsayer, / Sprite, by Bobtail.

Charlotte Buford — Kitty Clark — Lexington — *Glencoe — Alice Carneal — Boston

- **Timoleon.** { Sir Archy, by * Diomed. / Daughter of * Saltram.
- **Sister to Tuckahoe.** { Ball's Florizel, by * Diomed. / Daughter of * Alderman.
- ***Sarpedon.** { Emilius, by Orville. / Icaria, by The Flyer.
- **Rowena.** { Sumpter, by Sir Archy. / Lady Grey, by Robin Grey.

Miss Obstinate — *Glencoe

- **Sultan.** { Selim, by Buzzard. / Bacchante, by Williamson's Ditto.
- **Trampoline.** { Tramp, by Dick Andrews. / Web, by Waxy.
- **Sumpter.** { Sir Archy, by * Diomed. / Flirtilla's dam by * Robin Redbreast.
- **Jenny Slamerkin.** { Tiger, by Blackburn's Whip. / Hannah Harris, by *Buzzard.

Seventh dam, Indiana by Columbus; Eighth dam, Jane Hunt by Hampton's Paragon; Ninth dam by *Figure; Tenth dam, Maria Slamerkin by *Wildair; Eleventh dam, *Mare by Cub; Twelfth dam, Amaranthus' dam by Second; Thirteenth dam (dam of Leede's Flash, Fop, &c.) by Starling; Fourteenth dam (Sister to Vane's Little Partner) by Croft's Partner; Fifteenth dam (Sister to Guy) by Greyhound; Sixteenth dam, Brown Farewell by Makeless; Seventeenth dam by Brimmer; Eighteenth dam by Place's White Turk; Nineteenth dam by Dodsworth; Twentieth dam, Layton Barb Mare.

FLORENCE FONSO.

At two years old started seven times, winning the Moet and Chandon Champagne Stakes at Monmouth Park, beating Kalula, Laura Garrison, The Bard and four others; ran second to Preciosa in the Autumn Stakes at Coney Island, beating Electric, The Bard and seven others; ran third to The Bard in the Boquet Stakes, same place, thirteen starters; second once and unplaced three times. At three years old started six times, running second to Brown Duke in a one-and-one-eighth miles Sweepstakes at Coney Island, six starters, and unplaced five times. At four years old started six times, running third once and unplaced five times.

PRODUCE.

1889, Barren to *Rayon d'Or.

1890, by *Kantaka or Algerine.

FLORENCE I.
Chestnut mare, foaled 1869. Bred by Mr. A. J. Alexander, Kentucky.

- ***Australian.**
  - **West Australian.**
    - **Melbourne.**
      - **Humphrey Clinker.**
        - Comus. { Sorcerer, by Trumpator. / Houghton Lass, by Sir Peter.
        - Clinkerina. { Clinker, by Sir Peter. / Pewet, by Tandem.
      - **Daughter of**
        - Cervantes. { Don Quixote, by Eclipse. / Evelina, by Highflyer.
        - Daughter of { Golumpus, by Gohanna. / Daughter of Paynator.
    - **Mowerina.**
      - **Touchstone.**
        - Camel. { Whalebone, by Waxy. / Daughter of Selim and Maiden.
        - Banter. { Master Henry, by Orville. / Boadicea, by Alexander.
      - **Emma.**
        - Whisker. { Waxy, by Pot-8-os. / Penelope, by Trumpator.
        - Gibside Fairy. { Hermes, by Mercury. / Vicissitude, by Pipator.
  - **Emilia.**
    - **Young Emilius.**
      - **Emilius.**
        - Orville. { Beningbrough, by King Fergus. / Evelina, by Highflyer.
        - Emily. { Stamford, by Sir Peter. / Daughter of Whisker.
      - **Shoveler.**
        - Scud. { Beningbrough, by King Fergus. / Eliza, by Highflyer.
        - Goosander. { Hambletonian, by King Fergus. / Rally, by Trumpator.
    - **Persian.**
      - **Whisker.**
        - Waxy. { Pot-8-os, by Eclipse. / Maria, by Herod.
        - Penelope. { Trumpator, by Conductor. / Prunella, by Highflyer.
      - **Variety.**
        - Selim, or Soothsayer. { Sorcerer, by Trumpator. / Goldenlocks, by Delpini.
        - Sprite. { Bobtail, by Precipitate. / Catherine by Woodpecker.

- **Charlotte Beford.**
  - **Lexington.**
    - **Boston.**
      - **Timoleon.**
        - Sir Archy. { * Diomed, by Florizel. / * Castianira, by Rockingham.
        - Daughter of { * Saltram, by Eclipse. / Daughter of Symme's Wildair.
      - **Sister to Tuckahoe.**
        - Ball's Florizel. { * Diomed, by Florizel. / Daughter of * Sbark.
        - Daughter of { *Alderman, by Pot-8-os. / Daughter of * Clockfast.
    - **Alice Carneal.**
      - ***Sarpedon.**
        - Emilius. { Orville, by Beningbrough. / Emily, by Stamford.
        - Icaria. { The Flyer, by VanDyke, jr. / Parma, by Dick Andrews.
      - **Rowena.**
        - Sumpter. { Sir Archy, by * Diomed. / Daughter of * Robin Redbreast.
        - Lady Gray. { Robin Gray, by * Royalist. / Maria, by Melzar.
  - **Kittle Clark.**
    - ***Glencoe.**
      - **Sultan.**
        - Selim. { Buzzard, by Woodpecker. / Castrel's dam, by Alexander.
        - Bacchante. { Williamson's Ditto, by Sir Peter. / Sister to Calomel, by Mercury.
      - **Trampoline.**
        - Tramp { Dick Andrews, by Joe Andrews. / Daughter of Gohanna.
        - Web. { Waxy, by Pot-8-os. / Maria, by Herod.
    - **Miss Obstinate.**
      - **Sumpter.**
        - Sir Archy. { * Diomed, by Florizel. / * Castianira, by Rockingham.
        - Flirtilla's dam. { * Robin Redbreast, by Sir Peter. / Daughter of * Obscurity.
      - **Jennie Slamerkin.**
        - Tiger. { Blackburn's Whip, by * Whip. / Jane Hunt, by Hampton's Paragon.
        - Hannah Harris. (Paragon). { * Buzzard, by Woodpecker. / Indiana (Columbia), by Columbus.

Seventh dam, Jane Hunt, by Hampton's Paragon; Eighth dam by * Figure; Ninth dam, Maria Slamerkin, by * Wildair; Tenth dam, * Mare by Cub; Eleventh dam, Amaranthus' dam, by Second; Twelfth dam (dam of Leedes, Flash, Fop, &c.) by Starling; Thirteenth dam (sister to Vane's Little Partner), by Croft's Partner; Fourteenth dam (sister to Guy), by Greyhound; Fifteenth dam, Brown Farewell by Makeless; Sixteenth dam by Brimmer; Seventeenth dam by Place's White Turk; Eighteenth dam by Dodsworth; Nineteenth dam, Layton Barb mare.

FLORENCE I.

Did not start at two years old. At three years old started six times, won once, was second once, and unplaced three times. At four years old started three times, running second once and third twice.

PRODUCE.

1875, ch. f., FLORENCE PAYNE, by Blarneystone.

1876, ch. f., FLORENCE LAMERTINE, (Flora A,), by Tom Bowling.

1877, Barren.

1878, ch. f., FLORENCE COOK, by War Dance.

1879, Barren.

1880, ch. c., by King Lear.

1881, b. c., POWHATTAN II., by *Glenelg.

1882, b. or br. f., FLORIO, by Virgil.

1883, ch. f., FLORENCE FONSO, by King Alfonso.

1884, Missed to *Rayon d'Or.

1885, Missed to *Kantaka and *Rayon d'Or.

1886, ch. c., BELLAIRE, (Florenzo), by *Rayon d'Or.

1887, Missed to *Rayon d'Or.

1888, ch. c., FLORIMOR, by *Rayon d'Or.

1889, ch. c., (Died 1889), by *Rayon d'Or.

1890,   by *Rayon d'Or.

FLORIO.

Brown mare, foaled 1882. Bred by W. L. Scott, Erie, Pa.

- **Virgil.**
  - **Vandal.**
    - ***Glencoe.**
      - **Sultan.**
        - Selim. { Buzzard, by Woodpecker. / Castrel's dam, by Alexander.
        - Bacchante. { Williamson's Ditto, by Sir Peter. / Sister to Calomel, by Mercury.
      - **Trampoline.**
        - Tramp. { Dick Andrews, by Joe Andrews. / Daughter of Gohanna.
        - Web. { Waxy, by Pot-8-os. / Penelope, by Trumpator.
    - **Tranby Mare.**
      - ***Tranby.**
        - Blacklock. { Whitelock, by Hambletonian. / Daughter of Coriander.
        - Daughter of { Orville, by Beningbrough. / Miss Grimstone, by Weasel.
      - **Lucilla.**
        - Trumpator. { Sir Solomon, by Tickle Toby. / Daughter of Hickory.
        - Lucy. { Orphan, by Ball's Florizel. / Lady Grey, by Robin Grey.
  - **Hymenia.**
    - ***Yorkshire.**
      - **St. Nicholas.**
        - Emilius. { Orville, by Beningbrough. / Emily, by Stamford.
        - Scamew. { Scud, by Beningbrough. / Goosander, by Hambletonian.
      - **Miss Rose.**
        - Tramp. { Dick Andrews, by Joe Andrews. / Daughter of Gohanna.
        - Daughter of { Sancho, by Don Quixote. / Blacklock's dam, by Coriander.
    - **Little Peggy.**
      - **Cripple.**
        - Medoc. { Am. Eclipse, by Duroc. / Young Maid of the Oaks, by *Expedition.
        - Grecian Princess. { Cook's Whip, by * Whip. / Jane Hunt, by Hampton's Paragon.
      - **Peggy Stewart.**
        - Cook's Whip. { * Whip, by Saltram. / Speckleback, by Randolph's Celer.
        - Mary Bedford. { Duke of Bedford, by * Bedford. / Daughter of * Speculator.
- **Florence I.**
  - ***Australian.**
    - **West Australian.**
      - **Melbourne.**
        - Humphrey Clinker. { Comus, by Sorcerer. / Clinkerina, by Clinker.
        - Daughter of { Cervantes, by Don Quixote. / Daughter of Golumpus.
      - **Mower-ina.**
        - Touchstone. { Camel, by Whalebone. / Banter, by Master Henry.
        - Emma. { Whisker, by Waxy. / Gibside Fairy, by Hermes.
    - **Emilia.**
      - **Young Emilius.**
        - Emilius. { Orville, by Beningbrough. / Emily, by Stamford.
        - Shoveler. { Scud, by Beningbrough. / Goosander, by Hambletonian.
      - **Per-sian.**
        - Whisker. { Waxy, by Pot-8-os. / Penelope, by Trumpator.
        - Variety. { Selim or Soothsayer, / Sprite, by Bobtail.
  - **Charlotte Buford.**
    - **Lexington.**
      - **Boston.**
        - Timoleon. { Sir Archy, by * Diomed. / Daughter of * Saltram.
        - Sister to Tuckahoe. { Ball's Florizel, by * Diomed. / Daughter of * Alderman.
      - **Alice Carneal.**
        - *Sarpedon. { Emilius, by Orville. / Icaria, by The Flyer.
        - Rowena. { Sumpter, by Sir Archy. / Lady Grey, by Robin Grey.
    - **Kitty Clark.**
      - ***Glencoe.**
        - Sultan. { Selim, by Buzzard. / Bacchante, by Williamson's Ditto.
        - Trampoline. { Tramp, by Dick Andrews. / Web, by Waxy.
      - **Miss Obstinate.**
        - Sumpter. { Sir Archy, by * Diomed. / Flirtilla's dam by * Robin Redbreast.
        - Jenny Slamerkin. { Tiger, by Blackburn's Whip. / Hannah Harris, by *Buzzard.

Seventh dam, Indiana by Columbus; Eighth dam, Jane Hunt by Hampton's Paragon; Ninth dam by *Figure; Tenth dam, Maria Slamerkin by *Wildair; Eleventh dam, Mare by Cub; Twelfth dam, Amaranthus' dam by Second; Thirteenth dam (dam of Leede's Flash, Fop, &c.) by Starling; Fourteenth dam (Sister to Vane's Little Partner) by Croft's Partner; Fifteenth dam (Sister to Guy) by Greyhound; Sixteenth dam, Brown Farewell by Makeless; Seventeenth dam by Brimmer; Eighteenth dam by Place's White Turk: Nineteenth dam by Dodsworth: Twentieth dam, Layton Barb Mare.

FLORIO.

At two years old started twelve times, winning the Youthful Stakes and Brentwood Stakes at Washington ; the Foam Stakes, Great Post Stakes, and a purse race at Sheepshead Bay ; second to Volante in the Flash Stakes at Saratoga ; third twice and unplaced four times. At three years old started five times, running unplaced each time.

PRODUCE.

1887, ch. c., FRANCO, by *Rayon d'Or.

1888, b. f., (Died February, 1889), by *Rayon d'Or.

1889, ch. f., (Died 1889), by *Rayon d'Or.

1890,　　　　　　　　by *Rayon d'Or.

FREDDY. (IMPORTED.)
Brown mare, foaled 1873. Bred by W. S. Cartwright. Imported by F. R. Sherwin.

- **George Frederick.**
  - **Marsyas.**
    - **Orlando.**
      - **Touchstone.**
        - Camel. — { Whalebone, by Waxy. / Daughter of Selim.
        - Banter. — { Master Henry, by Orville. / Boadicea, by Alexander.
      - **Vulture.**
        - Langar. — { Selim, by Buzzard. / Daughter of Walton.
        - Kite. — { Bustard, by Castrel. / Olympia, by Sir Oliver.
    - **Malibran.**
      - **Whisker.**
        - Waxy. — { Pot-8-os, by Eclipse. / Maria, by Herod.
        - Penelope. — { Trumpator, by Conductor. / Prunella, by Highflyer.
      - **Garcia.**
        - Octavian. — { Stripling, by Phenomenon. / Daughter of Oberon.
        - Daughter of — { Shuttle, by Y. Marske. / Catherine, by Delpini.
  - **Princess of Wales.**
    - **Stockwell.**
      - **The Baron.**
        - Irish Birdcatcher. — { Sir Hercules, by Whalebone. / Guiccioli, by Bob Booty.
        - Echidna. — { Economist, by Whisker. / Miss Pratt, by Blacklock.
      - **Pocahontas.**
        - Glencoe. — { Sultan, by Selim. / Trampoline, by Tramp.
        - Marpessa. — { Muley, by Orville. / Clare, by Marmion.
    - **The Bloomer.**
      - **Melbourne.**
        - Humphrey Clinker. — { Comus, by Sorcerer. / Clinkerina, by Clinker.
        - Daughter of — { Cervantes, by Don Quixote. / Daughter of Golumpus.
      - **Lady Sarah.**
        - Velocipede. — { Blacklock, by Whitelock. / Daughter of Juniper.
        - Lady Moore Carew. — { Tramp, by Dick Andrews. / Kite, by Bustard.
- **Phoebe Athol.**
  - **Blair Athol.**
    - **Stockwell.**
      - **The Baron.**
        - Irish Birdcatcher — { Sir Hercules, by Whalebone. / Guiccioli, by Bob Booty.
        - Echidna. — { Economist, by Whisker. / Miss Platt, by Blacklock.
      - **Pocahontas.**
        - *Glencoe. — { Sultan, by Selim. / Trampoline, by Tramp.
        - Marpessa. — { Muley, by Orville. / Clare, by Marmion.
    - **Blink Bonny.**
      - **Melbourne.**
        - Humphrey Clinker. — { Comus, by Sorcerer. / Clinkerina, by Clinker.
        - Daughter of — { Cervantes, by Don Quixote. / Daughter of Golumpus.
      - **Queen Mary.**
        - Gladiator. — { Partizan, by Walton. / Pauline, by Moses.
        - Daughter of — { Plenipotentiary, by Emilius. / Myrrha, by Whalebone.
  - **Phoebe.**
    - **Touchstone.**
      - **Camel.**
        - Whalebone. — { Waxy, by Pot-8-os. / Penelope, by Trumpator.
        - Daughter of — { Selim, by Buzzard. / Maiden, by Sir Peter.
      - **Banter.**
        - Master Henry. — { Orville, by Beningbrough. / Miss Sophia, by Stamford.
        - Boadicea. — { Alexander, by Eclipse. / Brunette, by Amaranthus.
    - **Netherton Maid.**
      - **Sheet Anchor.**
        - Lottery. — { Tramp, by Dick Andrews. / Mandane, by Pot-8-os.
        - Morgiana. — { Muley, by Orville. / Miss Stevenson, by Scud or Sorcerer.
      - **Daughter of**
        - Tantivity. — {
        - Myrtilla. — { The Flyer, by Van Dyke, Jr. / Myrtle, by Abjer.

Seventh dam, Mite, by Meteor; eighth dam, Nike, by Alexander; ninth dam, Nimble, by Florizel; tenth dam, Rantipole, by Blank; eleventh dam, sister to Careless, by Regulus; twelfth dam, Silvertail, by Henage's White Nose; thirteenth dam by Rattle; fourteenth dam by the Darley Arabian; fifteenth dam, Old Child mare, by Sir T. Greeley's Bay Arabian; sixteenth dam, Cook's Vixen, by the Hensley Turk; seventeenth dam, Dodsworth's dam.

FREDDY.

Never ran.

PRODUCE.

1882, lost foal by Monseigneur.

1883-'84-'85-'86 '87-'88-'89, Barren.

1890,   by *Rayon d'Or.

HONEY BEE (IMPORTED).

Black mare, foaled 1877. Bred by Mr. W. W. Blenkiron, England. Imported 1881, by Mr. W. Easton.

Beeswing, 1861.	Saunterer.	Irish Birdcatcher, 1833.	Sir Hercules, 1826.	Whalebone, 1807.	Waxy.	{ Pot-8-os, by Eclipse. / Maria, by Herod.	
					Penelope.	{ Truimpator, by Conductor. / Prunella, by Highflyer.	
				Peri, 1822.	Wanderer.	{ Gohanna by Mercury. / Catherine, by Woodpecker.	
					Thalestris.	{ Alexander, by Eclipse. / Rival, by Sir Peter.	
			Guiccioli.	Rob Booty, 1804.	Chanticleer.	{ Woodpecker, by Herod. / Daughter of Eclipse.	
					Ierne.	{ Bagot, by Herod. / Daughter of Gamahoe.	
				Flight, 1809.	Escape.	{ Commodore, by Tug. / Daughter of Highflyer.	
					Young Heroine.	{ Bagot, by Herod. / Heroine, by Hero.	
		Ennui.	Bay Middleton, 1833.	Sultan, 1816.	Selim.	{ Buzzard, by Woodpecker. / Castrel's dam, by Alexander.	
					Bacchante.	{ Williamson's Ditto, by Sir Peter. / Sister to Calomel, by Mercury.	
				Cobweb, 1821.	Phantom.	{ Walton, by Sir Peter. / Julia, by Whiskey.	
					Filagree.	{ Soothsayer, by Sorcerer. / Web, by Waxy.	
			Blue Devils.	Velocipede, 1825.	Blacklock.	{ Whitelock, by Hambletonian. / Daughter of Coriander.	
					Daughter of	{ Juniper, by Whiskey. / Daughter of Sorcerer.	
				Care.	Woful.	{ Waxy, by Pot-8-os. / Penelope, by Trumpator.	
					Daughter of	{ Rubens, by Buzzard. / Tippitywitchet, by Waxy.	
Honey.	Knight of Kars.	Nutwith.	Tomboy.		Jerry.	{ Smolensko, by Sorcerer. / Louisa, by Orville.	
					Beeswing's dam.	{ Ardrossan, by John Bull. / Lady Eliza, by Whitworth.	
			Daughter of		Comus.	{ Sorcerer, by Trumpator. / Houghton Lass, by Sir Peter.	
					Plumper's dam.	{ Delpini, by Highflyer. / Miss Muston, by King Fergus.	
		Pocahontas, 1837.	Glencoe, 1837.		Sultan.	{ Selim, by Buzzard. / Bacchante, by Williamson's Ditto.	
					Trampoline.	{ Tramp, by Dick Andrews. / Web, by Waxy.	
			Marpeesa.		Muley.	{ Orville, by Benningbrough. / Eleanor, by Whiskey.	
					Clare.	{ Marmion, by Whiskey. / Harpalice, by Gohanna.	
	Melbourne or Cossack.	Hetman Platoff.			Brutandorf.	{ Blacklock, by Whitelock. / Mandane, by Pot-8-os.	
					Daughter of	{ Comus, by Sorcerer. / Marciana, by Stamford.	
		Joannina.			Priam.	{ Emilius, by Orville. / Cresida, by Whiskey.	
					Joanna.	{ Sultan, by Selim. / Filagree, by Soothsayer.	
Honeydew.	Touchstone.				Camel.	{ Whalebone, by Waxy. / Daughter of Selim.	
					Banter.	{ Master Henry, by Orville. / Boadicea, by Alexander.	
Beeswing.	Doctor Syntax.				Doctor Syntax.	{ Paynator, by Trumpator. / Daughter of Beningbrough.	
					Daughter of	{ Ardrossan, by John Bull. / Lady Eliza, by Whitworth.	

Seventh dam, X Y Z's dam by Spadille; Eighth dam, Sylvia by Young Marske; Ninth dam, Sylvia by Regulus; Tenth dam by Regulus; Eleventh dam by Lord Morton's Arabian; Twelfth dam by Mixbury; Thirteenth dam by Mulso Bay Turk; Fourteenth dam by Bay Bolton; Fifteenth dam by Coneyskins; Sixteenth dam by Hutton's Grey Barb; Seventeenth dam by Byerly Turk; Eighteenth dam by Bustler.

HONEY BEE.

Started but once and then as a two-year-old, running unplaced to Dreamland at Sandown Park, England.

————————

PRODUCE.

1884, Missed to Algerine.

1885, Missed to Algerine.

1886, ch. c., J. C. BURNETT, by *Rayon d'Or or Algerine.

1887, ch. c., HONEYMAN, by *Rayon d'Or.

1888, b. f., FUGITIVE, by Wanderer.

1889, Barren to Algerine.

1890,   by Wanderer.

IONE.

Bay mare, foaled 1876. Bred by Mr. R. W. Cameron, N. Y.

- **Inverary** (sire side label) / ***Eclipse**
  - **Orlando.**
    - **Touchstone.**
      - **Camel.**
        - Whalebone. { Waxy, by Pot-8-os. / Penelope, by Trumpator. }
        - Daughter of { Selim, by Buzzard. / Maiden, by Sir Peter. }
      - **Banter.**
        - Master Henry. { Orville, by Beningbrough. / Miss Sophia, by Stamford }
        - Boadicea. { Alexander, by Eclipse. / Brunette, by Amaranthus. }
    - **Vulture.**
      - **Langar.**
        - Selim. { Buzzard, by Woodpecker. / Castrel's dam, by Alexander. }
        - Daughter of { Walton, by Sir Peter. / Young Giantess, by Diomed }
      - **Kite.**
        - Bustard. { Castrel, by Buzzard. / Mishap, by Shuttle. }
        - Olympia. { Sir Oliver, by Sir Peter. / Scotilla, by Anvil. }
  - **Gaze.**
    - **Bay Middleton.**
      - **Sultan.**
        - Selim. { Buzzard by Woodpecker. / Castrel's dam, by Alexander. }
        - Bacchante. { Williamson's Ditto, by Sir Peter. / Sister to Calomel, by Mercury. }
      - **Cobweb.**
        - Phantom. { Walton, by Sir Peter. / Julia, by Whiskey. }
        - Filagree. { Soothsayer, by Sorcerer. / Web, by Waxy. }
    - **Fly-catcher.**
      - **Go-dolphin.**
        - Partisan. { Walton, by Sir Peter. / Parasol, by Pot-8-os. }
        - Ridicule. { Shuttle, by Young Marske. / Daughter of Dungannon. }
      - **Sister to Cobweb.**
        - Phantom. { Walton, by Sir Peter. / Julia, by Whiskey. }
        - Filagree. { Soothsayer, by Sorcerer. / Web, by Waxy. }
- ***Stolen Kisses**
  - ***Leamington.**
    - **Faugh-a-Ballagh.**
      - **Sir Hercules.**
        - Whalebone. { Waxy, by Pot-8-os. / Penelope, by Trumpator. }
        - Peri. { Wanderer, by Gohanna. / Thalestris, by Alexander. }
      - **Guiccioli.**
        - Bob Booty. { Chanticleer, by Woodpecker. / Ierne, by Bagot. }
        - Flight. { I. Escape, by Commodore. / Young Heroine, by Bagot. }
    - **Daughter of**
      - **Panta-loon.**
        - Castrel. { Buzzard, by Woodpecker. / Selim's dam, by Alexander. }
        - Idalia. { Peruvian, by Sir Peter / Musidora, by Meteor. }
      - **Daphne.**
        - Laurel. { Blacklock, by Whitelock. / Wagtail, by Prime Minister. }
        - Maid of Honor. { Champion, by Selim. / Etiquette, by Orville. }
  - **Defamation.**
    - **Knight of Kars.**
      - **Nut-with.**
        - Tomboy. { Jerry, by Smolensko. / Beeswing's dam, by Ardrossan. }
        - Daughter of { Comus, by Sorcerer. / Plumper's dam, by Delpini. }
      - **Poca-hontas.**
        - Glencoe. { Sultan, by Selim. / Trampoline, by Tramp. }
        - Marpessa. { Muley, by Orville. / Clare, by Marmion. }
    - **Iago.**
      - Don John. { Tramp or Waverly. / Hetman Platoff's dam, by Comus. }
      - Scandal. { Selim, by Buzzard. / Daughter of Haphazard. }
    - **Cari-cature.**
      - Pantaloon. { Castrel, by Buzzard. / Idalia, by Peruvian. }
      - Pasquinade. { Camel, by Whalebone. / Banter, by Master Henry. }

Seventh dam, Boadicea by Alexander; Eighth dam, Brunette by Amaranthus; Ninth dam, Mayfly by Matchem; Tenth dam, Pidgeon's dam by Starling; Eleventh dam by Grasshopper; Twelfth dam by Newton's Arabian; Thirteenth dam by Pert; Fourteenth dam by St. Martin's; Fifteenth dam by Sir E. Hale's Arabian; Sixteenth dam, the Old Field mare.

IONE.

Never ran.

.

PRODUCE.

1881, b. f., IONA, (Mollie B.), by Alarm or Lyttleton.

1882, br. f., ISLETTE, by *Strachino.

1883, Missed to Erdenheim.

1884, b. f.,   by Algerine.

1885, twins, b. c. (dead), and ch. c., KINGSFORD, by *Rayon d'Or.

1886, b. f., MISS OLIVE, (Ionia), by *Rayon d'Or.

1887, Missed to *Rayon d'Or.

1888, ch. c., INCA, by *Kantaka.   (Gelded.)

1889, Barren to *Kantaka.

1890,   by *Rayon d'Or.

JUDITH, (IMPORTED)

Bay Mare, foaled 1877. Bred by the Baroness Rothschild, England. Imported by Wm. Easton in 1881.

- **Verdure.**
  - **Macaroni.**
    - **Sweetmeat.**
      - **Gladiator.**
        - **Parti-san.**
          - Walton. { Sir Peter, by Highflyer. / Arethusa, by Dungannon. }
          - Parasol. { Pot-8-os, by Eclipse. / Prunella, by Highflyer. }
        - **Pauline.**
          - Moses. { Whalebone or Seymour. / Daughter of Gohanna. }
          - Quadrille. { Selim, by Buzzard. / Canary Bird, by Sorcerer. }
      - **Lollypop.**
        - **Starch or Voltaire.**
          - Blacklock. { Whitelock, by Hambletonian. / Daughter of Coriander. }
          - Daughter of { Phantom, by Walton. / Daughter of Overton. }
        - **Belinda.**
          - Blacklock. { Whitelock, by Hambletonian. / Daughter of Coriander. }
          - Wagtail. { Prime Minister, by Sancho. / Daughter of Orville. }
    - **Jocose.**
      - **Pantaloon.**
        - **Castrel.**
          - Buzzard. { Woodpecker, by Herod. / Misfortune, by Dux. }
          - Daughter of { Alexander, by Eclipse. / Daughter of Highflyer. }
        - **Idalia.**
          - Peruvian. { Sir Peter, by Highflyer. / Daughter of Boudrow. }
          - Musidora. { Meteor, by Eclipse. / Maid of all Work, by Highflyer. }
      - **Banter.**
        - **Master Henry.**
          - Orville. { Beningbrough, by King Fergus. / Evelina, by Highflyer. }
          - Miss Sophia. { Stamford, by Sir Peter. / Sophia, by Buzzard. }
        - **Boa-dicea.**
          - Alexander. { Eclipse, by Marske. / Grecian Princess, by Forester. }
          - Brunette. { Amaranthus, by Old England / Mayfly, by Matchem. }
  - **King Tom.**
    - **Harkaway.**
      - **Econo-mist.**
        - Whisker. { Waxy, by Pot-8-os. / Penelope, by Trumpator. }
        - Floranthe. { Octavian, by Stripling. / Caprice, by Anville. }
      - **Fanny Dawson.**
        - Nabocklish. { Rugantino, by Commodore. / Butterfly, by Master Bagot. }
        - Miss Tooley. { Teddy the Grinder, by Asparagus. / Lady Jane, by Sir Peter. }
    - **Pocahontas.**
      - **Glencoe.**
        - Sultan. { Selim, by Buzzard. / Bacchante, by Williamson's Ditto. }
        - Trampoline. { Tramp, by Dick Andrews. / Web, by Waxy. }
      - **Mar-pessa.**
        - Muley. { Orville, by Beningbrough. / Eleanor, by Whiskey. }
        - Clare. { Marmion, by Whiskey. / Harpalice, by Gohanna. }
- **Maybloom.**
  - **Newminster.**
    - **Touch-stone.**
      - Camel. { Whalebone, by Waxy. / Daughter of Selim. }
      - Banter. { Master Henry, by Orville. / Boadicea, by Alexander. }
    - **Bees-wing.**
      - Doctor Syntax. { Paynator, by Trumpator. / Daughter of Beningbrough. }
      - Daughter of { Ardrossan, by John Bull. / Lady Eliza, by Whitworth. }
  - **Lady Hawthorn.**
    - **Wind-hound.**
      - Pantaloon. { Castrel, by Buzzard. / Idalia, by Peruvian. }
      - Phryne. { Touchstone, by Camel. / Decoy, by Filho-da-Puta. }
    - **Alice Hawthorn.**
      - Muley Moloch. { Muley, by Orville. / Nancy, by Dick Andrews. }
      - Rebecca. { Lottery, by Tramp. / Daughter of Cervantes. }

Seventh dam, Anticipation by Beningbrough; Eighth, Expectation by Herod; Ninth by Skim; Tenth by Janus; Eleventh, Spinster by Crab; Twelfth, Sister to Squirrel's dam by Bloody Buttocks; Thirteenth, Sister to Guy by Greyhound (Barb); Fourteenth, Brown Widdrington Mare by Partner; Fifteenth, Brown Farewell by Makeless; Sixteenth by Brimmer; Seventeenth, Trumpet's dam by Place's White Turk; Eighteenth by the Dodsworth Barb; Nineteenth, Layton Barb Mare.

JUDITH.

Never ran.

PRODUCE.

1882, Missed to Kisber.

1883, Lost foal by Aureolus.

1884, Missed to *Rayon d'Or.

1885, b. f., by *Rayon d'Or. (Dead.)

1886, b. c., JULIEN, by *Rayon d'Or.

1887, Missed to *Rayon d'Or.

1888, ch. f.,   by Wanderer. (Died October, 1888.)

1889, ch. c.,   by Wanderer.

1890,   by Wanderer.

KATE WALKER.

Brown mare, foaled 1868. Bred by Mr. Sidney Taylor, Ky.

- Embry's Lexington.
  - Lexington.
    - Boston.
      - Timoleon.
        - Sir Archy.
          - *Diomed, by Florizel.
          - *Castianira, by Rockingham.
        - Daughter of
          - *Saltram, by Eclipse.
          - Daughter of Symme's Wildair.
      - Sister to Tuckahoe.
        - Ball's Florizel.
          - *Diomed, by Florizel.
          - Daughter of *Shark.
        - Daughter of
          - *Alderman, by Pot-8-os.
          - Daughter of *Clockfast.
    - Alice Carneal.
      - *Sarpedon.
        - Emilius.
          - Orville, by Beningbrough.
          - Emily, by Stamford.
        - Icaria.
          - The Flyer, by VanDyke, jr.
          - Parma, by Dick Andrews.
      - Rowena.
        - Sumpter.
          - Sir Archy, by *Diomed.
          - Daughter of *Robin Redbreast.
        - Lady Grey.
          - Robin Gray, by * Royalist.
          - Maria, by Melzar.
  - Bellamira.
    - *Monarch.
      - *Priam.
        - Emilius.
          - Orville, by Beningbrough.
          - Emily, by Stamford.
        - Cressida.
          - Whiskey, by Saltram.
          - Young Giantess, by Diomed.
      - *Delphine.
        - Whisker.
          - Waxy, by Pot-8-os.
          - Penelope, by Trumpator.
        - My Lady.
          - Comus, by Sorcerer.
          - The Colonel's dam, by Delpini.
    - Kitty Heath.
      - American Eclipse.
        - Duroc.
          - *Diomed, by Florizel.
          - Amanda, by Gray Diomed.
        - Miller's Damsel.
          - Messenger, by Mambrino.
          - Daughter of Pot-8-os, by Eclipse.
      - American Pomona.
        - Sir Alfred.
          - *Sir Harry, by Sir Peter.
          - Lady Chesterfield, by *Diomed.
        - Daughter of
          - *Sir Harry, by Sir Peter.
          - *Pomona, by Worthy.
- Carrie D.
  - Don Juan.
    - Berthune.
      - Sidi Hamet.
        - Virginian.
          - Sir Archy, by *Diomed.
          - Meretrix, by Magog.
        - Lady Burton.
          - Sir Archy, by *Diomed.
          - Sultana, by Jefferson's Barb.
      - Sussette.
        - Aratus.
          - Director, by Sir Archy.
          - Betsey Haxall, by * Sir Harry.
        - Jenny Cockracy.
          - Potomac, by *Diomed.
          - Timoleon's dam, by * Saltram.
    - Ariel.
      - *Sarpedon.
        - Emilius.
          - Orville, by Beningbrough.
          - Emily, by Stamford.
        - Icaria.
          - The Flyer, by VanDyke, Jr.
          - Parma, by Dick Andrews.
      - Lancess.
        - Lance.
          - American Eclipse, by Duroc.
          - Young Empress, by Financier.
        - Aurora.
          - Aratus, by Director.
          - Paragon, by *Buzzard.
  - Romance.
    - Sir Leslie.
      - Sir William of Transport.
        - Sir Archy.
          - * Diomed, by Florizel.
          - * Castianira, by Rockingham.
        - Transport.
          - Virginius, by *Diomed.
          - Nancy Air, by *Bedford.
      - Miss Dowden.
        - *Buzzard.
          - Woodpecker, by Herod.
          - Misfortune, by Dux.
        - Daughter of
          - *Speculator, by Dragon.
          - Daughter of Damon, by *Fearnaught.
    - Arian.
      - Trumpator.
        - Sir Solomon.
          - *Tickle Toby, by Alfred.
          - Vesta, by Dreadnaught.
        - Daughter of
          - Hickory, by *Whip.
          - *Trumpetta, by Trumpator.
      - Mary Jones.
        - Kosciusko.
          - Sir Archy, by *Diomed.
          - Lottery, by *Bedford.
        - Daughter of
          - Young Bedford, by *Bedford.
          - Daughter of Arion.

Seventh dam by Brilliant, son of *Marplot.

KATE WALKER.

Started but once and then as a two-year-old under the name of Cricket Walker and ran third in a mile dash at Lexington, Ky., won by Hollywood, Saucebox second; nine starters; time, 1:45¾.

--- ---

PRODUCE.

1874, bl. c., ED. TURNER, by Enquirer.

1875, Barren.

1876, b. f., ANN FIEF, by Alarm. (Tremont's dam.)

1877, NANCY FOSTER, by *Buckden. (Died February 17, 1880.)

1878, b. c., BEND 'OR, by *Buckden.

1879, br. f., MAGGIE H., by Bob Woolly

1880, Barren.

1881, b. c., by King Alfonso. (Dead.)

1882, Barren.

1883, b. f., HATTIE D. H., by *Buckden.

1884, Missed to Ten Broeck.

1885 b. f., by Ten Broeck. (Dead.)

1886, Missed to *Rayon d'Or.

1887, Missed to *Rayon d'Or.

1888, Missed to *Rayon d'Or and Algerine.

1889, Missed to Wanderer, Algerine, *Kantaka and *Rayon d'Or.

1890,   by *Rayon d'Or, *Kantaka and Algerine.

KINLOCH. Chestnut mare, foaled 1878. Bred by Jas. A. Grinstead, Ky.

Humphrey Clinker.	{	Comus, by Sorcerer. / Clinkerina, by Clinker.
Daughter of	{	Cervantes, by Don Quixote. / Daughter of Golumpus.
Touchstone.	{	Camel, by Whalebone. / Banter, by Master Henry.
Emma.	{	Whisker, by Waxy. / Gibside Fairy, by Hermes.
Emilius.	{	Orville, by Beningbrough. / Emily, by Stamford.
Shoveler.	{	Scud, by Beningbrough. / Goosander, by Hambletonian.
Whisker.	{	Waxy, by Pot-8-os. / Penelope, by Trumpator.
Variety.	{	Selim, or Soothsayer. / Sprite, by Bobtail.
Lottery.	{	Tramp, by Dick Andrews. / Mandane, by Pot-8-os.
Morgianna.	{	Muley, by Orville. / Miss Stephenson, by Scud or Sorcerer.
*Priam.	{	Emilius, by Orville. / Cressida, by Whiskey.
Daughter of	{	Orville, by Beningbrough. / Daughter of Buzzard.
Sir Hercules.	{	Whalebone, by Waxy. / Peri, by Wanderer.
Guiccioli.	{	Bob Booty, by Chanticleer. / Flight, by Escape.
Liverpool.	{	Tramp, by Dick Andrews. / Daughter of Whisker.
Rachel.	{	Muley, by Orville. / Daughter of Comus.
Whalebone.	{	Waxy, by Pot-8-os. / Penelope, by Trumpator.
Peri.	{	Wanderer, by Gohanna. / Thalestris, by Alexander.
Bob Booty.	{	Chanticleer, by Woodpecker. / Icrue, by Irish Escape.
Flight.	{	Escape, by Highflyer. / Young Heroine, by Bagot.
Brutandorf.	{	Blacklock, by Whitelock. / Mandane, by Pot-8-os.
Daughter of	{	Comus, by Sorcerer. / Mariana, by Stamford.
Sir Hercules.	{	Whalebone, by Waxy. / Peri, by Wanderer.
Mary Ann.	{	Waxy Pope, by Waxy. / Witch, by Sorcerer.
Orville.	{	Beningbrough, by King Fergus. / Evelina, by Highflyer.
Emily.	{	Stamford, by Sir Peter. / Daughter of Whiskey.
Tramp.	{	Dick Andrews, by Joe Andrews. / Daughter of Gohanna.
Remembrance.	{	Sir Solomon, by Sir Peter. / Queen Mab, by Eclipse.
Orville.	{	Beningbrough, by King Fergus. / Evelina, by Highflyer.
Eleanor.	{	Whiskey, by Saltram. / Young Giantess, by Diomed.
Dick Andrews.	{	Joe Andrews, by Eclipse. / Daughter of Highflyer.
Spitfire.	{	Beningbrough, by King Fergus. / Daughter of Young Sir Peter.

Ancestral line names: *Australian. West Australian. Australian. Emilia. Young Emilius. Persian. Waverly. Cicily Jopson. Weatherbit. Sheet Anchor. Miss Lettie. Cestren. Fanghe-Balloch. Daughter of Sir Hercules. *Knight of St. George. Irish Birdcatcher. Guiccioli. Maltese. Hetman Platoff. Water Witch. St. George's dam. Variation. *Ambassador. Britannia. Muley. Nancy. *Trapes. Mel-bourne. Mower-ina.

KINLOCH.

Never ran.

PRODUCE.

1883, ch. c., BILL BOND, (Ed. Gilman), by St. Martin.

1884, ch. c., CYCLONE, by St. Martin.

1885, ch. f.,   by *Athlete.

1886-'87-'88, Barren.

1889, ch. c.,   by Aristides.

1890,   by *Rayon d'Or.

LADY SCARBROUGH.
Bay mare, foaled 1876. Bred by Mr. A. Welch, Pa.

*Leamington.

Faugh-a-Ballagh.

Sir Hercules.
- Whale bone.
  - Waxy. { Pot-8-os, by Eclipse. / Maria, by Herod. }
  - Penelope. { Trumpator, by Conductor. / Prunella, by Highflyer. }
- Peri.
  - Wanderer. { Gohanna, by Mercury. / Catherine, by Woodpecker. }
  - Thalestris. { Alexander, by Eclipse. / Rival, by Sir Peter. }

Guiccioli.
- Bob Booty.
  - Chanticleer. { Woodpecker, by Herod. / Daughter of Eclipse. }
  - Ierne. { Bagot, by Herod. / Daughter of Gamahoe. }
- Flight.
  - Irish Escape. { Commodore, by Tug. / Daughter of Highflyer. }
  - Young Heroine. { Bagot, by Herod. / Heroine, by Hero. }

Daughter of —

Pantaloon.
- Castrel.
  - Buzzard. { Woodpecker, by Herod. / Misfortune, by Dux. }
  - Daughter of { Alexander, by Eclipse. / Daughter of Highflyer. }
- Idalia.
  - Peruvian. { Sir Peter, by Highflyer. / Popinjay's Dam, by Boudrow. }
  - Musidora. { Meteor, by Eclipse. / Maid-of-all-Work, by Highflyer. }

Daphne.
- Laurel.
  - Blacklock. { Whitelock, by Hambletonian. / Daughter of Coriander. }
  - Wagtail. { Prime Minister, by Sancho. / Daughter of Orville. }
- Maid of Honor.
  - Champion. { Selim, by Buzzard. / Podagra, by Gouty. }
  - Etiquette. { Orville, by Beningbrough. / Boadicea, by Alexander. }

The Baron.
- Irish Bird-catcher.
  - Sir Hercules. { Whalebone, by Waxy. / Peri, by Wanderer. }
  - Guiccioli. { Bob Booty, by Chanticleer. / Flight, by Escape. }
- Echidna.
  - Economist. { Whisker, by Waxy. / Florauthe, by Octavian. }
  - Miss Pratt. { Blacklock, by Whitelock. / Gadabout, by Orville. }

Rataplan.

Pocahontas.
- *Glencoe.
  - Sultan. { Selim, by Buzzard. / Bacchante, by Williamson's Ditto. }
  - Trampoline. { Tramp, by Dick Andrews. / Web, by Waxy. }
- Mar-pessa.
  - Muley. { Orville, by Beningbrough / Evelina, by Highflyer. }
  - Clare. { Marmion, by Whiskey. / Harpalice, by Gohanna. }

*Lady Lumley.

Schottische.

Fandango.
- Baru-ton.
  - Voltaire. { Blacklock, by Whitelock. / Daughter of Phantom. }
  - Martha Lynn. { Mulatto, by Catton. / Leda, by Filho da Puta. }
- Casta-nette.
  - Don John. { Tramp or Waverly. / Daughter of Comus. }
  - Nickname. { Ishmael, by Sultan. / Misnomer, by Merlin. }

Charlemagne's Dam.
- Sleight of Hand.
  - Pantaloon. { Castrel, by Buzzard. / Idalia, by Peruvian. }
  - Decoy. { Filho da Puta, by Haphazard. / Finesse, by Peruvian. }
- Daughter of
  - Comus. { Sorcerer, by Trumpator. / Houghton Lass, by Sir Peter. }
  - Daughter of { Oiseau, by Camillus. / Anna Maria, by Stamford. }

Eeventh dam, Stella by Phoenomenon; Eighth dam, Skypeeper by Highflyer; Ninth dam, Miss West by Matchem; Tenth dam by Regulus: Eleventh dam by Orab; Twelfth dam by Childers; Thirteenth dam by Basto.

LADY SCARBROUGH.

Never ran.

- - - ——————

PRODUCE.

1880, b. c., WELSHMAN, by Alarm.   (Gelded.)

1881, b. f., ALCINA, by Alarm.

1882, b. f., FIDELE, by Alarm.

1883, b. f., PETTICOAT, by Alarm.

1884, Missed to Algerine.

1885, b. c., TOM McCOOK, by Algerine.   (Gelded.)

1886, Missed to *Kantaka.

1887, b. c., ZOR, by *Kantaka.   (Gelded.)

1888, ch. f.,   by *Kantaka.

1889, Barren to *Rayon d'Or.

1890,   by *Kantaka.

L'ARGENTINE.

Chestnut mare, foaled 1873. Bred by A. K. Richards, Kentucky.

- **War Dance.**
  - **Lexington.**
    - **Boston.**
      - **Timoleon.**
        - **Sir Archy.** { * Diomed, by Florizel, / * Castianira, by Rockingham.
        - **Daughter of** { * Saltram, by Eclipse. / Daughter of Symme's Wildair.
      - **Sister to 'tuckahoe.**
        - **Ball's Florizel.** { * Diomed, by Florizel. / Daughter of * Shark.
        - **Daughter of** { * Alderman, by Pot-8-os. / Daughter of * Clockfast.
    - **Alice Carneal.**
      - *** Sarpedon.**
        - **Emilius.** { Orville, by Beningbrough. / Emily, by Stamford.
        - **Icaria.** { The Flyer, by Van Dyke, jr. / Parma, by Dick Andrews.
      - **Rowena.**
        - **Sumpter.** { Sir Archy, by * Diomed. / Daughter of * Robin Redbreast.
        - **Lady Grey.** { Robin Grey, by * Royalist. / Maria, by Melzar.
  - **Reel.**
    - *** Glencoe.**
      - **Sultan.**
        - **Selim.** { Buzzard, by Woodpecker. / Castrel's dam, by Alexander.
        - **Bacchante.** { Williamson's Ditto, by Sir Peter. / Sister to Calomel, by Mercury.
      - **Trampoline.**
        - **Tramp.** { Dick Andrews, by Joe Andrews. / Daughter of Gohanna.
        - **Web.** { Waxy, by Pot-8-os. / Penelope, by Trumpator.
    - *** Gallopade.**
      - **Catton.**
        - **Golumpus.** { Gohanna, by Mercury. / Catherine, by Woodpecker.
        - **Lucy Grey.** { Timothy, by Delpini. / Lucy, by Florizel.
      - **Camilline.**
        - **Camillus.** { Hambletonian, by King Fergus. / Faith, by Pacolet.
        - **Daughter of** { Smolensko, by Sorcerer. / Miss Cannon, by Orville.
- **Miss Grey.**
  - **Daughter of**
    - **Revill.**
      - **Vandall.**
        - *** Glencoe.**
          - **Sultan.** { Selim, by Buzzard. / Bacchante, by Williamson's Ditto
          - **Trampoline.** { Tramp, by Dick Andrews. / Web, by Waxy.
        - **Daughter of**
          - *** Tranby.** { Blacklock, by Whitelock. / Daughter of Orville.
          - **Lucilla.** { Trumpator, by Sir Solomon. / Lucy, by Orphan.
      - **Mary Ellen.**
        - **Mirabeau.**
          - **Medoc.** { Am. Eclipse, by Duroc. / Y. Maid of the Oaks, by *Expedi-[tion.
          - **Ann Merry.** { Sumpter, by Sir Archy. / Grecian Princess, by Blackburn's [Whip.
        - **Arrabella.**
          - **Bertrand.** { Sir Archy, by *Diomed. / Eliza, by *Bedford.
          - **President's Dam.** { Hancock's Hambletonian. / Daughter of Whip.
    - *** Sovereign.**
      - **Emilius.**
        - **Orville.** { Beningbrough, by King Fergus. / Evelina, by Highflyer.
        - **Emily.** { Stamford, by Sir Peter. / Daughter of Whiskey.
      - **Fleur de Lis.**
        - **Bourbon.** { Sorcerer, by Trumpator. / Daughter of Precipitate.
        - **Lady Rachel.** { Stamford, by Sir Peter. / Young Rachel, by Volunteer.
  - **Daughter of**
    - **Grey Medoc.**
      - **Medoc.** { Am. Eclipse, by Duroc. / Y. Maid of the Oaks, by *Expedi-[tion.
      - **Grey Fanny.** { Bertrand, by Sir Archy. / Daughter of *Buzzard.
    - **Marvis.**
      - **Wagner.** { Sir Charles, by Sir Archy. / Maria West, by Marion.
      - **Daughter of** { Medoc, by American Eclipse. / Daughter of Blackburn's Whip.

Seventh dam by Sumpter; eighth dam, Virago, by *Shark; ninth dam, *Gunilda (Virago), by Star; tenth dam, Virago, by the Phantom Arabian; eleventh dam, Crazy, by Lath; twelfth dam, sister to Snip, by Childers; thirteenth dam, sister to Soreheels, by Basto; fourteenth dam, sister to Mixbury, by Curwen's Bay Barb; fifteenth dam by Curwen's *Spot; sixteenth dam by the White-legged Lowther Barb; seventeenth dam, Old Vintner mare.

L'ARGENTINE.

Did not start at two years old. At three years old started six times, winning four times and unplaced twice. At four years old started six times, winning them all. At five years old started three times, winning twice and unplaced once. At six years old started fifteen times, winning eight times, second four times, and unplaced three times. At seven years old started seven times, winning four times, second once, third once, and unplaced once.

PRODUCE.

1882, b. c., BILL STERITT, by Jack Hardy. (Gelded.)

1883, Barren to Jack Hardy.

1884, Barren to Jack Hardy.

1885, b. f., LOTTIE F., by Jack Hardy.

1886, Barren to Jack Hardy.

1887, ch. c., LEIGHTON, by *Rayon d'Or.

1888, Barren to *Rayon d'Or.

1889, ch. f.,   by *Rayon d'Or.

1890,   by *Rayon d'Or.

LIATUNAH.—(LAH-TU-NAH.)

Bay mare, foaled 1876. Bred by Gen. Wm. G. Harding, of Tennessee.

- **John Morgan.**
  - ***Sovereign.**
    - **Emilius.**
      - **Orville.**
        - Beningbrough. { King Fergus, by Eclipse. / Daughter of Herod. }
        - Evelina. { Highflyer, by Herod. / Termagant, by Tantrum. }
      - **Emily.**
        - Stamford. { Sir Peter, by Highflyer. / Horatio, by Eclipse. }
        - Daughter of { Whiskey, by Saltram. / Grey Dorimant, by Dorimant. }
    - **Fleur de Lis.**
      - **Bourbon.**
        - Sorcerer. { Trumpator, by Conductor. / Young Giantess, by Diomed. }
        - Daughter of { Precipitate, by Mercury. / Daughter of Highflyer. }
      - **Lady Rachel.**
        - Stamford. { Sir Peter, by Highflyer. / Horatio, by Eclipse. }
        - Young Rachel. { Volunteer, by Young Belgrade. / Rachel, by Highflyer. }
  - **Sally Lewis.**
    - ***Glencoe.**
      - **Sultan.**
        - Selim. { Buzzard, by Woodpecker. / Castrel's dam, by Alexander. }
        - Bacchante. { Williamson's Ditto, by Sir Peter. / Sister to Calomel, by Mercury. }
      - **Trampoline.**
        - Tramp. { Dick Andrews, by Joe Andrews. / Daughter of Gohanna. }
        - Web. { Waxy, by Pot-8-os. / Penelope, by Trumpator. }
    - **Motto.**
      - ***Barefoot.**
        - Tramp. { Dick Andrews, by Joe Andrews. / Daughter of Gohanna. }
        - Rosamond. { Buzzard, by Woodpecker. / Roseberry by Phenomenon. }
      - **Lady Thompkins.**
        - American Eclipse. { Duroc, by *Diomed. / Miller's Damsel, by *Messenger. }
        - Katy Ann. { Ogle's Oscar, by * Gabriel. / Medoc's dam, by * Expedition. }

- **Lautana.**
  - **Capt. Elgee.**
    - ***Leviathan.**
      - **Muley.**
        - Orville. { Beningbrough, by King Fergus. / Evelina, by Highflyer. }
        - Eleanor. { Whiskey, by Saltram. / Young Giantess, by Diomed. }
      - **Daughter of**
        - Windle. { Beningbrough, by King Fergus. / Mary Ann, by Sir Peter. }
        - Daughter of { Anvil, by Herod. / Virago, by Snap. }
    - **Reel.**
      - ***Glencoe.**
        - Sultan. { Selim, by Buzzard. / Bacchante, by Williamson's Ditto. }
        - Trampoline. { Tramp, by Dick Andrews. / Web, by Waxy. }
      - ***Gallopade.**
        - Catton. { Golumpus, by Gohanna. / Lucy Grey, by Timothy. }
        - Camillina. { Camillus, by Hambletonian. / Daughter of Smolensko. }
  - **Angeline.**
    - ***Albion.**
      - **Cain or Actæon.**
        - Scud. { Beningbrough, by King Fergus. / Eliza, by Highflyer. }
        - Diana. { Stamford, by Sir Peter / Daughter of Whiskey }
      - **Pan-thea.**
        - Comus or Blacklock. { Whitelock, by Hambletonian. / Daughter of Coriander. }
        - Manuella. { Dick Andrews, by Joe Andrews, / Mandane, by Pot-8-os, }
    - **Clara Howard.**
      - ***Barefoot.**
        - Tramp. { Dick Andrews, by Joe Andrews. / Daughter of Gohanna. }
        - Rosamond. { Buzzard, by Woodpecker, / Roseberry by Phenomenon. }
      - ***Alarm.**
        - Thunderbolt. { Sorcerer, by Trumpator. / Wamski, by Mentor. }
        - Zadora. { Trafalgar, by / Nike, by Alexander. }

Seventh dam, Nimble by Florizel; Eighth dam, Rantipole by Blank; Ninth dam, Sister to Careless by Careless by Regulus; Tenth dam, Silvertail by Henage's White-nose; Eleventh dam by Rattler; Twelfth dam by Darley Arabian: Thirteenth dam by Sir T. Gresley's Bay Arabian; Fourteenth dam by the Helmsley Turk. Fifteenth dam, Dodsworth's dam.

LIATUNAH.

At two years old started in seven races, winning two—the Filly Stakes at Lexington, and the Lucas and Hunt Stakes at St. Louis—ran second twice, third three times, and unplaced once. At three years old started four times, winning the Oaks at Louisville and the Illinois Oaks at Chicago, ran third once, and unplaced once. At four years old started in five races and was unplaced in all. At five years old started in fourteen races, winning two—mile dash at Louisville and Board of Trade Handicap at Chicago—ran second once, third once, and unplaced ten times. At six years old started in thirteen races, won none, was second three times, third once, and unplaced in nine. At seven years old started six times, winning two, third in three, and unplaced once. Winnings, $13,910.

PRODUCE.

1885, ch. c., by *Prince Charlie or *Rayon d'Or. (Died 1886.)

1886, b. f., GYPSY QUEEN, by *Rayon d'Or.

1887, ch. c., GYPSY KING, by *Rayon d'Or.

1888, ch. f.,   by *Kantaka. (Died August, 1888.)

1889, b. c.,   by *Rayon d'Or.

1890,   by *Rayon d'Or.

LILLY B.

- **sire: *Hurrah.**
  - **Newminster.**
    - **Touchstone.**
      - **Camel.**
        - Whalebone. { Waxy, by Pot-8-os. / Penelope, by Trumpator.
        - Daughter of { Selim, by Buzzard. / Maiden, by Sir Peter.
      - **Bauter.**
        - Master Henry. { Orville, by Beningbrough. / Miss Sophia, by Stamford.
        - Bondicea. { Alexander, by Eclipse. / Brunette, by Amaranthus.
    - **Beeswing.**
      - **Dr. Syntax.**
        - Paynator. { Trumpator, by Conductor. / Daughter of Mark Anthony.
        - Daughter of { Beningbrough, by King Fergus. / Jennie Mole, by Carbuncle.
      - **Daughter of.**
        - Ardrossan. { John Bull, by Fortitudes. / Miss Whip, by Volunteer.
        - Lady Eliza. { Whitworth, by Agonistes. / X.Y.Z.'s dam, by Spadille.
  - **Jovial.**
    - **Bay Middleton.**
      - **Sultan.**
        - Selim. { Buzzard, by Woodpecker. / Daughter of Alexander.
        - Bacchante. { Williamson's Ditto, by Sir Peter. / Sister to Calomel, by Mercury.
      - **Cobweb.**
        - Phantom. { Walton, by Sir Peter. / Julia, by Whiskey.
        - Filagree. { Soothsayer, by Sorcerer. / Web, by Waxy.
    - **Sister to Grey Momus.**
      - **Conus.**
        - Sorcerer. { Trumpator, by Conductor. / Young Giantess, by Diomed.
        - Houghton Lass. { Sir Peter, by Highflyer. / Alexina, by King Fergus.
      - **Daughter of.**
        - Cervantes. { Don Quixote, by Eclipse. / Evelina, by Highflyer.
        - Emma. { Don Cossock, by Haphazard. / Vesta, by Delpini.
- **dam: Sally Newton.**
  - **John Morgan.**
    - ***Sovereign.**
      - **Emilius.**
        - Orville. { Beningbrough, by King Fergus. / Evelina, by Highflyer.
        - Emily. { Stamford, by Sir Peter. / Daughter of Whiskey.
      - **Fleur de Lis.**
        - Bourbon. { Sorcerer, by Trumpator. / Daughter of Precipitate.
        - Lady Rachel. { Stamford, by Sir Peter. / Young Rachel, by Volunteer.
    - **Sally Lewis.**
      - ***Glencoe.**
        - Sultan. { Selim, by Buzzard. / Bacchante, by Williamson's Ditto.
        - Trampoline. { Tramp, by Dick Andrews. / Web, by Waxy.
      - **Motto.**
        - *Barefoot. { Tramp, by Dick Andrews. / Rosamond, by Buzzard.
        - Lady Tompkins. { American Eclipse, by Duroc. / Katy Ann, by Ogle's Oscar.
  - **Nellie Grey.**
    - **Oliver.**
      - **Wagner.**
        - Sir Charles. { Sir Archy, by *Diomed. / Daughter of *Citizen.
        - Maria West. { Marion, by Sir Archy. / Ella Crump, by *Citizen.
      - **Flight.**
        - *Leviathan. { Muley, by Orville. / The Dandy's dam, by Windle.
        - Charlotte Hamilton. { Sir Charles, by Sir Archy. / Lady of the Lake, by *Sir Harry.
    - **Blue Bell.**
      - **Chorister.**
        - *Contract. { Catton, by Golumpus. / Helen, by Humbletonian.
        - Jenny Grey. { Robin Grey, by *Royalist. / Richmond Jenny, by *Diomed.
      - **Blue Filly (Fior.).**
        - *Hedgefood. { Filho-da-Puta, by Haphazard. / Miss Craigie, by Orville.
        - Lady Tompkins. { American Eclipse, by Duroc. / Katy Ann, by Ogle's Oscar.

Seventh dam, Young Maid of the Oaks, by *Expedition; eighth dam, Old Maid of the Oaks, by *Spread Eagle; ninth dam, Annette (Nancy Air's dam), by *Shark; tenth dam by Rockingham; eleventh dam by Baylor's Gallant; twelfth dam by True Whig; thirteenth dam by *Regulus; fourteenth dam by *Diamond.

LILLY B.

Did not run until four years old, and then started thirteen times, running first once, second twice, third once, and unplaced nine times. At five years old started twenty-six times, winning eight times, second four times, third seven times, and unplaced seven times. At six years old started ten times, winning four times, second once, and unplaced five times.

PRODUCE.

1887, Slipped ch. c., by *Kantaka.

1888. Missed to *Kantaka.

1889, ch. c.,   by *Kantaka.

LILLY R.

Chestnut mare, foaled 1876. Bred by Mr. D. Swigert, Ky.

Florine or Florence (Hindoo's dam).

*Glenelg.

- Citadel.
  - Stockwell.
    - The Baron.
      - Irish Birdcatcher. { Sir Hercules, by Whalebone. / Guiciolli, by Bob Booty.
      - Echidna. { Economist, by Whisker. / Miss Pratt, by Blacklock.
    - Pocahontas.
      - Glencoe. { Sultan, by Selim. / Trampoline, by Tramp.
      - Marpessa. { Muley, by Orville. / Clare, by Marmion.
  - Sortie.
    - Melbourne.
      - Humphrey Clinker. { Comus, by Sorcerer. / Clinkerina, by Clinker.
      - Daughter of { Cervantes, by Don Quixote / Daughter of Golumpus, by Gohanna
    - Escalade.
      - Touchstone. { Camel, by Whalebone. / Banter, by Master Henry.
      - Ghuznee. { Pantaloon, by Castrel. / Languish, by Cain.
- *Rapta.
  - Kingston.
    - Venison.
      - Partisan. { Walton, by Sir Peter. / Parasol, by Pot-8-os.
      - Fawn. { Smolensko, by Sorcerer. / Jerboa, by Gohanna.
    - Queen Anne.
      - Slane. { Royal Oak, by Catton. / Daughter of Orville.
      - Garcia. { Octavian, by Stripling. / Daughter of Shuttle, by Catherine.
  - Alice Lowe.
    - Defence.
      - Whalebone. { Waxy, by Pot-8-os, / Penelope, by Trumpator.
      - Defiance. { Rubens, by Buzzard. / Little Follie, by Highland Fling.
    - Pet.
      - Gainsborough. { Rubens, by Buzzard. / Tiny, by Sir Peter Teazle.
      - Daughter of { Topsey Turvey, by St. George. / Agnes, by Bolton.

Lexington.

- Boston.
  - Timoleon.
    - Sir Archy. { *Diomed, by Florizel. / *Castianira, by Rockingham.
    - Daughter of { *Saltram, by Eclipse. / Daughter of Symme's Wildair.
  - Sister to Tuckahoe.
    - Ball's Florizel. { *Diomed, by Florizel. / Daughter of *Shark.
    - Daughter of { *Alderman, by Pot-8-os. / Daughter of *Clockfast.
- Alice Carneal.
  - Sarpedon.
    - Emilius. { Orville, by Beningbrough. / Emily, by Stamford.
    - Icaria. { The Flyer, by VanDyke, jr. / Parma, by Dick Andrews.
  - Rowena.
    - Sumpter. { Sir Archy, by *Diomed. / Daughter of *Robin Redbreast.
    - Lady Grey. { Robin Gray, by * Royalist. / Maria, by Melzar.

*Weatherwitch.

- Weatherbit.
  - Sheet Anchor.
    - Lottery. { Tramp, by Dick Andrews. / Mandane, by Pot-8-os.
    - Morgiana. { Muley, by Orville. / Miss Stevenson, by Scud.
  - Miss Letty.
    - Priam. { Emilius, by Orville. / Cressida, by Whiskey.
    - Miss Fanny's dam. { Orville, by Beningbrough. / Daughter of Buzzard by Hornpipe.
- Daughter of
  - Birdcatcher.
    - Sir Hercules. { Whalebone, by Waxy. / Peri, by Wanderer.
    - Guiciolli. { Bob Booty, by Chanticleer. / Flight, by Irish Escape.
  - Colocynth.
    - Physician. { Brutandorf, by Blacklock. / Primetta, by Prime Minister.
    - Camelina. { Whalebone, by Waxy. / Daughter of Selim.

Seventh dam, Maiden by Sir Peter; Eighth dam by Phenomenon; Ninth dam, Matron by Florizel; Tenth dam, Maiden by Matchem; Eleventh dam by Squirt, Twelfth dam, Lot's dam by Mogul; Thirteenth dam, Camilla by Bay Bolton; Fourteenth dam, Old Lady by the Pulleine Arabian; Fifteenth dam by Rockwood: Sixteenth dam by Bustler.

LILLY R.

At two years old started in seven races, winning the Filly Stakes at Lexington, ran second once, third once and unplaced four times. At three years old started nine times, winning one, second in one, third in two, and unplaced in five. At four years old started five times, winning three, third in one, and unplaced in one. At five years old started in eleven races, winning two, ran second in two, third in three, and unplaced in four.

PRODUCE.

1883, Missed to Algerine.

1884, ch. f., REINE D'OR, by *Rayon d'Or.

1885, ch. c., ALCHEMIST, (Sheriff O'Neill—Dangu), by *Rayon d'Or.

1886, Missed to *Rayon d'Or.

1887, ch. c., CHAOS, by *Rayon d'Or.   (Gelded.)

1888. ch. f., TURMOIL, by *Rayon d'Or.

1889, Barren to *Rayon d'Or.

1890,   by *Rayon d'Or.

LISON (IMPORTED).

Chestnut mare, foaled 1881. Bred at Dangu Stud, Haras, France. Imported by C. J. Osborn, 1885.

Laure, 1874.

Nongat, 1872.

Consul

Monarque.

The Baron, Sting or The Emperor.

{ Defence. — { Whalebone, by Waxy. / Defiance by Rubens.
{ Daughter of — { Reveler, by Comus. / Design, by Tramp.

Poetess.

{ Royal Oak. — { Catton, by Golumpus / Daughter of Smolensko.
{ Ada. — { Whisker, by Waxy. / Anna Bella, by Shuttle.

Lady Lift.

Sir Hercules.

{ Whalebone. — { Waxy, by Pot-8-os. / Penelope, by Trumpator.
{ Peri. — { Wanderer, by Gohanna, / Thalestris, by Alexander.

Sylph.

{ Spectre. — { Phantom, by Walton. / Fillikius, by Gouty.
{ Fanny Leigh, sister to Bustard. — { Castrel, by Buzzard. / Mishap, by Shuttle.

Nebuleuse, 1857.

Gladiator, 1833.

Partisan.

{ Walton. — { Sir Peter, by Highflyer. / Arethusa, by Dungannon.
{ Parasol. — { Pot-8-os, by Eclipse. / Prunella, by Highflyer.

Pauline.

{ Moses. — { Whalebone or Seymour. / Sister to Castanea, by Gohanna.
{ Quadrille. — { Selim, by Buzzard. / Canary Bird, by Whiskey or Sorcerer.

Belle de Nuit, 1844.

Young Emilius.

{ Emilius. — { Orville, by Beningbrough. / Emily, by Stamford.
{ Shoveler. — { Seud, by Beningbrough. / Goosander, by Hambletonian.

Odine, 1852.

{ Tigris, — { Quiz, by Buzzard. / Persepolis, by Alexander.
{ Miss Ann. — { Figaro, by Haphazard. / Daughter of Tramp.

Knight of the Garter, 1844.

The Prime Minister, 1856.

Melbourne.

{ Humphrey Clinker. — { Comus, by Sorcerer. / Clinkerina, by Clinker.
{ Daughter of — { Cervantes, by Don Quixote. / Daughter of Golumpus.

Pantalonade.

{ Pantaloon. — { Castrel, by Buzzard. / Idalia, by Peruvian.
{ Festival. — { Camel by Whalebone. / Michaelmas, by Thunderbolt.

Rosa Bonheur.

Touchstone.

{ Camel. — { Whalebone, by Waxy. / Daughter of Selim.
{ Banter. — { Master Henry, by Orville. / Boadicea, by Alexander.

Boarding School Miss.

{ Plenipotentiary. — { Emilius, by Orville. / Harriet, by Pericles.
{ Marpessa. — { Muley, by Orville. / Clare, by Marmion.

Lady Hilda, 1867.

Lord of the Isles.

Touchstone.

{ Camel. — { Whalebone, by Waxy. / Daughter of Selim.
{ Banter. — { Master Henry, by Orville. / Boadicea, by Alexander.

Fair Helen.

{ Pantaloon. — { Castrel, by Buzzard. / Idalia, by Peruvian.
{ Rebecca. — { Lottery, by Tramp. / Daughter of Cervantes.

Rigolboche. (Cremorne's dam).

Skirmisher's dam.

Kataplan.

{ The Baron. — { Irish Birdcatcher, by Sir Hercules. / Echidna, by Economist.
{ Pocahontas. — { Glencoe, by Sultan. / Marpessa, by Muley.

{ Gardham. — { Falcon, by Bustard. / Muta, sister to Lottery, by Tramp.
{ Daughter of — { Langar, by Selim. / Sister to Busto, by Clinker.

Seventh dam, Bronze (sister to Castrel, &c.) by Buzzard; Eighth dam by Alexander; Ninth dam by Highflyer; Tenth dam by Alfred; Eleventh dam by Engineer; Twelfth dam, Bay Malton's dam by Cade; Thirteenth dam, Lass of the Mill by Old Traveler; Fourteenth dam, Miss Makeless by Son of Grey-hound (Barb); Fifteenth dam by Partner; Sixteenth dam, Brown Woodcock by Woodcock; Seventeenth dam, Lusty Thornton by Croft's Bay Barb; Eighteenth dam, Chestnut Thornton by Makeless; Nineteenth dam, Old Thornton by Brimmer; Twentieth dam by Dickey Pierson; Twenty-first dam Burton Barb mare.

LISON.

Was disabled by an accident at two years old.

———— ——— ···· ———

PRODUCE.

1885, ch. c., HARBOR LIGHTS, by *Rayon d'Or.   (Gelded.)

1886, Missed to *Rayon d'Or.

1887, ch. c., by *Kantaka.   (Died 1888.)

1888, ch. f., SEASHORE, by Wanderer.

1889, ch. f., by Wanderer.   (Killed 1889.)

1890,   by Wanderer.

LIZZIE COX.

Chestnut mare, foaled 1879. Bred by Mr. M. H. Sanford, Preakness Stud.

- ***Glenelg**
  - **Citadel**
    - **Stockwell**
      - **The Baron**
        - Irish Birdcatcher { Sir Hercules, by Whalebone. / Guiciolli, by Bob Booty.
        - Echidna. { Economist, by Whisker. / Miss Pratt, by Blacklock.
      - **Pocahontas**
        - Glencoe. { Sultan, by Selim. / Trampoline, by Tramp.
        - Marpessa. { Muley, by Orville. / Clare, by Marmion.
    - **Sortie**
      - **Melbourne**
        - Humphrey Clinker. { Comus, by Sorcerer. / Clinkerina, by Clinker.
        - Daughter of { Cervantes, by Don Quixote. / Daughter of Golumpus, by Gohanna.
      - **Escalade**
        - Touchstone { Camel, by Whalebone. / Banter, by Master Henry.
        - Ghuznee. { Pantaloon, by Castrel. / Languish, by Cain.
  - ***Bapta**
    - **Kingston**
      - **Venison**
        - Partisan. { Walton, by Sir Peter. / Parasol, by Pot-8-os.
        - Fawn. { Smolensko, by Sorcerer. / Jerboa, by Gohanna.
      - **Queen Anne**
        - Slane. { Royal Oak, by Catton. / Daughter of Orville.
        - Garcia { Octavian, by Stripling. / Daughter of Shuttle, by Catherine.
    - **Alice Lowe**
      - **Defence**
        - Whalebone. { Waxy, by Pot-8-os. / Penelope, by Trumpator.
        - Defiance. { Rubens, by Buzzard. / Little Folic, by Highland Fling.
      - **Pet**
        - Gainsborough. { Rubens, by Buzzard. / Tiny, by Sir Peter Teazle.
        - Daughter of { Topsey Turvey, by St. George. / Agnes, by Shuttle.
- **Retort**
  - **Lever**
    - **Lexington**
      - **Boston**
        - Timoleon. { Sir Archy, by * Diomed. / Daughter of * Saltram.
        - Sister to Tuckahoe. { Ball's Florizel, by * Diomed. / Daughter of * Alderman.
      - **Alice Carneal**
        - * Sarpedon. { Emilius, by Orville. / Icaria, by The Flyer.
        - Rowena. { Sumpter, by Sir Archy. / Lady Grey, by Robin Grey.
    - **Levity**
      - ***Trustee**
        - Catton. { Golumpus, by Gohanna. / Lucy Grey, by Timothy.
        - Emma. { Whisker, by Waxy. / Gibside Fairy, by Hermes.
      - **Vandal's Dam**
        - *Tranby. { Blacklock, by Whitelock. / Daughter of Orville.
        - Lucilla. { Trumpator, by Sir Solomon. / Lucy, by Orphan.
  - **Return**
    - **Commodore**
      - **Boston**
        - Timoleon. { Sir Archy, by * Diomed. / Daughter of * Saltram.
        - Sister to Tuckahoe. { Ball's Florizel, by * Diomed / Daughter of * Alderman.
      - **Rosalie Somers**
        - Sir Charles. { Sir Archy, by *Diomed. / Daughter of * Citizen.
        - Mischief. { Virginian, by Sir Archy. / Daughter of * Bedford.
    - **Reunion**
      - **Union**
        - *Glencoe. { Sultan, by Selim. / Trampoline, by Tramp.
        - Giantess. { *Leviathan, by Muley. / Virginia, by Sir Archy.
      - **Galla-pade, Jr.**
        - *Glencoe. { Sultan, by Selim. / Trampoline, by Tramp.
        - Catillion. { *Leviathan, by Muley. / *Gallopade, by Catton.

Seventh dam, Camillus by Camillus; Eighth dam by Smolensko; Ninth dam, Miss Cannon by Orville; Tenth dam by Weathercock; Eleventh dam, Cora by Matchem; Twelfth dam by Turk; Thirteenth dam by Cub; Fourteenth dam by Allworthy; Fifteenth dam by Starling; Sixteenth dam by Bloody Buttocks; Seventeenth dam by Greyhound; Eighteenth dam, Brocklesby Betty by Curwen's Bay Barb; Nineteenth dam, Leede's Hobby Mare by The Lister Turk.

LIZZIE COX.

Never ran.

PRODUCE.

1883, ch. c., by *King Ban.   (Died.)

1884, Missed to Onondaga.

1885, ch. f., MONEY BOX, by Onondaga or *Rayon d'Or.

1886, Missed to *Rayon d'Or.

1887, ch. f., PARADOX, by *Rayon d'Or.

1888, ch. c., by *Rayon d'Or.   (Died 1889.)

1889, ch. c.,   by *Rayon d'Or.

1890,   by *Rayon d'Or.

LUCY WALLACE.

Chestnut mare, foaled 187.. Bred by J. M. McClelland, Ky.

Ballinkeel or War Dance.

- **Lexington.**
  - **Boston.**
    - **Timoleon.**
      - Sir Archy. — { * Diomed, by Florizel. / * Castianira, by Rockingham.
      - Daughter of — { * Saltram, by Eclipse. / Daughter of Symme's Wildair.
    - **Sister to Tuckahoe.**
      - Ball's Florizel. — { * Diomed, by Florizel. / Daughter of * Shark.
      - Daughter of — { * Alderman, by Pot-8-os. / Daughter of * Clockfast.
  - **Alice Carneal.**
    - **Sarpedon.**
      - Emilius — { Orville, by Beningbrough. / Emily, by Stamford.
      - Icaria. — { The Flyer, by Van Dyke, jr. / Parma, by Dick Andrews.
    - **Rowena.**
      - Sumpter. — { Sir Archy, by * Diomed. / Daughter of * Robin Redbreast.
      - Lady Grey. — { Robin Grey, by * Royalist. / Maria, by Melzar.
- **Reel.**
  - *** Glencoe.**
    - **Sultan.**
      - Selim. — { Buzzard, by Woodpecker. / Castrel's dam, by Alexander.
      - Bacchante. — { Williamson's Ditto, by Sir Peter. / Sister to Calomel, by Mercury.
    - **Trampoline.**
      - Tramp. — { Dick Andrews, by Joe Andrews. / Daughter of Gohanna.
      - Web. — { Waxy, by Pot-8-os. / Penelope, by Trumpator.
  - *** Gallopade.**
    - **Catton.**
      - Golumpus. — { Gohanna, by Mercury. / Catherine, by Woodpecker.
      - Lucy Grey. — { Timothy, by Delpini. / Lucy, by Florizel.
    - **Camilline.**
      - Camillus. — { Hambletonian, by King Fergus. / Faith, by Pacolet.
      - Daughter of — { Smolensko, by Sorcerer. / Miss Cannon, by Orville.

Blanche Rosseau.

- *** Mickey Free.**
  - **Irish Birdcatcher.**
    - **Sir Hercules.**
      - Whalebone. — { Waxy, by Pot-8-os. / Penelope, by Trumpator.
      - Peri. — { Wanderer, by Gohanna. / Thalestris, by Alexander.
    - **Gulcci-oli.**
      - Bob Booty. — { Chanticleer, by Woodpecker. / Ierne, by Bagot.
      - Flight. — { Irish Escape, by Commodore. / Young Heroine, by Bagot.
  - **Annie (Colley).**
    - **Wanderer.**
      - Gohanna. — { Mercury, by Eclipse. / Daughter of Herod.
      - Catherine. — { Woodpecker, by Herod. / Camilla, by Trentham.
    - **Caroline.**
      - Whalebone. — { Waxy, by Pot-8-os. / Penelope, by Trumpator.
      - Marianne. — { Mufti, by Damascus Arabian. / Maria, by Telemachus.
- **Ada Tevis.**
  - *** Albion.**
    - **Cain or Octaeon.**
      - Scud. — { Beningbrough, by King Fergus. / Eliza, by Highflyer.
      - Diana. — { Stamford, by Haphazard. / Daughter of Whiskey.
    - **Panthea.**
      - Comus or Blacklock. — { Whitelock, by Hambletonian. / Daughter of Coriander.
      - Manuella. — { Dick Andrews, by Joe Andrews. / Mandane, by Pot-8-os.
  - **Daughter of**
    - *** Leviathan.**
      - Muley. — { Orville, by Beningbrough. / Daughter of Whiskey
      - The Dandy's Dam. — { Windle, by Beningbrough. / Daughter of Anvil.
    - **Daughter of**
      - Jerry. — { Pacolet, by Spark. / Black Sophia, by Top Gallant.
      - Daughter of — { Sir Archy, by * Diomed. / Daughter of * Dare Devil.

Seventh dam, Lady Bolingbroke by * Pantaloon; Eighth dam, Cades by Warmsley's King Herod: Ninth dam, Stella by * Othello; Tenth dam, * Selim, by the Godolphin Arabian.

LUCY WALLACE

Never ran.

PRODUCE.

1882, b. c., LEAD, by Lelaps.   (Died 1886.)

1883, Barren

1884, b. f., ALMA, by Himyar.

1885, ch. c., by *Rayon d'Or.   (Dead.)

1886, ch. c., SPARLING, by *Rayon d'Or.

1887, ch. f., MARTHA, by *Rayon d'Or.

1888, ch. f., LUMINOUS, by *Rayon d'Or.

1889, Barren to *Rayon d'Or.

1890,   by *Kantaka.

LUNE D'OR.
Chestnut mare, foaled 1844. Bred by W. L. Scott, Erie, Pa.

- ***Rayon D'Or.**
  - **Flageolet.**
    - **Plutus.**
      - **Daughter Trumpeter.**
        - **Orlando.** { Touchstone, by Camel. / Vulture, by Langar.
        - **Cavatina.** { Redshank, by Sandbeck. / Oxygen, by Emilius.
      - **of**
        - **Planet.** { Bay Middleton, by Sultan. / Plenary, by Emilius.
        - **Alice Bray.** { Venison, by Partisan. / Darkness, by Glencoe.
    - **La Favorite.**
      - **Monarque.**
        - **The Baron Sting. or the Emperor.** { Defense, by Whalebone. / Delight, by Reveller.
        - **Poetess.** { Royal Oak, by Catton. / Ada, by Whisker.
      - **Constance.**
        - **Gladiator.** { Partisan, by Walton. / Pauline, by Mose..
        - **Lanterne.** { Hercules, by Rainbow. / Elvira, by Eryx.
  - **Araucaria.**
    - **Ambrose.**
      - **Touchstone.**
        - **Camel.** { Whalebone, by Waxy. / Daughter of Selim
        - **Banter.** { Master Henry, by Orville. / Boadicea, by Alexander.
      - **Annette.**
        - **Priam.** { Emilius, by Orville. / Cressida, by Whiskey.
        - **Potentate's Dam.** { Don Juan, by Orville. / Moll in the Wad, by Hambletonian
    - **Pocahontas.**
      - **Glencoe.**
        - **Sultan.** { Selim, by Buzzard. / Bacchante, by Williamson's Ditto.
        - **Trampoline.** { Tramp, by Dick Andrews. / Web, by Waxy.
      - **Marpessa.**
        - **Muley.** { Orville, by Beningbrough / Eleanor, by Whiskey.
        - **Clare.** { Marmion, by Whiskey. / Harpalice, by Gohanna.
- **Mary Constance.**
  - **War Dance.**
    - **Lexington.**
      - **Boston.**
        - **Timoleon.** { Sir Archy, by *Diomed. / Daughter of *Saltram.
        - **Sister to Tuckahoe.** { Ball's Florizel, by *Diomed. / Daughter of *Alderman.
      - **Alice Carneal.**
        - ***Sarpedon.** { Emilius, by Orville. / Icaria, by The Flyer.
        - **Rowena.** { Sumpter, by Sir Archy. / Lady Gray, by Robin Gray.
    - **Reel.**
      - ***Glencoe.**
        - **Sultan.** { Selim, by Buzzard. / Bacchante, by Williamson's Ditto.
        - **Trampoline.** { Tramp, by Dick Andrews. / Web, by Waxy.
      - ***Gallopade.**
        - **Catton.** { Golumpus, by Gohanna. / Lucy Grey, by Timothy.
        - **Camillina.** { Camillus, by Hambletonian. / Daughter of Smolensko.
  - **Lass of Sydney.**
    - **Hillsborough's dau.***
      - ***Knight of St. George.**
        - **Irish Birdcatcher.**
          - **Sir Hercules.** { Whalebone, by Waxy. / Peri, by Wanderer.
          - **Guiccioli.** { Bob Booty, by Chanticleer. / Flight, by Escape.
        - **Maltese.**
          - **Hetman Platoff.** { Brutandorf, by Blacklock. / Daughter of Comus.
          - **Waterwitch.** { Sir Hercules, by Whalebone. / Mary Ann, by Waxy Pope.
    - **The Nun.**
      - **Lancercost.**
        - **Liverpool.** { Tramp, by Dick Andrews. / Daughter of Whisker.
        - **Otis.** { Bustard, by Buzzard. / Gayhurst's dam, by Election.
      - **Catton.**
        - **Daughter of** { Paynator, by Trumpator. / Sister to Zodiac, by St. George.

Seventh dam, Abigail, by Woodpecker; eighth dam, Firetail, by Eclipse: ninth dam by Blank; tenth dam by Cade; eleventh dam Spectator's dam, by Partner; twelfth dam, Bonnie Lass, by Bay Bolton; thirteenth dam by the Darley Arabian; fourteenth dam by the Byerly Turk; fifteenth dam by the Taffolet Barb; sixteenth dam by Place's White Turk; seventeenth dam, Natural Barb mare.

LUNE D'OR.

Ran only at two years old and then started but twice, winning a Sweepstakes at Coney Island, and unplaced once.

PRODUCE.

1888, Barren to *Kantaka.

1889, ch. c.,   by *Kantaka.

1890,   by Algerine.

MARY CONSTANT.

Bay mare, foaled 1870. Bred by Mr. A. Keene Richards, Kentucky.

Lass of Sidney.

Hillsborough's dam. *

War Dance.

Reel.

*Gallopade.

Lexington.

Alice Carneal.

*Glencoe.

Knight of St. George.

Irish Birdcatcher.

Maltese.

Lanercost.

The Nun.

Boston.
Sister to Tuckahoe.
* Sarpedon.
Rowena.
Sultan.
Trampoline.
Catton.
Camillina.
Sir Hercules.
Griccioli.
Hetman Platoff.
Water Witch.
Liverpool.
Otis.
Catton.
Daughter of

Timoleon.

Sir Archy.	{ Diomed, by Florizel. / { Castianira, by Rockingham.
Daughter of	{ Saltram, by Eclipse. / { Daughter of Symmes Wildair.
Ball's Florizel.	{ Diomed, by Florizel. / { Daughter of * Shark.
Daughter of	{ *Alderman, by Pot-8-os. / { Daughter of * Clockfast.
Emilius	{ Orville, by Beningbrough. / { Emily, by Stamford.
Icaria.	{ The Flyer, by VanDyke, jr. / { Parma, by Dick Andrews.
Sumpter.	{ Sir Archy, by * Diomed. / { Flirtilla's dam, by Robin Redbreast.
Lady Gray.	{ Robin Gray, by * Royalist. / { Maria, by Melzar.
Selim.	{ Buzzard, by Woodpecker. / { Castrel's dam, by Alexander.
Bacchante.	{ Williamson's Ditto, by Sir Peter. / { Sister to Calomel, by Mercury.
Tramp	{ Dick Andrews, by Joe Andrews. / { Daughter of Gohanna.
Web.	{ Waxy, by Pot-8-os, / { Penelope, by Trumpator.
Golumpus.	{ Gohanna, by Mercury. / { Catherine, by Woodpecker.
Lucy Gray.	{ Timothy, by Whisker or P. Minister. / { Lucy, by Florizel.
Camillus.	{ Hambletonian, by King Fergus. / { Faith, by Pacolet.
Daughter of	{ Smolensko, by Sorcerer. / { Miss Cannon, by Orville.
Whalebone.	{ Waxy, by Pot-8-os. / { Penelope, by Trumpator.
Peri.	{ Wanderer, by Gohanna. / { Thalestris, by Alexander.
Bob Booty.	{ Chanticleer, by Woodpecker. / { Ierne, by Bagot.
Flight.	{ Escape, by Commodore. / { Young Heroine, by Bagot.
Brutandorf.	{ Blacklock, by Whitelock. / { Mandane, by Pot-8-os.
Daughter of	{ Comus, by Sorcerer. / { Marciana, by Stamford.
Sir Hercules.	{ Whalebone, by Waxy. / { Peri, by Wanderer.
Mary Anne.	{ Waxy Pope, by Waxy. / { Witch, by Sorcerer.
Tramp	{ Dick Andrews, by Joe Andrews. / { Daughter of Gohanna.
Daughter of	{ Whisker, by Waxy. / { Mandane, by Pot-8-os.
Bustard.	{ Buzzard, by Woodpecker. / { Gipsey, by Trumpator.
Gayhurst's dam.	{ Eection, by Gohanna. / { Sister to Skysweeper, by Highflyer.
Golumpus.	{ Gohanna, by Mercury. / { Catherine, by Woodpecker.
Lucy Gray.	{ Timothy, by Delpini. / { Lucy, by Florizel.
Paynator.	{ Trumpator, by Conductor. / { Daughter of Marc Anthony.
Sister to Zodiac.	{ St. George, by Highflyer. / { Abigail, by Woodpecker.

Seventh Dam, Firetail by Eclipse; Eighth dam by Blank; Ninth dam by Cade; Tenth dam, Spectator's dam by Partner; Eleventh dam, Bonnie Lass by Bay Bolton; Twelfth dam by the Darley Arabian; Thirteenth dam by the Taffolet Barb; Fourteenth dam by the Byerly Turk; Fifteenth dam by Place's White Turk; Sixteenth dam, Natural Barb mare.

MARY CONSTANT. Sister to Tubman.

As a two-year-old started in two races and was unplaced in both. At three years old started seven times, won once (mile heats), third once, and unplaced five times. At four years old started four times, running third in two, and unplaced in two.

PRODUCE.

1880, b. f., IDA GREEN, by *Saxon.

1881, Barren.

1882, b. c., CINCINNATUS, by Falsetto.

1883, b. f., CONSTANCY, by *Saxon.

1884, ch. f., LUNE D'OR, by *Rayon d'Or.

1885, ch. f.,   by *Kantaka.

1886, ch. f., IVEYDOR, by *Rayon d'Or.

1887, b. f., KALAVALA, (Hebe), by *Kantaka.

1888, Barren to *Kantaka.

1889, Barren to *Kantaka.

1890,   by *Kantaka.

MAURINE.

Bay mare, foaled 1882. Bred by Mr. P. Lorillard, N. J.

Carrie Atherton.

- **Complegne.** (Fitz Gladiator / Zarah.)
  - Gladiator.
    - **Partisan.** { Walton, by Sir Peter. / Parasol, by Pot-8-os.
    - **Pauline.** { Moses, by Whalebone or Seymour. / Quadrille, by Selim.
  - Zarah.
    - **Reveler.** { Comus, by Sorcerer. / Rosette, by Beningbrough.
    - **Sister to Wouvermans.** { Rubens, by Buzzard. / Brightonia, by Gohanna.
- **Maid of Hart.** (The Provost)
  - **The Saddler.** { Waverly, by Whalebone. / Castrellina, by Castrel.
  - **Rebecca.** { Lottery, by Tramp. / Daughter of Cervantes.
- **Martha Lynn.**
  - **Mulatto.** { Catton, by Golumpus. / Desdemona, by Orville.
  - **Leda.** { Filho-da-Puta, by Haphazzard. / Treasure, by Camillus.

*Mortemer.

- **The Baron, or Nuncio.**
  - Plenipotentiary.
    - **Emilius.** { Orville, by Beningbrough. / Emily, by Stamford.
    - **Harriet.** { Pericles, by Evander. / Daughter of Selim.
  - Ally.
    - **Partisan.** { Walton, by Sir Peter. / Parasol, by Pot-8-os.
    - **Jest.** { Waxy, by Pot-8-os. / Scotia, by Delpini.
- **Comtesse.** (Eusebia)
  - Emilius.
    - **Orville.** { Beningbrough, by King Fergus. / Evelina, by Highflyer.
    - **Emily.** { Stamford, by Sir Peter. / Daughter of Whiskey.
  - Mangel Wurzel.
    - **Merlin.** { Castrel, by Buzzard. / Miss Newton, by Delpini.
    - **Morel.** { Sorcerer, by Trumpator. / Hornby Lass, by Buzzard.

Glycera.

- **Lexington.**
  - Boston.
    - Timoleon.
      - **Sir Archy.** { * Diomed, by Florizel. / * Castianira, by Rockingham.
      - **Daughter of** { * Saltram, by Eclipse. / Daughter of Symme's Wildair.
    - Sister to Tuckahoe.
      - **Ball's Florizel.** { * Diomed, by Florizel. / Daughter of * Shark.
      - **Daughter of** { * Alderman, by Pot-8-os. / Daughter of * Clockfast.
  - **Alice Carneal.**
    - *Sarpedon.
      - **Emilius** { Orville, by Beningbrough. / Emily, by Stamford.
      - **Icaria.** { The Flyer, by Van Dyke, jr. / Parma, by Dick Andrews.
    - Rowena.
      - **Sumpter.** { Sir Archy, by * Diomed. / Daughter of * Robin Redbreast.
      - **Lady Grey.** { Robin Grey, by * Royalist. / Maria, by Melzar.
- **Sister to Pryor.**
  - *Sovereign.
    - Emilius.
      - **Orville.** { Beningbrough, by King Fergus. / Evelina, by Highflyer.
      - **Emily.** { Stamford, by Sir Peter. / Daughter of Whiskey.
    - Fleur de Lis.
      - **Bourbon.** { Sorcerer, by Trumpator. / Daughter of Precipitate.
      - **Lady Rachel.** { Stamford, by Sir Peter. / Young Rachel, by Volunteer.
  - Gipsey.
    - *Glencoe.
      - **Sultan.** { Selim, by Buzzard. / Bacchante, by Williamson's Ditto.
      - **Trampoline.** { Tramp, by Dick Andrews. / Web, by Waxy.
    - **American Eclipse.** { Duroc, by *Diomed. / Miller's Damsel, by *Messenger;
    - **Young Maid of the Oaks.** { *Expedition, by Pegassus. / Old Maid of the Oaks, by *Spread Eagle.

Seventh dam, Annette (Nancy Air's dam) by *Shark: Eighth dam by Rockingham; Ninth dam by Baylor's Gallant; Tenth dam by True Whig; Eleventh dam by Regulus; Twelfth dam by Spottswood's Diamond.

MAURINE.

Never ran.

PRODUCE.

1886, Missed to *Rayon d'Or.

1887, ch. c., CANTEEN, by *Kantaka.   (Gelded)

1888, Missed to *Kantaka.

1889, ch. c.,   by *Rayon d'Or.

1890,   by *Rayon d'Or.

MISS NEILSON (IMPORTED.) Bred by Mr. R. Peck, England. Imported 1882 by Mr. W. L. Scott, Erie, Pa.
Bay mare, foaled 1878.

- **La Fille de Ma Mie**
  - **Scottish Chief**
    - **Lord of the Isles**
      - **Touchstone**
        - **Camel**
          - Whalebone. { Waxy, by Pot-8-os. / Penelope, by Trumpator. }
          - Daughter of { Selim, by Buzzard. / Maiden, by Sir Peter. }
        - **Banter**
          - Master Henry. { Orville, by Beningbrough. / Miss Sophia, by Stamford. }
          - Boadicea. { Alexander, by Eclipse. / Brunette, by Amaranthus. }
      - **Fair Helen**
        - **Pantaloon**
          - Castrel. { Buzzard, by Woodpecker. / Selim's dam, by Alexander. }
          - Idalia. { Peruvian, by Sir Peter. / Musidora, by Meteor. }
        - **Rebecca**
          - Lottery. { Tramp, by Dick Andrews. / Mandane, by Pot-8-os. }
          - Daughter of { Cervantes, by Don Quixote. / Anticipation, by Beningbrough. }
    - **The Little Known**
      - **Muley**
        - Orville. { Beningbrough, by King Fergus. / Evelina, by Highflyer. }
        - Eleanor. { Whiskey, by Saltram. / Young Giantess, by Diomed. }
      - **Lacerta**
        - Zodiac. { St. George, by Highflyer. / Abigail, by Woodpecker. }
        - Jerboa. { Gohanna, by Mercury. / Camilla, by Trentham. }
  - **Miss Ann**
    - **Bay Missy**
      - **Bay Middleton**
        - Sultan. { Selim, by Buzzard. / Bacchante, by Williamson's Ditto. }
        - Cobweb. { Phantom, by Walton. / Fillagree, by Soothsayer. }
      - **Camilla**
        - Young Phantom. { Phantom, by Walton. / Emmerline, by Waxy. }
        - Sister to Speaker. { Camillus, by Hambletonian. / Sister to Prime Minister, by Sancho. }
    - **The Baron**
      - **Irish Birdcatcher**
        - Sir Hercules. { Whalebone, by Waxy. / Peri, by Wanderer. }
        - Guiccioli. { Bob Booty, by Chanticleer. / Flight, by Escape. }
      - **Echidna**
        - Economist. { Whisker, by Waxy. / Floranthe, by Octavian. }
        - Miss Pratt. { Blacklock, by Whitelock. / Gadabout by Orville. }
- **Ma Mie**
  - **Kataplan**
    - **Pocahontas**
      - **Glencoe**
        - Sultan. { Selim, by Buzzard. / Bacchante, by Williamson's Ditto. }
        - Trampoline. { Tramp, by Dick Andrews. / Web, by Waxy. }
      - **Marpessa**
        - Muley. { Orville, by Beningbrough. / Eleanor, by Whiskey. }
        - Clare. { Marmion, by Whiskey. / Harpalice, by Gohanna. }
    - **Jerry**
      - **Smolensko**
        - Sorcerer. { Trumpator, by Conductor. / Young Giantess, by Diomed. }
        - Wowski. { Mentor, by Justice. / Maria, by Herod. }
      - **Louisa**
        - Orville. { Beningbrough, by King Fergus. / Evelina, by Highflyer. }
        - Thomasina. { Timothy, by Delpini. / Violet, by Shark. }
  - **Fanchon**
    - **Lapdog**
      - Whalebone. { Waxy, by Pot-8-os. / Penelope, by Trumpator. }
      - Daughter of { Canopus, by Gohanna. / Daughter of Y. Woodpecker. }
    - **Scuffle**
      - Partisan. { Walton, by Sir Peter. / Parasol, by Pot-8-os. }
      - Scratch. { Selim, by Buzzard. / Daughter of Haphazard. }

Seventh dam, by Precipitate; Eighth dam, Colibri by Woodpecker; Ninth dam, Camilla by Trentham; Tenth dam, Coquette by the Compton Barb.

MISS NEILSON.

At two years old started in three races in England, winning the Two-Year-Old Selling Plate at Manchester, and running unplaced in Tyro Stakes at Liverpool and Juvenile Stakes at Lewes.

PRODUCE.

1883, Missed to Coltness.

1884, Missed to Algerine.

1885, ch. c.,   by Stratford.

1886, b. f., LADY HEMPHILL, by *Rayon d'Or.

1887, Missed to *Rayon d'Or.

1888, ch. f., STRAY MISS, by Wanderer.

1889, Barren to Wanderer.

1890,   by Wanderer.

MONEY BOX.

Chestnut mare, foaled 1883. Bred by W. L. Scott, Erie, Pa.

- **Onondaga or *Rayon D'Or.**
  - **Flageolet.**
    - **Plutus.**
      - **Daughter of Trumpeter.**
        - Orlando. — Touchstone, by Camel. / Vulture, by Langar.
        - Cavatina. — Redshank, by Sandbeck. / Oxygen, by Emilius.
      - Planet. — Bay Middleton, by Sultan. / Plenary, by Emilius.
      - Alice Bray. — Venison, by Partisan. / Darkness, by Glencoe.
    - **La Favorite.**
      - **Monarque.**
        - The Baron Sting. or the Emperor. — Defense, by Whalebone. / Delight, by Reveller.
        - Poetess. — Royal Oak, by Catton. / Ada, by Whisker.
      - **Constance.**
        - Gladiator. — Partisan, by Walton. / Pauline, by Moses.
        - Lanterne. — Hercules, by Rainbow. / Elvira, by Eryx.
  - **Araucaria.**
    - **Ambrose.**
      - **Touchstone.**
        - Camel. — Whalebone, by Waxy. / Daughter of Selim.
        - Banter. — Master Henry, by Orville. / Boadicea, by Alexander.
      - **Annette.**
        - Priam. — Emilius, by Orville. / Cressida, by Whiskey.
        - Potentate's Dam. — Don Juan, by Orville. / Moll in the Wad, by Hambletonian.
    - **Pocahontas.**
      - **Glencoe.**
        - Sultan. — Selim, by Buzzard. / Bacchante, by Williamson's Ditto.
        - Trampoline. — Tramp, by Dick Andrews. / Web, by Waxy.
      - **Marpessa.**
        - Muley. — Orville, by Beningbrough. / Eleanor, by Whiskey.
        - Clare. — Marmion, by Whiskey. / Harpalice, by Gohanna.
- **Lizzie Cox.**
  - ***Glenelk.**
    - **Citadel.**
      - **Stockwell.**
        - The Baron. — Irish Birdcatcher, by Sir Hercules. / Echidna, by Economist.
        - Pocahontas. — Glencoe, by Sultan. / Marpessa, by Muley.
      - **Sortie.**
        - Melbourne. — Humphrey Clinker, by Comus. / Daughter of Cervantes.
        - Escalade. — Touchstone, by Camel. / Ghuznee, by Pantaloon.
    - ***Bapta.**
      - **Kingston.**
        - Venison. — Partisan, by Walton. / Fawn, by Smolensko.
        - Queen Anne. — Slane, by Royal Oak. / Garcia, by Octavian.
      - **Alice Lowe.**
        - Defence. — Whalebone, by Waxy. / Defiance, by Rubens.
        - Pet. — Gainsborough, by Rubens. / Daughter of Topsey Turvey.
  - **Retort.**
    - **Lever.**
      - **Lexington.**
        - Boston. — Timoleon, by Sir Archy. / Sister to Tuckahoe, by Ball's Florizel.
        - Alice Carneal. — *Sarpedon, by Emilius. / Rowena, by Sumpter.
      - **Levity.**
        - *Trustee. — Catton, by Golumpus. / Emma, by Whisker.
        - Vandal's dam. — *Trauby, by Blacklock. / Lucilla, by Trumpator.
    - **Return.**
      - **Commodore.**
        - Boston. — Timoleon, by Sir Archy. / Sister to Tuckahoe, by Ball's Florizel.
        - Rosalie Somers. — Sir Charles, by Sir Archy. / Mischief, by Virginian.
      - **Re-union.**
        - Union. — *Glencoe, by Sultan. / Giantess, by *Leviathan.
        - Gallopade, Jr. — *Glencoe, by Sultan. / Cotillion, by *Leviathan.

Seventh dam, *Gallopade, by Catton; eighth dam, Camillina, by Camillus; ninth dam, by Smolensko; tenth dam, Miss Cannon, by Orville; eleventh dam by Weathercock; twelfth dam, Cora, by Matchem; thirteenth dam by Turk; fourteenth dam by Cub; fifteenth dam by Allworthy; sixteenth dam by Starling; seventeenth dam by Bloody Buttocks; eighteenth dam by Greyhound; nineteenth dam, Brocklesby Betty, by Curwen's Bay Barb; twentieth dam, Leede's Hobby Mare, by the Lister Turk.

MONEY BOX.

Never ran.

PRODUCE.

1889, ch. c ,	by *Kantaka.
1890,	by Algerine.

MONOPOLY.

Chestnut mare, foaled 1876. Bred by A. K. Richards, Ky.

Sir Archy.
{ * Diomed, by Florizel.
{ * Castianira, by Rockingham.

Daughter of
{ * Saltram, by Eclipse.
{ Daughter of Symme's Wildair.

Ball's Florizel.
{ * Diomed, by Florizel.
{ Daughter of * Shark.

Daughter of
{ * Alderman, by Pot-8-os.
{ Daughter of * Clockfast.

Emilius.
{ Orville, by Beningbrough.
{ Emily, by Stamford.

Icaria.
{ The Flyer, by Van Dyke, jr.
{ Parma, by Dick Andrews.

Sumpter.
{ Sir Archy, by * Diomed.
{ Daughter of * Robin Redbreast.

Lady Grey.
{ Robin Grey, by * Royalist.
{ Maria, by Melzar.

Selim.
{ Buzzard, by Woodpecker.
{ Castrel's dam, by Alexander.

Bacchante.
{ Williamson's Ditto, by Sir Peter.
{ Sister to Calumel, by Mercury.

Tramp.
{ Dick Andrews, by Joe Andrews.
{ Daughter of Gohanna.

Web.
{ Waxy, by Pot-8-os.
{ Penelope, by Trumpator.

Golumpus.
{ Gohanna, by Mercury.
{ Catherine, by Woodpecker.

Lucy Grey.
{ Timothy, by Delpini.
{ Lucy, by Florizel.

Camillus.
{ Hambletonian, by King Fergus.
{ Faith, by Pacolet.

Daughter of
{ Smolensko, by Sorcerer.
{ Miss Cannon, by Orville.

Sir Hercules.
{ Whalebone, by Waxy.
{ Peri, by Wanderer.

Guiccioli.
{ Bob Booty, by Chanticleer.
{ Flight, by Escape.

Hetman Platoff.
{ Brutandorf, by Blacklock.
{ Daughter of Comus.

Waterwitch.
{ Sir Hercules, by Whalebone.
{ Mary Ann, by Waxy Pope.

Humphrey Clinker.
{ Comus, by Sorcerer.
{ Clinkerina, by Clinker.

Daughter of
{ Cervantes, by Don Quixote.
{ Daughter of Golumpus.

Muley Moloch.
{ Muley, by Orville.
{ Nancy, by Spitfire.

Sister to Righton.
{ Palmerin, by Amadis.
{ Oceana, by Cerebus.

Blacklock.
{ Whitelock, by Hambletonian.
{ Daughter of Coriander.

Manuella.
{ Dick Andrews, by Joe Andrews.
{ Mandane, by Pot-8-os.

* Trustee.
{ Catton, by Golumpus.
{ Emma, by Whisker.

Alice Carneal.
{ * Sarpedon, by Emilius.
{ Rowena, by Sumpter.

Muley.
{ Orville, by Beningbrough.
{ Eleanor, by Whiskey.

Daughter of
{ Election, by Gohanna.
{ Fair Helen, by Hambletonian.

Sir Leslie.
{ Sir William of Transport, by Sir Archy.
{ Miss Dowden, by * Buzzard.

Little Peggy.
{ Gallatin, by * Diomed.
{ Trumpetta, by Hephestion.

Intermediate ancestors (left to right columns): War Dance. Reel. Monomania. Young Utilla. Utilla. Boston. Lexington. Alice Carneal. Sister to Tuckahoe. Sarpedon. Rowena. Glencoe. Sultan. Trampoline. Gallopade. Catton. Camilline. * Knight of St. George. Irish Birdcatcher. Maltese. Melbourne, Jr. Melbourne. Clarkia. * Melrose. Hurricane. * Belshazzar. Miss Trustee. * Margrave. Too Soon.

Seventh dam, Peggy, by * Bedford; Eighth dam, * Peggy (Sister to Postmaster) by Herod; Tenth dam by Snap; Eleventh dam by Gower Stallion; Twelfth dam by Childers.

MONOPOLY.

At two years old started but twice, running unplaced in Louisville Ladies' Stake and Cincinnati Jockey Club Stakes. At three years old started twice, unplaced in each. At four years old started nine times, winning Citizens' Cup and mile heat purse at Moberly, Mo., and a mile-and-a-quarter sweepstakes at Springfield, Ills.; ran second four times and third twice. At five years old started eight times, running second three times, third once, and unplaced four times.

PRODUCE.

1883, Missed to Voltigeur.

1884, b. f., BERTHA C., by Versailles.

1885, b. f., RETTA, by Versailles.

1886, b. c., JAKE MILLER, by *Rayon d'Or.

1887, Missed to *Rayon d'Or.

1888, b. f., EXCLUSION, by *Rayon d'Or.

1889, ch. c.,   by *Rayon d'Or.

1890,   by *Kantaka.

NANNIE H.

Chestnut mare, foaled 1874. Bred by W. F. Harper, Ky.

- **Sally Watson.**
  - *** Glen Athol.**
    - **Blair Athol.**
      - **Stockweil.**
        - **The Baron.**
          - Irish Bird-catcher. { Sir Hercules, by Whalebone. / Guiccioli, by Bob Booty.
          - Echidna. { Economist, by Whisker. / Miss Pratt, by Blacklock.
        - **Pocahontas.**
          - * Glencoe. { Sultan, by Selim. / Trampoline, by Tramp.
          - Marpessa. { Muley, by Orville. / Clare, by Marmion.
      - **Blink Bonny.**
        - **Melbourne.**
          - Humphrey Clinker. { Comus, by Sorcerer. / Clinkerina, by Clinker.
          - Daughter of { Cervantes, by Don Quixote. / Daughter of Golumpus.
        - **Queen Mary.**
          - Gladiator. { Partizan, by Walton. / Pauline, by Moses.
          - Daughter of { Plenipotentiary, by Emilius. / Myrrha, by Whalebone.
    - **Greta.**
      - **Voltigeur.**
        - **Voltaire.**
          - Blacklock. { Whitelock, by Humbletonian / Daughter of Coriander.
          - Daughter of { Phantom, by Walton. / Daughter of Overton.
        - **Martha Lynn.**
          - Mulatto. { Catton, by Golumpus. / Desdemona, by Orville.
          - Leda. { Filho-da-Puta, by Haphazard. / Treasure, by Camillus.
      - **Mountain Flower.**
        - **Ithurial.**
          - Touchstone. { Camel, by Whalebone. / Banter, by Master Henry.
          - Verbena. { Velocipede, by Blacklock. / Rosalba, by Milo.
        - **Heather Bell.**
          - Bay Middleton { Sultan, by Selim. / Cobweb, by Phantom.
          - Maid of Lune. { Whisker, by Waxy. / Gibside Fairy, by Hermes.
  - **Ringgold.**
    - **Boston.**
      - **Timoleon.**
        - Sir Archy. { * Diomed, by Florizel. / * Castianira, by Rockingham.
        - Daughter of { * Saltram, by Eclipse. / Daughter of Symme's Wildair.
      - **Sister to Tuckahoe.**
        - Ball's Florizel. { * Diomed, by Florizel. / Daughter of * Shark.
        - Daughter of { * Alderman, by Pot-8-os. / Daughter of * Clockfast.
    - **Flirtilla, Jr.**
      - **Sir Archy.**
        - * Diomed. { Florizel, by King Herod. / Sister to Juno, by Spectator.
        - * Castianira. { Rockingham, by Highflyer. / Tibitha, by Trentham.
      - **Flirtilla.**
        - Sir Archy, { * Diomed, by Florizel. / * Castianira, by Rockingham.
        - Sumpter's dam. { * Robin Redbreast, by Sir Peter. / Daughter of * Obscurity.
- **Ann Watson.**
  - ***Glencoe.**
    - **Sultan.**
      - Selim. { Buzzard, by Woodpecker. / Castrel's dam, by Alexander
      - Bacchante. { Williamson's Ditto, by Sir Peter. / Sister to Calomel, by Mercury.
    - **Trampoline.**
      - Tramp. { Dick Andrews, by Joe Andrews. / Daughter of Gohanna.
      - Web. { Waxy, by Pot-8-os / Penelope, by Trumpator.
  - ***Clink.**
    - **Humphrey Clinker.**
      - Comus. { Sorcerer, by Trumpator. / Houghton Lass, by Sir Peter.
      - Clinkerina. { Clinker, by Sir Peter. / Pewet, by Tandem.
    - **Lady Newton.**
      - Oiscau. { Camillus by Humbletonian. / Daughter of Ruler.
      - Daughter of { Haphazard, by Sir Peter. / Daughter of Stamford.

Seventh dam, Alexina by King Fergus; Eighth dam, Lardella by Young Marske; Ninth dam by Cade: Tenth dam by brother to Fearnaught: Eleventh dam Miss Wyndham, by Wyndham: Twelfth dam by Belgrade Turk; Thirteenth dam, Old Scarboro mare by Makeless; Fourteenth dam by Brimmer.

NANNIE H.

As a two-year-old did not run. At three years started in seven races, won one at three-quarter mile heats, third in one, and unplaced in five. At four years old ran sixteen times, won six and was unplaced in ten. At five years old started four times, running second twice and unplaced twice.

PRODUCE.

1880, bl. f., LUCRETIA, by Virginius.

1881, br. c., SIMOON, by Algerine. (Gelded.)

1882, ch. f., RADIIA, by Algerine.

1883, b. c., BINNACLE, by Algerine.

1884, b. c., SOMERSET, by *Rayon d'Or or Algerine.

1885, ch. c. (dead), by *Kantaka or *Rayon d'Or.

1886, ch. f., MY FAVORITE, by *Rayon d'Or.

1887, Missed to *Rayon d'Or.

1888, ch. c., THE TURK, by *Kantaka. (Gelded.)

1889, ch. f.,   by *Kantaka.

1890,   by *Rayon d'Or.

NELLIE RANSOM.
Chestnut mare, foaled 1868. Bred by Gen. Harding, Ky.

Vesper Light. — Jack Malone — Bude Light.

Lexington — Sister to Tuckahoe. — Timo-leon. / Hoston. — Icon.

Sir Archy.	{ * Diomed, by Florizel. / * Castianira, by Rockingham.
Daughter of	{ * Saltram, by Eclipse. / Daughter of Symme's Wildair.
Ball's Florizel.	{ * Diomed, by Florizel. / Daughter of * Shark.
Daughter of	{ * Alderman, by Pot-8-os. / Daughter of * Clockfast.

Alice Carneal — Emilius. / Icaria.

| Emilius. | { Orville, by Beningbrough. / Emily, by Stamford. |
| Icaria. | { The Flyer, by Van Dyke, jr. / Parma, by Dick Andrews. |

*Sarpedon. — Rowena. — Sumpter. / Lady Grey.

| Sumpter. | { Sir Archy, by * Diomed. / Daughter of * Robin Redbreast. |
| Lady Grey. | { Robin Grey, by * Royalist. / Maria, by Melzar. |

Glorlana — American Eclipse — Duroc. — Miller's Damsel.

*Diomed.	{ Florizel, by Herod. / Sister to Juno, by Spectator.
Amanda.	{ Grey Diomed, by *Medley. / Daughter of Virginia Cade.
" Messenger.	{ Mambrino, by Engineer. / Daughter of Turf.
Daughter of	{ Pot-8-os, by Eclipse. / Daughter of Gimcrack.

Triffe — Sir Charles — Daughter of.

Sir Archy.	{ * Diomed, by Florizel. / * Castianira, by Rockingham.
Daughter of	{ *Citizen, by Pacolet. / Daughter of Commutation.
Cicero.	{ Sir Archy, by *Diomed. / Daughter of *Diomed.
Daughter of	{ *Bedford, by Dungannon. / Daughter of Bellair.

Childe Harold — *Sovereign — Fleur de Lis — Emilius.

Orville.	{ Beningbrough, by King Fergus. / Evelina, by Highflyer.
Emily.	{ Stamford, by Sir Peter. / Daughter of Whiskey.
Bourbon.	{ Sorcerer, by Trumpator. / Daughter of Precipitate.
Lady Rachel.	{ Stamford, by Sir Peter. / Young Rachel, by Volunteer.

Maria West — Marion — Ella Crump.

Sir Archy.	{ * Diomed, by Florizel. / * Castianira, by Rockingham.
Daughter of	{ *Citizen, by Pacolet. / Daughter of *Alderman.
* Citizen.	{ Pacolet, by Blank. / Princess, by Turk.
Daughter of	{ Huntsman, by * Mousetrap. / Daughter of Symme's Wildair.

*Gilencoe. — Sultan. — Trampoline.

Selim.	{ Buzzard, by Woodpecker. / Castrel's dam, by Alexander.
Bacchante.	{ Williamson's Ditto, by Sir Peter. / Sister to Calomel, by Mercury.
Tramp.	{ Dick Andrews, by Joe Andrews. / Daughter of Gohanna.
Web.	{ Waxy, by Pot-8-os. / Penelope, by Trumpator.

Gaslight — *Leviathen. — Pigeon.

Muley.	{ Orville, by Beningbrough. / Eleanor, by Whiskey.
The Dandy's Dam.	{ Windle, by Benningbrough. / Daughter of Anvil.
Pacolet.	{ * Citizen, by Pacolet. / Daughter of Tippoo Saib.
*Mermald.	{ Waxy, by Pot-8-os. / Mother Shipton, by Anvil.

Seventh dam, Jemima by Satellite: Eighth dam, Maria by Herod; Ninth dam, Lisette by Snap; Tenth dam, Miss Windsor by The Godolphin Arabian.

NELLIE RANSOM.

Started but once as a two-year-old, running third to McKinney and Susan Beane second. At three years old started in ten races, winning two, including the Monmouth Sequel Stakes, ran second in one, third in one, and unplaced in six. At four years old started four times, won once, second once, and third twice. Winnings, $3,650.

PRODUCE.

1877, ch. c., FERNCLIFF, by *Leamington.

1878, Missed to Frederick the Great.

1879, ch. f., THECLA, by Baden-Baden.

1880-'81-'82-'83, Barren.

1884, ch. f., by *Rayon d'Or. (Died.)

1885, Missed to *Rayon d'Or.

1886, ch. c., RANSOM, by *Rayon d'Or.

1887, Missed to *Rayon d'Or.

1888, ch. f., MISS RANSOM, by *Rayon d'Or.

1889, Barren to *Rayon d'Or.

1890,   by *Rayon d'Or.

NETTIE STERLING.

Bay mare, foaled 1868. Bred by A. J. Alexander, Ky.

Eissler (Young).

- **Lexington.**
  - **Boston.**
    - **Timoleon.**
      - **Sir Archy.**
        - *Diomed.
          - Florizel, by Herod.
          - Sister to Juno, by Spectator.
        - *Castianira.
          - Rockingham, by Highflyer.
          - Tabitha, by Trentham.
      - **Daughter of**
        - *Saltram.
          - Eclipse, by Marske.
          - Virago, by Snap.
        - Daughter of
          - Symme's Wildair, by *Fearnaught.
          - Daughter of Tyler's Driver (by *Othello.)
    - **Sister to Tuckahoe.**
      - **Ball's Florizel.**
        - *Diomed.
          - Florizel, by Herod.
          - Sister to Juno, by Spectator.
        - Daughter of
          - *Shark, by Marske.
          - Daughter of Harris' Eclipse.
      - **Daughter of**
        - *Alderman.
          - Pot-8-os, by Eclipse.
          - Lady Bolingbroke, by Squirrel.
        - Daughter of
          - *Clockfast, by Gimcrack.
          - Daughter of Symme's Wildair.
  - **Alice Carneal.**
    - ***Sarpedon.**
      - **Emilius.**
        - Orville.
          - Beningbrough, by King Fergus.
          - Evelina, by Highflyer.
        - Emily.
          - Stamford, by Sir Peter.
          - Daughter of Whiskey.
      - **Icaria.**
        - The Flyer.
          - VanDyke, Jr., by Walton.
          - Azalia, by Beningbrough.
        - Parma.
          - Dick Andrews, by Joe Andrews.
          - May, by Beningbrough.
    - **Rowena.**
      - **Sumpter.**
        - Sir Archy.
          - *Diomed, by Florizel.
          - *Castianira, by Rockingham.
        - Flirtilla's dam.
          - Robin Redbreast, by Sir Peter.
          - Daughter of *Obscurity.
      - **Lady Grey.**
        - Robin Grey.
          - *Royalist, by Saltram.
          - Belle Mariah, by Grey Diomed.
        - Maria,
          - Melzar, by *Medley.
          - Daughter of Highflyer.

Fanny Eissler.

- ***Yorkshire.**
  - **St. Nicholas.**
    - **Emilius.**
      - Orville.
        - Beningbrough, by King Fergus.
        - Evelina, by Highflyer.
      - Emily.
        - Stamford, by Sir Peter.
        - Daughter of Whiskey.
    - **Sea-mew.**
      - Scud.
        - Beningbrough, by King Fergus.
        - Eliza, by Highflyer.
      - Goosander.
        - Hambletonian, by King Fergus.
        - Rally, by Trumpator.
  - **Miss Rose.**
    - **Tramp.**
      - Dick Andrews.
        - Joe Andrews, by Eclipse.
        - Daughter of Highflyer.
      - Daughter of
        - Gohanna, by Mercury.
        - Fraxinella, by Trentham.
    - **Daughter of**
      - Sancho.
        - Don Quixote, by Eclipse.
        - Daughter of Highflyer.
      - Blacklock's dam.
        - Corlander, by Pot-8-os.
        - Wildgoose, by Highflyer.
- **Elborak.**
  - **Cripple.**
    - **Medoc.**
      - American Eclipse.
        - Duroc, by *Diomed.
        - Miller's Damsel, by *Messenger.
      - Young Maid of the Oaks.
        - *Expedition, by Pegassus.
        - Maid of the Oaks, by *Spread Eagle.
    - **Grecian Princess.**
      - Blackburn's Whip,
        - *Whip, by Saltram.
        - Speckleback, by Randolph's Celer.
      - Daughter of
        - Hampton's Paragon, by *Flimnap.
        - Moll, by *Figure.
  - **Mary Bedford.**
    - **Sumpter.**
      - Sir Archy.
        - *Diomed, by Florizel.
        - *Castianira, by Rockingham.
      - Flirtilla's dam.
        - *Robin Redbreast, by Sir Peter.
        - Daughter of *Obscurity.
    - **Daughter of**
      - Duke of Bedford.
        - *Bedford, by Dungannon.
        - Daughter of Voltaire.
      - Daughter of
        - *Speculator, by Dragon.
        - Alexander's Dare Devil Mare (*see note).

*This Dare Devil Mare was taken from Virginia to Kentucky by Stephen Bullock, Esq., and from her much good stock has descended. Her pedigree has not been reliably extended, but the Stud Book adds that she was "said to have been bred by Col. J. Hoomes, and out of *Trumpetta." If this is true, the extension of Nettie Sterling's pedigree would be: Seventh dam, *Trumpetta by Trumpator; Eighth dam, Sister to Lambinos by Highflyer; Ninth dam by Eclipse; Tenth dam, Vauxhall's dam by Young Cade; Eleventh dam by Bolton Little John; Twelfth dam, Darham's Favorite by Son or Bald Galloway; Thirteenth dam, Daffodil's dam by Sir T. Garcoine's foreign horse.

NETTIE STERLING.

Never ran.

PRODUCE.

1875, ch. f., FANNIE ELSSLER, by Lord Chesterfield.   (Trotter.)

1876, ch. f., TILLIE, by Lord Chesterfield.   (Trotter.)

1877 and 1878, not bred.

1879, b. c., HUDSON, by Baden-Baden.   (Gelded.)

1880-'81-'82-'83, Barren.

1884, Missed to *Rayon d'Or or Algerine.

1885, ch. c., by *Kantaka.   (Dead.)

1886, b. c., LOUIS D'OR, by *Rayon d'Or.

1887, b. c., STERLING, by *Rayon d'Or.

1888, b. f., CASTANET, by *Kantaka.

1889, Barren to *Rayon d'Or.

1890,   by Algerine.

NIRVANA.

Bay mare, foaled 1881. Bred by Mr. A. J. Alexander, Ky.

- **King Alfonso.**
  - ***Phaeton.**
    - **King Tom.**
      - **Harkaway.**
        - Economist { Whisker, by Waxy. / Floranthe, by Octavian. }
        - Daughter of { Nabocklish, by Rugantino, / Miss Tooley, by Teddy-the-Grinder. }
      - **Pocahontas.**
        - Glencoe. { Sultan, by Selim. / Trampoline, by Tramp. }
        - Marpessa. { Muley, by Orville. / Clare, by Marmion. }
    - **Merry Sunshine.**
      - **Storm.**
        - Touchstone. { Camel, by Whalebone. / Banter, by Master Henry. }
        - Ghuznee. { Pantaloon, by Castrel. / Languish, by Cain. }
      - **Daughter of.**
        - Falstaff. { Touchstone, by Camel. / Decoy, by Filho-da-Puta. }
        - Sister to Pompey { Emilius, by Orville. / Variation, by Bustard. }
  - **Capitola.**
    - **Vandal.**
      - ***Glencoe.**
        - Sultan. { Selim, by Buzzard. / Bacchante, by Williamson's Ditto. }
        - Trampoline. { Tramp, by Dick Andrews. / Web, by Waxy. }
      - **Alaric's Dam.**
        - *Tranby. { Blacklock, by Whitelock. / Daughter of Orville. }
        - Lucilla. { Trumpator, by Sir Solomon. / Lucy, by Orphan. }
    - **Daughter of.**
      - ***Margrave.**
        - Muley. { Orville, by Beningbrough. / Eleanor, by Whiskey. }
        - Chatham's Dam. { Election, by Gohanna. / Fair Helen, by Hambletonian. }
      - **Mistletoe.**
        - Cherokee. { Sir Archy, by *Diomed. / Roxana, by Hephestion. }
        - Black-Eyed Susan. { Tiger, by Blackburn's Whip. / Daughter of Albert. }
- **Margie Hunter.**
  - ***Australian.**
    - **West Australian.**
      - **Melbourne.**
        - Humphrey Clinker. { Comus, by Sorcerer. / Clinkerina, by Clinker. }
        - Daughter of { Cervantes, by Don Quixote. / Daughter of Golumpus. }
      - **Mowerina.**
        - Touchstone. { Camel, by Whalebone. / Banter, by Master Henry. }
        - Emma. { Whisker, by Waxy. / Gibside Fairy, by Hermes. }
    - **Emilia.**
      - **Young Emilius.**
        - Emilius. { Orville, by Beningbrough. / Emily, by Stamford. }
        - Shoveler. { Scud, by Beningbrough. / Goosander, by Hambletonian. }
      - **Persian.**
        - Whisker. { Waxy, by Pot-8-os. / Penelope, by Trumpator. }
        - Variety. { Selim or Soothsayer, / Sprite, by Bobtail. }
  - **Heads I Say.**
    - ***Heads or Tails.**
      - ***Glencoe.**
        - Selim. { Buzzard, by Woodpecker. / Castrel's dam, by Alexander. }
        - Bacchante. { Williamson's Ditto, by Sir Peter. / Sister to Calomel, by Mercury. }
      - **Trampoline.**
        - Tramp. { Dick Andrews, by Joe Andrews. / Daughter of Gohanna. }
        - Web. { Waxy, by Pot-8-os. / Penelope, by Trumpator. }
    - **Active.**
      - **Lottery.**
        - Tramp. { Dick Andrews, by Joe Andrews. / Daughter of Gohanna. }
        - Mandane. { Pot-8-os, by Eclipse. / Young Camilla, by Woodpecker. }
      - Partisan. { Walton, by Sir Peter. / Parasol, by Pot-8-os. }
      - Eleanor. { Whiskey, by Saltram. / Young Giantess, by Diomed. }

Seventh dam, Giantess by Matchem; Eighth dam, Molly Longlegs by Babraham; Ninth dam by Cole's Fox Hunter; Tenth dam (Sister to Cato) by Partner; Eleventh dam (Sister to Roxana) by Bald Galloway; Twelfth dam (Sister to Chaunter) by Akaster Turk; Thirteenth dam by Leede's Arabian; Fourteenth dam by Spanker.

NIRVANA.

Ran only as a two-year-old, and started four times, running third at Latonia in the Clipsetta Stakes to Eva S. and Mona, beating Encore, Hanap and two others ; in the Spinaway Stakes at Saratoga, ran unplaced to Tolu, ten starters; same place in six-furlong purse was unplaced to Brad, eleven starters; same place in Misses' Stakes ran unplaced to Tolu, ten starters.

PRODUCE.

1886, Missed to *Rayon d'Or.

1887, Missed to *Kantaka.

18-8, Slipped foal December, 1887, by Wanderer and *Kantaka.

1889, ch. c.,   by *Kantaka.

1890,   by *Kantaka.

NUMA. Bay mare, foaled 1881. Bred by Rufus Lisle, Kentucky.

Longfellow.

- **Leamington.**
  - **Faugh-a-Ballagh.**
    - **Sir Hercules.**
      - Whalebone. { Waxy, by Pot-8-os. / Penelope, by Trumpator.
      - Peri. { Wanderer, by Gohanna. / Thalestris, by Alexander.
    - **Guiccioli.**
      - Bob Booty. { Chanticleer, by Woodpecker. / Ierne, by Bagot.
      - Flight. { 1. Escape, by Commodore. / Young Heroine, by Bagot.
  - **Daughter of** (Pantaloon — Daphne.)
    - **Pantaloon.**
      - Castrel. { Buzzard, by Woodpecker. / Selim's dam, by Alexander.
      - Idalia. { Peruvian, by Sir Peter. / Musidora, by Meteor.
    - **Daphne.**
      - Laurel. { Blacklock, by Whitelock. / Wagtail, by Prime Minister.
      - Maid of Honor. { Champion, by Selim. / Etiquette, by Orville.
- **Nantura.**
  - **Brawner's Eclipse.**
    - **Am. Eclipse.**
      - Duroc. { *Diomed, by Florizel. / Amanda, by Grey Diomed.
      - Miller's Damsel. { Messenger, by Mambrino. / Daughter of Pot-8-os.
    - **Daughter of.**
      - Henry. { Sir Archy, by *Diomed. / Daughter of *Diomed.
      - Y. Romp. { Duroc, by *Diomed. / Romp, by Duroc.
  - **Queen Mary.**
    - **Bertrand.**
      - Sir Archy. { *Diomed, by Florizel. / Castianira, by Rockingham.
      - Eliza. { Bedford, by Dungannon. / Mambrina, by Mambrino.
    - **Lady Fortune.**
      - Brim. or Blue Beard. { *Brimmer, by Blue Beard. / Daughter of Lamplighter.
      - Woodpecker's dam. { Buzzard, by Woodpecker. / The Fawn, by Craig's Alfred.

Witchery.

- **Waverly.**
  - ***Australian.**
    - **West Australian.**
      - Melbourne. { Humphrey Clinker, by Comus. / Daughter of Cervantes.
      - Mowerina. { Touchstone, by Camel. / Emma, by Whisker.
    - **Emilia.**
      - Young Emilius. { Emilius, by Orville. / Shoveler, by Scud.
      - Persian. { Whisker, by Waxy. / Variety, by Selim.
  - ***Vicity Jopson.**
    - **Weatherbit.**
      - Sheet Anchor. { Lottery, by Tramp. / Morgiana, by Muley.
      - Miss Letty. { Priam, by Emilius, / Daughter of Orville.
    - **Cestrea.**
      - Faugh-a-Ballagh. { Sir Hercules, by Whalebone. / Guiccioli, by Bob Booty.
      - Daughter of. { Liverpool, by Tramp. / Rachel, by Muley.
- **Danger's dam.**
  - **War Dance.**
    - **Lexington.**
      - Boston. { Timoleon, by Sir Archy. / Sis. to Tuckahoe, by Ball's Florizel.
      - Alice Carneal. { *Sarpedon, by Emilius. / Rowena, by Sumpter.
    - **Reel.**
      - *Glencoe. { Sultan, by Selim. / Trampoline, by Tramp.
      - *Gallopade. { Catton, by Golumpus. / Camillina, by Camillus.
  - **Daughter of.**
    - **Ma bonnet.**
      - *Sovereign. { Emilius, by Orville. / Fleur de Lis, by Bourbon.
      - Flight. { *Leviathan, by Muley. / Charlotte Hamilton, by Sir Charles.
    - **Fay.**
      - *Yorkshire. { St. Nicholas, by Emilius. / Miss Rose, by Tramp.
      - *Fury. { *Priam, by Emilius. / Sister to Ainderley, by Velocipede.

Seventh dam, Kate, by Catton; eighth dam, Miss Garforth, by Walton; ninth dam by Hyacinthus; tenth dam, Zora, by Delpini; eleventh dam, Flora, by King Fergus; twelfth dam, Atalanta, by Matchem; thirteenth dam, Lass of the Mill, by Oroonoko; fourteenth dam by Old Traveler; fifteenth dam, Miss Makeless, by Young (greyhound); sixteenth dam by Old Partner; seventeenth dam by Woodcock; eighteenth dam by Croft's Bay Barb; nineteenth dam by Makeless; twentieth dam by Brimmer; twenty-first dam by Dickey Pierson.

NUMA.

Never ran.

PRODUCE.

1889, Barren to *Kantaka.

1890,   by *Kantaka.

POMONA. Roan mare, foaled 1884. Bred by W. L. Scott, Erie, Pa.

- **Ten Broeck.**
  - ***Phaeton.**
    - **King Tom.**
      - **Hark-away.**
        - Economist. { Whisker, by Waxy. / Floranthe, by Octavian.
        - Fanny Dawson. { Nabocklish, by Rugantino. / Miss Tooley, by Teddy the Grinder.
      - **Poca-hontas.**
        - Glencoe. { Sultan, by Selim. / Trampoline, by Tramp.
        - Marpessa. { Muley, by Orville. / Clare, by Marmion.
    - **Merry Sun-shine.**
      - **Storm.**
        - Touchstone. { Camel, by Whalebone. / Banter, by Master Henry.
        - Ghuznee. { Pantaloon, by Castrel. / Languish, by Cain.
      - **Daughter of**
        - Falstaff. { Touchstone, by Camel. / Decoy, by Filho-da-Puta.
        - Sister to Pompey. { Emilius, by Orville. / Variation, by Bustard.
  - **Fanny Holton.**
    - **Lexington.**
      - **Boston.**
        - Timoleon. { Sir Archy, by *Diomed. / Daughter of *Saltram.
        - Sis. to Tuckahoe. { Ball's Florizel, by *Diomed. / Daughter of *Alderman.
      - **Alice Carneal.**
        - Sarpedon. { Emilius, by Orville. / Icaria, by The Flyer.
        - Rowena. { Sumpter, by Sir Archy. / Lady Grey, by Robin Grey.
    - **Naturna.**
      - **Brawner's Eclipse.**
        - Am. Eclipse. { Duroc, by *Diomed. / Miller's Damsel, by *Messenger.
        - Daughter of { Henry, by Sir Archy. / Young Romp, by Duroc.
      - **Queen Mary.**
        - Bertrand. { Sir Archy, by *Diomed. / Eliza, by Bedford.
        - Lady Fortune. { Brimmer, or Blue Beard. / Woodpecker's dam, by *Buzzard.
- **Fannie Moore.**
  - **Lightning.**
    - **Lexington.**
      - **Boston.**
        - Timoleon. { Sir Archy, by.*Diomed / Daughter of *Saltram.
        - Sis. to Tuckahoe. { Ball's Florizel, by *Diomed. / Daughter of *Alderman.
      - **Alice Carneal.**
        - Sarpedon. { Emilius, by Orville. / Icaria, by The Flyer.
        - Rowena. { Sumpter, by Sir Archy. / Lady Grey, by Robin Grey.
    - **Blue Bonnet.**
      - ***Hedg-ford.**
        - Filho-du-Putn. { Haphazard, by Sir Peter. / Mrs. Barnet, by Waxy.
        - Miss Cragie. { Orville, by Beningbrough. / Marchioness, by Lurcher.
      - **Grey Fanny.**
        - Bertrand. { Sir Archy, by *Diomed. / Eliza, by *Bedford.
        - Daughter of { *Buzzard, by Woodpecker. / Arminda, by *Medley.
  - **Lady Sovereign.**
    - ***Sovereign.**
      - **Emilius.**
        - Orville. { Beningbrough, by King Fergus. / Evelina, by Highflyer.
        - Emily. { Stamford, by Sir Peter. / Daughter of Whiskey.
      - **Fleur-de-lis.**
        - Bourbon. { Sorcerer, by Trumpator. / Daughter of Precipitate.
        - Lady Rachel. { Stamford, by Sir Peter. / Young Rachel, by Volunteer.
    - **Crops.**
      - **Meteor.**
        - Am. Eclipse. { Duroc, by *Diomed. / Miller's Damsel, by *Messenger.
        - Young Maid of the Oaks. { *Expedition, by Pegasus. / Old Maid of the Oaks, by *Spread Ea-[gle].
      - **Daughter of**
        - Thornton's Rat-tler. { Sir Archy, by *Diomed. / Sumpter's dam, by *Robin Redbreast.
        - Daughter of { *Spread Eagle, by Volunteer. / Daughter of Boxer.

Seventh dam, Rose of Sharon, by *Pantaloon; eighth dam, Queen of Diamonds, by Meade's Celer; ninth dam, Philadelphia, by Meade's Pilgrim; tenth dam by Lee's Mare Anthony; eleventh dam by Silvereye; twelfth dam by *Jolly Roger; thirteenth dam by *Monkey; fourteenth dam by *Childers.

POMONA.

At two years old started three times, running unplaced each time. At three years old started twenty-one times, winning a purse at Saratoga, second to Joe Cotton in the Welter Stakes at Saratoga, second in a purse, third to Firenzi in the Hunter Stakes, third in a purse, and unplaced sixteen times.

PRODUCE.

1889, b. f.,   by *Rayon d'Or.

1890,   by *Rayon d'Or.

PRESTO (IMPORTED).

Brown mare, foaled 1876. Bred by Mr. Carew Gibson, England. Imported by Mr. Tattersall.

- **Aslauga**
  - **Adventurer**
    - **Newminster**
      - **Touchstone**
        - Camel. { Whalebone, by Waxy. / Daughter of Selim. }
        - Banter. { Master Henry, by Orville. / Boadicea, by Alexander. }
      - **Beeswing**
        - Dr. Syntax. { Paynator, by Trumpator. / Daughter of Beningbrough. }
        - Daughter of { Ardrossan, by John Bull. / Lady Eliza, by Whitworth. }
    - **Palma**
      - **Emilius**
        - Orville. { Beningbrough, by King Fergus. / Evelina, by Highflyer. }
        - Emily. { Stamford, by Sir Peter. / Daughter of Whiskey. }
      - **Francesca**
        - Partisan. { Walton, by Sir Peter. / Parasol, by Pot-8-os. }
        - Miss Fanny's dam. { Orville, by Beningbrough. / Golden Leg's dam, by Buzzard. }
  - **Ferina**
    - **Pretender**
      - **Partisan**
        - Walton { Sir Peter, by Highflyer. / Arethusa, by Dungannon. }
        - Parasol. { Pot-8-os, by Eclipse. / Prunella, by Highflyer. }
      - **The Fawn**
        - Smolensko. { Sorcerer, by Trumpator. / Wowski, by Mentor. }
        - Jerboa. { Gohanna, by Mercury. / Camilla, by Trentham. }
    - **Partiality**
      - **Middleton**
        - Orville. { Beningbrough, by King Fergus. / Evelina, by Highflyer. }
        - Lampedosa. { Precipitate by Mercury. / Bobtail, by Eclipse. }
      - **Favorite**
        - Blucher. { Waxy, by Pot-8-os. / Pautina, by Buzzard. }
        - Scheherazede { Selim, by Buzzard. / Gipsy, by Trumpator. }
- **Sorceress**
  - **Rataplan**
    - **The Baron**
      - **Irish Birdcatcher**
        - Sir Hercules. { Whalebone, by Waxy. / Peri, by Wanderer. }
        - Guiccioli. { Bob Booty, by Chanticleer. / Flight, by Escape. }
      - **Echidna**
        - Economist. { Whisker, by Waxy. / Floranthe, by Octavian. }
        - Miss Pratt. { Blacklock, by Whitelock. / Gadabout, by Orville. }
    - **Pocahontas**
      - **Glencoe**
        - Sultan. { Selim, by Buzzard. / Bacchante, by Williamson's Ditto. }
        - Trampoline. { Tramp, by Dick Andrews. / Web, by Waxy. }
      - **Marpessa**
        - Muley. { Orville, by Beningbrough. / Eleanor, by Whiskey. }
        - Clare. { Marmion, by Whiskey. / Harpalice, by Gohanna. }
  - **Sister to Grey Momus** (Contract's dam)
    - **Sleight of Hand**
      - **Pantaloon**
        - Castrel. { Buzzard, by Woodpecker. / Selim's dam, by Alexander. }
        - Idalia. { Peruvian, by Sir Peter / Musidora, by Meteor. }
      - **Decoy**
        - Filho-da-Puta. { Haphazard, by Sir Peter. / Mrs. Barnett, by Waxy. }
        - Finesse. { Peruvian, by Sir Peter. / Violante, by John Bull. }
    - **Comus**
      - Sorcerer. { Trumpator, by Conductor. / Young Giantess, by Diomed. }
      - Houghton Lass. { Sir Peter, by Highflyer. / Alexina, by King Fergus. }
      - Cervantes. { Don Quixote, by Eclipse. / Evalina, by Highflyer. }
      - Emma. { Don Cossock, by Haphazard. / Vesta, by Delpini. }

Seventh dam, Faith by Pacolet; Eighth dam Atalanta, by Matchem; Ninth dam, Lass of the Mill by Oroonoko; Tenth dam by Traveler; Eleventh dam, Miss Makeless by son of Greyhound; Twelfth dam, Miss Doe's dam by Cottingham; Thirteenth dam, Warlock Galloway by Snake; Fourteenth dam (sister to Carlisle gelding) by Bald Galloway; Fifteenth dam (Squirrel's dam) by Carlisle Turk; Sixteenth dam by Bald Galloway; Seventeenth dam by the Byerly Turk.

PRESTO.

Started only as a two-year-old, running eight times in England, winning the Town Selling Stakes at Northampton, half a mile, beating Startle and Wellington ; same place ran second to Firefly in the Wakefield Lawn Stakes; at Wolverhampton ran second to Flyaway Dick in Wrottesley Plate, six starters ; at Liverpool ran third in the Starkie Stakes ; at Warwick ran third in the Juvenile Flying Plate, eight starters, and ran unplaced three times.

PRODUCE.

1880, br. c., PALMERSTON, by Vedette.

1881, br. f., CHANGE, by Alarm.

1882, br. f., JONGLEUSE, by Alarm.

1883, b. c., POCOMOKE, by Reform. (Gelded.)

1884, Missed to Algerine.

1885, bl. c.. DEFENSE (Satan), by *Rayon d'Or.

1886, br. c., SIN, by *Rayon d'Or.

1887, Slipped colt foal, by *Rayon d'Or.

1888, br. f., AMULET, by *Rayon d'Or.

1889, Slipped bl. f., by *Rayon d'Or.

1890,   by Wanderer.

QUARANTINE (IMPORTED).

Bay mare, foaled 1876. Bred by Mr. Blenkiron, England. Imported 1882 by Mr. W. L. Scott, Erie, Pa.

- **Kinderpest**
  - **Victorious**
    - **Newminster**
      - **Touchstone**
        - **Camel**
          - Whalebone.
            - Waxy, by Pot-8-os.
            - Penelope, by Trumpator.
          - Daughter of
            - Selim, by Buzzard.
            - Maiden, by Sir Peter.
        - **Banter**
          - Master Henry.
            - Orville, by Beningbrough.
            - Miss Sophia, by Stamford.
          - Boadicea.
            - Alexander, by Eclipse.
            - Brunette, by Amaranthus.
      - **Beeswing**
        - **Doctor Syntax**
          - Paynator.
            - Trumpator, by Conductor.
            - Daughter of Marc Anthony.
          - Daughter of
            - Beningbrough, by King Fergus.
            - Jennie Mole, by Carbuncle.
        - **The Lame Mare**
          - Ardrossan.
            - John Bull, by Fortitude.
            - Miss Whip, by Volunteer.
          - Lady Eliza.
            - Whitworth, by Agonistes.
            - Daughter of Spadille.
    - **Daughter of**
      - **Jeremy Diddler**
        - **Jerry**
          - Smolensko.
            - Sorcerer, by Trumpator.
            - Wowski, by Mentor.
          - Louisa.
            - Orville, by Beningbrough.
            - Thomasina, by Timothy.
        - **Marpessa**
          - Muley.
            - Orville, by Beningbrough.
            - Eleanor, by Whiskey.
          - Clare.
            - Marmion, by Whiskey.
            - Harpalice, by Gohanna.
      - **Daughter of**
        - **Voltaire**
          - Blacklock.
            - Whitelock, by Hambletonian.
            - Daughter of Coriander.
          - Daughter of
            - Phantom, by Walton.
            - Daughter of Overton.
        - **Lightning's dam**
          - Blucher.
            - Waxy, by Pot-8-os.
            - Paulina, by Buzzard.
          - Opal.
            - Sir Peter, by Highflyer.
            - Olivia, by Justice.
- **Adine**
  - **Alarm**
    - **Venison**
      - **Partisan**
        - Walton.
          - Sir Peter, by Highflyer.
          - Arethusa, by Dungannon.
        - Parasol.
          - Pot-8-os, by Eclipse.
          - Prunella, by Highflyer.
      - **Fawn**
        - Smolensko
          - Sorcerer, by Trumpator.
          - Wowski, by Mentor.
        - Jerboah.
          - Gohanna, by Mercury.
          - Camilla, by Trentham.
    - **Southdown**
      - **Defence**
        - Whalebone.
          - Waxy, by Pot-8-os.
          - Penelope, by Trumpator.
        - Defiance.
          - Rubens, by Buzzard.
          - Little Folly, by Highland Fling.
      - **Feltona**
        - X. Y. Z.
          - Haphazard, by Sir Peter.
          - Daughter of Spadille.
        - Janetta.
          - Beningbrough, by King Fergus.
          - Daughter of Drone.
  - **Daughter of**
    - **Slane**
      - **Royal Oak**
        - Catton.
          - Golumpus, by Gohanna.
          - Lucy Grey, by Timothy.
        - Daughter of
          - Smolensko, by Sorcerer.
          - Lady Mary, by Beningbrough.
      - **Daughter of**
        - Orville.
          - Beningbrough, by King Fergus.
          - Evelina, by Highflyer.
        - Epsom Lass.
          - Sir Peter, by Highflyer.
          - Alexina, by King Fergus.
    - **Glencoe**
      - Sultan.
        - Selim, by Buzzard.
        - Bacchante, by Williamson's Ditto.
      - Trampoline.
        - Tramp, by Dick Andrews.
        - Web, by Waxy.
    - **Ales.**
      - Whalebone.
        - Waxy, by Pot-8-os.
        - Penelope, by Trumpator.
      - Hazardess.
        - Haphazard, by Sir Peter.
        - Daughter of Orville.

QUARANTINE.

At two years old started in seven races in England, running third in one and unplaced in six.   At three years old started but once and ran unplaced to Cremation in
Wickham Plate at Croydon, ten starters.

PRODUCE.

1880, b. f., (dead), by Dutch Skater.

1881, Barren.

1882, Barren.

1883, b. f., HOMEWARD BOUND, by Coltness.   (Imp. in utero.)

1884, b. c., BRIAN BORU, by Algerine.

1885, ch. f., QUOTATION, by *Rayon d'Or.

1886, ch. c.,   by *Rayon d'Or or Algerine.

1887, Missed to Wanderer.

1888, b. c., PESTILENCE, by Wanderer.

1889, b. c.,   by Algerine.

1890,   by *Rayon d'Or.

QUEEN T.

Chestnut mare, foaled 1881. Bred in Belle Meade Stud, Tenn.

- **Bryonia.**
  - ***Great Tom.**
    - **King Tom.**
      - **Harkaway.**
        - **Economist.**
          - Whisker. — { Waxy, by Pot-8-os. / Penelope, by Trumpator. }
          - Floranthe. — { Octavian, by Stripling. / Caprice, by Anvil. }
        - **Fanny Dawson.**
          - Naboklish. — { Rugantino, by Commodore. / Butterfly, by Master Bagot. }
          - Miss Tooley. — { Teddy the Grinder, by Asparagus. / Lady Jane, by Sir Peter. }
      - **Pocahontas.**
        - ***Glencoe.**
          - Sultan. — { Selim, by Buzzard. / Bacchante, by Williamson's Ditto. }
          - Trampo'ine. — { Tramp, by Dick Andrews. / Web, by Waxy. }
        - **Marpessa.**
          - Muley. — { Orville, by Beningbrough. / Eleanor, by Whiskey. }
          - Clare. — { Marmion, by Whiskey. / Harpalice, by Gohanna. }
    - **Woolcraft.**
      - **Voltigeur.**
        - **Voltaire.**
          - Blacklock. — { Whitelock, by Hambletonian. / Daughter of Coriander. }
          - Daughter of — { Phantom, by Walton. / Daughter of Overton. }
        - **Martha Lynn.**
          - Mulatto. — { Catton, by Golumpus. / Desdemona, by Orville. }
          - Leda. — { Filho-da-Puta, by Haphazard. / Treasury, by Camillus. }
      - **Daughter of**
        - **Venison.**
          - Partisan. — { Walton, by Sir Peter. / Parasol, by Pot-8-os. }
          - Fawn. — { Smolensko, by Sorcerer. / Jerboa, by Gohanna. }
        - **Wedding Day.**
          - Camel. — { Whalebone, by Waxy. / Daughter of Selim. }
          - Margellina. — { Whisker, by Waxy. / Manuella, by Dick Andrews. }
  - **Arnica.**
    - **Astoroid.**
      - **Lexington.**
        - **Boston.**
          - Timoleon. — { Sir Archy, by *Diomed. / Daughter of *Saltram. }
          - Sis. to Tuckahoe. — { Ball's Florizel, by *Diomed. / Daughter of *Alderman. }
        - **Alice Carneal.**
          - *Sarpedon. — { Emilius, by Orville. / Icaria, by The Flyer. }
          - Rowena. — { Sumpter, by Sir Archy. / Lady Grey, by Robin Grey. }
      - **Nebula.**
        - *Glencoe. — { Sultan, by Selim. / Trampoline, by Tramp. }
        - Blue Bonnet. — { *Hedgeford, by Filho-da-Puta. / Grey Fanny, by Bertrand. }
    - **Iodine.**
      - ***Sovereign.**
        - Emilius. — { Orville, by Beningbrough. / Emily, by Stamford. }
        - Fleur-de-Lis. — { Bourbon, by Sorcerer. / Lady Rachel, by Stamford. }
      - **Compromise's dam.**
        - Stockholder. — { Sir Archy, by *Diomed. / Daughter of *Citizen. }
        - Sis. to Geranium. — { Pacolet, by *Citizen. / Nell Saunders, by Wilke's Wonder. }
- **Jack Malone.**
  - **Lexington.**
    - Boston. — { Timoleon, by Sir Archy. / Sis. to Tuckahoe, by Ball's Florizel. }
    - Alice Carneal. — { *Sarpedon, by Emilius. / Rowena, by Sumpter. }
  - **Gloriana.**
    - **American Eclipse.**
      - Duroc. — { *Diomed, by Florizel. / Amanda, by Grey Diomed. }
      - Miller's Damsel. — { *Messenger, by Mambrino. / Daughter of Pot-8-os. }
    - **Trifle.**
      - Sir Charles. — { Sir Archy, by *Diomed. / Daughter of *Citizen. }
      - Daughter of — { Cicero, by Sir Archy. / Daughter of *Bedford. }

Seventh dam, Julietta, by *Dare Devil; eighth dam, Rosetta, by *Centinel; ninth dam, Diana, by Clodius; tenth dam, Sally Painter, by Evan's *Sterling; eleventh dam, *Silver, by Belzize Arabian; twelfth dam by Croft's Partner; thirteenth dam, sister to Roxana, by Bald Galloway; fourteenth dam, sister to Chaunter, by Akaster Turk; fifteenth dam by Leede's Arabian; sixteenth dam by Spanker.

QUEEN T.

Started only at two years old, running ten times, second once, third once, and unplaced eight times.

PRODUCE.

1885, Slipped foal by *Rapture.

1886, b. c., by *Uhlan.   (Died.)

1887, Barren.

1888, b. f.,	by *Uhlan.
1889, b. f.,	by *Uhlan.
1890,	by *Rayon d'Or.

QUITS. Chestnut mare, foaled 1870. Bred by Mr. John Hunter, N. Y.

Columbia.

- * Eclipse.
  - Orlando.
    - Touchstone.
      - Camel.
        - Whalebone. { Waxy, by Pot-8-os. / Penelope, by Trumpator.
        - Daughter of { Selim, by Buzzard. / Maiden, by Sir Peter.
      - Banter.
        - Master Henry. { Orville, by Beningbrough. / Miss Sophia, by Stamford.
        - Boadicea. { Alexander, by Eclipse. / Brunette, by Amaranthus.
    - Vulture.
      - Langar.
        - Selim. { Buzzard, by Woodpecker. / Castrel's dam, by Alexander.
        - Daughter of { Walton, by Sir Peter. / Young Giantess, by Diomed.
      - Kite.
        - Bustard. { Castrel, by Buzzard. / Mishap, by Shuttle.
        - Olympia. { Sir Oliver, by Sir Peter. / Scotilla, by Anvil.
  - Gaze.
    - Bay Middleton.
      - Sultan.
        - Selim. { Buzzard, by Woodpecker. / Castrel's dam, by Alexander.
        - Bacchante. { Williamson's Ditto, by Sir Peter. / Sister to Calomel, by Mercury.
      - Cobweb.
        - Phantom. { Walton, by Sir Peter. / Julia, by Whiskey.
        - Filagree. { Soothsayer, by Sorcerer. / Web, by Waxy.
    - Fly-catcher.
      - Godolphin.
        - Partisan. { Walton, by Sir Peter. / Parasol, by Pot-8-os.
        - Ridicule. { Shuttle, by Young Marske. / Daughter of Dungannon.
      - Sister to Cobweb.
        - Phantom. { Walton, by Sir Peter. / Julia, by Whiskey.
        - Filagree. { Soothsayer, by Sorcerer. / Web, by Waxy.
- * Glencoe.
  - Sultan.
    - Selim.
      - Buzzard. { Woodpecker, by Herod. / Misfortune, by Dux.
      - Castrel's dam. { Alexander, by Eclipse. / Daughter of Highflyer.
    - Bacchante.
      - Williamson's Ditto. { Sir Peter, by Highflyer. / Arethusa, by Dungannon.
      - Sister to Calomel. { Mercury, by Eclipse. / Daughter of Herod.
  - Trampoline.
    - Tramp.
      - Dick Andrews. { Joe Andrews, by Eclipse. / Daughter of Highflyer.
      - Daughter of { Gohanna, by Mercury. / Fraxinella, by Trentham.
    - Web.
      - Waxy. { Pot-8-os, by Eclipse. / Maria, by Herod.
      - Penelope. { Trumpator, by Conductor. / Prunella, by Highflyer.

Maria West. (Wagner's dam.)

- Fleur de Lis.
  - * Sovereign.
    - Emilius.
      - Orville. { Beningbrough, by King Fergus. / Evelina, by Highflyer.
      - Emily. { Stamford, by Sir Peter. / Daughter of Whiskey.
    - Fleur de Lis.
      - Bourbon. { Sorcerer, by Trumpator. / Daughter of Precipitate.
      - Lady Rachel. { Stamford, by Sir Peter. / Young Rachel, by Volunteer.
- Ella Crump.
  - Marion.
    - Sir Archy. { * Diomed, by Florizel. / * Castianira, by Rockingham.
    - Daughter of { * Citizen, by Pacolet. / Daughter of * Alderman.
  - * Citizen.
    - * Citizen. { Pacolet, by Blank. / Princess, by Turk.
    - Daughter of { Huntsman, by * Mousetrap. / Daughter of Symme's Wildair.

Seventh dam by * Fearnaught; Eighth dam by * Janus.

QUITS.

Did not run at two years old. At three years old started fourteen times, winning three, second in three, third in two, and unplaced in six. At four years old started in twenty-one races, won six, was second in seven, third in one, and unplaced in seven.

--- --- --- ---

PRODUCE.

1877, ch. f.,   by War Dance.

1878, ch. c., QUARTZ, by Limestone.

1879, ch. f., MAGGIE J., by Limestone.

1880, ch. c., FIGARO (Laredo), by *Glenlyon.

1881, b. f., LAST TAG, by *Glenlyon.

1882, ch. c., COL. SINN, by *Mortemer.

1883, ch. c., QUITO, by Duke of Magenta.

1884, ch. f., CLIO, by *Rayon d'Or.

1885, ch. c., QUIBBLER, by *Rayon d'Or. (Gelded.)

1886, ch. c., by *Rayon d'Or. (Died 1887.)

1887, Dead ch. c., by *Rayon d'Or.

1888, Sick and not bred.

1889, ch. f.,   by *Rayon d'Or.

1890,   by Wanderer.

RED GIRL. Chestnut mare, foaled 1857, Bred in McGrathiana Stud.

					Sir Archy.		{ Diomed, by Florizel. { Castianira, by Rockingham.
				Boston.	Daughter of		{ Saltram, by Eclipse. { Daughter of Symme's Wildair.
				Timoleon.	Ball's Florizel.		{ Diomed, by Florizel. { Daughter of *Shark.
			Lexington.	Robin Brown's dau.	Daughter of		{ *Alderman, by Pot-8-os. { Daughter of *Clockfast.
		Duke of Magenta.	Alice Carneal.	Sarpedon.	Emilius.		{ Orville, by Beningbrough. { Emily, by Stamford.
					Icaria.		{ The Flyer, by Van Dyke, Jr. { Parma, by Dick Andrews.
				Rowena.	Sumpter.		{ Sir Archy, by Diomed. { Flirtilla's dam, by Robin Redbreast.
					Lady Grey.		{ Robin Grey, by Royalist. { Maria, by Melzar.
			*Yorkshire.	St. Nicholas.	Emilius.		{ Orville, by Beningbrough. { Emily, by Stamford.
					Seamew.		{ Send, by Beningbrough. { Goosander, by Hambletonian.
*Malvina.		Magenta.		Miss Rose.	Tramp.		{ Dick Andrews, by Joe Andrews. { Daughter of Gohanna.
					Daughter of		{ Sancho, by Herod. { Blacklock's dam, by Coriander.
			Marian.	Glencoe.	Sultan.		{ Selim, by Buzzard. { Bacchante, by Williamson's Ditto.
					Trampoline.		{ Tramp, by Dick Andrews. { Web, by Waxy.
				Minerva Anderson.	*Luzborough.		{ Williamson's Ditto, by Sir Peter. { Daughter of Dick Andrews.
					Daughter of		{ Sir Charles, by Sir Archy. { Daughter of Bess' Brimmer.
	Scottish Chief.	Lord of the Isles.	Touchstone.	Camel.			{ Whalebone, by Waxy. { Daughter of Selim.
				Banter.			{ Master Henry, by Orville. { Boadicea, by Alexander.
			Fair Helen.	Pantaloon.			{ Castrel, by Buzzard. { Idalia, by Peruvian.
				Rebecca.			{ Lottery, by Tramp. { Daughter of Cervantes.
		Miss Ann.	The Little Known.	Muley.			{ Orville, by Beningbrough. { Eleanor, by Whiskey.
				Lacerta.			{ Zodiac, by St. George. { Jerboa, by Gohanna.
			Bay Missy.	Bay Middleton.			{ Sultan, by Selim. { Cobweb, by Phantom.
				Camilla.			{ Young Phantom, by Phantom. { Sister to Speaker, by Camillus.
Maid of the Glen.	Kingston.	Venison.	Partisan.				{ Walton, by Sir Peter. { Parasol, by Pot-8-os.
			Fawn.				{ Smolensko, by Sorcerer. { Jerboa, by Gohanna.
		Queen Anne.	Slane.				{ Royal Oak, by Catton. { Daughter of Orville.
			Garcia.				{ Octavian, by Stripling. { Daughter of Shuttle, by Catherine.
	Glencairne.	Touchstone.	Camel.				{ Whalebone, by Waxy. { Daughter of Selim.
			Banter.				{ Master Henry, by Orville. { Boadicea, by Alexander.
		Venison.	Sultan.				{ Selim, by Buzzard. { Bacchante, by Williamson's Ditto.
			Trampoline.				{ Tramp, by Dick Andrews. { Web, by Waxy.

Seventh dam, Penelope, by Trumpator; eighth dam, Prunella, by Highflyer; ninth dam, Promise, by Snap; tenth dam, Julia, by Blank; eleventh dam, Spectator's dam, by Partner; twelfth dam, Bonny Lass, by Bay Bolton; thirteenth dam, by the Darley Arabian; fourteenth dam by the Byerly Turk; fifteenth dam by Taffolet Barb; sixteenth dam by Place's White Turk; seventeenth dam, Natural Barb Mare.

RED GIRL.

At two years old started sixteen times, winning four times, second twice, third three times, and unplaced seven times. At three years old started sixteen times, winning the Keneshaw Stakes at Nashville and two purse races at Saratoga ; ran second twice, third once, and unplaced ten times. At four years old started but once, running unplaced.

PRODUCE.

1889, Barren to *Rayon d'Or.
1890,   by *Kantaka.

REEL DANCE.
Chestnut Mare foaled 1879. Bred by J. M. McClelland, Ky.

War Dance.
- **Lexington.**
  - **Boston.**
    - **Timoleon.**
      - Sir Archy. { * Diomed, by Florizel. / * Castianira, by Rockingham. }
      - Daughter of { * Saltram, by Eclipse. / Daughter of Symme's Wildair. }
    - **Sister to Tuckahoe.**
      - Ball's Florizel. { * Diomed, by Florizel. / Daughter of * Shark. }
      - Daughter of { * Alderman, by Pot-8-os. / Daughter of * Clockfast. }
  - **Alice Carneal.**
    - **Sarpedon.**
      - Emilius { Orville, by Beningbrough. / Emily, by Stamford. }
      - Icaria. { The Flyer, by Van Dyke, jr. / Purina, by Dick Andrews. }
    - **Rowena.**
      - Sumpter. { Sir Archy, by * Diomed. / Daughter of * Robin Redbreast. }
      - Lady Grey. { Robin Grey, by * Royalist. / Maria, by Melzar. }
- **Reel.**
  - *** Glencoe.**
    - **Sultan.**
      - Selim. { Buzzard, by Woodpecker. / Castrel's dam, by Alexander. }
      - Bacchante. { Williamson's Ditto, by Sir Peter. / Sister to Calomel, by Mercury. }
    - **Trampoline.**
      - Tramp. { Dick Andrews, by Joe Andrews. / Daughter of Gohanna. }
      - Web. { Waxy, by Pot-8-os. / Penelope, by Trumpator. }
  - *** Gallopade.**
    - **Cation.**
      - Golumpus. { Gohanna, by Mercury. / Catherine, by Woodpecker. }
      - Lucy Grey. { Timothy, by Delpini. / Lucy, by Florizel. }
    - **Camilline.**
      - Camillus. { Hambletonian, by King Fergus. / Faith, by Pacolet. }
      - Daughter o' { Smolensko, by Sorcerer. / Miss Cannon, by Orville. }

Blanche Rosseau.
- *** Mickey Free.**
  - **Irish Birdcatcher.**
    - **Sir Hercules.**
      - Whalebone { Waxy, by Pot-8-os. / Penelope, by Trumpator. }
      - Peri. { Wanderer, by Gohanna. / Thalestris, by Alexander. }
    - **Guiccioli.**
      - Bob Booty. { Chanticleer, by Woodpecker. / Ierne, by Bagot. }
      - Flight. { Irish Escape, by Commodore. / Young Heroine, by Bagot. }
  - **Annie (Colley).**
    - **Wanderer.**
      - Gohanna. { Mercury, by Eclipse. / Daughter of Herod. }
      - Catherine. { Woodpecker, by Herod. / Camilla, by Trentham. }
    - **Caroline.**
      - Whalebone. { Waxy, by Pot-8-os. / Penelope, by Trumpator. }
      - Marianne. { Mufti, by Damascus Arabian. / Maria, by Telemachus. }
- **Ada Tevis.**
  - *** Albion.**
    - **Cain or Octaeon.**
      - Scud. { Beningbrough, by King Fergus. / Eliza, by Highflyer. }
      - Diana. { Stamford, by Haphazard. / Daughter of Whiskey. }
    - **Panthea.**
      - Comus or Blacklock. { Whitelock, by Hambletonian. / Daughter of Coriander. }
      - Manuella. { Dick Andrews, by Joe Andrews. / Mandane, by Pot-8-os. }
  - **Daughter of**
    - *** Leviathan.**
      - Muley. { Orville, by Beningbrough. / Daughter of Whiskey. }
      - The Dandy's Dam. { Windle, by Beningbrough. / Daughter of Anvil. }
    - **Daughter of**
      - Jerry { Pacolet, by Spark. / Black Sophia, by Top Gallant. }
      - Daughter of { Sir Archy, by * Diomed. / Daughter of * Dare Devil. }

Seventh dam, Lady Bolingbroke by * Pantaloon; Eighth dam, Cades by Warmsley's King Herod; Ninth dam, Stella by * Othello; Tenth dam, * Selima by the Godolphin Arabian.

REEL DANCE.

Never ran.

PRODUCE.

1884, ch. c., TROY, by Lelaps.

1885, ch. f.,   by *Rayon d'Or.

1886, ch. f., COTILLION, by *Rayon d'Or.

1887, ch. f., MINUET, by *Rayon d'Or.

1888, ch. c., FANDANGO, by *Kantaka.   (Gelded.)

1889, ch. c. (died 1889), by *Kantaka.

1890,   by *Rayon d'Or.

REINE D'OR.
Chestnut mare, foaled 1884. Bred by W. L. Scott, Erie, Pa.

- ***Rayon D'Or.**
  - **Flageolet.**
    - **Plutus.**
      - Daughter of Trumpeter.
        - Orlando. { Touchstone, by Camel. / Vulture, by Langar.
        - Cavatina. { Redshank, by Sandbeck / Oxygen, by Emilius.
      - Daughter of —
        - Planet. { Bay Middleton, by Sultan. / Plenary, by Emilius.
        - Alice Bray. { Venison, by Partisan. / Darkness, by Glencoe.
    - **La Favorite.**
      - Monarque.
        - The Baron Sting. or the Emperor. { Defense, by Whalebone. / Delight, by Reveller.
        - Poetess. { Royal Oak, by Catton. / Ada, by Whisker.
      - Constance.
        - Gladiator. { Partisan, by Walton. / Pauline, by Moses.
        - Lanterne. { Hercules, by Rainbow. / Elvira, by Eryx.
  - **Araucaria.**
    - **Ambrose.**
      - Touchstone.
        - Camel. { Whalebone, by Waxy. / Daughter of Selim.
        - Banter. { Master Henry, by Orville. / Boadicea, by Alexander.
      - Annette.
        - Priam. { Emilius, by Orville. / Cressida, by Whiskey.
        - Potentate's Dam. { Don Juan, by Orville. / Moll in the Wad, by Hambletonian.
    - **Pocahontas.**
      - Glencoe.
        - Sultan. { Selim, by Buzzard. / Bacchante, by Williamson's Ditto.
        - Trampoline. { Tramp, by Dick Andrews. / Web, by Waxy.
      - Marpessa.
        - Muley. { Orville, by Beningbrough. / Eleanor, by Whiskey.
        - Clare. { Marmion, by Whiskey. / Harpalice, by Gohanna.
- **Lilly R.**
  - ***Glenelg.**
    - **Citadel.**
      - Stockwell.
        - The Baron. { Irish Birdcatcher, by Sir Hercules. / Echidna, by Economist.
        - Pocahontas. { Glencoe, by Sultan. / Marpessa, by Muley.
      - Sortie.
        - Melbourne. { Humphrey Clinker, by Comus. / Daughter of Cervantes.
        - Escalade. { Touchstone, by Camel. / Ghuznee, by Pantaloon.
    - ***Bapta.**
      - Kingston.
        - Venison. { Partisan, by Walton. / Fawn, by Smolensko.
        - Queen Anne. { Slane, by Royal Oak. / Garcia, by Octavian.
      - Alice Lowe.
        - Defense. { Whalebone, by Waxy. / Defiance, by Rubens.
        - Pet. { Gainsborough, by Rubens. / Daughter of Topsey Turvey.
  - **Florine or Florence (Hindoo's dam).**
    - **Lexington.**
      - Boston.
        - Timoleon. { Sir Archy, by *Diomed. / Daughter of *Saltram.
        - Sister to Tuckahoe. { Ball's Florizel, by *Diomed. / Daughter of *Alderman.
      - Alice Carneal.
        - Sarpedon. { Emilius, by Orville. / Icaria, by The Flyer.
        - Rowena. { Sumpter, by Sir Archy. / Lady Gray, by Robin Gray.
    - ***Weatherwitch.**
      - Weatherbit.
        - Sheet Anchor. { Lottery, by Tramp. / Morgiana, by Muley.
        - Miss Lettie. { Priam, by Emilius. / Miss Fanny's dam, by Orville.
      - Daughter of —
        - Birdcatcher. { Sir Hercules, by Whalebone. / Guiciolli, by Bob Booty.
        - Colocynth. { Physician, by Brutandorf. / Camelina, by Whalebone.

Seventh dam by Selim; eighth dam, Maiden, by Sir Peter; ninth dam by Phenomenon; tenth dam, Matron, by Florizel; eleventh dam, Maiden, by Matchem; twelfth dam by Squirt; thirteenth dam, Lot's dam, by Mogul; fourteenth dam, Camilla, by Bay Bolton; fifteenth dam, Old Lady, by the Pulleine Arabian; sixteenth dam by Rockwood; seventeenth dam by Bustler.

REINE D'OR.

At two years old started but once, running unplaced in the Moet and Chandon Champagne Stakes at Monmouth Park. At three years old started but twice, winning once and unplaced once.

PRODUCE.

1889, ch f.   by *Kantaka.
1890.   by Algerine.

SANTA LUCIA (IMPORTED).

Chestnut mare, foaled 1873. Bred by Mr. John Watson, England. Imported 1881, by Mr. W. Easton.

Lady Margarette.

Lord Lyou.

- Stockwell
  - The Baron
    - Irish Bird-catcher
      - Sir Hercules. { Whalebone, by Waxy. / Peri, by Wanderer.
      - Guiccioli. { Bob Booty, by Chanticleer. / Flight, by Escape.
    - Ech-idna.
      - Economist. { Whisker, by Waxy. / Floranthe, by Octavian.
      - Miss Pratt. { Blacklock, by Whitelock. / Gadabout, by Orville.
  - Pocahontas.
    - Glen-coe.
      - Sultan. { Selim, by Buzzard. / Bacchante, by Ditto.
      - Trampoline { Tramp, by Dick Andrews. / Web, by Waxy.
    - Mar-pessa.
      - Muley. { Orville, by Benningbrough. / Eleanor, by Whiskey.
      - Clare. { Marmion, by Whiskey. / Harpalice, by Gohanna.

Paradigm.

- Paragone 1843.
  - Touch-stone, 1831.
    - Camel. { Whalebone, by Waxy. / Daughter of Selim.
    - Banter. { Master Henry, by Orville. / Boadicea, by Alexander.
  - Hoyden, 1837.
    - Tomboy. { Jerry, by Smolensko. / Beeswing's dam, by Ardrossan.
    - Rochana. { Velocipede, by Blacklock. / Miss Garforth, by Walton.
- Ellen Horne.
  - Red-shank.
    - Sandbeck. { Catton, by Golumpus. / Orvilina, by Benningbrough.
    - Johanna. { Selim, by Buzzard. / Skyscraper Mare.
  - Delhi.
    - Plenipoten-tiary. { Emilius, by Orville. / Harriet, by Pericles.
    - Pawn, jr. { Waxy, by Pot-8-os. / Pawn, by Trumpator.

Honiton.

- Stockwell.
  - The Baron.
    - Irish Bird-catcher. { Sir Hercules, by Whalebone. / Guiccioli, by Bob Booty.
    - Echidna. { Economist, by Whisker. / Miss Pratt, by Blacklock.
  - Poca-hontas.
    - Glencoe. { Sultan, by Selim. / Trampoline, by Tramp.
    - Marpessa. { Muley, by Orville. / Clare, by Marmion.
- Flax.
  - Sur-plice.
    - Touchstone. { Camel, by Whalebone. / Banter, by Master Henry.
    - Crucifix. { Priam, by Emilius. / Octaviana, by Octavian.
  - Odessa.
    - Sultan. { Selim, by Buzzard. / Bacchante, by Wm's Ditto.
    - Sister to Cob-web. { Phantom, by Walton. / Filligree, by Soothsayer.

Retreat.

- Flight.
- Oriando.
  - Touch-stone.
    - Camel. { Whalebone, by Waxy. / Daughter of Selim.
    - Banter. { Master Henry, by Orville. / Boadicea, by Alexander.
  - Vul-ture.
    - Langar. { Selim, by Buzzard. / Daughter of Walton.
    - Kite. { Bustard, by Castrel. / Olympia, by Sir Oliver.
- Jereed.
  - Sultan.
    - Sultan. { Selim, by Buzzard. / Bacchante, by Wm's Ditto.
    - My Lady. { Comus, by Sorcerer. / The Colonel's dam, by Delpini.
  - Elope-ment.
    - Velocipede. { Blacklock, by Whitelock. / Daughter of Juniper.
    - Scandal. { Selim, by Buzzard. / Daughter of Haphazard.

Seventh dam, Daughter of Precipitate; Eighth dam, Daughter of Woodpecker; Colibri by Woodpecker; Ninth dam, Camilla by Trentham; Tenth dam, Coquette by the Compton Barb; Eleventh dam, sister to Regulus, by the Godolphin Arabian.

SANTA LUCIA.

As a two-year-old started in ten races; ran unplaced four times, second three times, and at Newcastle, England, won the Gibside Selling Plate, beating May Blossom, Strathcomon, and four others; at Liverpool won The Liver Stakes, beating Minsterdale and Procris; at Redcar won the Tradesman's Plate, beating Kite, Lemon and eight others.

PRODUCE.

1883, ch. f., MADELAINE, (Aureole), by Aureolus.   (Died 1887.)

1884, ch. f , AURELIA, by Algerine.

1885, ch. c., by Algerine or *Rayon d'Or.   (Died 1886.)

1886, Missed to Algerine.

1887, ch. c., TORSO, by Algerine.

1888, ch. f., MILLRACE, by Wanderer.

1889, b. c.,   by Algerine.

1890,   by *Rayon d'Or.

SCOTTISH LASS

Bay mare, sired in England, and foaled in 1883 at Algeria Stud Farm, Erie, Pa.

- **Scottish Chief.**
  - **Lord of the Isles.**
    - **Touchstone.**
      - **Camel.**
        - Whalebone. { Waxy, by Pot-8-os. / Penelope, by Trumpator.
        - Daughter of { Selim, by Buzzard. / Maiden, by Sir Peter.
      - **Banter.**
        - Master Henry. { Orville, by Beningbrough. / Miss Sophia, by Stamford.
        - Boadicea. { Alexander, by Eclipse. / Brunette, by Amaranthus.
    - **Fair Helen.**
      - **Panta-loon.**
        - Castrel. { Buzzard, by Woodpecker. / Daughter of Alexander.
        - Idalia. { Peruvian, by Sir Peter / Musidora, by Meteor.
      - **Rebecca.**
        - Lottery. { Tramp, by Dick Andrews. / Mandane, by Pot-8-os.
        - Daughter of { Cervantes, by Don Quixote. / Anticipation, by Beningbrough.
  - **Miss Ann.**
    - **The Little Known.**
      - **Muley.**
        - Orville. { Beningbrough, by King Fergus. / Evelina, by Highflyer.
        - Eleanor. { Whiskey, by Saltram. / Young Giantess, by Diomed.
      - **Lacerta.**
        - Zodiac. { St. George, by Highflyer. / Abigail, by Woodpecker.
        - Jerboa. { Gohanna, by Mercury. / Camilla, by Trentham.
    - **Bay Missy.**
      - **Bay Middle-ton.**
        - Sultan. { Selim, by Buzzard. / Bacchante, by Williamson's Ditto.
        - Cobweb. { Phantom, by Walton. / Filagree, by Soothsayer.
      - **Camilla.**
        - Young Phantom. { Phantom, by Walton. / Emmeline, by Waxy.
        - Sister to Speaker { Camillus, by Hambletonian. / Sister to Prime Minister, by Sancho.

- ***Doncaster Lass.**
  - **Doncaster.**
    - **Stockwell.**
      - **The Baron.**
        - Irish Birdcatcher. { Sir Hercules, by Whalebone. / Guiciolli, by Bob Booty.
        - Echidna. { Economist, by Whisker. / Miss Pratt, by Blacklock.
      - **Poca-hontas.**
        - Glencoe. { Sultan, by Selim. / Trampoline, by Tramp.
        - Marpessa. { Muley, by Orville. / Clare, by Marmion.
    - **Marigold.**
      - **Tedding-ton.**
        - Orlando. { Touchstone, by Camel. / Vulture, by Langar.
        - Miss Twickenham. { Rockingham, by Humphrey Clinker. / Electress, by Election.
      - **Daugh-ter of.**
        - Ratan. { Buzzard, by Blacklock. / Daughter of Picton.
        - Daughter of { Melbourne, by Humphrey Clinker. / Lizbeth, by Phantom.
  - **Our Mary Ann.**
    - **Voltigeur.**
      - **Vol-taire.**
        - Blacklock. { Whitelock, by Hambletonian. / Daughter of Coriander.
        - Daughter of { Phantom, by Walton. / Daughter of Overton.
      - **Mar-tha Lynn.**
        - Mulatto. { Catton, by Golumpus. / Desdemona, by Orville.
        - Leda. { Filho-da-Puta, by Haphazard. / Treasure, by Camillus.
    - **Garnish.**
      - **Faugh-a-Bal-lagh.**
        - Sir Hercules. { Whalebone, by Waxy. / Peri, by Wanderer.
        - Guiciolli. { Bob Booty, by Chanticleer. / Flight, by Irish Escape.
      - **Gaiety.**
        - Touchstone. { Camel, by Whalebone. / Banter, by Master Henry.
        - Cast Steel. { Whisker, by Waxy. / The Twinkle, by Walton.

Seventh dam by Orville; Eighth dam, Lisette by Hambletonian; Ninth dam, Constantia by Walnut; Tenth dam, Contessina by Young Marske; Eleventh dam, Tuberose by Herod; Twelfth dam, Grey Starling by Starling; Thirteenth dam, Coupling Polly by Bartlett's Childers; Fourteenth dam, Sister to Thunderbolt by Counsellor; Fifteenth dam by Snake; Sixteenth dam by Luggs; Seventeenth dam by Davill's Old Woodcock.

SCOTTISH LASS.

At two years old started eleven times, winning a five-eighths mile purse at Saratoga, six starters, ran second five times, third three times, and unplaced twice. At three years old started four times, running unplaced each time.

PRODUCE.

1888, b. f., NOMAD, by Wanderer.

1889, Slipped foal by Wanderer.

1890,   by Wanderer.

SHEBOYGAN.
Brown mare, foaled 1880. Bred by Mr. R. F. Johnson. Ky.

- **Virgil**
  - **Vandal**
    - ***Glencoe**
      - **Sultan**
        - Selim. { Buzzard, by Woodpecker. / Castrel's dam, by Alexander. }
        - Bacchante. { Williamson's Ditto, by Sir Peter. / Sister to Calomel, by Mercury. }
      - **Trampoline**
        - Tramp. { Dick Andrews, by Joe Andrews. / Daughter of Gohanna. }
        - Web. { Waxy, by Pot-8-os. / Penelope, by Trumpator. }
    - **Tranby Mare**
      - ***Tranby**
        - Blacklock. { Whitelock, by Hambletonian. / Daughter of Coriander. }
        - Daughter of { Orville, by Beningbrough. / Miss Grimstone, by Weasel. }
      - **Lucilla**
        - Trumpator. { Sir Solomon, by Tickle Toby. / Daughter of Hickory. }
        - Lucy. { Orphan, by Ball's Florizel. / Lady Grey, by Robin Grey. }
  - **Hymenia**
    - ***Yorkshire**
      - **St. Nicholas**
        - Emilius. { Orville, by Beningbrough. / Emily, by Stamford. }
        - Seamew. { Scud, by Beningbrough. / Goosander, by Hambletonian. }
      - **Miss Rose**
        - Tramp. { Dick Andrews, by Joe Andrews. / Daughter of Gohanna. }
        - Daughter of { Sancho, by Don Quixote. / Blacklock's dam, by Coriander. }
    - **Little Peggy**
      - **Cripple**
        - Medoc. { Am. Eclipse, by Duroc. / Young Maid of the Oaks, by *Expedition }
        - Grecian Princess. { Cook's Whip, by * Whip. / Jane Hunt, by Hampton's Paragon. }
      - **Peggy Stewart**
        - Cook's Whip. { * Whip, by Saltram. / Speckleback, by Randolph's Celer. }
        - Mary Bedford. { Duke of Bedford, by * Bedford. / Daughter of * Speculator. }
- **Millie J.**
  - **Lexington**
    - **Boston**
      - **Timoleon**
        - Sir Archy. { * Diomed, by Florizel. / * Castianira, by Rockingham. }
        - Daughter of { * Saltram, by Eclipse. / Daughter of Symme's Wildair }
      - **Sister to Tuckahoe**
        - Ball's Florizel. { * Diomed, by Florizel. / Daughter of *Shark. }
        - Daughter of { * Alderman, by Pot-8-os. / Daughter of *Clockfast. }
    - **Alice Carneal**
      - ***Sarpedon**
        - Emilius. { Orville, by Beningbrough. / Emily, by Stamford. }
        - Icaria. { The Flyer, by Van Dyke, jr. / Parma, by Dick Andrews. }
      - **Rowena**
        - Sumpter. { Sir Archy, by * Diomed. / Daughter of * Robin Redbreast }
        - Lady Grey. { Robin Grey, by * Royalist. / Maria, by Melzar. }
  - **Daughter of (Cracker's Dam)**
    - **Cripple**
      - **Medoc**
        - American Eclipse. { Duroc, by *Diomed. / Miller's Damsel, by *Messenger. }
        - Young Maid of the Oaks. { *Expedition, by Pegassus. / Maid of the Oaks, by *Spread Eagle. }
      - **Grecian Princess**
        - Blackburn's Whip. { *Whip, by Saltram. / Speckleback, by Randolph's Celer. }
        - Daughter of { Hampton's Paragon, by *Flimnap. / Moll, by *Figure. }
    - **Daughter of**
      - **Lance**
        - American Eclipse. { Duroc, by *Diomed. / Miller's Damsel, by *Messenger. }
        - Daughter of { Financier, by *Buzzard. / Empress, by *Baronet. }
      - **Daughter of**
        - Blackburn's Buzzard. { *Buzzard, by Woodpecker. / Daughter of *Speculator. }
        - Lady Gray. { Greyhound, by Stockholder / Daughter of *Spread Eagle. }

Seventh dam (Sister to Lamplighter) by *Medley; Eighth dam by *Lonsdale; Ninth dam, *Kitty Fisher by Cade; Tenth dam, Grey Mare by Somerset Arab: Eleventh dam, Bald Charlotte by Old Royal; Twelfth dam by Bethell's Castaway; Thirteenth dam by Brimmer.

SHEBOYGAN.

Never ran.

PRODUCE.

1885, Missed to *Kantaka.
1886, Missed to *Kantaka.
1887, b. c., INDEX, by *Kantaka. (Gelded.)
1888, bl. c., NUBIAN, by *Kantaka.
1889, b. f.,   '   by *Kantaka.
1890,   by *Rayon d'Or.

SPARK. Gray mare, foaled 1878. Bred by Mr. A. Welch, Pa.

Ancestor	Sire / Dam
Waxy.	Pot-8-os, by Eclipse. / Maria, by Herod.
Penelope.	Trumpator, by Conductor. / Prunella, by Highflyer.
Wanderer.	Gohanna, by Mercury. / Catherine, by Woodpecker.
Thalestris.	Alexander, by Eclipse. / Rival, by Sir Peter.
Chanticleer.	Woodpecker, by Herod. / Daughter of Eclipse.
Ierne.	Bagot, by Herod. / Daughter of Gamahoe.
Irish Escape.	Commodore, by Tug. / Daughter of Highflyer.
Young Heroine.	Bagot, by Herod. / Heroine, by Hero.
Buzzard.	Woodpecker, by Herod. / Misfortune, by Dux.
Daughter of	Alexander, by Eclipse. / Daughter of Highflyer.
Peruvian.	Sir Peter, by Highflyer. / Popinjay's Dam, by Boudrow.
Musidora.	Meteor, by Eclipse. / Maid-of-all-Work, by Highflyer.
Blacklock.	Whitelock, by Hambletonian. / Daughter of Coriander.
Wagtail.	Prime Minister, by Sancho. / Daughter of Orville.
Champion.	Selim, by Buzzard. / Podagra, by Gouty.
Etiquette.	Orville, by Beningbrough. / Boadicea, by Alexander.
Sir Archy.	* Diomed, by Florizel. / * Castianira, by Rockingham
Daughter of	* Saltram, by Eclipse. / Daughter of Symme's Wildair.
Ball's Florizel.	* Diomed, by Florizel. / Daughter of * Shark.
Daughter of	*Alderman, by Pot-8-os. / Daughter of * Clockfast.
Emilius.	Orville, by Beningbrough. / Emily, by Stamford.
Icaria.	The Flyer, by VanDyke, jr. / Parma, by Dick Andrews.
Sumpter.	Sir Archy, by * Diomed. / Daughter of * Robin Redbreast.
Lady Grey.	Robin Gray, by * Royalist. / Maria, by Melzar.
Selim.	Buzzard, by Woodpecker. / Castrel's dam, by Alexander.
Bacchante.	Williamson's Ditto, by Sir Peter. / Sister to Calomel, by Mercury.
Tramp.	Dick Andrews, by Joe Andrews. / Daughter of Gohanna.
Web.	Waxy, by Pot-8-os. / Penelope, by Trumpator.
Woodpecker.	Bertrand, by Sir Archy. / Daughter of * Buzzard.
Ophelia.	Wild Medley, by Mendoza. / Daughter of Sir Archy.
Medoc.	Am. Eclipse, by Duroc. / Young Maid of the Oaks, by * Expedition.
Miss Obstinate.	Sumpter, by Sir Archy. / Jennie Slamerkin, oy Tiger.

Intermediate ancestors in the tree: Faugh-a-Ballagh; Guiccioli; Sir Hercules; Whalebone; Peri; Bob Booty; Ierne; Flight; Castrel; Pantaloon; Idalia; Laurel; Daphne; Maid of Honor; Timoleon; Boston; Sister to Tuckahoe; * Sarpedon; Rowena; Lexington; Alice Carneal; Sultan; Trampoline; * Glencoe; Grey Eagle; Mary Morris; Eagless; Daughter of; * Leamington; Mary Clark.

Seventh dam, Paragon by * Buzzard; Eighth dam, Columbia by Columbus; Ninth dam by Hampton's Paragon; Tenth dam by * Figure; Eleventh dam, Maria Slamerkin by * Wildair; Twelfth dam,* Mare by Cub; Thirteenth dam, Amaranthus dam by Second; Fourteenth dam by Starling; Fifteenth dam by Croft's Partner; Sixteenth dam by Greyhound; Seventeenth dam, Brown Farewell by Makeless; Eighteenth dam by Brimmer; Nineteenth dam by Place's White Turk; Twentieth dam by Dodsworth; Twenty-first dam, Layon Barb mare.

SPARK.

At two years old started in twelve races, won three, was second in three, third in three and unplaced in three. At three years old started in twenty-five races, winning five, including the Hunter Stakes at Jerome Park, second in nine, third in three and unplaced in seven. At four years old started in thirteen races, won one, ran second in one, third in two, and unplaced in nine. Winnings, $7,950.

`

PRODUCE.

1884, ch. f., DAPHNE, by *Rayon d'Or.

1885, ch. f., LOUISA T., by *Rayon d'Or.

1886, ch. f., GRETCHEN, by *Rayon d'Or.

1887, Missed to *Rayon d'Or.

1888, Missed to *Kantaka.

1889, Missed to *Kantaka and *Rayon d'Or.

1890,   by Algerine.

SPRINGLET. Chestnut mare, foaled 1872. Bred by Mr. M. B. Gratz, of Kentucky.

- **Springbrook.**
  - ***Australian.**
    - **West Australian.**
      - **Melbourne.**
        - **Humphrey Clinker.**
          - Comus. { Sorcerer, by Trumpator. / Houghton Lass, by Sir Peter. }
          - Clinkerina. { Clinker, by Sir Peter. / Pewet, by Tandem. }
        - **Daughter of**
          - Cervantes. { Don Quixote, by Eclipse. / Evelina, by Highflyer. }
          - Daughter of { Golumpus, by Gohanna. / Daughter of Paynator. }
      - **Mowerina.**
        - **Touchstone.**
          - Camel. { Whalebone, by Waxy. / Daughter of Selim and Maiden. }
          - Banter. { Master Henry, by Orville. / Boadicea, by Alexander. }
        - **Emma.**
          - Whisker. { Waxy, by Pot-8-os. / Penelope, by Trumpator. }
          - Gibside Fairy. { Hermes, by Mercury. / Vicissitude, by Pipator. }
    - **Emilia**
      - **Young Emilius.**
        - **Emilius.**
          - Orville. { Beningbrough, by King Fergus. / Evelina, by Highflyer. }
          - Emily. { Stamford, by Sir Peter. / Daughter of Whiskey, by Saltram. }
        - **Shoveler.**
          - Scud. { Beningbrough, by King Fergus. / Eliza, by Highflyer. }
          - Goosander. { Hambletonian, by King Fergus. / Rally, by Trumpator. }
      - **Persian.**
        - **Whisker.**
          - Waxy. { Pot-8-os, by Eclipse. / Maria, by Herod. }
          - Penelope. { Trumpator, by Conductor. / Prunella, by Highflyer. }
        - **Variety.**
          - Selim, or Soothsayer. { Sorcerer, by Trumpator. / Golden Locks, by Delpini. }
          - Sprite. { Bobtail, by Precipitate. / Catherine by Woodpecker. }
  - **Lexington.**
    - **Boston.**
      - **Timoleon.**
        - Sir Archy. { * Diomed, by Florizel. / * Castianira, by Rockingham. }
        - Daughter of { * Saltram, by Eclipse. / Daughter of Symmes Wildair. }
      - **Sister to Tuckahoe.**
        - Ball's Florizel. { * Diomed, by Florizel. / Daughter of * Shark. }
        - Daughter of { *Alderman, by Pot-8-os, / Daughter of * Clockfast. }
    - **Alice Carneel.**
      - **Sarpedon.**
        - Emilius { Orville, by Beningbrough. / Emily, by Stamford. }
        - Icaria. { The Flyer, by VanDyke, jr. / Parma, by Dick Andrews. }
      - **Rowena.**
        - Sumpter. { Sir Archy, by * Diomed. / Flirtilla's dam, by Robin Redbreast. }
        - Lady Gray. { Robin Gray, by * Royalist. / Maria, by Melzar. }
- **Emuchfaw.**
  - **Mambrino.**
    - **American Eclipse.**
      - Duroc. { * Diomed, by Florizel. / Amanda, by Gray Diomed. }
      - Millers Damsel. { *Messenger, by Mambrino, / Daughter of Pot-8-os, by Eclipse. }
    - **Grand Duchess.**
      - Gracchus. { * Diomed, by Florizel. / Daughter of Chanticleer. }
      - * Duchess. { Grouse, by Highflyer. / Daughter of Magnet. }
  - **Diana.**
    - **Virginian.**
      - Sir Archy. { * Diomed, by Florizel. / * Castianira, by Rockingham. }
      - Meretrix. { Magog, by Chanticleer. / Narcissa, by * Shark. }
    - **Daughter of**
      - * Knowsley. { Sir Peter, by Highflyer. / Capella, by King Herod. }
      - Daughter of { * Dion, by Spadille. / Daughter of Meade's Celer, by * Janus. }

Seventh dam by Tristan Shandy.

SPRINGLET.

At two years old started but once, running second to Aniella, Ravenna third. At three years old started fourteen times, won five times, three of them at mile heats, ran second six times, and unplaced three times. At four years old started ten times, won once, was second twice, third three times, and unplaced four times. At five years old did not start, but at six years started in eighteen races, running first in six, second in five, and unplaced in seven.

———————

PRODUCE.

1880, ch. c., TUNIS, by Algerine. (Died.)

1881, ch. f., OASIS, by Algerine.

1882, ch. f., SITA, by Algerine.

1883, Missed to Algerine.

1884, Missed to *Rayon d'Or.

1885, ch. f., CANTOLET, by *Kantaka.

1886, ch. c., KOKO, (Capulet), by *Kantaka.

1887, Missed to *Rayon d'Or.

1888, ch. c., CASCADE, by *Kantaka. (Gelded.)

1889, ch. f.,   by *Kantaka.

1890,   by *Kantaka.

SWEET SONGSTRESS (IMPORTED).

Bay mare, foaled 1879. Bred by Mr. Carew Gibson, England. Imported 1881, by Wm. Easton.

- **Melodious.**
  - **Forester or Peppermint.**
    - **Doncaster.**
      - **Stockwell.**
        - **The Baron**
          - Irish Birdcatcher
            - **Sir Hercules.** { Whalebone, by Waxy. / Peri, by Wanderer.
            - **Guiccioli.** { Bob Booty, by Chanticleer. / Flight, by Escape.
          - **Echidna**
            - **Economist.** { Whisker, by Waxy. / Floranthe, by Octavian.
            - **Miss Pratt.** { Blacklock, by Whitelock. / Gadabout, by Orville.
        - **Pocahontas.**
          - **Glencoe**
            - **Sultan.** { Selim, by Buzzard. / Bacchante, by Williamson's Ditto.
            - **Trampoline.** { Tramp, by Dick Andrews. / Web, by Waxy.
          - **Marpessa**
            - **Muley.** { Orville, by Beningbrough. / Eleanor, by Whiskey.
            - **Clare.** { Marmion, by Whiskey. / Harpalice, by Gohanna.
      - **Marigold.**
        - **Teddington.**
          - **Orlando**
            - **Touchstone.** { Camel, by Whalebone. / Banter, by Master Henry.
            - **Vulture.** { Langar, by Selim. / Kite, by Bustard.
          - **Miss Twickenham**
            - **Rockingham.** { Humphrey Clinker, by Comus. / Medora, by Swordsman.
            - **Electress.** { Election, by Gohanna. / Daughter of Stamford.
        - **Daughter of**
          - **Ratan**
            - **Buzzard.** { Blacklock, by Whitelock. / Miss Newton, by Delpini.
            - **Daughter of** { Picton, by Smolensko. / Daughter of Selim.
          - **Daughter of**
            - **Melbourne.** { Humphrey Clinker, by Comus. / Daughter of Cervantes.
            - **Lizbeth.** { Phantom, by Walton. / Elizabeth, by Rainbow.
  - **Pantalonade.**
    - **Sweetmeal.**
      - **Gladiator**
        - **Partisan.** { Walton, by Sir Peter. / Parasol, by Pot-8-os.
        - **Pauline.** { Moses, by Seymour. / Quadrille, by Selim.
      - **Lollypop**
        - **Starch or Voltaire.** { Blacklock, by Whitelock. / Daughter of Phantom.
        - **Belinda.** { Blacklock, by Whitelock. / Wagtail, by Prime Minister.
    - **Daughter of**
      - **Pantaloon**
        - **Castrel.** { Buzzard, by Woodpecker. / Selim's dam, by Alexander.
        - **Idalia.** { Peruvian, by Sir Peter. / Musidora, by Meteor.
      - **Festival**
        - **Camel.** { Whalebone, by Waxy. / Daughter of Selim.
        - **Michaelmas.** { Thunderbolt, by Sorcerer. / Plover, by Sir Peter.
- **Harp.**
  - **Kremlin.**
    - **Sultan**
      - **Selim.** { Buzzard, by Woodpecker. / Castrel's dam, by Alexander.
      - **Bacchante.** { Williamson's Ditto, by Sir Peter. / Sister to Calomel, by Mercury.
    - **Francesca**
      - **Partisan.** { Walton, by Sir Peter. / Parasol, by Pot-8-os.
      - **Miss Fanny's dam.** { Orville, by Beningbrough. / Golden Leg's dam, by Buzzard.
  - **Harmony.**
    - **Reveller**
      - **Comus.** { Sorcerer, by Trumpator. / Houghton Lass, by Sir Peter.
      - **Rosette.** { Beningbrough, by King Fergus. / Rosamond, by Tandem.
    - **Daughter of**
      - **Orville.** { Beningbrough, by King Fergus. / Evelina, by Highflyer.
      - **Mirth.** { Trumpator, by Conductor. / Hoity-toity, by Highflyer.

Seventh dam by Goldfinder; Eighth dam, Lady Bolingbroke by Squirrel; Ninth dam, Cyphron by Blaze; Tenth dam, Selima by Bethel's Arabian; Eleventh dam by Graham's Champion; Twelfth dam by the Darley Arabian.

SWEET SONGSTRESS.

Never started and was never trained.

PRODUCE.

1881, Missed to Algerine.

1885, b. c., by Stratford.

1886, b. f , MARGERINE. by Algerine.

1887, b. c., OZONE, by Algerine. (Gelded.)

1888, Missed to Wanderer.

1889, Slipped twin fillies, by Wanderer.

1890, by Algerine.

SONCY LASS.

Bay mare, foaled 1886. Bred by Mr. P. Lorillard.

Partisan.	{ Walton, by Sir Peter. { Parasol, by Pot-8-os.
Pauline.	{ Moses, by Whalebone or Seymour. { Quadrille, by Selim.
Reveler.	{ Comus, by Sorcerer. { Rosette, by Beningbrough.
Sister to Wouvermans.	{ Rubens, by Buzzard. { Brightonia, by Gohanna.
The Saddler.	{ Waverly, by Whalebone. { Castrellina, by Castrel.
Rebecca.	{ Lottery, by Tramp. { Daughter of Cervantes.
Mulatto.	{ Catton, by Golumpus. { Desdemona, by Orville.
Leda.	{ Filho-da-Puta, by Haphazzard. { Treasure, by Camillus.
Emilius	{ Orville, by Beningbrough. { Emily, by Stamford.
Harriet.	{ Pericles, by Evander. { Daughter of Selim.
Partisan.	{ Walton, by Sir Peter. { Parasol, by Pot-8-os.
Jest.	{ Waxy, by Pot-8-os. { Scotia, by Delpini.
Orville.	{ Beningbrough, by King Fergus. { Evelina, by Highflyer.
Emily.	{ Stamford, by Sir Peter. { Daughter of Whiskey.
Merlin.	{ Castrel, by Buzzard. { Miss Newton, by Delpini.
Morel.	{ Sorcerer, by Trumpator. { Hornby Lass, by Buzzard.
The Baron.	{ Irish Birdcatcher, by Sir Hercules. { Echidna, by Economist.
Pocahontas.	{ Glencoe, by Sultan. { Marpessa, by Muley.
Melbourne.	{ Humphrey Clinker, by Comus. { Daughter of Cervantes.
Escalade.	{ Touchstone, by Camel. { Ghuznee, by Pantaloon.
Venison.	{ Partisan, by Walton. { Fawn, by Smolensko.
Queen Anne.	{ Slane, by Royal Oak. { Garcia, by Octavian.
Defence.	{ Whalebone, by Waxy. { Defiance, by Rubens.
Pet.	{ Gainsborough, by Rubens. { Daughter of Topsey Turvey.
Timoleon.	{ Sir Archy, by * Diomed. { Daughter of * Saltram.
Sister to Tuckahoc.	{ Ball's Florizel, by * Diomed. { Daughter of * Alderman.
* Sarpedon.	{ Emilius, by Orville. { Icaria, by The Flyer.
Rowena.	{ Sumpter, by Sir Archy. { Lady Grey, by Robin Grey.
Sultan.	{ Selim, by Buzzard. { Bacchante, by Wm's Ditto.
Trampoline.	{ Tramp, by Dick Andrews. { Web, by Waxy.
Trustee.	{ Catton, by Golumpus. { Emma, by Whisker.
Vandal's Dam.	{ Tranby, by Blacklock. { Lucilla, by Trumpator.

Right-margin note: Seventh dam, Lucy by Orphan; Eighth dam, Lady Grey by Robin Grey; Ninth dam, Maria by Melzar; Tenth dam by *Highflyer; Eleventh dam by *Fearnaught; Twelfth dam by Ariel (Brother to Partner); Thirteenth dam by *Jack of Diamonds; Fourteenth dam, Old Diamond (called Duchess) by Cullen's Arabian; (Both Jack of Diamonds and Old Diamond were imported by Gen. Spottswood, and both were by Cullen's Arabian); Fifteenth dam, Grisewood's Lady Thigh by Croft's Partner; Sixteenth dam by Greyhound; Seventeenth dam (Sophonisba's dam) by Curwen's Bay Barb; Eighteenth dam by D'Arcy's Chestnut Arabian; Nineteenth dam by Whiteshirt; Twentieth dam Montague Mare.

Left-margin lineage labels (read top to bottom): Gladiator. Fitz Gladiator. Zarah. Compiegne. Maid of Hart. The Provost. Martha Lynn. Plenipotentiary. Ally. Emilius. Mangel Wurzel. Stockwell. Sortie. Kingston. Alice Lowe. Boston. Alice Carneal. Glencoe. — Mortemer. The Baron, or Nuncio. Compiegne. Euseba. Citadel. *Glenelg. *Barta. Lexington. — Mildred. *Stamps. Bertha. Levity.

SONCY LASS.

At two years old started but once, running unplaced to Madstone at Monmouth Park. At three years old started four times, running third in the Harlem Stakes, six starters, at Jerome Park, and unplaced three times.

PRODUCE.

THREE CHEERS.

Chestnut mare, foaled 1882. Bred by P. R. Harness, Ohio.

- **Chance.**
  - **Revolver.**
    - **Revenue.**
      - *Trustee.
        - Catton.
          - Golumpus, by Gohanna.
          - Lucy Grey, by Timothy.
        - Emma.
          - Whisker, by Waxy.
          - Gibside Fairy, by Hermes.
      - Rosalie Somers.
        - Sir Charles.
          - Sir Archy, by *Diomed.
          - Daughter of *Citizen.
        - Mischief.
          - Virginian, by Sir Archy.
          - Daughter of *Bedford.
    - **Balloon.**
      - *Yorkshire.
        - St. Nicholas.
          - Emilius, by Orville.
          - Seamew, by Scud.
        - Miss Rose.
          - Tramp, by Dick Andrews.
          - Daughter of Sancho.
      - Heraldry.
        - Herald.
          - Plenipotentiary, by Emilius.
          - Delpini, by Whisker.
        - Margaret Woods.
          - *Priam, by Emilius.
          - Maria West, by Marion.
  - **Syren.**
    - **Oliver.**
      - Wagner.
        - Sir Charles.
          - Sir Archy, by *Diomed.
          - Daughter of *Citizen.
        - Maria West.
          - Marion, by Sir Archy.
          - Ella Crump, by *Citizen.
      - Flight.
        - *Leviathan.
          - Muley, by Orville.
          - Daughter of Windle.
        - Charlotte Hamilton.
          - Sir Charles, by Sir Archy.
          - Lady of the Lake, by *Sir Harry.
    - **Nebraska.**
      - *Sovereign.
        - Emilius.
          - Orville, by Beningbrough.
          - Emily, by Stamford.
        - Fleur-de-Lis.
          - Bourbon, by Sorcerer.
          - Lady Rachel, by Stamford.
      - Mary Banim's dam.
        - Stockholder.
          - Sir Archy, by *Diomed.
          - Daughter of *Citizen.
        - Rosetta.
          - Wilkes' Wonder, by *Diomed.
          - Rosy Clack, by *Saltram.

- ***Hurrah.**
  - **Newminster.**
    - Touchstone.
      - Camel.
        - Whalebone.
          - Waxy, by Pot-8-os.
          - Penelope, by Trumpator.
        - Daughter of
          - Selim, by Buzzard.
          - Maiden, by Sir Peter.
      - Banter.
        - Master Henry.
          - Orville, by Beningbrough.
          - Miss Sophia, by Stamford.
        - Boadicea.
          - Alexander, by Eclipse.
          - Brunette, by Amaranthus.
    - Beeswing.
      - Dr. Syntax.
        - Paynator.
          - Trumpator, by Conductor.
          - Daughter of Mark Anthony.
        - Daughter of
          - Beningbrough, by King Fergus.
          - Jennie Mole, by Carbuncle.
      - Daughter of
        - Ardrossan.
          - John Bull, by Fortitudes.
          - Miss Whip, by Volunteer.
        - Lady Eliza.
          - Whitworth, by Agonistes.
          - X. Y. Z.'s dam, by Spadille.
  - **Jovial.**
    - Bay Middleton.
      - Sultan.
        - Selim.
          - Buzzard, by Woodpecker.
          - Daughter of Alexander.
        - Bacchante.
          - Williamson's Ditto, by Sir Peter.
          - Sister to Calomel, by Mercury.
      - Cobweb.
        - Phantom.
          - Walton, by Sir Peter.
          - Julia, by Whiskey.
        - Filagree.
          - Soothsayer, by Sorcerer.
          - Web, by Waxy.
    - Sister to Grey Momus.
      - Conus.
        - Sorcerer.
          - Trumpator, by Conductor.
          - Young Giantess, by Diomed.
        - Houghton Lass.
          - Sir Peter, by Highflyer.
          - Alexina, by King Fergus.
      - Daughter of
        - Cervantes.
          - Don Quixote, by Eclipse.
          - Evelina, by Highflyer.
        - Emma.
          - Don Cossack, by Haphazard.
          - Vesta, by Delpini.

Seventh dam, Camilla, by Metzar; eighth dam, Jet, by Flimnap; ninth dam, Diana, by Clodius; tenth dam, Sally Painter, by *Sterling; eleventh dam, *Silver, by Belsize Arabian; twelfth dam, by Croft's Partner; thirteenth dam, sister to Roxana, by Bald Galloway; fourteenth dam, sister to Chaunter, by the Akaster Turk; fifteenth dam, by Leede's Arabian; sixteenth dam by Spanker.

THREE CHEERS.

At two years old started eight times, winning once, third twice and unplaced five times. At three years old started twenty-eight times, winning twice, second six times, third seven times, and unplaced thirteen times. At four years old started eleven times, winning a Handicap Sweepstakes at Monmouth Park, second once, third once, and unplaced eight times. At five years old started ten times, without securing a place.

PRODUCE.

1889, ch. c.,   by *Rayon d'Or.

1890,   by *Rayon d'Or.

TROMMEL. (IMPORTED.)

Brown mare, foaled 1874. Bred by W. S. Crawford. Imported by Wm. Easton.

				Final cross
Gladiator	Partisan	Walton.		{ Sir Peter, by Highflyer. / Arethusa, by Dungannon.
		Parasol.		{ Pot-8-os, by Eclipse. / Prunella, by Highflyer.
	Pauline	Moses.		{ Whalebone, or Seymour. / Daughter of Gohanna.
		Quadrille.		{ Selim, by Buzzard. / Canary Bird, by Sorcerer.
Sweetmeat	Lollypop	Blacklock.		{ Whitelock, by Hambletonian. / Daughter of Coriander.
	Starch or Val-tire	Daughter of		{ Phantom, by Walton. / Daughter of Overton.
	Belinda	Blacklock.		{ Whitelock, by Hambletonian. / Daughter of Coriander.
		Wagtail.		{ Prime Minister, by Sancho. / Daughter of Orville.
Parmesan	Verulam	Lottery	Tramp.	{ Dick Andrews, by Joe Andrews. / Daughter of Gohanna.
			Mandane.	{ Pot-8-os, by Eclipse. / Young Camilla, by Woodpecker.
		Wire	Waxy.	{ Pot-8-os, by Eclipse. / Maria, by Herod.
			Penelope.	{ Trumpator, by Conductor. / Prunella, by Highflyer.
Gruyere	Jennin	Touch-stone	Camel.	{ Whalebone, by Waxy. / Daughter of Selim.
			Banter.	{ Master Henry, by Orville. / Boadicea, by Alexander.
	Emma		Whisker.	{ Waxy, by Pot-8-os. / Penelope, by Trumpator.
			Gibside Fairy.	{ Hermes, by Mercury. / Vicissitude, by Pipator.
Rataplan	The Baron	Irish Bird-catcher	Sir Hercules.	{ Whalebone, by Waxy. / Peri, by Wanderer.
			Guiccioli.	{ Bob Booty, by Chanticleer. / Flight, by Escape.
		Ech-idna	Economist.	{ Whisker, by Waxy. / Floranthe, by Octavian.
			Miss Pratt.	{ Blacklock, by Whitelock. / Gadabout, by Orville.
	Pocahontas	Glencoe	Sultan.	{ Selim, by Buzzard. / Bacchante, by Williamson's Ditto.
			Trampoline.	{ Tramp, by Dick Andrews. / Web, by Waxy.
		Marpessa	Muley.	{ Orville, by Beningbrough. / Eleanor, by Whiskey.
			Clare.	{ Marmion, by Whiskey. / Harpalice, by Gohanna.
Rub-a-dub.	Tightfit	Teddington	Orlando	Touchstone.	{ Camel, by Whalebone. / Banter, by Master Henry.
				Vulture.	{ Langar, by Selim. / Kite, by Bustard.
		Miss Twick-ingham	Rockingham.	{ Humphrey Clinker, by Comus. / Medora, by Swordsman.
			Electress.	{ Election, by Gohanna. / Daughter of Stamford.
	Daughter of	Gladiator	Partisan.	{ Walton, by Sir Peter. / Parasol, by Pot-8-os.
			Pauline.	{ Moses, by Whalebone or Seymour. / Quadrille, by Selim.
	Daughter of		Cadland.	{ Andrew, by Orville. / Sorcery, by Sorcerer.
			Widgeon.	{ Whisker, by Waxy. / Daughter of Dick Andrews.

Seventh dam, Desdemona, by Sir Peter; eighth dam, Princess, by Eclipse; ninth dam, Heroine, by Phenomenon; tenth dam by Bosphorus; eleventh dam, sister to Grecian Princess, by W. Williams' Forester; twelfth dam by the Coalition Colt; thirteenth dam by Bustard; fourteenth dam, Lord Leigh's Charming Molly, by Second; fifteenth dam, Mr. Hangar's brown mare, by Stanyan's Arabian; sixteenth dam, Ginsey, by King William's No-Tongued Barb; seventeenth dam by Makeless; eighteenth dam, Royal Mare.

TROMMEL.

At two years old started twice in England, winning a Sweepstakes, Criterion course, at Newmarket, and ran second to Young Roscius in the Bentwick Memorial Stakes at Goodwood. At three years old started in England five times, running third to Carthusian in the Fourth Welter Handicap at Newmarket, third to Sir Hugh in the Oxfordshire Stakes at Oxford, third to Hasper in the Cleveland Handicap at Doncaster, and unplaced twice. At four years old started three times, running unplaced each time.

PRODUCE.

1881, b. f., SKATRESS, by Dutch Skater.

1882, Barren.

1883, Slipped twins by Sensation.

1884, Barren.

1885, Slipped foal by Sensation.

1886, ch. f., SASIN, by Sensation.

1887, b. f., by Sensation. (Dead.)

1888, Barren to Sensation.

1889, Barren to *Rayon d'Or and Wanderer.

1890,   by Algerine.

TWILIGHT.

Bay mare, foaled 1881. Bred by W. L. Scott, Erie, Pa.

Seventh dam, daughter of Quicksilver, son of *Medley ; eighth dam, daughter of Meade's Celer, son of *Janus.

Ella T.	Algerine.	Abd-el-Kader.	*Australian.	West Australian.	Melbourne.	{ Humphrey Clinker, by Comus. / Daughter of Cervantes.
					Mowerina.	{ Touchstone, by Camel. / Emma, by Whisker.
				Emilia.	Young Emilius.	{ Emilius, by Orville. / Shoveler, by Scud.
					Persian.	{ Whisker, by Waxy. / Variety, by Selim or Soothsayer.
			Reserve.	Berthune.	Sidi Hamet.	{ Virginian, by Sir Archy. / Lady Burton, by Sir Archy.
					Susette.	{ Aratus, by Director. / Jenny Cockracy, by Potomac.
				Alice Carneal.	*Sarpedon.	{ Emilius, by Orville. / Icaria, by The Flyer.
					Rowena.	{ Sumpter, by Sir Archy. / Lady Grey, by Robin Grey.
	Ninn (Planet's dam.)	Boston.	Timoleon.	Sir Archy.		{ *Diomed, by Florizel. / *Castianira, by Rockingham.
				Daughter of		{ *Saltram, by Eclipse. / Daughter of Symme's Wildair.
			Sister to Tuckahoe.	Ball's Florizel.		{ *Diomed, by Florizel. / Daughter of *Shark.
				Daughter of		{ *Alderman, by Pot-8-os. / Daughter of *Clockfast.
		*Frolicsome Fanny.	Lottery.	Tramp.		{ Dick Andrews, by Joe Andrews. / Daughter of Gohanna.
				Mandane.		{ Pot-8-os, by Eclipse. / Young Camilla, by Woodpecker.
			Sister to Catterick.	Whisker.		{ Waxy, by Pot-8-os. / Penelope, by Trumpator.
				Daughter of		{ Bay Trophonius, by Beningbrough. / Daughter of Slope.
Bonnie Kate.	War Dance.	Lexington.	Boston.	Timoleon.		{ Sir Archy, by *Diomed. / Daughter of *Saltram.
				Sister to Tuckahoe.		{ Ball's Florizel, by *Diomed. / Daughter of *Alderman.
			Alice Carneal.	*Sarpedon.		{ Emilius, by Orville. / Icaria, by The Flyer.
				Rowena.		{ Sumpter, by Sir Archy. / Lady Gray, by Robin Gray.
		Reel.	*Glencoe.	Sultan.		{ Selim, by Buzzard. / Bacchante, by Williamson's Ditto.
				Trampoline.		{ Tramp, by Dick Andrews. / Web, by Waxy.
			*Gallopade.	Catton.		{ Golumpus, by Gohanna. / Lucy Grey, by Timothy.
				Camillina.		{ Camillus, by Hambletonian. / Daughter of Smolensko.
	*Knight of St. George.	Irish Birdcatcher.	Sir Hercules.			{ Whalebone, by Waxy. / Peri, by Wanderer.
			Guiccioli.			{ Bob Booty, by Chanticleer. / Flight, by Escape.
		Maltese.	Hetman Platoff.			{ Brutandorf, by Blacklock. / Daughter of Comus.
			Waterwitch.			{ Sir Hercules, by Whalebone. / Mary Ann, by Waxy Pope.
Eagle.	Zenith.	American Eclipse.				{ Duroc, by *Diomed. / Miller's Damsel, by *Messenger.
		Belle Anderson.				{ Sir William of Transp't, by Sir Archy / Butterfly, by Sumpter.
	Eagletta.	Grey Eagle.				{ Woodpecker, by Bertrand. / Ophelia, by Wild Medley.
		Mary Howe.				{ Tiger, by Blackburn's Whip. / Lady Robin, by Robin Grey.

•

TWILIGHT.

Was never trained on account of severe distemper.

PRODUCE.

1885, b. f.,   by *Rayon d'Or.

1886, ch. c.,   by *Kantaka.

1887, b. c., by *Rayon d'Or.   (Dead.)

1888, b. f., by *Rayon d'Or.   (Died October, 1888.)

1889, ch. c.,   by *Rayon d'Or.

1890,   by *Rayon d'Or.

VALLERIA. Brown Mare, foaled 1878. Bred by Mr M. H. Sanford, Ky.

*Glenelg or Virgil.

- **Sire line (*Glenelg or Virgil):**
  - **Vandal.**
    - **Glencoe.**
      - **Sultan.**
        - Selim. { Buzzard, by Woodpecker. / Castrel's dam, by Alexander. }
        - Bacchante. { Williamson's Ditto, by Sir Peter. / Sister to Calomel, by Mercury. }
      - **Trampoline.**
        - Tramp. { Dick Andrews, by Joe Andrews. / Daughter of Gohanna. }
        - Web. { Waxy, by Pot-8-os. / Penelope, by Trumpator. }
    - **Tranby Mare.**
      - ***Tranby.**
        - Blacklock. { Whitelock, by Hambletonian. / Daughter of Coriander. }
        - Daughter of. { Orville, by Beningbrough. / Miss Grimstone, by Weasel. }
      - **Lucilla.**
        - Trumpator. { Sir Solomon, by Tickle Toby. / Daughter of Hickory. }
        - Lucy. { Orphan, by Ball's Florizel. / Lady Grey, by Robin Grey. }
  - **Hymenia.**
    - ***Yorkshire.**
      - **Eng. St. Nicholas.**
        - Emilius. { Orville, by Beningbrough. / Emily, by Stamford. }
        - Seamew. { Scud, by Beningbrough. / Goosander, by Hambletonian. }
      - **Miss Rose.**
        - Tramp. { Dick Andrews, by Joe Andrews. / Daughter of Gohanna. }
        - Daughter of. { Sancho, by Don Quixote. / Blacklock's dam, by Coriander. }
    - **Little Peggy.**
      - **Cripple.**
        - Medoc. { Am. Eclipse, by Duroc. / Young Maid of the Oaks, by * Expedition. }
        - Grecian Princess. { Cook's Whip by * Whip. / Jane Hunt, by Hampton's Paragon. }
      - **Peggy Stewart.**
        - Cook's Whip. { * Whip, by Saltram. / Speckleback, by Randolph's Coler. }
        - Mary Bedford. { Duke of Bedford, by * Bedford. / Daughter of * Speculator. }

- **Dam line (Stamps):**
  - **Lexington.**
    - **Boston.**
      - **Timoleon.**
        - Sir Archy. { * Diomed, by Florizel. / * Castianira, by Rockingham. }
        - Daughter of. { * Saltram, by Eclipse. / Daughter of Symme's Wildair. }
      - **Sister to Tuckahoe.**
        - Ball's Florizel. { * Diomed, by Florizel. / Daughter of * Shark. }
        - Daughter of. { * Alderman, by Pot-8-os. / Daughter of * Clockfast. }
    - **Alice Carneal.**
      - **Sarpedon.**
        - Emilius. { Orville, by Beningbrough. / Emily, by Stamford. }
        - Icaria. { The Flyer, by Van Dyke, jr. / Parma, by Dick Andrews. }
      - **Rowena.**
        - Sumpter. { Sir Archy, by * Diomed. / Daughter of * Robin Redbreast. }
        - Lady Grey. { Robin Grey, by * Royalist. / Maria, by Melzar. }
  - **Mildred.**
    - **Levity.**
      - ***Glencoe.**
        - Sultan.
          - Selim. { Buzzard, by Woodpecker. / Castrel's dam, by Alexander. }
          - Bacchante. { Williamson's Ditto, by Sir Peter. / Sister to Calomel, by Mercury. }
        - Trampoline.
          - Tramp. { Dick Andrews, by Joe Andrews. / Daughter of Gohanna. }
          - Web. { Waxy, by Pot-8-os. / Penelope, by Trumpator. }
      - ***Trustee.**
        - Catton. { Golumpus, by Gohanna. / Lucy Grey, by Timothy. }
        - Emma. { Whisker, by Waxy. / Gibside Fairy, by Hermes. }
    - **Vandal's Dam.**
      - *Tranby. { Blacklock, by Whitelock. / Daughter of Orville. }
      - Lucilla. { Trumpator, by Sir Solomon. / Lucy, by Orphan. }

Seventh dam, Lady Grey by Robin Grey; Eighth dam, Maria by Melzar; Ninth dam, Maria by Robin Grey by *Highflyer; Tenth dam by *Fearnaught; Eleventh dam by Artel; Twelfth dam by *Jack of Diamonds; Thirteenth dam *Diamond (Called Duchess) by the Cullen Arabian, (Both Jack of Diamonds and Old Diamond were imported by Gen. Spottswood, and both were by the Cullen Arabian); Fourteenth dam, Grisewood's Lady Thigh by Croft's Partner; Fifteenth dam by Grey-hound; Sixteenth dam (Sophonisba's dam) by Curwen's Bay Barb; Seventeenth dam by D'Arcy's Chestnut Arabian; Eighteenth dam by Whiteshirt; Nineteenth dam, Montague Mare.

VALLERIA.

At two years old started in nine races, winning two, second in four, and unplaced in three. At three years old started in twenty-one races, won one at one mile and 500 yards at Saratoga, beating Cinderella and Sir Walter in 2:12½ ; ran second in two, third in five and unplaced in thirteen.

— —

PRODUCE.

1883, b. c., VELVET, by Algerine. (Gelded.)

1884, b. c., by *Rayon d'Or. (Dead.)

1885, b. f., BAYLIGHT, by *Rayon d'Or.

1886, b. f., LAURA STONE, (Madonna), by *Rayon d'Or.

1887, Dead filly, by *Rayon d'Or.

1888, b. c., VERSATILE, by *Rayon d'Or.

1889, Barren to *Rayon d'Or.

1890,   by *Rayon d'Or.

VERDICT.

Chestnut mare, foaled 1876. Bred by H. P. McGrath, Kentucky.

```
Jury.
 *Leamington.
  Faugh-a-Ballagh.
   Sir Hercules.
    Whalebone.
     Waxy. ........... { Pot-8-os, by Eclipse.
                       { Maria, by Herod.
     Penelope. ....... { Trumpator, by Conductor.
                       { Prunella, by Highflyer.
    Peri.
     Wanderer. ....... { Gohanna, by Mercury.
                       { Catherine, by Woodpecker.
     Thalestris. ..... { Alexander, by Eclipse.
                       { Rival, by Sir Peter.
   Guiccioli.
    Bob Booty.
     Chanticleer. .... { Woodpecker, by Herod.
                       { Daughter of Eclipse.
     Ierne. .......... { Bagot, by Herod.
                       { Daughter of Gumahoe.
    Irish Flight.
     Irish Escape. ... { Commodore, by Tug.
                       { Daughter of Highflyer.
     Young Heroine. .. { Bagot, by Herod.
                       { Heroine, by Hero.
  Daughter of Pantaloon.
   Castrel.
    Buzzard. ......... { Woodpecker, by Herod.
                       { Misfortune, by Dux.
    Daughter of ...... { Alexander, by Eclipse.
                       { Daughter of Highflyer.
   Idalia.
    Peruvian. ........ { Sir Peter, by Highflyer.
                       { Popinjay's Dam, by Boudrow.
    Musidora. ........ { Meteor, by Eclipse.
                       { Maid-of-all-Work, by Highflyer.
   Laurel.
    Blacklock. ....... { Whitelock, by Hambletonian.
                       { Daughter of Coriander.
    Wagtail. ......... { Prime Minister, by Sancho.
                       { Daughter of Orville.
   Maid of Honor.
    Champion. ........ { Selim, by Buzzard.
                       { Podagra, by Gouty.
    Etiquette. ....... { Orville, by Beningbrough.
                       { Boadicea, by Alexander.

 Daphne.
  Lexington.
   Boston.
    Timoleon.
     Sir Archy. ...... { * Diomed, by Florizel.
                       { * Castianira, by Rockingham.
     Daughter of ..... { * Saltram, by Eclipse.
                       { Daughter of Symme's Wildair.
    Sister to Tuckahoe.
     Ball's Florizel. . { * Diomed, by Florizel.
                       { Daughter of * Shark.
     Daughter of ..... { * Alderman, by Pot-8-os.
                       { Daughter of * Clockfast.
   Alice Carneal.
    Sarpedon.
     Emilius. ........ { Orville, by Beningbrough.
                       { Emily, by Stamford.
     Icara. .......... { The Flyer, by Van Dyke, jr.
                       { Parma, by Dick Andrews.
    Rowena.
     Sumpter. ........ { Sir Archy, by * Diomed.
                       { Daughter of * Robin Redbreast.
     Lady Grey. ...... { Robin Grey, by * Royalist.
                       { Maria, by Melzar.

Roxana.
 * Chesterfield.
  * Priam.
   Emilius. .......... { Orville, by Beningbrough.
                       { Emily, by Stamford.
   Cressida. ......... { Whiskey, by Saltram.
                       { Young Giantess, by Diomed.
  Worthless.
   Walton. ........... { Sir Peter, by Highflyer.
                       { Arethusa, by Dungannon.
   Altisidora. ....... { Dick Andrews, by Joe Andrews.
                       { Mandane, by Pot-8-os.

 Levia.
  Tolevia.
   * Tranby.
    Blacklock. ....... { Whitelock, by Hambletonian
                       { Daughter of Coriander.
    Daughter of ...... { Orville, by Beningbrough.
                       { Miss Grimstone, by Weasle.
   * Contract.
    * Contract ....... { Catton, by Golumpus.
                       { Helen, by Hambletonian.
    Diamond. ......... { Turpin's Florizel.
                       { Daughter of Lewis' Eclipse.
```

Seventh dam, Minerva by Melzar; Eighth dam by Hall's Union; Ninth dam, the Kirtley mare by Madison's Milo; Tenth dam by Fearnaught.

VERDICT

At two years old started in five races, winning two, including the Ladies' Stakes at Louisville, second in two and unplaced in one. At three years old started in ten races, won one—the Vestal Stakes at Baltimore—ran third once and unplaced eight times. At four years old started four times, running second once and unplaced three times. At five years old started in three races and was unplaced in each.

PRODUCE.

1883, b. c., I. H. D., (Juryman), by Algerine.

1884, Missed to *Rayon d'Or.

1885, Missed to *Kantaka.

1886, ch. c., TIPSTAFF, by *Rayon d'Or or *Kantaka.

1887, Missed to *Rayon d'Or.

1888, Missed to *Rayon d'Or.

1889, ch. f.,   by *Kantaka.

1890,   by *Kantaka.

VESTA.

Grey mare, foaled 1883. Bred by McH. Meadar, Kentucky.

Congressman

- War Dance
  - Lexington
    - Boston
      - Timoleon { Sir Archy, by *Diomed. / Daughter of *Saltram.
      - Sister to Tuckahoe. { Ball's Florizel, by *Diomed. / Daughter of *Alderman.
    - Alice Carneal
      - *Sarpedon. { Emilius, by Orville. / Icaria, by The Flyer.
      - Rowena. { Sumpter, by Sir Archy. / Maria, by Melzar.
  - Reel
    - *Glencoe
      - Sultan. { Selim, by Buzzard. / Bacchante, by Williamson's Ditto.
      - Trampoline. { Tramp, by Dick Andrews. / Web, by Waxy.
    - Gallopade
      - Catton. { Golumpus, by Gohanna. / Lucy Grey, by Timothy.
      - Camillina. { Camillus, by Hambletonian. / Daughter of Smolensko.
- Saratoga
  - *Knight of St. George
    - Irish Birdcatcher
      - Sir Hercules. { Whalebone, by Waxy. / Peri, by Wanderer.
      - Guiccioli. { Bob Booty, by Chanticleer. / Flight, by Escape.
    - Maltese
      - Hetman Platoff. { Brutandorf, by Blacklock. / Daughter of Comus.
      - Waterwitch. { Sir Hercules, by Whalebone. / Mary Ann, by Waxy Pope.
  - Daughter of *Glencoe
    - Gipsy
      - Sultan. { Selim, by Buzzard. / Bacchante, by Williamson's Ditto.
      - Trampoline. { Tramp, by Dick Andrews, / Web, by Waxy.
    - American Eclipse { Duroc, by *Diomed. / Miller's Damsel, by *Messenger.
    - Young Maid of the Oaks. { *Expedition, by Pegassus. / Maid of the Oaks, by *Spread Eagle.

Chinchilla

- War Dance
  - Lexington
    - Boston
      - Timoleon. { Sir Archy, by *Diomed. / Daughter of *Saltram.
      - Sister to Tuckahoe. { Ball's Florizel, by *Diomed, / Daughter of *Alderman.
    - Alice Carneal
      - *Sarpedon. { Emilius, by Orville. / Icaria, by The Flyer.
      - Rowena. { Sumpter, by Sir Archy. / Lady Grey, by Robin Gray.
  - Reel
    - *Glencoe
      - Sultan. { Selim, by Buzzard. / Bacchante, by Williamson's Ditto.
      - Trampoline. { Tramp, by Dick Andrews. / Web, by Waxy.
    - *Gallopade
      - Catton. { Golumpus, by Gohanna. / Lucy Grey, by Timothy.
      - Camillina. { Camillus, by Hambletonian / Daughter of Smolensko.

Black Eyes

- *Mickey Free, 1871.
  - Irish Birdcatcher
    - Sir Hercules. { Whalebone, by Waxy. / Peri, by Wanderer.
    - Guiccioli. { Bob Booty, by Chanticleer. / Flight, by I. Escape.
  - Annie (Colly)
    - Wanderer. { Gohanna, by Mercury. / Catherine, by Woodpecker.
    - Caroline. { Whalebone, by Waxy. / Marianne, by Mufti.,
- Peggy.
  - Paddy Burns, 1843.
    - Grey Eagle, 1835. { Woodpecker, by Bertrand. / Ophelia, by Wild Medley.
    - Julia Ann. { Medoc, by Am. Eclipse. / Daughter of *Eagle.
  - Bridget, 1858.
    - Boston. { Timoleon, by Sir Archy. / Sister to Tuckahoe, by Ball's Florizel.
    - Too Soon. { Sir Leslie, by Sir William of Transport. / Little Peggy, by Gallatin.

Seventh dam, Trumpetta, by Herbestion; eighth dam, Peggy by *Bedford; ninth dam, *Peggy by Trumpator; tenth dam, Peggy by Herod; eleventh dam by Snap; twelfth dam by Gower Stallion; thirteenth dam by Childers.

VESTA.

Never ran.

.

PRODUCE.

1889, bl. c.,	by Joe S. (Trotter.)
1890,	by Algerine.

VIOLA.

Chestnut mare, foaled 1874. Bred by Mr. P. Lorillard.

- **VIOLA.**
  - ***Eclipse.**
    - **Orlando.**
      - **Touchstone.**
        - **Camel.**
          - Whalebone. { Waxy, by Pot-8-os. | Penelope, by Trumpator. }
          - Daughter of. { Selim, by Buzzard. | Maiden, by Sir Peter. }
        - **Banter.**
          - Master Henry. { Orville, by Beningbrough. | Miss Sophia, by Stamford. }
          - Boadicea. { Alexander, by Eclipse. | Brunette, by Amaranthus. }
      - **Vulture.**
        - **Langar.**
          - Selim. { Buzzard, by Woodpecker. | Castrel's dam, by Alexander. }
          - Daughter of. { Walton, by Sir Peter. | Young Giantess, by Diomed. }
        - **Kite.**
          - Bustard. { Castrel, by Buzzard. | Mishap, by Shuttle. }
          - Olympia. { Sir Oliver, by Sir Peter. | Scottilla, by Anvil. }
    - **Gaze.**
      - **Bay Middleton.**
        - **Sultan.**
          - Selim. { Buzzard, by Woodpecker. | Castrel's dam, by Alexander. }
          - Bacchante. { Williamson's Ditto, by Sir Peter. | Sister to Calomel, by Mercury. }
        - **Cobweb.**
          - Phantom. { Walton, by Sir Peter. | Julia, by Whiskey. }
          - Filagree. { Soothsayer, by Sorcerer. | Web, by Waxy. }
      - **Fly-Catcher.**
        - **tic-dolphin.**
          - Partisan. { Walton, by Sir Peter. | Parasol, by Pot-8-os. }
          - Ridicule. { Shuttle, by Young Marske. | Daughter of Dungannon. }
        - **Sister to Cobweb.**
          - Phantom. { Walton, by Sir Peter. | Julia, by Whiskey. }
          - Filagree. { Soothsayer, by Sorcerer. | Web, by Waxy. }
  - **Coquette.**
    - **Lexington.**
      - **Boston.**
        - **Timoleon.**
          - Sir Archy. { *Diomed, by Florizel. | *Castianira, by Rockingham. }
          - Daughter of. { *Saltram, by Eclipse. | Daughter of Symme's Wildair. }
        - **Sister to Tuckahoe.**
          - Ball's Florizel. { *Diomed, by Florizel. | Daughter of *Shark. }
          - Daughter of. { *Alderman, by Pot-8-os. | Daughter of *Clockfast. }
      - **Alice Carneal.**
        - ***Sarpedon.**
          - Emilius. { Orville, by Beningbrough. | Emily, by Stamford. }
          - Icaria. { The Flyer, by VanDyke, Jr. | Parma, by Dick Andrews. }
        - **Rowena.**
          - Sumpter. { Sir Archy, by *Diomed. | Daughter of *Robin Redbreast. }
          - Lady Gray. { Robin Gray, by *Royalist. | Maria, by Melzar. }
    - **Sportsmistress.**
      - **Revenue.**
        - ***Trustee.**
          - Catton. { Golumpus, by Gohanna. | Lucy Grey, by Timothy. }
          - Emma. { Whisker, by Waxy. | Gibside Fairy, by Hermes. }
        - **Rosalie Somers.**
          - Sir Charles. { Sir Archy, by *Diomed. | Daughter of *Citizen. }
          - Mischief. { Virginian, by Sir Archy. | Daughter of *Bedford. }
      - **Susan Harris.**
        - **American Eclipse.**
          - Duroc. { *Diomed, by Florizel. | Amanda, by Grey Diomed. }
          - Miller's Damsel. { *Messenger, by Membrino. | *Daughter of Pot-8-os. }
        - **Cub.**
          - Medoc. { Am. Eclipse, by Duroc. | Young Maid of the Oaks. }
          - Ann Merry. { Sumpter, by Sir Archy. | Grecian Princess, by Blackburn's Whip. }

Seventh dam, by Hampton's Paragon; eighth dam, Moll, by *Figure; Ninth dam, Maria Slamerkin, by Wildair; tenth dam, *Mare by Cub; eleventh dam, Amaranthus' dam by Second; twelfth dam (dam of Leedes, &c.) by Starling; thirteenth dam (sister to Vane's Little Partner) by Croft's Partner; fourteenth dam (sister to Guy) by Greyhound; fifteenth dam, Brown Farewell, by Makeless; sixteenth dam by Brimmer; seventeenth dam by Place's White Turk; eighteenth dam by Dodsworth; nineteenth dam, Layton Barb mare.

VIOLA.

Never ran.

PRODUCE.

1878, b. f., MAMIE M., by *Saxon.

1879, Barren.

1880, b. c.,   by *Saxon.

1881, Barren.

1882, ch. c.,   by Duke of Magenta

1883, ch. c., BLAZE DUKE, by Duke of Magenta.

1884, Barren.

1885, ch. f., PROSPERITY, by Onondaga.

1886, ch. c., GRAYSON, by Onondaga or Gilroy.

1887, ch. f.,   by *London.

1888, Barren to *London.

1889, ch. c.,   by *Rayon d'Or.

1890,   by *Rayon d'Or.

VIVID (IMPORTED).
Bay mare, foaled 1879. Bred by Mr. P. Right, England. Imported 1882, by Mr. W. L. Scott, Erie, Pa.

- **Vitula.**
  - **Speculum.**
    - **Vedette.**
      - **Voltigeur.**
        - **Voltaire.**
          - Blacklock. { Whitelock, by Hambletonian. / Daughter of Coriander. }
          - Daughter of { Phantom, by Walton. / Daughter of Overton. }
        - **Martha Lynn.**
          - Mulatto. { Catton, by Golumpus. / Desdemona, by Orville. }
          - Leda. { Filho-da-Puta, by Haphazard. / Treasure, by Camillus. }
      - **Daughter of**
        - **Irish Bird-catcher.**
          - Sir Hercules. { Whalebone, by Waxy. / Peri, by Wanderer. }
          - Guiccioli. { Bob Booty, by Chanticleer. / Flight, by Escape. }
        - **Nan Darrell.**
          - Inheritor. { Lottery, by Tramp. / Handmaiden, by Walton. }
          - Nell. { Blacklock, by Whitelock. / Madam Vestris, by Comus. }
    - **Doralice.**
      - **Alarm, or Orlando.**
        - **Touchstone.**
          - Camel. { Whalebone, by Waxy. / Daughter of Selim. }
          - Banter. { Master Henry, by Orville. / Boadicea, by Alexander. }
        - **Vulture.**
          - Langar. { Selim, by Buzzard. / Daughter of Walton. }
          - Kite. { Bustard, by Castrel. / Olympia, by Sir Oliver. }
      - **Preserve, (Sister to Imported Pickle).**
        - **Emilius.**
          - Orville. { Beningbrough, by King Fergus. / Evelina, by Highflyer. }
          - Emily. { Stamford, by Sir Peter. / Daughter of Whiskey. }
        - **Mustard.**
          - Merlin. { Castrel, by Buzzard. / Miss Newton, by Delpini. }
          - Morel. { Sorcerer, by Trumpator. / Hornby Lass, by Buzzard. }
  - **Arthur Wellesley.**
    - **Melbourne.**
      - **Humphrey Clinker.**
        - Comus. { Sorcerer, by Trumpator. / Houghton Lass, by Sir Peter. }
        - Clinkerina. { Clinker, by Sir Peter. / Pewet, by Tandem. }
      - **Daughter of**
        - Cervantes. { Don Quixote, by Eclipse. / Evalina, by Highflyer. }
        - Daughter of { Golumpus, by Gohanna. / Daughter of Paynator. }
    - **Lady Barbara.**
      - **Launcelot.**
        - Camel. { Whalebone, by Waxy. / Daughter of Selim. }
        - Banter. { Master Henry, by Orville. / Boadicea, by Alexander. }
      - **Daughter of**
        - Buzzard. { Blacklock, by Whitelock. / Miss Newton, by Delpini. }
        - Donna Maria. { Partisan, by Walton. / Donna Clara, by Cesario. }
- **Prairie Bird.**
  - **Zillah.**
    - **Touchstone.**
      - **Camel.**
        - Whalebone. { Waxy, by Pot-8-os. / Penelope, by Trumpator. }
        - Daughter of { Selim, by Buzzard. / Maiden, by Sir Peter. }
      - **Banter.**
        - Master Henry. { Orville, by Beningbrough. / Miss Sophia, by Stamford. }
        - Boadicea. { Alexander, by Eclipse. / Brunette, by Amaranthus. }
    - **Reveller.**
      - Comus. { Sorcerer, by Trumpator. / Houghton Lass, by Sir Peter. }
      - Rosette. { Beningbrough, by King Fergus. / Rosamond, by Tandem. }
  - **Morisca.**
    - Morisco. { Muley, by Orville. / Aquelina, by Eagle. }
    - Waltz. { Election, by Gohanna. / Penelope, by Trumpator. }

Seventh dam, Prunella by Highflyer; Eighth dam, Promise by Snap; Ninth dam, Julia by Blank; Tenth dam, Spectator's dam by Partner; Eleventh dam, Bonny Lass by Bay Bolton; Twelfth dam, by the Darley Arabian; Thirteenth dam, by the Byerly Turk; Fourteenth dam, by Taffolet Barb; Fifteenth dam, by Place's White Turk; Sixteenth dam, Natural Barb mare.

VIVID.

Ran but twice, and then as a two-year-old, at Warwick, England, ran third to Strelitzia, three years, in Kenilworth Plate, twelve starters, and at Manchester ran unplaced to Mattock in Eglinton Nursery Handicap, eleven starters.

— — — —

PRODUCE.

1883, b. c., VOTARY, by Exminster. (Imp. in utero.)

1884, Missed to Algerine.

1885, b. c., VELVETEEN, by Algerine. (Gelded.)

1886, ch. f., KANTA, by *Kantaka.

1887, Slipped b. c., by Algerine.

1888, b. c., VAGABOND, by Wanderer.

1889, Barren to Wanderer.

1890,   by Wanderer.

VOILÀ.

Bay mare, foaled 1881. Bred by Clay & Woodford, K'y.

					Sire and dam
*Billet.	Voltigeur.	Voltaire.	Blacklock.	Whitelock.	{ Hambletonian, by King Fergus / Rosalind, by Phenemenon.
				Daughter of	{ Coriander, by Pot-8-os. / Wildgoose, by Highflyer.
			Daughter of	Phantom.	{ Walton, by Sir Peter. / Julia, by Whiskey.
				Daughter of	{ Overton, by King Fergus. / Gratitude's dam, by Walnut.
		Martha Lynn.	Mulatto.	Catton.	{ Golumpus, by Gohanna. / Lucy Grey, by Timothy.
				Desdemona.	{ Orville, by Beningbrongh. / Fanny, by Sir Peter.
			Leda.	Filho-da-Puta.	{ Haphazard, by Sir Peter. / Mrs. Barnet, by Waxy.
				Treasure.	{ Camillus, by Hambletonian. / Daughter of Hyacinthus.
	Calcutta.	Flatcatcher.	Touchstone.	Camel.	{ Whalebone, by Waxy. / Daughter of Selim.
				Banter.	{ Master Henry, by Orville. / Boadicea, by Alexander.
			Decoy.	Filho-da-Puta.	{ Haphazard, by Sir Peter. / Mrs. Barnet, by Waxy.
				Finesse.	{ Peruvian, by Sir Peter. / Violanthe, by John Bull.
		Miss Martin.	St. Martin.	Actæon.	{ Scud, by Beningbrough. / Diana, by Stamford.
				Galena.	{ Walton, by Sir Peter. / Comedy, by Comus.
			Wagtail.	Whisker.	{ Waxy, by Pot-8-os. / Penelope, by Trumpator.
				Daughter of	{ Sorcerer, by Trumpator. / Daughter of Sir Solomon.
Belle Palmer.	*Bonny Scotland.	Iago.	Don John.	Tramp or Waverly.	{ Whalebone, by Waxy. / Margaretta, by Sir Peter.
				Hetman, Platoff's dam	{ Comus, by Sorcerer. / Marciana, by Stamford.
			Scandal.	Selim.	{ Buzzard, by Woodpecker. / Castrel's dam, by Alexander.
				Daughter of	{ Haphazard, by Sir Peter. / Daughter of Precipitate.
		Queen Mary.	Gladiator.	Partisan.	{ Walton, by Sir Peter. / Parasol, by Pot-8-os.
				Pauline.	{ Moses, by Whalebone or Seymour. / Quadrille, by Selim.
			Daughter of	Plenipotentiary.	{ Emilius, by Orville. / Harriet, by Pericles.
				Myrrha	{ Whalebone, by Waxy. / Gift, by Young Gohanna.
	Fanny Cheatham.	Lexington.	Boston.	Timoleon.	{ Sir Archy, by *Diomed. / Daughter of *Saltram.
				Sister to Tuckahoe.	{ Ball's Florizel, by *Diomed. / Daughter of *Alderman.
			Alice Carneal.	*Sarpedon.	{ Emilius, by Orville. / Icaria, by The Flyer.
				Rowena.	{ Sumpter, by Sir Archy. / Lady Grey, by Robin Grey.
		Laura.	*Leviathan.	Muley.	{ Orville, by Beningbrough. / Eleanor, by Whiskey.
				Daughter of	{ Windle, by Beningbrough. / Daughter of Anvil.
			Daughter of	Stockholder.	{ Sir Archy, by *Diomed. / Daughter of *Citizen.
				Daughter of	{ Pacolet, by *Citizen. / Nell Saunders, by Wilkes' Wonder

Seventh dam, Jolietta by *Dare Devil; Eighth dam, Rosetta by *Centinel; Ninth dam, Diana by Clodius; Tenth dam, Sallie Painter by Evans' 'Sterling,' Eleventh dam, *Silver by Belsize Arabian; Twelfth dam by Croft's Partner; Thirteenth dam (sister to Roxana) by Bald Galloway: Fourteenth dam (Sister to Chaunter) by Akaster Turk; Fifteenth dam by Leede's Arabian: Sixteenth dam by Spanker.

VOILA.

At two years old started three times, winning five furlong purse at Chicago, and second to Mona in Ladies' Stakes, same place, and unplaced once. At three years old started three times, and ran unplaced in each.

PRODUCE.

1886, Missed to *Rayon d'Or.

1887, ch. c.. JOHN ATWOOD, (Volo), by *Rayon d'Or.

1888, ch. c., VOID, by *Rayon d'Or. (Gelded.)

1889, b. c.. killed 1889, by *Rayon d'Or.

1890, by Algerine.

WAITAWAY.

Bay Mare, sired in England and foaled in 1883 at Algeria Stud Farm, Erie, Pa.

Rosicrucian.
- Beadsman.
  - Weatherbit.
    - Sheet Anchor.
      - Lottery. { Tramp, by Dick Andrews. / Mandane, by Pot-8-os.
      - Morgiana. { Muley, by Orville. / Miss Stevenson, by Sorcerer
    - Miss Letty.
      - Priam. { Emilius, by Orville. / Cressida, by Whiskey.
      - Daughter of { Orville, by Beningbrough. / Daughter of Buzzard.
  - Mendicant.
    - Touchstone.
      - Camel. { Whalebone, by Waxy. / Daughter of Selim.
      - Banter. { Master Henry, by Orville. / Boadicea, by Alexander.
    - Lady Moor Carew.
      - Tramp. { Dick Andrews, by Joe Andrews. / Daughter of Gohanna.
      - Kite. { Bustard, by Castrel. / Olympia, by Sir Oliver.
- Madame Eglentine.
  - Cowl.
    - Bay Middleton.
      - Sultan. { Selim, by Buzzard. / Bacchante, by Williamson's Ditto.
      - Cobweb. { Phantom, by Walton. / Filagree, by Soothsayer.
    - Crucifix.
      - Priam. { Emilius, by Orville. / Cressida, by Whiskey.
      - Octaviana. { Octavian, by Stripling. / Daughter of Shuttle.
  - Diversion.
    - Defence.
      - Whalebone. { Waxy, by Pot-8-os. / Penelope, by Trumpator.
      - Defiance. { Rubens, by Buzzard. / Little Folly, by Highland Fling.
    - Folly.
      - Middleton. { Phantom, by Walton. / Web, by Waxy.
      - Little Folly. { Highland Fling, by Spadille. / Harriet, by Volunteer.

*Bordelaise.
- Brown Bread.
  - Weatherbit.
    - Sheet Anchor.
      - Lottery. { Tramp, by Dick Andrews. / Mandane, by Pot-8-os.
      - Morgiana { Muley, by Orville. / Miss Stevenson, by Sorcerer.
    - Miss Letty.
      - Priam. { Emilius, by Orville. / Cressida, by Whiskey.
      - Daughter of { Orville, by Beningbrough. / Daughter of Buzzard.
  - Brown Agnes.
    - West Australian.
      - Melbourne. { Humphrey Clinker, by Comus. / Daughter of Cervantes.
      - Mowerina. { Touchstone, by Camel. / Emma, by Whisker.
    - Miss Agnes.
      - Irish Birdcatcher. { Sir Hercules, by Whalebone. / Guiccioli, by Bob Booty.
      - Agnes. { Clarion, by Sultan. / Annette, by Priam.
- Aline.
  - Claret.
    - Touchstone.
      - Camel. { Whalebone, by Waxy. / Daughter of Selim.
      - Banter. { Master Henry, by Orville. / Boadicea, by Alexander.
    - Mountain Sylph.
      - Belshazzer. { Blacklock, by Whitelock. / Manuella, by Dick Andrews.
      - Stays. { Whalebone, by Waxy. / Daughter of Frolic.
  - Weatherside.
    - Weatherbit.
      - Sheet Anchor. { Lottery, by Tramp. / Morgiana, by Muley.
      - Miss Letty. { Priam, by Emilius. / Daughter of Orville.
    - Lady Alice.
      - Chanticleer. { Irish Birdcatcher, by Sir Hercules. / Whim, by Drone.
      - Agnes. { Clarion, by Sultan. / Annette, by Priam.

Seventh dam, Potentate's dam by Don Juan (by Orville); Eighth dam, Moll-in-the-Wad by Hambletonian; Ninth dam, Spitfire by Pipator; Tenth dam, Farewell by Slope; Eleventh dam by Young Marske; Twelfth dam by Brother to Silvio; Thirteenth dam, Sister to Stripling by Hutton's Spot.

IMPORTED WAITAWAY.

At two years old started twice, running unplaced both times. At three years old started but once, running unplaced in the Withers Stakes at Jerome Park.

--- ---

PRODUCE.

1888, b. f., WENDAWAY, by Wanderer.
1889, b. f.,   by Wanderer.
1890,   by Wanderer.

INDEX.